LOVE
AND OTHER
CONSPIRACIES

Mallory Marlowe

Berkley Romance
New York

BERKLEY ROMANCE
Published by Berkley
An imprint of Penguin Random House LLC
penguinrandomhouse.com

Library of Congress Cataloging-in-Publication Data

Names: Marlowe, Mallory, author.
Title: Love and other conspiracies / Mallory Marlowe.
Description: First edition. | New York: Berkley Romance, 2024.
Identifiers: LCCN 2023051463 (print) | LCCN 2023051464 (ebook) |
ISBN 9780593640081 (trade paperback) | ISBN 9780593640098 (ebook)
Subjects: LCGFT: Romance fiction. | Novels.
Classification: LCC PS3613.A76638 L68 2024 (print) |
LCC PS3613.A76638 (ebook) | DDC 813/.6—dc23/eng/20231214
LC record available at https://lccn.loc.gov/2023051463
LC ebook record available at https://lccn.loc.gov/2023051464

First Edition: August 2024

Printed in the United States of America
1st Printing

Book design by Shannon Nicole Plunkett

For all the believers

• AUTHOR'S NOTE •

Love and Other Conspiracies is a romantic comedy with humor, hijinks, and a guaranteed happily-ever-after. However, it does also contain the following themes and content: overcoming a past toxic relationship, workplace harassment by an ex-partner, past death of a parent from a terminal illness, mentions of caretaking for an ill family member, discussions of depression, recreational alcohol and marijuana usage, sexual content, and language. For anyone who may be sensitive to these topics, please read with care.

CHAPTER 1

*L*os Angeles is a city of believers. Whether it be the belief that you'll wait on the right producer's table at the right time and land that big break or that there'll miraculously be no traffic on the 405, everyone has *something* they believe in with their whole being.

Nearly everyone working at Skroll came here believing in their shot at the fifteen minutes of internet fame the company all but guarantees. For them, it's clearly just another day at the office. Interns chatter over catered lunch, and a member of the video team skateboards through the stark white, open-concept office.

And me? I wholeheartedly believe I am about to get fired.

Can we chat?

Few phrases strike fear into my heart the way "Can we chat?" does. It's not good when it comes from a partner or parent, and it's even less fun when it comes from my boss. Chloe is less of a "boss" and more like a cool older friend who sometimes offers me raises and puts my name on org charts as Skroll undergoes yet another restructuring. She joins us producers for drinks and always compliments my blue hair, noticing when I touch it up or experiment with the shade.

But Chloe *also* has the power to fire me.

Today, it wouldn't shock me if she did. After a month and a half of busywork instead of the producing I was hired to do, I'm expendable.

"Do you think hashtag 'NoraLicks' or 'LicksWithNora' would sell more of these guys?"

I yank myself from my bout of shaking hands and a churning stomach to answer my coworker and recent roommate, Nora. She taps hesitantly at her keyboard, writing and deleting the hashtags several times. I glance at her screen. In the Wild West that is millennial start-up culture, deciding how to sponsor and market fake rubber tongues to lick cats with *does* demand my serious consideration. Except right now, my brain is a broken record of: "Can we chat?," "Time to pack up your desk now," and "Do you have any retail experience?"

"Oh . . . I didn't think it was that triggering of a question," she says now that she's seen my face. "Hallie, is everything okay?"

Nora's screen shows a thumbnail where she and Amita— one of our other coworkers—are corralled by an army of kittens, with said licking tools bitten between their teeth. I think these cats look more nervous than anything, but at least Nora has something to *do*. While other staffed producers and contributors spend their nine-to-fives making clickbait videos and writing their fun listicles, I've spent the past month and a half logging video stats and online traffic reports because that's all there is for me to do. It's far below my pay grade and producer job title, but since my plans to produce one of Skroll's most hyped shows were derailed, I feel lucky to be hanging on to their payroll by even a thread.

"Uh, Chloe wants to talk to me."

". . . Oh." Nora nips her bottom lip and traces her fingers

around the flowered ink on her wrist, a nervous habit. She embraces the quirky tattoos up and down her arms and is constantly tipping her mousy brown hair with bold and bright colors. I've never seen her in business casual wear—always trendy crop tops and high-waisted shorts, fun rompers, and overdramatic shoes. There's no part of Nora that's afraid to be herself.

Meanwhile, lately, every part of myself feels like clothing that needs a run through the wash with fabric softener.

"Maybe she found another show for you."

"Doubtful."

Nora doesn't refute my doubt because she knows I'm right. Instead, we sit in silence until I bite the bullet.

Yep. Coming!!

The second exclamation point feels excessive, but I'll blame it on my shaking hands.

I stand and look out at the high-tech office in front of me. This office feels like home, and not just because of the horrifying amount of time I spend here.

No, *spent*.

Eight years ago, Skroll was little more than a pop culture news site full of listicles and personality quizzes. Now it's a multimedia conglomerate that could catapult random millennials to internet superstardom over a single viral video.

I didn't come to Skroll looking for my own fame, but instead to be the one pulling all the strings behind the scenes. I wanted to produce, and Skroll filled my past several years with late-night shoots, the video team scrambling for fresh takeout after-hours, and delirious foosball games while we spitballed ideas. Now I spend my days in the office killing time, all because one person decided I didn't matter enough.

Over the past four years, I worked my way up the video team's ladder from an office PA—making coffee runs and ordering snacks for the office—to associate producer, and then finally a real, shiny producer. When Skroll began to dip its toes into video content and longer-form series, it ran like a small, quirky movie studio. I brainstormed and developed, organized schedules, booked our studios and equipment, and made sure everyone showed up on time. I've helmed so many of those videos that launched talent into the digital spotlight. And I was damn good at it.

I meander through the stark white desks and overpriced ergonomic chairs to Chloe's office beside the Doge conference room. She yells for me to enter after two knocks, and I shimmy my way in. Her workspace always manages to make microwave meals smell like five-star cuisine, seasoned with the light scent of Nag Champa. Her cactus-shaped humidifier puffs and I catch a whiff of calming lavender.

But I do not feel calm.

I am a bundle of shaky hands, impending boob sweat, and a stress-induced eye twitch.

I take a seat on one of her toadstool-shaped chairs, which she insists promote better posture. I slump anyway.

She spins the screen out of the way as I offer her a meek wave. "Hi."

"Hey, Hal. Glad you were available. So, there's something we should talk about . . ."

I can't read her expression. Is she letting me go? Am I getting put on a PIP, where I'll have to log every minute of my day, down to every time I go to the bathroom?

"Sure, what is it?"

"So, your show . . ."

I furrow my brows. "Uh, do I have a show I don't know about? Because . . ."

She chews the corner of her lip. "Yeah . . . *that's* the part I wanted to discuss."

"Okay," I say.

"We are full steam ahead here on the Skroll Series Program, and Kevin is funneling a good amount of our department funds into show budgets and all of our current series are staffed."

"So, I'm getting let go?"

Chloe sucks in a breath that does not reassure me. "That's what I'm trying to avoid. You're a damn good producer, Hallie, and I don't want to lose you. But if I don't have anything for you to do? It's going to be hard to justify keeping you if layoffs come. I need *you* to come up with a show for the program."

The Skroll Series Program was like pilot season for web series. Each year, producers and on-camera talent would pitch their shows and record a pilot episode and, if it tested well with corporate, a trial first season. The chosen programs would receive a meager budget and a small gang of producers and assistants in the office, and their stars would be catapulted into the digital spotlight in hopes of gaining the highest content engagement. Skroll fans tuned in religiously and engaged in fandom squabbles—the full Like, Comment, Subscribe—in hopes their favorite show would get a second season, full of higher budgets, higher promotion, and, hell, merchandise if the show did *really* well.

This year was supposed to be my first competing as a lead producer. I'd laid out schedules, episode ideas, and aesthetics and visuals for the team. *Noobie Brothers* would feature a group of newbie tabletop players fumbling their way through a game campaign. I'd be pulling every string behind the scenes and would claim that victory for myself, even if I never appeared on camera. It wasn't about the attention for me.

Cade Browning—the onscreen ringleader—went viral one night and has yet to be cured. A single silly video of him getting his chest waxed made him Skroll's resident clickbait snack. It's obvious why. He's a perfect cocktail of an All-American Boy with a nip of edge. Blond hair, blue eyes, and a dizzying smile. He can switch his personalities at the drop of a hat—calculating and deliberate one moment, self-effacing and charming the next.

Everyone fell for it; even me.

I should have seen it coming when Cade swooped in like a hawk just days after my first solo-produced short went viral. Though, when you're twenty-two, fresh out of school, determined to climb the ladder, and the office heartthrob starts paying attention to you, you pay attention back.

When you're twenty-two and said heartthrob tells you how brilliant you are, flirts with you, and suggests hopping in bed together, you do.

When you're twenty-five and no longer the cute fresh meat you used to be, you end up logging traffic reports all day instead of producing a show.

Two months ago, I *had* a show and a guaranteed role for at least six months. Then Cade dropped the fatal blow. He thought a cozy night in with a bottle of wine and my favorite takeout would soften the hit that he didn't want me on the show anymore, but after I ended our relationship over it, he sure wasted no time slandering me to the crew.

You're hard to work with.

You just don't stand out.

I need people with real substance on this show. People who matter.

Now I'm an adrift producer without a show as my buoy.

My pen drops off my lap and rolls under Chloe's desk. "Me? A ... show?"

"Yes. This isn't public knowledge yet, so don't say a damn thing. Eric got arrested for public indecency at the Denny's down the road, so we won't be moving forward with his show."

Shame. What the world truly needed was a web series where a fuckboy calculated how many blunts it'd take to blow certain objects up. It was like *MythBusters* for stoners.

"... Which leaves an open spot in the Series Program that we haven't filled yet."

I don't even stop to think about if it's mine. It *will* be mine. There was a spot with my name and creative touch all over it from the get-go. If I create my own show, I'll not only get to reclaim what's mine, but I'll compete side by side against Cade. If I do this, I could beat his ass. I *have* to beat his ass.

"We're on a time crunch here, Hal. Get me an idea by the end of the week and, if we like it, you'll have to hustle to get a pilot together for the board. If we pick you up for the season, you'll get Eric's production budget and full use of our studios to produce your first season."

That doesn't leave much time to come up with a concept, find the right talent, and convince them to hop on board with my half-baked idea.

Shit. I'm going to have to make a deck.

I can kiss my bed goodbye for the rest of the week. But for the chance to shove my show so far up Cade's ass it'll show up on a strep test? I'll forgo sleep for as long as humanly possible to get back at him and prove to Skroll I am useful for far more than just logging metadata (though I like to think I'm good at that, too).

My heart speeds up, hands beginning to sweat and shake. "You've got yourself a deal. Friday. I'll have a show ready to go for you then."

"That's what I like to hear!"

Show. Beating Cade. Winning. I just have no idea where to begin.

I bumble out of Chloe's office in a haze, my brain operating like a too-fast hamster wheel. I hadn't even thought over accepting Chloe's offer. I just *did* it. Now I have to follow through.

The Brain-Hamster has been flung off the wheel by the time I return to my desk. I sink behind my monitor.

"You good?" Nora asks. She flashes me a thumbs-up, then a thumbs-down.

I provide her with a so-so. "I'm good, but I need a show idea."

That's when I realize I didn't grab my pen from the floor in Chloe's office. Dammit. I liked that pen.

"A show idea?" she yelps. "*Really*?"

"Yes. By Friday—"

Nora immediately deflates. "Well . . . shit."

"I'll figure it out," I say, but I am not convinced. I don't know where to start.

"You know what we should do?"

"What?"

"We should get high and watch *Agent Cody Banks*. Frankie Muniz really brings out my creativity."

❡ ❡ ❡

We *do* get high and watch *Agent Cody Banks*. A few hours and a half a bottle of five-dollar wine later, when Nora has gone to bed, I am deep in internet hell.

I listened to podcasts, I watched vlogs, I hunted Instagram for charismatic influencers. I only broke for our brief movie. I feel like I've consumed every bit of media under the sun, yet I still haven't made a dent in my ever-growing list of TV show recommendations.

I slurp a chopstick full of noodles into my mouth as the alcohol hits me suddenly. The clock on my computer flashes two a.m. I'll feel this in the morning, though I don't have time for a hangover. I slip my headphones out of my ears and notice the TV in front of me has descended into late-night madness. I'm an hour away from the impending infomercials for discreet adult diapers.

I zero in on the screen as the show returns from a commercial break.

Cosmic Conspiracies.

Yep, I've hit the middle-of-the-night trash TV. Animated planets whirl across the screen and large-headed aliens bobble forward like unsteady bowling pins.

"Sightings of apelike creatures have been reported on nearly every continent on Earth," says an overdramatic narrator. "From the Himalayan Yeti to the Florida Skunk Ape and the most famous of all beasts—Bigfoot—cultures across the world tell stories of something they can't explain lurking in the woods . . ."

Oh, Jesus.

"In ancient drawings, you'll find large, hairy creatures

intermingled with humans." The show cuts to a portly British man. "If you look at the footprints, they aren't so different from ours. Could we be closer to Bigfoot than we think? Could Bigfoot even be an extraterrestrial from another planet?"

"What the fuck," I mutter into my ramen. Yet, at the same time, I suddenly understand how people religiously watch shows like this. I feel no urge to change the channel. Bigfoot is not real, and neither are aliens, but I *have* to know how they're going to justify this.

Then a man far too hot to be offering *any* opinion on Bigfoot appears onscreen. He's young, probably late twenties, with shaggy, dark hair falling in front of his face; a sharp, stubble-coated jawline; and a square pair of black glasses. His bright green eyes are ablaze with excitement and an analytical seriousness that can't be feigned.

"When we think about Bigfoot," he begins, in the smoothest, sexiest voice I've ever heard. It's a clear baritone, simultaneously soothing and commanding. The man is full of dramatic hand gestures to help him paint a picture. "We think about a flesh and blood creature not so different from ourselves. When we think of aliens, we think of Greys or little green men. Those are vastly different visuals. But the idea that Bigfoot could have come from somewhere else, or that he's not native to this world, raises the question: If we share genetic links with Bigfoot, as we do apes, what does that make us?"

Noodles drop out of my mouth. I choke on a bean sprout. The most handsome man I've ever seen has just publicly proposed that Bigfoot is an alien and that, de facto, *we* are aliens as well. And I am fucking enthralled. I rewind the clip to the man's name and title onscreen.

HAYDEN HARGROVE
HOST, THE OUT THERE

I type "The Out There" into Google and it brings me to a website. I'm half expecting a nineties HTML horror show, but it's sharp, professional, and functional. It links to an active Subreddit, a few news articles, and a tab called "Critter Spottings" that I'm too afraid to click on. I learn that *The Out There* is a long-running cryptid and conspiracy theories podcast with an alarmingly large fan base consisting of many teenage girls. A quick look through the Tumblr tag is full of edited photos of their swoony host in flower crowns. Looking at the headshot of Hayden at the bottom of his website, it's clear why he gets the attention. He sits behind a microphone in a small, dimly lit recording studio, midnarration. For someone who exists mainly behind the mic, he has a magnetic enthusiasm and passion to him on-camera.

This is what Skroll needs.

Skroll needs a hot monster hunter.

' THE OUT THERE '

EP #187 "Encounters with the Men in Black"

On this week's episode of The Out There, *Hayden digs into the mysterious history of the fabled Men in Black. He breaks down the myths and rumors lurking in the shadows and talks with*

an anonymous tipster who had a recent run-in with suited
saboteurs.

HAYDEN

So, you mean to tell me the person who harassed you was not
Will Smith?

[REDACTED]

No, I can confirm that the man in question was not the star of
any major film franchise.

HAYDEN

I figured—

[REDACTED]

Nor the star of a minor film franchise.

HAYDEN

Perfect, that was my next question. Whenever someone sees
something mysterious, I like to make sure neither an A-list actor
nor a C-list actor was responsible. For the new kids, the Men in
Black are alleged government agents that tend to appear
following alien or UFO sightings in an effort to keep witnesses
quiet. They often rely on intimidation techniques, but in a few
cases, they've done things that are a little . . . shall we say, Out
There? What was your experience, [REDACTED]?

[REDACTED]

I was driving home one night when I saw a disc with lots of
lights in the sky flying above my car. I had never seen anything

like it. At first I thought it might have been a plane going down, so I was ready to call for help. I pulled over and started taking pictures. I didn't get many good ones, but a few of them were good enough to put up on the Facebook.

HAYDEN

You can just call it Facebook. No need for "the."

[REDACTED]

The pictures got taken down quickly, and the next day, this man shows up at my house. Dressed in a suit, tie, hat, suspenders.

HAYDEN

Aside from the clothing, what did he look like? There are some theories that the Men in Black are actually aliens themselves. There have been descriptions mentioning glowing eyes and pale skin with no hair and features that look almost painted on. Was that your experience, too?

[REDACTED]

No, he didn't look like an alien. He looked like a man. Very clean-cut and normal looking. He told me to delete the pictures from my phone and to never talk about what I saw again. At first I refused, because I knew it meant I'd seen something good, you know? Then he kept showing up. Outside my house, at work.

My wife kept wondering why this other man was standing outside our house all the time. Asking for me. I didn't know how to explain it to her and it really harmed our marriage. I think she suspected I was having an affair.

HAYDEN

Hmm, yeah, if I explained that to my hypothetical wife, I wouldn't really bank on her believing me either. It's like a Jake from State Farm situation, but with aliens, huh? See, when I got my visit from the alleged Men in Black, I think I accidentally scared him away.

[REDACTED]

Then consider yourself very, very lucky, my friend.

[*THE OUT THERE* THEME MUSIC]

HAYDEN

Hi, guys, welcome to another episode of The Out There. A few quick updates before we get started—

I did a little more research on that Fresno Nightcrawler sighting I got a tip about last week, but I haven't been able to turn up any other eyewitnesses or recent sightings, so unfortunately this trail goes cold for now. I will keep an eye on it, and if anyone else has any other info to report—you know where to send it.

There is an escalation on last week's Florida Man headline, and it's wild—here it is as a refresher: "In Bitter H.O.A. Battle, Florida Man Claims Bigfoot Put Unsanctioned Lawn Flamingos in His Yard." The H.O.A. lobbed some hefty fines at this Florida Man, but lawyers are now involved after a twelve-foot skeleton decoration from Home Depot appeared in the man's yard overnight. His defense is that at five-four and a hundred and fifty pounds, he's not at all capable of carrying or constructing the skeleton himself. So, naturally the only other option is Bigfoot. But I did find several recent upticks in

Sasquatch sightings in Northern Florida, so I really can't rule it out. I'll do the responsible thing and keep up with this story and keep you all updated.

On that note, this week's episode is sponsored by BeatBuds, headphones that go where you do. I spend a lot of time on the phone making this podcast happen, and having a Bluetooth headset that lets me do my job while on the go makes that possible. Click the link in our show bio and use the promo code OUTTHERE for twenty percent off your order. So, now that that's Out There—let's get into it—

So, say you saw something you couldn't explain . . .

CHAPTER 2

In another Cosmic Conspiracy, Hayden Hargrove lives in LA as well.

He doesn't disclose what part of the city he calls home, but he doesn't argue when I pitch meeting in Hollywood. The wonder of LA is that each neighborhood has a personality of its own. Silver Lake is for the hipsters. Santa Monica is where the popular kids from high school live. And I'm not sure anyone actually *lives* in Century City. I'm fairly certain it's just office buildings and ostentatious fountains.

I'm not sure what neighborhood lends itself best to the local Bigfoot hunters.

Although the Skroll offices are in Hollywood, I try to spend as little time here as possible. It's a neighborhood full of strip malls, the occasional way-too-fancy-for-Hollywood bar, and terrifying gift shops. The sidewalks look like the San Andreas Fault has buckled through them and are filled with people in dirty superhero costumes selling overpriced photos to tourists.

Hollywood is a necessary evil of living in LA.

It is also the only place that would naturally have an alien-themed pop-up bar.

"Earthling, can I get you anything?"

The bartender, wearing a tinfoil hat and antennae, hovers in front of me. I eye the sticky menu. All the cocktails have space-themed names, and I'm too flabbergasted by the titles to dig into what is *in* the drinks. I panic and order something called a Space Oddity.

I receive a neon blue drink that might earn me a lecture at my next dentist appointment, but tastes fine enough that I'm not as mad about paying seventeen dollars for it. I turn around and skim the crowd. Unsurprisingly, there are not many people in an alien-themed bar on a Wednesday night, but none of them seem to be Hayden.

I told him to look for the girl with the blue hair.

I seem to fit in at a place like this, with the glittery walls and floating UFO mobiles above, even if I don't believe aliens are real.

"Oh my god, you're *that* guy!" the bouncer says behind me. Somehow, I feel like I already know who he's talking to. "My girlfriend and I went to your panel at CON-Spiracy last year—the one on alien autopsies—man . . . That was unreal."

"Uh, thank you. Can I . . . can I have my ID back, please?"

Less than twenty-four hours ago, I'd heard the same silky and spooky voice spew ridiculous conspiracy theories as a guest on a late-night docuseries. No wonder the guy went into podcasting. Who wouldn't want to spend hours listening to him? In fact, listening to him was how I spent *my* day.

The Out There is surprisingly engaging for someone like me, who does not believe in monsters or aliens or ghosts. My producer brain *knows* ghost-hunting shows are bullshit, and if aliens are real, how come they haven't made contact or killed us all yet? But Hayden presents information clearly, and he makes the most outlandish theories feel normal.

Hayden makes me *wish* I believed.

Somehow, his voice is even nicer in person.

"Hallie?"

As I turn around, I realize he is even more *attractive* in person, too. Hayden towers over me with a lanky but muscled build, hidden underneath a well-fitted plaid button-down. A few days of scruff coat his cheeks and jaw, his chestnut hair longer than it was on TV. The early February chill turns his cheeks pink and windblown beneath the frames of his glasses. This man is way too handsome to spend his life hunting aliens. But for my sake, I'm glad he does.

"Um." It was easy to draft an email and schedule a meeting, but now I feel at a loss for words. Perhaps because he is one of the most handsome men I've seen in my life, but I also realize I don't know what the two of us could have in common. Certainly not a mutual love of aliens.

Hayden's eyes hold mine. Maybe he's wondering if he chose the wrong blue-haired girl at the bar. His emerald stare makes my skin feel warm, like what I imagine being struck by a UFO laser beam must feel like. He looks just as struck, and I don't know what to make of it.

I clear my throat. "Yes. Hi. I'm Hallie. That'd make you Hayden."

"Sure does. It's good to meet you." He slides into the seat next to me.

"Can I get you a drink?"

Hayden digs his hands into the pockets of his down vest and surveys the menu. He looks like Mr. October in the sexy version of the REI calendar, which I don't believe exists, but I suddenly think it should. Dark ink extends down his left forearm, a line-art deer, its antlers stretching into skeletal trees. Its eyes feel too far apart, or its mouth is a little too open. I can't put my finger on what unsettles me about this deer, since I typically have a neutral relationship with them, if they remain a safe distance away. There's also a small UFO tattooed along the outside of his wrist. "Sure. Whatever the UFO Fuel is."

"I just hope these drinks don't get us abducted and probed," I joke.

Hayden shrugs, straight-faced. "It'd be interesting for science."

Even in the name of science, I'd like to avoid being probed. I want to know nothing about this man's kinks. "R-right . . ."

When the bartender returns, I order his drink, which looks like it should glow in the dark—a neon green concoction of God knows what. There's a small plastic alien floating in the drink, riding the single large ice cube like a mechanical bull.

"Hey." I frown. "*Mine* didn't come with an alien."

After a sip of his drink, Hayden turns to me. "So, you wanted to talk about your proposal. But before we do . . ."

Oh no.

Hayden leans in close and glances covertly over one shoulder. "You're not trying to scam me into giving you classified info—"

His wariness makes *me* glance over my shoulder, too. "*You* have classified information?"

Hayden's eyes shift back and forth, debating if he should keep going or not. Then his shoulders and hands rise in surrender. "I know a guy."

"Is it you?"

"You never know who is trying to scam you for black market Bigfoot footage."

"Seems like you've had a few bad run-ins with foreign princes asking for your bank info." Does that count as a conspiracy? I don't know, but the smile peeking at the corners of his lips indicates *maybe* I've tapped this conspiracy theorist's funny bone.

Hayden laughs as he takes another sip of his drink. "Hey, it's serious business. Old people fall for it all the time. Might be a conspiracy."

Ha, bingo.

"Well, fortunately for you, I do not look like a nefarious royal trying to take your money . . . At least, I don't think so."

"No," he says. The word is sharp, and the hardened gaze he gives me cauterizes it like a hot knife. "No, you do not."

I'm too busy drowning in the tone of Hayden's words and the piercing look he's giving me to come up with another quip, so I take a sip of my drink. I've spent all day wondering how tough of a sell this man might be or if the vibrant conspiracy theorist persona is an act. I'm guessing now that it isn't, but there is something human and grounded about Hayden that reassures me we might be able to make something work here.

Hayden clears his throat. "So, the show . . ."

"Right. Every year, Skroll does their Series Program, where our in-house creators pitch and produce a season of a web series. There's usually around ten shows. The most popular series gets picked up for a second season and everything that comes with it. Skroll judges based on viewership and engagement, social media buzz . . . I've seen creators gain up to a million new followers from their shows. It can make an entire career.

"We have one spot open, and my boss wants me to find a show that I think will be wildly successful. Obviously, *The Out There* already has a huge following, but it could be even bigger if we adapt it to a web series. There's a lot about the podcast that's already working, but we could make it more visual. I mean, you were great on *Cosmic Conspiracies*. I'm thinking for certain episodes, you could do real ghost hunts or Mothguy—"

Hayden's shoulders rise eagerly when I mention the phrase "ghost hunts," like I've scratched a hard-to-reach itch, and then deflate. "Mothman."

"Right. Mothman hunts. I think that the monster market might be untapped—"

"I mean, *clearly*, if we haven't found Bigfoot yet."

"Of course," I play along, but he is genuinely vexed that there are mysteries still out there. "There's *clearly* work to do. We'd work together over the next few months—you'd be a freelance contractor for Skroll for the duration of the season and I'd be your producer. We'd have part-time production staff working with us, and a modest budget for our first season, so that can cover the travel and lodging for those on-location shoots. You'd still have full creative control over the series. Look, I don't believe in any of this stuff—the aliens, the cryptids, or ghosts—but I really liked *The Out There*, and I think you could be a *great* internet personality if we use this platform."

Hayden's quiet, sipping his drink and contemplating what I've said. The legal discussions can come later, but all I need is for him to at least give this a chance. If he sees how successful this show could be, we'll be golden. But I *am* asking him to step away from his podcasting career to morph it into something else. It isn't an easy ask.

Finally, he sets his drink down.

"You mean, you really don't believe in any of it?"

Suddenly, the blasphemous conspiracy theorist I discovered on *Cosmic Conspiracies* is back. His eyes are alight with questions and theories. This . . . this is what Skroll needs. Pure, unbridled passion—even if it is for aliens.

"Excuse me?"

His fingers rake through his hair, pupils blown out.

"None of it? You don't believe in aliens or Bigfoot or ghosts or—I . . . I don't know . . . the Denver airport?"

"The Denver airport? What . . . I've never been, but I guess I believe in it. I know it exists—"

"*Obviously*, it exists," Hayden cuts in. "It's a secret base for *something*. Like, I don't like talking that much about the Illuminati because they're problematic, but I have many questions about the airport's size. The bunkers. The mural. The *horse*."

Images flash through my brain, and none of them connect, but I want them to. Desperately.

"Right," I agree. "Uh, no. I don't believe in any of it."

Hayden rubs the bridge of his nose beneath his glasses. "That's a lot to swallow."

"So was hearing that Bigfoot might have been an alien—"

His hands smack down on the bar. Our glasses jingle. The alien riding his ice cube sinks beneath the surface. "Mind-blowing, isn't it?" He looks at me like he's finally discovered a kindred conspiratorial spirit, someone who will complement all his weirds with their own.

I chew my bottom lip. "Not the word I'd use."

He deflates. His fingers tap the edge of his glass as the TV screen behind him lights with poorly animated aliens dabbing in the middle of the desert. It's hard to look at anything else. A speech bubble pops up above one of the aliens: "ayyy lmao."

"But regardless of whether or not *I* believe in this stuff, I think you have talent and I think Skroll's viewers would really enjoy you."

"*The Out There* has only ever been a podcast," he begins. "It's what I know how to do. I'm not . . . I'm no actor, Hallie. I highly doubt a handful of episodes of *Cosmic Conspiracies* count as acting. My fans know it as a podcast. What if they don't *want* to see it adapted?"

"If I'm being honest, I don't think your listeners, or anyone, really, would have any issue with looking at you more."

Help.

My face flushes—probably a horrible tomato red—but Hayden's brows rise as he runs his fingers along his stubbled jaw. I catch a smile tug at the corner of his lips, a dimple popping beneath his scruffy cheeks as he bites down on one side of his mouth. Fuck, I suddenly *hope* the Bermuda Triangle is real. This would be a great time for it to do a girl a solid and suck me in. I can't tell if he's intrigued, or shocked, or if he *knows* how good-looking he is.

He must. Unless he's one of those guys who holds strong conspiracies about every mirror being a two-way mirror.

I toss back a long sip of my drink and clear my throat. "And if this is successful, it'll rake in a lot more money than a podcast. You could be on more TV shows—ones that aren't just on in the middle of the night."

"To be fair, I think you caught a rerun."

"Sure. Who doesn't love syndication? This is good exposure. Just think: if you hit it big, you could be a *regular* on *Cosmic Conspiracies*. Hell, you could have your own show on TV. With better graphics!"

He finishes his drink, pensive and silent.

"I need to think about it, Hallie. I'm on hiatus between seasons of the podcast, so I *do* have the time right now, but . . ."

"Do you think you'd be able to think about it at a secondary location?"

His eyebrow quirks. I mean, I get it. It's not the type of question *I'd* respond well to on a first date. "Huh?"

"If you're done with your drink, come with me."

Hayden warily sets his glass down and rescues the plastic alien from the bottom as I close out our tab. I have another trick up my sleeve that he might like more than alien-themed alcohol.

* * *

"Are we going on a *ghost tour*?"

"Indeed. I hear Hollywood is full of haunted shit, huh?"

Hayden's boots scuff beside me, and he buries his hands deeper into his pockets. "Are you trying to woo me into doing your show?"

"Is it working? Are you wooed?"

"I said I'd *think* about it." His voice is terse, but he offers a soft laugh that sends a shiver down my spine.

We pause as we reach the tour kiosk. When we halt, our eyes lock. I reach deep into the part of my brain that's watched a lot of interrogations on cop shows. I narrow my eyes. "I need you to think about it faster. I need to have something by Friday morning. A pitch deck, episode plans, *something*."

"I'm *thinking* about it—"

The tour guide—a chirpy, middle-aged man named Gary—interrupts and leads us through the cavernous back halls of the Chinese Theatre to a gaudy, topless van painted to look like a hearse, which does not, in fact, look like a hearse.

A couple in matching *Ghost Adventures* shirts funnel into the back seat. Another two pairs take the middle, leaving Hayden and me to the front row. The smallest row. Thankfully, *I'm* small, but Hayden is not. I'm already daunted by the proximity I'm about to be sucked into.

"Ladies first," he says.

I hop into the van, sliding all the way to the window as he climbs in after me. His long legs hardly fit behind the passenger seat and the tip bucket placed between the driver and Gary. As he readjusts, our knees brush—worn denim against my thin, patterned tights. The van itself smells like plastic and cigarette smoke, but Hayden smells like amber and whiskey with a note of old books.

The touch sends a tingle up my back. It's been a long time since I've been attracted to someone, and in the past, I've experienced it so rarely that I've started viewing men as paint swatches in various neutral tones. When I look at Hayden, I see deep forest greens and warm browns like mulled wine and fall leaves. Color, for the first time in so long.

There is something about Hayden that interests me, and not just because of the odd way he came into my life. It could be either untapped horniness or feeling that I'm on the right track in learning to feel something again. It also comes with the fear of something new and the boundary of keeping my professional distance.

"Sorry," he mutters, yanking his leg away. He shoves his hands back into his vest pockets and bites down on his lip. He looks out the window and feigns fascination with the Baja Fresh across the street. Gary loads into the van with us and sits in the passenger seat, tapping on his tinny microphone a few times.

"Hello, ghouls, gals, and other ethereal pals. Welcome to Haunted Hollywood, the best tour of Tinsel Town's dark side. My name's Gary and I'll be your crypt keeper as we visit several notoriously haunted locations around the city. So . . . buckle up and please refrain from screaming."

The tour bus takes off, explaining the history of Grauman's Chinese Theatre and the native ghosts, Fritz and Annabelle, and how Marilyn Monroe haunts the halls of the Roosevelt Hotel. Hayden listens intently, and I watch *him* just as intently. It's obvious he already knows all of this. So much for wooing him with my ghost tour.

We snake farther into the Hollywood Hills, catching an illuminated look at the Hollywood Sign. The tourists behind us snap photos religiously, but I look at the Hollywood Sign from the Skroll offices every day.

"While it might preside over Hollywood like a calling, the sign has a grisly history. It was originally built as an advertisement for the Hollywoodland housing development." Sinister music plays beneath Gary's narration. "In 1929, a young actress—"

"It was 1932."

I turn to Hayden. Gary scowls. "What was that?"

At first I think he might be nervous with the attention on him, then I realize Hayden's not nervous. He's frustrated. I mean, how could we *not* know this? We are absolute fools.

"It was 1932. Peg Entwistle jumped off the H in *1932*, not 1929. Now hikers see her apparition in her *1930s* clothing haunting the park."

"Anything else to share?" Gary prods.

"It's also just a legend that, the day after her death, she received a role offer. It's never been proven."

Gary throws a fiery stare Hayden's way. "This guy'll take tips at the end of the tour, I guess."

Hayden rubs the bridge of his nose beneath his glasses while the bus leads us deeper into Griffith Park. He grumbles to himself as Gary feeds the tourists an overdramatic story about the random body parts that showed up in the park over the years. Gary alleges that the mysterious body parts were credited to the Night Stalker, to which Hayden hisses a soft "no" under his breath.

I already know this man will do half of my job for me. He's a hot human encyclopedia of weird knowledge.

We weave through the hills past the Old Zoo in Griffith Park and the Hollywood Forever Cemetery, where stars are laid to rest. As we round out the tour, the van leads us up Benedict Canyon, past commuters stuck in traffic heading into the Valley.

Poor suckers.

"As idyllic as these hills might seem, they are home to one of the grisliest murders in history. In August 1969, cult leader Charles Manson and his followers murdered actress Sharon Tate and four friends. Manson's orders were to 'do it as gruesome as you can.' And boy, did they! The world was horrified

by the images of 'pig' written in blood on the front door and
to hear of the death of Tate, who was eight and a half months
pregnant at the time. The house remains a tough sell for real
estate agents all over Los Angeles. Can't imagine why—"

"The house isn't even there anymore," Hayden interrupts.
"It was torn down in 1994."

"It's still there, kid. 10050 Cielo Drive. Plug it into Google."

Hayden slips his glasses off, dropping them into his lap.
Years come off his face instantly. I note the small indents on
the bridge of his nose left behind from the frames. I don't get
to fixate on his oddly charming features before I realize that
Hayden taking his glasses off is akin to a cowboy cocking his
gun before a duel.

Hayden is about to throw it down over Charles Manson.

I can't tell if I'm horrified or horrifically amused.

Hayden digs the bases of his palms into his eyes. "No, it's
not. The house was demolished. Now the David Oman House
is the closest location to the site of the murders. A hundred
and fifty feet away. *That* is where most of the hauntings take
place now. Apparitions of the murder victims have been seen
in the house and in the area. It's one of the best-documented
paranormal locations in Los Angeles. Plug it into Google."

Oh my god. Oh my god, no.

Not only is Hayden not enjoying the ghost tour, but we are
about to get banned from every ghost tour in Los Angeles. I
doubt he'll want to work with me in any capacity if this is the
first hangout activity I come up with. However, I am beginning to wonder if I did get ripped off with these tickets. Gary
hasn't known a rat's ass about any of the places we went.

"Did *you* write the script for this tour, kid?"

"Obviously not," he replies. His voice slips into a lilt of a

Boston accent. It should not be hot, but boy, is it. "But I could have. If I did, it'd at least be factually correct. At least people would be getting their money's worth."

"Who are you going to trust?" Gary poses to the rest of the van. "Me, a professional, or some nitwit millennial?"

I clear my throat. "Uh . . . the nitwit millennial."

Hayden stifles a laugh beside me. His smile is a bright but hidden secret, and when his gaze reaches mine, I feel like I've been let in on it. The older woman sitting behind us ponders, too, before conceding that she would side with the nitwit millennial as well. Gary drops his microphone and buckles his seat belt.

We ride in silence back to the theater, Gary occasionally pointing out locations like The Viper Room and The Comedy Store and explaining their history. Hayden remains quiet this time, but part of me wishes he'd speak up. At least I'd get a bit of my money's worth if he gave out the info.

We tip Gary regardless and pace in silence over the names of stars long dead until we reach the parking garage.

"I'm parked here."

He nods. "I'm around the corner. Thanks for tonight. It was . . ."

"That was kind of a disaster."

His shoulders rise, and my shame fades when he breaks into a quiet laugh. "I wouldn't say that."

"Really?"

"No, it's not your fault Gary doesn't know the difference between an apparition and a possession."

"Neither do I."

Instead of giving a know-it-all retort, he smiles. "There's time to learn."

Hayden had not offered Gary the same kind of grace. Another beat of silence. *Have I somehow made this conspiracy theorist trust the local nonbeliever?*

"So, what do you think about the show?" I finally ask.

Hayden stiffens but nods slowly. "Hallie, it's a compelling proposal, but let me sleep on it—"

"Remember, I need to present this to my boss by Friday morning. If it's a no, I need to know soon. But . . . I hope it's *not* a no."

"I know. I won't hold you up too long, I promise. This is new, and I don't know yet if I'm the person you think I am. On camera, at least."

"Do you think the person behind the mic is going to be so different in front of a camera?"

He jingles his keys in the palm of his hand with a nervous jitter. "I might need help."

I smile. "Well, that's what I'm here for."

Instead of answering, Hayden reaches into his vest pocket and tosses something my direction. My hand-eye coordination fails me, and I fumble to catch what he's thrown. It's the tiny alien from his drink. "Talk to you soon, Hallie."

• CHAPTER 3 •

I have a Pavlovian response to the sound of my email dinging, so despite the late night I had, when it pings, I am, regretfully, awake.

My laptop is still open on my bed, a half-fleshed-out deck on my screen and two new emails in my inbox. There's another candle sale at Bath & Body Works, and I can trim three inches off my waist, apparently, by clicking a suspicious link from someone named Chaz8762o06@6mail.biz. But there is no email from Hayden yet.

I know I'd asked a lot of him, but for most people the opportunity to have this kind of platform would be a no-brainer. But to Hayden, the existence of Bigfoot and aliens and Mothboy is a no-brainer, too. I missed that memo.

The clock reads eight thirty a.m. Nora left for the office early to help her best friend, Jamie, set up for a shoot. Skroll might be fast and loose with hours and policy, but with the thin ice I'm skating on, it won't help me to show up late. I scramble out of bed, hunting through my drawers for clothes and applying enough makeup to hide how I spent my whole night in front of my laptop, waiting for an email from a hot guy.

I've been living in Nora's apartment for a few months now,

and I'm still not fully used to this being *my* room. After sharing for so long, it's still strange to use the space and live in it how *I* want. After her last roommate left LA to do some soul-searching after Burning Man, Nora was a week or two away from finding a new place with Jamie, before I showed up two months ago asking for a place to stay. All I had then was smudged mascara, a single duffel bag of my belongings, and the resolve that I wouldn't let someone like Cade control my life any longer.

I step into the kitchen to grab a granola bar on the way out the door when something taps behind me from the other side of the living room.

Lizzie.

I'm getting used to most things about living with Nora, but I will never be used to her terrifying bearded dragon, Lizzie (short for Lizard) Borden. I don't love the way Lizzie stares at me while we watch TV, and I especially don't like how half the time I can't find her—it fosters the fear that she's escaped and will end up somewhere in my bed.

I do not like nature. I do not vibe well with wildlife.

I pad over to the case and make sure it's shut. Lizzie and I lock eyes. She blinks slowly.

"Goodbye," I hiss. Lizzie dive-bombs for a grape she's just discovered at the bottom of the terrarium.

Halfway into my commute, my phone buzzes with an email, and I nearly swerve off Mulholland Drive. I know emailing and driving is a bad idea, but the way Hayden's name pops up on my phone makes my stomach flutter. I'm ninety percent sure it's not my ibuprofen breakfast coming back to bite me.

FROM: Hayden Hargrove
SUBJECT: Re: Re: Re: Re: The Out There—Web Series Inquiry from Skroll

Sorry for the late reply, but I've done more thinking, and I would like to take you up on this project. I think The Out There has room to grow, and I'm eager to see what ideas you have for the series.

I've attached my documents that I use to pitch to sponsors. Feel free to use the materials as you see fit and keep me updated.

—H

I pull over, take a deep breath, and let out a relieved yell before veering back onto the road. I hunt through Spotify, find a playlist titled "yas bitch," and crank it. My brain rushes with potential slide ideas for my deck. If I work my ass off all day today, I can have a pitch ready for tomorrow morning. Chloe likes to give us Friday afternoons off, and she mostly does it to head to Joshua Tree early to do . . . well, *something* in the desert with her boyfriend.

The Skroll offices are still quiet by the time I reach my desk, just the early-morning bustle at the coffee machine and someone cursing at the office printer. Nora and Jamie are congregated over her neighboring desk as he troubleshoots something on her video-editing software. Most of us sit in one large room with desks side by side, our screens in clear sight of everyone else's at all times. It was particularly awkward when someone's assignment had them Googling things that would put them on a watch list.

I wonder if *The Out There* will get me put on a list.

I wonder if Hayden is *already* on a list.

Is that going to alter our ability to travel? I did not factor that into the budget.

"Morning, Hal," Nora says. Jamie waves as he sips his coffee. While Nora is hardly five foot and thin as a rail, her clothes and attitude are like trendy, untied sneakers or undone buttons at the top of a shirt. Meanwhile, Jamie Santos is laced up like a corset. He's shy with a warm affability that makes him malleable wherever he goes. He's also unfairly handsome. With dark wavy hair and golden-brown skin, he's a UK transplant who grew up across the world with his documentary filmmaker parents, and all the interns have massive crushes on him. He's the kind of person who wears button-downs and sometimes ties to the office each day, but it's hardly out of character with his lilt of a British accent and prep school background.

Yet somehow, he and Nora are inseparable.

Jamie is a fixture around our apartment, sometimes subjecting Nora to excessively boring movie marathons or absolutely crushing *Jeopardy!* with takeout after work. He's pleasant, unobtrusive, and picks up after himself, but I get the feeling he saves his most vibrant colors for Nora.

"So, you came home late last night? Hot date?" Nora reclaims her seat, munching on a muffin as Jamie snags the last part of the muffin top. She yanks it away from him, rolling her eyes. Instead of another heist attempt, he lets his gaze linger on her with an affectionate half smile.

My glare must speak for itself. Hot? Yes. Date? No way. Even if Hayden was the nicest guy in the entire world, "date" is still a terrifying word like "taxes" or "benefits open enroll-ment." I'm not sure I'm old enough to use any of them yet.

"No, I was meeting with someone whose show I might work on."

"Do tell," Nora pushes.

I Google *The Out There* and pull up Hayden's well-manicured website. For someone whose content is so balls to the wall, he spends good money making himself look completely legit. I let the two of them scroll through. Nora clicks on the "About" page, where Hayden's headshot and bio pop up. Heat rushes into my cheeks as my fingers curl around the tiny plastic alien in my jacket pocket.

"*Well*," she gasps. "Damn, this guy's a looker. And you had drinks with him last night?"

A drink, and then he argued with a hokey ghost tour guide for the rest of the night.

"Yeah. He's nice. Conspiracies and monsters aren't my thing, but there's something about him that I am compelled by."

"His face?"

"*Nora.*"

"Unhelpful, I know, but tell me I'm wrong. If this show gets picked up, I vote Jamie and I come help you work on it."

As Skroll contributors, Jamie and Nora are welcome to bounce around shows as needed in between writing their weekly listicles and think pieces. Last week, Nora wrote a riv-eting article on how many bath bombs it'd take to dye your skin purple, which still shows in our shared bathtub. Jamie, meanwhile, writes film reviews far too intelligent for a site that mostly offers critiques via GIFs. I think he sticks around for the camaraderie and health insurance he might not get freelancing.

"Oh, so *I* don't get to vote for myself?" Jamie mocks. "I feel so special."

Nora swivels her chair to hip-check him. He dodges her blow, leaning his elbow on top of her head before she wiggles from underneath him.

"Refill?" he asks.

"Please." Jamie departs with both of their mugs, and Nora turns to me. "Does he really look like this in person?"

My stomach jitters congeal. I think of squishing into the tour van with Hayden last night and the way our knees brushed. I think of how good he smelled and the bright greens in his eyes when he got excited about ghosts and cryptids. I knew how I physically felt when I was around him—pure, un-bridled attraction—but in the aftermath, I'm left with my contradictory thoughts.

It's uncouth to date someone I'm going to be working so closely with. It'd be wrong to let my emotions and baggage weigh down our professional relationship.

Besides, I'm not sure I believe I can let myself fall in love again.

"Yeah, he does, but it's irrelevant. I'm not sure I'm looking for . . ."

The dark and fuzzy corners of my brain know I won't be alone forever, but it's hard to convince myself of that some-times. Sometimes I think of how much easier it'd be to be alone. I can't fall for someone's pretty words ever again. I learned the hard way that red flags are like quicksand—easy to miss unless you know what to look for, too hard to pull yourself out of when you're in deep.

"I get it." She doesn't need to dwell on it more. We've had this conversation plenty of times. "Look, right now, I want you to focus on writing a killer pitch and getting yourself into this program. Believe in yourself."

Nora taps a magnet on her filing cabinet—a cat in space drinking wine with the caption "Believe in Yourself"—beside her "Chaotic Bisexual" decal.

I linger on her words. "Okay. If I'm going to get into the Series Program, I need to make a kick-ass deck."

* * *

By the following morning, I *have* made a kick-ass deck. The visuals are sharp, and I've supplemented the slides Hayden gave me with examples from his episodes—particularly funny clips, engaging storytelling moments, and anything that shows off his on-air charisma. I've started to hear Hayden's voice in my head more than my own. I send him the finished product, but I don't receive a response by the time Chloe calls me to the Sad Keanu conference room.

I know she and Kevin, Skroll's CEO, are sitting inside with notebooks, ready to pick my presentation apart, but I've practiced this. I know what I'm talking about. I know I have a good idea. This was what I'd wanted years ago—to pull random acts from the ether and bring them into the spotlight.

I remind myself that I am an asset. The videos I worked on at Skroll were regular viral hits and brought in money, viewers, and attention. Cade leeched off my talent and ideas for a reason—because he *knew* how good I was. It was *my* hard work that even got me the chance to vie for this spot. I'm valuable here, and I am going to be valuable in driving *The Out There* to first place. I need to be.

But that doesn't change the fact that Skroll has felt like a minefield for the past two months. Cade's gravitational pull is strong and Skroll revolves around him in orbit, and no matter how many times I tell myself I'm moving on, I will always fear his presence and the way he has nearly everyone wrapped around his finger.

I sense his approach like a rippling glass of water in *Jurassic Park*. Without seeing him right away, I can smell the familiar scent of overpriced cologne and mint gum with notes of sativa clinging to the air, and I know the low and smoky "hey" he offers to anyone he passes. At one point, it'd charmed me and made me feel special when I desperately wanted to mean something. When I'd felt the things I did for him so infrequently, how was I supposed to know it wasn't normal?

I clutch my laptop closer to my chest, ready for it to take a bullet for me. My funky patterned tights, jean shorts, and sweater feel like weak armor. There's nowhere to run right now. He stops in his tracks and turns to me with a cloying smile. I immediately think of everything wrong with me today.

Does my hair look greasy?

Is my concealer creasing at my eyes, showing how tired I am?

Have I put on enough weight for Cade to notice?

Is there enough on my hips for him to pinch and snipe at?

I try to stop spiraling and instead brainstorm everything I like about myself. I like my fun hair and I like my body. I love my offbeat style and I know I am a damn good producer. But with Cade standing in front of me, I can't believe any of my own affirmations. I'm left thinking of all the places I don't measure up.

"Are . . . are you meeting with Chloe and Kevin?" Cade asks, damn well knowing the answer.

"No, I'm loitering outside of Sad Keanu for no reason."

"They offered you Eric's spot, didn't they?"

"I'm pitching *my* show."

"Really now?" Cade rubs his jaw with a laugh, but behind the laugh, I watch his blue eyes steel over with intimidation. Cade knows as well as anyone that *I* was the skill and tact behind his videos and shows. If I'm competing on my own, I'm going to kick his ass.

I *have* to kick his ass.

"Don't sound so shocked," I spit back. "I have a show and it's going to be good."

"Hallie," he sighs, "you really think you're ready for something like this?"

His voice says "you know you aren't" and "are you sure you want to compete against me?" It took too long to learn that what looked like support from the surface at Skroll was a slow degradation of my confidence underneath. Since the night I left him, I have resolved that I don't need to listen to him. I don't need to believe him when I hear his words in my head over and over again. *I'm hard to work with. I don't stand out. I don't matter.* I still feel every word like daggers between my ribs, even as I'm trying my best to heal. Stupid, shitty armor in the form of a blush-pink polyester sweater.

But I recite my own affirmations in my head nevertheless. One day, I'll believe them.

"I . . ."

His eyebrows pop as I stutter. It shouldn't be this hard to face him. I did it once before, but I am still paying the price. I'll be paying that price for a while. The girl he was with before me, Sam, another Skroll producer, stuck by him for a year before leaving him. It was impossible for her to find a job in digital media after he dragged her name through the mud. By the time I learned this, his claws were already in too deep and I couldn't bear to lose everything I'd worked for.

I wonder what kind of person gets off on hurting people— perhaps the same kind of person that drinks his coffee completely black and literally never wears socks. "Use your words, babe."

"I'm not going to be on camera. I found my own hot white guy to host, and I'm going to win."

Cade's lips turn up with another condescending smile. "Very mature—"

The door to Sad Keanu swings wide open and Chloe stands in the doorway. She glances between Cade and me. While Kevin sucks Cade's proverbial artistic dick, Chloe merely tolerates him. If Chloe had more sway, I don't imagine Cade would have a job.

"Hallie, we're ready for you. Cade, can I help you?"

Cade's eyes light up with the same fake affection he's used to keep Skroll wrapped around his finger. He smiles at Chloe, but his eyes serve as a reminder to me. *Don't shine too bright on your own.* Too bad, Cade. Too damn bad. "No, just wishing Hallie good luck, is all. You guys are in for a real treat with her pitch."

Cade gives my arm a reassuring pat and it takes everything in me to not cringe.

"Right. Well, bye."

She tugs me into the conference room and takes her seat at the other end of the boardroom table with Kevin. Kevin Chadwick doesn't like the title "CEO" and instead prefers to be called "Champ," which I think is arguably worse. He's five-foot-eight worth of smooth talking with dollar signs for eye-balls. Skroll has always been a boys' club, and part of me worries if he'll even consider what a girl like me has to say, so with this chance I have, I need to stand out and bring him something he can't look away from.

"Hi, Champ. Hi, Chloe." I set my computer up to present my slides and suck in a few deep breaths, wishing I'd taken Nora up on her vape pen earlier. At least I'd feel less sweaty, and I wouldn't be back to thinking of all the worst-case scenarios.

Believe in yourself. Do not disappoint space wine cat.

Believe in yourself the way Hayden believes in Bigfoot.

I can't believe I smile at the thought, but as I look back down at my opening slide, I *can* believe there is something better around the corner for me.

"Thank you for giving me this opportunity. I'm really excited to bring you this pitch because I *know* this show will be an amazing addition to the Skroll family. Now, in the wake of the current true-crime craze, people are compelled by the unknown and unexplained more than ever. But how about we go a little deeper? A little more . . . *out there*?"

Both pick their heads up as I start my deck.

"*The Out There* is a long-running conspiracy theories podcast that looks at a new mystery or monster each episode, digs into the origins, and lays out the theories. It's hosted by Hayden Hargrove, who I think will make a great on-camera talent for the Series Program. Hayden not only has a great voice for podcasting, but I discovered him on an episode of *Cosmic Conspiracies*, and he has such a relatable, passionate on-camera presence, as well. Every episode is framed like a story—supplemented with real audio files from famous cases, interviews with experts, and other materials."

I run through some of the stats Hayden's provided me, from his weekly listeners to some vague financial details and sponsorship info. I expected his sponsorships to be odd organizations hunting for aliens, and he *does* have those, but most of them are normal: Bluetooth headphones, audio-editing programs, glasses manufacturers. Both Kevin and Chloe are impressed.

"I think there is serious potential in adapting *The Out There* to a web series. We can elevate the listening experience to a viewing experience, including actual video footage, doing deep investigative dives and in-person paranormal hunts. As an example of the fun but engaging tone of the show, I have a couple of clips for you to listen to."

I run them through a few quick clips from episodes—one about Bigfoot; another about a haunted hospital, where Hayden interviewed a paranormal medium on her experiences there; and another about the Denver airport. Because he'd mentioned it, I investigated the place myself. I learned a lot of far-fetched shit, but some of the segments on the episode were a blast to listen to.

"We can create a new kind of investigation show—not like the overdramatic staged shows on TV, something fun and accessible for a wider audience—"

"Hallie, I didn't take you for a conspiracy theorist," Kevin teases.

"I'm not. I'm actually a pretty big skeptic."

"So why did you bring this to us?"

"Because I think Hayden is a great talent and has a way with words, and if he can convince someone like me to listen to hours of his podcast, I think he'd convince a lot of our viewers to tune in, too. Whether or not you believe what he's saying, it *is* entertaining. Hell, why do you think *Cosmic Conspiracies* has seventeen seasons?"

"He's hot, too," Chloe whispers, jotting notes.

"Hargrove . . ." Kevin muses. "Where do I know that name from?"

"Have *you* been listening to *The Out There*?" I jab.

This gets a small chuckle out of him. I've never made Kevin chuckle before. Fuck yeah.

"So . . . what do you say?" I ask.

* * *

Minutes later, I dip out of Sad Keanu and into Success Kid and pull out my phone. I linger over Hayden's number, but instead I set the phone down and scrub my hands over my face with a few giddy bounces. I will need another reapply of deodorant, but I *will* be going for one of the beers in the kitchen. I want to "cheers!" everyone I see.

I calm myself and wait for Hayden to answer.

"Hello?"

"Hey, Hayden. It's Hallie . . . you know, from Skroll."

He laughs softly on the other end of the line, and I feel like a puddle. "Hi—did you present the deck to your boss?"

"I did."

"And?"

"We're in," I say, trying to hide my giddiness.

"Really?"

"You sound shocked."

"I'm surprised such a mainstream company wants to pick up my show about Mothman," he says. There's a sense of

bewilderment in his voice, until he clears his throat and levels himself out. "I mean, wow . . . that's great. So, what are our
next steps?"

"They want a pilot episode by the end of next week. It's a
bit of a crunch, but we're joining the game late. We can reuse
one of your old episodes so we don't have to do the research
from scratch. We can set up a time to get to work."

He's quiet for a moment. "Yeah, we've got a lot of work to
do. What are you up to tomorrow?"

"Nothing."

"Good. We've got to catch you up to speed."

He hangs up before I can ask what the hell he means.

CHAPTER 4

*H*ayden might live in LA, but he lives *downtown*.

With how large LA is, downtown might as well be in a different state. It reminds me of being back home in New York, minus the quaint bodegas and endless good food at every corner. Instead, there are so many unidentifiable office buildings, apartments meant to look like lavish Italian villas overlooking the cluttered LA freeways, and the full gauntlet of niche restaurants and bars.

I round the corner and park in Hayden's guest lot. His building is straight out of a history book on Art Deco architecture. A decorative marquee hangs in front of the entryway—which has a *doorman*—and gold-plated revolving doors. It looks more like a high-end hotel than an apartment building. Hell, it beats the two-story stucco monstrosity of my apartment building. The inside is industrial-chic, with exposed brick and aesthetically placed pipes. There are flatscreens on the walls, playing what looks like artistic sensory videos for babies. I watch them, mesmerized, as I wait for an elevator up to the twelfth floor.

I follow the hall to the corner apartment, hesitating before knocking. It's real now. We have *work* to do and both of our careers hinge on it. Well, at least if all else fails, Hayden can go back to podcasting. Judging by the type of apartment he lives in, he's doing fine talking about cryptids and monsters.

Me, though . . . I'll be out of a job. I'll have proved Cade right. I don't matter. I wasn't special enough on my own.

I finally knock, and the door swings open. Today, Hayden's wearing a heather-gray T-shirt with "West Virginia State Cryptozoology Department" and who I *think* is Mothdude on it. After a bit of Googling, I can now successfully identify several notable cryptids. Bigfoot's easy, so is the Loch Ness Monster. I'm still working on the rest.

The T-shirt shows that the odd deer tattoo on his forearm is hardly the end of the artwork. Ink extends up to a massive piece on his upper arm. There are waves, a ship, and . . . tentacles? They wrap around his bicep and shoulder, where other tiny shop minimum–type tattoos paint the inside of his bicep down to his forearm.

Fiddlesticks.

He has nice biceps.

"Hey, come on in," Hayden invites. I step inside and slip my jacket off. He quickly takes it and hangs it on an honest-to-god coatrack. *I* don't even have a coatrack.

I'm expecting Hayden's apartment to be much like the other twenty-something guy apartments I've been in—messy, disorganized, with sad attempts at furniture and décor—but it's not. Hayden's apartment is so *bright*. Huge windows line the back wall. My eyes leap from rooftop bar to rooftop pool to glowing billboards. It looks like an old warehouse, gutted and retrofitted into a trendy loft. The open-concept living room and kitchen have exposed brick walls and more industrial beams and pipes.

He also knows how to decorate. The walls are decked with

expensive-looking art, there's a basket of decorative balls and scented pinecones on the coffee table, and an extensive built-in bookcase along the back wall near the flatscreen. Who the hell is this man?

He smells good, dresses well, and looks like he moisturizes.

I bet he even has a bed frame.

"You found it okay?"

"Yeah." I take in the scent of warm cinnamon and leather-bound books. "I don't come downtown often, but this is nice."

"It's home."

"And you afford this just from your podcast?"

It's complete word vomit, but the benefit of LA is that it's not actually uncouth to ask about people's rent. It's always high, and we are always sad about it.

"My dad owned the unit, but it's mine now. So, kind of, but not really."

"Right . . ." I trail off. Hayden shoves his hands in his pockets and we linger in silence. If we are going to work together, we have to be friendly. We have to trust one another. He needs to believe I'm guiding him on the best path, and I have to believe the content he's creating will make us both money. I've learned by now to never count on the nice guys. Friendly could be nothing more than an outfit.

Something about Hayden feels different, though. I debated meeting him somewhere public to keep a boundary in place, but when he mentioned he had a recording studio built in his apartment, it was hard to argue he wasn't well equipped. Yet I still feel anxiety roiling in my stomach at the idea of being alone with him. I fear the awkward small talk, the uncomfortable feeling of a first playdate with a new friend, and the tingling feeling he leaves in my chest. Even his emails and phone calls make my heart race in a way that scares me. It scares me most because I can't control it.

The last time I was in a man's apartment was the night I left Cade, and that didn't go well.

"Can I get you something to drink?"

"Just water is fine," I say.

He pours a glass of water from the Brita filter and passes me the cup. The side of the glass reads "Property of Area 51." I note the items stuck on his fridge—a newspaper clipping about a strange creature sighting, an alien-shaped bottle opener, and a sticky note with a number that reads "Dark Web Guy." As I take a sip, something hairy rubs against my leg. I jump back with a yelp and glance down. A well-fed gray cat gawks up at me with huge yellow pupils and meows, but it sounds more like a rabid raccoon in a garbage disposal.

"Hi," I appease the cat.

"That's Cthulhu."

At the sound of his name, Cthulhu flops over, and I'm concerned he won't be able to get back up. If so, do I flip him over again? Do I have to pick him up? I like cats in theory, but in practice, I end up with scratches *everywhere*. I squat beside the cat and give his tummy a rub. He simply accepts my gesture.

"Well, he doesn't *behave* like a Lovecraftian monster."

"No." Hayden laughs. "His sea monster days are long gone now. Right, buddy?"

Cthulhu successfully flips over and waddles in Hayden's direction, brushing himself against Hayden's jeans and leaping onto a short cat tree. I don't think he'd be able to jump much higher.

"So," Hayden transitions, tossing the cat a treat, "before

we get started, I think it might be a good idea to run you through some basics."

"Basics?"

He nods, moving into the living room. I follow, plopping myself on his smooth leather couch. Instead of sitting with me, he turns on the flatscreen and stands in front of it. Then I notice the clicker in his hands.

Oh no.

Nothing good comes of a man with a clicker.

The stiff, nervous guy who invited me in slides off like a jacket as he rubs his hands together.

"If we're going to make a show together, you should be on my level. See, I can make a deck, too." He winks. Does this man's personality only turn on when he's talking about cryptids?

"Nothing could ever put me on your level, Hayden."

"I encourage you to take notes." Hayden raises a small notepad and a pen beside his head, but I respond by reaching into my bag and taking out my own. I came prepared and he is delighted.

The TV lights up with a blank slide. Hayden hits a button on his remote, and a title pops up.

Suddenly, his dorky monster T-shirt fits him like a well-worn uniform and he's the guy I saw on TV a few days ago. Eager, passionate, and ready to spew some weird shit. This is like the world's strangest college lecture.

CRYPTIDS & CONSPIRACIES 101

I write the words in my notebook and feel shame.

"I'm ready," I say, but I am not sure I am. I'm willing to learn the ropes, identify the local cryptids of North America, but I have a deep-seated fear that, one day, I will buy into all of this. Maybe one day, I'll be the girl in the alien T-shirt, too.

He clears his throat and hits the next slide. "So, per Merriam-Webster, 'a cryptid is an animal, such as a Sasquatch or the Loch Ness Monster, which has been *claimed* to exist but never *proven* to exist—'"

"Because they're fake—" I mutter into my notepad.

"They are *not*!" he rejects, pointing the clicker at me like he caught me passing notes in class. "Now, 'contrary to popular belief, cryptids don't *have* to be supernatural, mythical, or all that strange—though many popular creatures acquire these characteristics as their legends grow.' I am quoting all of this, by the way; I didn't write this myself."

"Oh good," I mutter. "I was worried."

Yet, even as I dismiss Hayden, I'm amazed at the confidence he has when he gets on these topics. Even if he didn't write the definition himself, he knows it well enough to recite it from memory. I'm alarmingly turned on by this man, waving emphatically with a clicker in hand in front of a drawing of the Vitruvian man with an alien head.

I unbutton the top of my flannel.

"Moving on—some of the most popular cryptids include Bigfoot, the Loch Ness Monster, Mothman, El Chupacabra, the Yeti, and the Jersey Devil. Cryptids come from all over the world, and all cultures have their own mysterious creatures."

Even though he sounds batshit peculiar, I do like listening to Hayden talk. His voice is soothing and I enjoy watching the way his arms flex as he waves them around, pointing to different figures on the slides. He *does* whip out a laser pointer. He swirls the light around a horrific drawing of the Jersey Devil onscreen.

"See, *hooves*." He circles them with the laser pointer. "Horse *head*, *wings*, *antlers*. So, clearly, this is *not* your average horse."

Then Cthulhu waddles into the room before being informed the laser pointer is not for him.

Several slides later, I raise my hand.

"Uh . . . yes?"

"Which one is your favorite?"

Hayden frowns. His arms cross in front of his chest, and I wish he wouldn't do things like that. Or that he'd at least put on a jacket or long sleeves or *something*. "Really?"

"I want to know."

"Genuinely?"

I nod.

He scratches the back of his neck, like he hadn't been expecting my genuine interest. "I dunno, probably Bigfoot?"

"Boring."

He breaks into an even larger frown. "Yeah, says the girl who doesn't even think he's real! Look, would you fault someone who said their favorite superhero was Superman? They're iconic for a reason, duh. Any other questions?"

"So many . . ."

I spend the next hour learning everything from the origins of cryptozoology to whatever the fuck a Flatwoods Monster is before we transition.

"The other half of this podcast is conspiracy theories. I lump cryptozoology in with conspiracies because I personally think there's a bit of overlap. Like, for example, there are theories that Mothman came from a World War II munitions plant, but that's just a theory." He clicks to the next slide, featuring a Venn diagram with examples that feel like a foreign language, and laces his fingers together. "See? Overlap."

I *am* taking notes, but Hayden promises a printout of his deck to keep on hand as we work on episodes. I promise him I'll sleep with it under my pillow, but he doesn't find this amusing.

"So, when you talk conspiracy theories, you're talking like JFK assassination, Area 51, the fake moon landing . . ."

He nods, running his fingers through his hair. He's worked himself up at some point discussing the differences between types of Sasquatches, and he now has a faint sheen of sweat along his hairline. "Exactly. There are a lot of conspiracy theories that are steeped in racism and anti-Semitism, so I avoid those because they don't need airtime and I don't want to validate them. Unless I feel particularly vocal and want to disprove certain theories and point out why they suck."

"We love that," I say. "Woke conspiracy theorist."

I follow him through the rest of his slideshow, where he breaks down common conspiracies and the theories behind them. Through the duration of his presentation, I ponder if the man missed his calling as a cool, hot high school teacher. I ask for a refill of water when he begins to explain that we on Earth do not have the technological capabilities to mutilate cattle in the way aliens do. It's complete with vigorous hand motions that make it look like he's slaughtering a cow in his living room.

"Did you retain all of that?" Hayden asks.

"I think so. Now, where to begin?"

Finally, he joins me on the couch, his own notepad in hand. "So, some of my most popular podcast episodes were the four-part series I did on Area 51, the JFK assassination, and my episodes on Mothman. I did a two-part special on the *National Treasure* movies."

"Fuck, I love *National Treasure*."

"You mean the movie about a *conspiracy*," he jests, eyebrows raising over his glasses, "about the Founding Fathers?"

"It is a national treasure, and a fictional kids' movie starring Nicolas Cage. Moving on. If I were entirely new to this—"

"—which you are—"

"—where would you advise I begin?"

His eyes widen like I've asked him to teach me to reverse engineer a UFO or something. "Honestly, I might start with something basic—cases of alien abductions, the Roswell crash— or keep it classic and go with Bigfoot."

"Let's start with Roswell. I think there's some potential there. It's still grounded, but *definitely* out there. I think enough people know about it that it's attention grabbing."

"I mean, *yeah*." His eyes widen. "What's more attention grabbing than alien corpses?"

Perhaps I am wrong about Roswell being easy to digest. "Wow, you got me there."

"All right, let me pull up the episode."

We huddle around Hayden's computer as he plays the episode. Both of us sit on the couch with notebooks in hand, taking notes throughout. As with all his episodes, Hayden knows how to tell a story. He doesn't come across like a raving zealot on YouTube. He makes a conspiracy about a damn weather balloon compelling.

By the end of the episode, I have a vision. He'll give an abbreviated lesson—infographics, narration, images. We can shape it like a monster-of-the-week TV episode, full of his quips and jokes. Since it's our first episode and we're getting our feet wet, we'll use the Skroll studios. When we have the go-ahead for the season and a more concrete budget, we can eventually go on ghost hunts and monster hunts and take inspiration from the existing episodes and work our footage into it.

"We'd need to find the clip of Obama saying that the classified UFO stuff isn't really that interesting—because, you know, that's what he *has* to say, right?"

I roll my eyes. "What if it's not *actually* that interesting?"

Hayden slides onto the floor, resting his notebook on the coffee table and reading a book from the shelf. He doesn't look up to argue with me this time. "Sometimes the truth *is* the real story. It's all a matter of what you believe. Some people trust what they're told, some of us don't."

"Right," I say. Cade's face flashes in my mind and his insidious words echo in my brain. "And you're trusting your show with a known nonbeliever."

He shrugs, an obvious smile threatening to break out. "If we're both here, you obviously believe in something."

"I don't know about that."

"Well, why not?"

I think on his question. Hayden knows more about cryptids and conspiracies than even the deepest Wikipedia rabbit holes, but when he glances across the table, I feel warm inside, and when I realize he is genuinely asking for my opinion, my throat suddenly feels dry.

"I guess . . . I guess I don't want to fall for everything people tell me."

"It's not about *falling* for it," he corrects, with no condescension in his voice. "No one tricked me into believing in this stuff. There's no grand master plan with malicious intent in believing in Bigfoot. At least, I don't *think* so. There *could* be, but I'd have to do more research."

I leave Hayden vexed as he thinks all of this over.

"You mean Bigfoot is not running a phishing scam?"

He shakes his head with conviction. "I doubt it."

"How did you get into this stuff? It's a very . . . *niche* interest."

Instead of a snarky response, Hayden quiets, tapping his pen against his pad. His Adam's apple bobs as he looks away, back down at the Roswell book. Has he been abducted by aliens or had a traumatic run-in with Bigfoot?

He clears his throat. "My dad. Weird stuff was his thing."

Was. The past tense is not lost on me, nor was it lost on me when he said the apartment *used* to belong to his father. I can gather enough from that and the way Hayden clicks his pen repeatedly to fill the silence. The question is Out There, but I doubt I'll get an answer anytime soon.

"So . . ." Hayden's eyes skim the page in front of him, then life floods back into his eyes. He waves his pen in circles to pivot me back to Roswell. "There's this thing called the Ramey Memo we should talk about . . ."

CHAPTER 5

I wait for Hayden outside the Skroll offices on Monday morning. We're deep in one of LA's surprisingly hot winter weeks. The apartment I share with Nora is a sweltering sauna and my lone cactus shriveled up overnight. So much for *easy* plants.

My nerves don't help my sweatiness, either. I fan myself with my oversized flannel and sweep my short blue waves into a ponytail. Even my well-loved Docs feel prone to causing blisters today. When Hayden rounds the corner, I realize he must feel the same. He clutches our final scripts like they're the only buoy left in the ocean, and there's none of the loose, easy composure I saw all Saturday. He could recite the smallest details about the Roswell crash at the drop of a hat and his confidence never wavered; even when I had a fact to shoot holes in, he was a bulletproof vest of evidence and arguments.

"Morning," I say.

Hayden's shoulders relax like he's shrugging off a heavy backpack. Some part of him settles when he sees me, and I wonder why that is. Could he really trust me already?

"Hey."

There's still strain in his voice that confirms my suspicions. I am so drawn to those bold and bright moments he has, like a conspiratorial teakettle, spewing odd facts in that confident, deep lull. He's open and authentic in ways few people are, but today, it feels like he's been taken off the burner.

I tap my badge and let him inside, offering a reassuring smile. As his producer, he should know I *am* excited about what we're going to create together, even if I'm a little terrified too. He follows, eyeing the open-concept floorplan from the foosball tables to the cupcake vending machines.

"It looks like a see-through iPhone case in here."

I smirk. "All this money and they can't afford opaque walls."

"If only Area 51 had the same mindset," he mutters, thinking I can't hear it. I can't help but smile, but I hope he doesn't notice. Upstairs in studio three, Nora, Jamie, and I have spent the morning building our set. Thanks to next-day delivery and a few art prints Hayden sent me (sketches of something called a Wendigo, newspaper clippings about flying saucers, an annotated map of the US with different "critters" marked on it), we've created the perfect monster-hunting lair.

As we enter, Jamie scowls, ever the film kid, adjusting the lights on our camera. "It's dimly lit, which is honestly a bit of a pain in the ass. It looks like we've relegated the conspiracy theorist to the broom closet."

"It's a creative choice. I personally like the broom closet aesthetic," Nora remarks as we enter.

Hayden surveys the set, from the pictures hanging on the wall to the large wooden desk he'll sit behind with a stack of books on one side and a fake cast of a Bigfoot print we'd found online.

"This looks good." There's a small smile tugging at his lips.

Nora whips around, nearly colliding with Hayden, and grins.

"Hi, I'm Nora," she says. His height feels particularly staggering beside her. They exchange brief pleasantries and compliment each other's tattoos, but when Jamie guides Hayden behind the desk to test our sound and lighting, Nora turns to me. "I should start watching late-night conspiracy theory shows."

"Now," Jamie orders, keeping one eye fixed on his computer and the other on the camera screen in front of him, "say a few words from the script."

"Wait," Nora interrupts, "he's looking kind of dewy."

"Dewy?" Hayden asks. "What does 'dewy' mean?"

"It's a makeup thing," I assure him. "Don't worry about it."

Nora hops onto the desk and fishes some setting powder from her bag, dabbing Hayden's cheekbones and forehead. I catch myself wondering how soft his skin is or how good he smells up close, but I know a touch that simple and intimate would set my skin on fire.

"I bet they don't do your makeup in podcasting," she teases.

"No," Hayden agrees, "they do not."

"Now we're good."

We test our sound levels, and when Jamie shouts "Action!" Hayden clears his throat, and his eyes crash down to his script like a UFO in Roswell.

"In the summer of 1947, something crashed in the New Mexico desert that's been baffling the world ever since."

He *sounds* good, like a modern-day Orson Welles . . . but Orson Welles also knew when to look at the camera. Hayden narrates the intro we'd written together with ease on the oral front, but he's getting an F in the "presentation" column of the public speaking rubric.

"Whether it was a weather balloon, or something out of

this world, the answers are still Out There somewhere. On the premiere episode of *The Out There*, we investigate the crash at Roswell and how the US learned that you can't pull a no-take-backsies, especially when it comes to aliens."

"He didn't look up at the camera at all," Jamie whispers as Hayden continues into the body of the script. Nora elbows him in the side. "He *didn't*."

"He's nervous," I snap. "This is new for him."

But Jamie's right. It's possible that Hayden can't carry a *web series* the way he carries his podcast. I'd been so confident based off what I saw on TV, I knew he'd deliver here, too. He's charismatic and relatable and has a way of telling stories. I try to remind myself, before I panic, that this is his first take. It's my job to believe in him.

"Cut!" I call.

By the look on Hayden's face, he already knows. Shame weighs in each of his movements and he sinks into hiding behind his hair and glasses.

"It was bad, wasn't it?"

"No," I lie.

"You don't have to lie. It was bad."

"You need to rely on your script less. You know what you're talking about. I *know* you do." He sighs, crossing his arms in front of his chest. Again, the confidence is gone.

"Hallie, I don't think I am cut out to be on camera. I told you. That's not my area of expertise." Hayden's voice picks up like he's being played on one point five speed.

"You did it just fine on *Cosmic Conspiracies*."

"Yeah," he agrees, "but there was a guy there asking me questions! I just had to answer. I hardly knew they were filming me. Besides, I was *not* the headliner of that episode."

I sit on the side of the table in front of him. With his height, we're nearly eye level, and I hold his gaze. He swallows, looking at my leg just inches away from his fingertips, the slivers of brown in his bright green eyes clearer than ever in the studio lights. I smell his sharp cologne and, this close, I can see a tiny scar above his right eyebrow, usually hidden by his hair. I'm fighting every urge to nudge my knee closer to his hand just to know what his touch feels like.

Reality snaps me back when I remember we're working together. Feelings between coworkers and colleagues are bound to end in mess somehow. I learned the hard way with Cade. I nudge my leg away, creating space between us that I *know* needs to exist.

"You were to me," I say. The tightness in his throat loosens and his shoulders relax. "You spent an afternoon lecturing me about all the different cryptids and conspiracy theories out there. You made me—someone who does not believe in any of this—still want to work with you. You convinced *me*."

His head shoots up with a look in his eyes that screams "gotcha!" "That it's all real?"

My first thought—horrifyingly enough—is that none of this is real. I read a few articles about Simulation Theory the other night after he pitched it as a potential episode, and it *almost* slips out of my mouth.

"*No*, that you have this in you. I don't believe in any of this stuff. But I believe in *you*."

He chews on the words for a moment before clearing his throat. "I feel really sweaty."

Hayden clutches the collar of his shirt and fans himself. I catch peeks of tattoos on his chest, and I suddenly feel sweaty, too. Something about Hayden lights parts of me on fire I didn't think I could ever ignite again.

"That's okay. It happens in front of the cameras. These lights are hot."

"Right."

The world is full of mediocre men who never doubt themselves or their talent. Hell, Skroll employs a bunch of them. But Hayden has talent, and as his producer, it's my job to clear the clouds of doubt he's feeling.

"Remember, I'm just behind the camera. You can focus on me." His gaze shifts up as I continue. His Adam's apple bobs, and he studies me, eyes tracking from the desk over my hips and the rest of my body. Usually, an exploratory gaze would piss me off, but I like it when it's Hayden doing it, even if I shouldn't. "Tell it to me. Pretend it's just us talking in your living room."

"Okay, I can do that," Hayden says.

I step away, taking my place beside Jamie. Hayden takes a few deep breaths and finally looks up at the camera.

"In the summer of 1947, something crashed in the New Mexico desert that's been baffling the world ever since."

Several hours later, we've recorded half the episode, and I'm not sure any of it is usable.

Hayden is *better* when he recites the script to me, but he's still nothing like the charismatic host he is behind the mic. With each disappointing take, his energy level wanes, and he knows as well as we do how this is going.

"We'll break for lunch," I say. "All of you come back in an hour."

Nora and Jamie shut off the equipment and head for the kitchen and the weekly catered meals. Hayden lingers behind, flipping through his script in defeat. His shoulders sink, and he tears little fringes into his pages.

"You okay?"

"This is a disaster. I'm . . . I'm sorry. I really thought I could do this, but it's not that easy. I'm better when I can hide behind something. I just . . . You took a chance on me, and I'm blowing it. I was your shot at a show." His words hang heavy in his eyes. "God, and Nora and Jamie must think I'm an idiot. Like, where'd you find this guy?"

"Late-night TV. And not the fun talk-show kind," I tease.

He glances up with a weak smile.

"Lunch break goes for you, too. We'll come back in a bit and keep at it. You just have to get used to it."

"I don't have the *time* to get used to it. You've got a deadline to hit," he reminds me, as if I don't already know. I started sweating at the second take and haven't stopped. My bra is tragically sticky, and my Apple Watch has sent me two high heart rate notifications in the past hour.

"Trust me, I know. But we can spare an hour for you to relax before we get back to work, huh?"

His fingers rake through his dark hair, he rubs the bridge of his nose, and he finally stands. "Okay. I'm going to go take a walk or something. Clear my head."

Hayden slides out from behind the table and fumbles for his backpack, leaving me with just silence, doubt, and his marked-up scripts still resting on the table. My job at Skroll depends on how good he is, but I know what it's like to have someone holding something over my head. I can't do that to him. I plan to do my job well for both of us, not just myself.

This show is going to be a fucking hit, even if it kills me.

CHAPTER 6

*A*major smoking gun in this case comes right from the hand of Brigadier General Roger Ramey. In a photo from July 8, 1947, General Ramey is seen standing over a piece of the Roswell debris. In his hand is a sheet of paper that *seems* inconspicuous at first, but using modern technology, internet sleuths have been able to enhance the document in his hands, and what they've found could reveal out of this world information about what really happened at Roswell."

After returning from lunch, Hayden is better in front of the camera, but still doesn't jump off the screen. We'll be integrating infographics and recording ADR over some of the clips we plan to use, but something about Hayden running through the info alone leaves a lot to be desired.

At least he looked up from his script this time. At least we caught a few smiles.

The door opens. Chloe is one of the last people I want to see right now. Chloe will judge and evaluate our progress based off raw footage, and it could make or break the entire show.

Fuck.

Fuckity fuck.

"How's it going?" she whispers.

"Good!" I chirp, my voice cracking.

Nora marks a new take, and Hayden resumes explaining the findings of the Ramey Memo. I study Chloe's face the entire time, and I can't tell if she's bored or just absorbing it all.

"He *is* cute," she says. "But is the whole show going to be him telling us about aliens?"

"No. Of course not. We're going to edit it and include other sources and footage."

"Hmm . . ."

Hayden looks up, notices another person in the room, and begins to stumble over his words. He pauses, clearing his throat, but it's like he's forgotten everything he's ever known about aliens. Chloe's checked her phone four times in the last minute, so I know she's getting bored. I need to salvage this. Somehow.

What gets Hayden going and pulls him out of his shell? Then it hits me:

"So, this guy is just waving classified info about aliens out in the open?"

Hayden's gaze shoots up to me. His brows furrow behind his dark hair. I can't tell if he's more shocked by what I've said or that I've interrupted his take.

I know all of this.

He *knows* I know this.

But that doesn't matter. I need to get him fired up.

"What?"

I step closer, but make sure I'm still out of frame. Nora scratches her head, but motions for Jamie to keep rolling.

"This guy who is dealing with potentially classified information about aliens just has this written on a piece of paper for everyone to see?"

"Well, no. Everyone he was with was also in the know. They were looking at a crashed UFO, for god's sakes. I feel like the ship sailed on keeping the circle *that* small. And it wasn't being waved around. Look at him." Hayden flags me over, pulling up the picture of Roger Ramey on the laptop staged on the desk. I've seen the picture a hundred times now as we rehearsed the script. The camera lights glare in my eyes. I'm not used to being on this side of the lens. "He's squatting and surveying the UFO—"

"Weather balloon," I correct.

"UFO."

"Whatever."

"What do you mean, 'whatever'? If someone can decode this, it'd mean we'd know if this was actually a flying saucer and—"

"It looks like a sad kite."

"You know, before you interrupted me, I was going to say that we'd also know if there were little alien bodies inside the flying saucer."

Hayden's voice pitches down, and he's talking so quickly now that his Boston accent slips out. Across the studio, Chloe's smiling. Good. This is good. I need to poke the Bigfoot until it drags me into its den and eats me alive.

"If there *were* little alien bodies, what did the US government do with them?"

"Well." Hayden slips a pencil behind his ear. Then the glasses come off. Bingo. "According to some reports, they ran autopsies on them. This mortician came out like forty years later and alleged that he was getting calls from the air base, asking about little coffins."

"That's nice. The US was going to give them little alien funerals. But how awkward would it be if they . . . like . . . didn't decompose?"

"Are you insinuating that aliens *could* be real if you're wondering how they decompose?" Manic energy surges in his eyes.

"Absolutely not."

His fists thump on the table. "Goddammit."

"But I guess it wouldn't matter if they put them in caskets and buried them. Like 'well, let's hope nobody exhumes *that*.'"

Hayden coyly covers his mouth with his hand, continuing to play it serious as a smile spreads across his face.

"You're terrible."

"Could you imagine digging it up and being like, 'holy shit, that is the world's ugliest kid'?"

"'Oh man, this one never grew out of their newborn alien phase,'" he laughs. He rests his head on the desk, and my laughing fit prolongs his. After a moment, he takes a deep breath and sits up. "Okay, I'm fine. Any other questions?"

"Not at the moment. Thank you. Proceed."

Hayden makes it through the rest of his script, keeping his focus mostly on me and veering away from the script more often than before. It's natural and fun to watch. He looks *happy* doing it. I only butt in when he relies too heavily on his script or stumbles over his words.

The sun has gone down by the time we wrap, but before we can head out, Chloe calls both Hayden and me into her office. I eye Hayden as he walks through the Skroll offices, silently questioning the conference rooms named for memes and gawking at the internal recording studios. We both take a seat on the toadstool chairs and wait for Chloe to shut the door.

"That was an interesting shoot today, you two."

Hayden swallows and remains silent.

"Yeah?" I ask. I can do the driving in this conversation.

"Yeah. I don't know how much of your footage you'll end up using, but it was an intriguing look at your process."

"Were there any parts that stood out to you?"

"Yes, actually."

"Cool," I say, digging out my notebook. "What parts?"

"The two of you *together*—"

"Well, that's going to get cut," I butt in.

"I don't think it should . . ."

I look to Hayden, but he's a challenging book to read now. He stares at his nails, picking at the cuticles farther. He rocks back and forth on the mushroom stool, waiting for someone else to say something. I hope *he'll* butt in and assure Chloe this is *his* show and he will find a way to succeed at it on his own. But he doesn't . . .

"What . . . what do you mean?" I ask. "We went completely off-script, and I'm not supposed to be *on* the show, just producing it." I receive another high heart rate notification on my watch. Goddammit. "*The Out There* is Hayden's show. I was trying to make him feel less nervous."

"Did it work?" Chloe asks Hayden. He blinks a few times.

"Um . . . yeah," he concedes. "It did. I felt a lot more comfortable when Hallie was there with me."

Chloe's eyebrow quirks. "Uh-huh."

"This was *not* part of the pitch," I continue. "The format

was supposed to be *Hayden* hosting the show and controlling the content, not talking to someone off-screen the whole time, making bad jokes."

"Who says you have to be off-screen?"

My throat dries up like Death Valley. I'm suddenly so aware of every sound and sensation in the office. A puff of Chloe's cactus humidifier, her email dinging several times, Hayden sliding his glasses off and rubbing his eyes.

"You're suggesting I . . . co-host?"

"I am."

"Chloe, I'm not a host. You know that. I have always been the one behind the camera, calling the shots. I'm not the personality. I . . . don't . . . stand out."

At this, Hayden's head rises, brows knit together, lips pinched in a straight line. "You have blue hair," he says.

"That's not enough. That doesn't make me interesting or funny." Words from worse nights and worse people pop into my head. *I don't stand out. I'm not funny. I'm hard to work with.* It zaps any inspiration or confidence down to nothing. No one else wants me on their show. Why would Hayden? Am I even brave enough to step in front of the camera like this?

"Hayden, what do you think? Do you think the show would be better if Hallie was your co-host?"

I know the answer already. He didn't bust his ass for years to build a platform and fan base to hand half of his show over to some girl he met a week ago. Why would he want to give up the spotlight if he doesn't have to?

Why would he give it up for someone who doesn't believe in what's out there?

"I do," he finally says. "I'm stiff as a board up there alone. At least it'd give me someone to talk to. Hallie is smart and funny, and even though she doesn't believe in *any* of this stuff, the show had a hell of a lot more life when she was bantering with me."

Holy shit.

"I . . ." I can stammer nothing else.

Our eyes meet and heat rises in my chest. Instantly, I know he's telling the truth. He genuinely means it. He wants me as his co-host.

He thinks something I bring to it makes the show better. I think of the hundreds of episodes he's created entirely on his own and the rabid fans who hound his social media. He slept on if he wanted to even adapt the show but isn't hesitating to bring me on board.

"If she's open to it, I'd like Hallie to co-host the show with me. I need the help." Hayden's voice is solid with conviction as he proposes this to Chloe. "She has great ideas, and her personality is *so* bright and likable. She's a hell of a lot funnier than I am."

Bright.

Something that stands out.

Chloe beams. Hayden's gaze is as compelling as all his theories. Behind it, I can tell he doesn't want to do this alone. He knows *The Out There* better than anyone, and he seems to know in this moment what'll make it better.

I never expected it to be me.

"If she's not okay with that, we'll find a way to make it work as it was," Hayden finishes. "But I think the show would be far better if Hallie and I hosted it together."

"Of course," I finally say. I spit it out before I can talk myself out of it or let the fear of being seen convince me otherwise. "I'd love to be your co-host."

He cracks a relieved smile, and tension rolls out of his shoulders. "I was hoping you'd say that."

Chloe claps her hands together in victory. "Excellent! With that settled, as much as I like the Roswell idea, I'd prefer one of those on-location videos you pitched. Let's get the two of you out there and *doing* stuff. I'll buy your pilot an extra couple of days and a small budget for an on-location shoot. How does that sound?"

"Sure," I agree. "If we're doing an on-location video, where should we start?"

I turn to Hayden, who is already reaching into his pocket for a piece of paper. He waves it between us. "I've got us covered," he says.

CHAPTER 7

The Old Hollywood vibes are strong as I sink into a sleek leather chair and smooth jazz plays over the speakers.

"First built in 1926, the Hollywood Roosevelt Hotel was home to the first Academy Awards," a nearby tour guide whispers, trying to intrude as little as possible. "Back then, the ceremony lasted only five minutes. Imagine that! Yeah, you can look inside. It's the longest continuously running hotel in all of Los Angeles. It is also one of the most haunted hotels in the city."

I glance over my shoulder. A familiar tour guide pokes his head into the lobby. I am not confident Gary's daytime walking tour is any more informative than the one for which I shelled out serious cash.

"The hotel is home to some of the most kindred spirits in Tinsel Town, including one Marilyn Monroe— Oh, not *you* again!"

Behind the tour group, Hayden waits patiently for them to stop blocking the door.

"I have nothing to say! You're correct so far. Can I . . . ?"

Gary grumbles but guides the guests out of the way so that Hayden can enter. He lugs several large bags with him. Clearly, he's packed for more than one night away. Either that or he has a very intense skincare or haircare routine. He *does* have nice skin and hair. He meets me with an eager smile that I can't help but return.

"Are we moving in? Where's the Ouija board?"

Hayden glances at all his bags. "It'll make sense. Come on, let's check in."

I'm already on edge about spending an entire night alone with Hayden. Skroll wasn't willing to shell out the money for *two* rooms. Besides, if we're filming overnight, we should be together. I conquered my fear of being alone with him when we prepped the pilot episode, but there's something strangely intimate about being in a room alone with him for a whole night. He'll see me without makeup, in my pajamas, will know what position I sleep in. I'll shower in the bathroom, and he'll *know* I'm naked in there. He'll get my morning grumpy/grogginess. I will be sleeping in a bra.

As we reach our room, there's a childlike glee in his eyes as Hayden films discreet shots of the interior. Our travel budget only accommodates two people, so we're on our own for filming on location.

"I could not get us one of the more haunted rooms," he laments.

"Shame."

"*It is.*"

Our room is nicer than most hotel rooms I've stayed in. Two large beds with perfectly made sheets and colored pillows, a desk in the corner, and a flatscreen. There are even wood floors, which is a change from the usual horrifying hotel carpets. Our windows overlook Hollywood Boulevard and a parking structure. Classic Hollywood.

"Not bad. I see why the celebrities don't want to leave."

"Ha," I snark as he sets down the bags. "Did you bring our whole studio?"

Our.

Even if I weren't the host, it'd still be *our* studio. But I *am* a host now. The title is still kicking around in my mouth and I haven't settled on the aftertaste yet. It still doesn't feel real, and it especially doesn't when Hayden reaches into one of the bags and whips out a camera.

"Boom. Night vision."

I block my face with my hand like a celebrity trying to avoid the paparazzi. Hayden frowns.

"Come on. Don't tell me you're camera shy."

"Of course not."

I'm not used to being allowed in the spotlight.

No one's wanted me there before.

I lower my hand.

"We don't need night vision if the lights are on," I advise. Hayden sinks into one of the kitchenette chairs and dives into his bags again. He unloads the contents onto the table.

"Whoa, are we going full Watergate here?"

"No, just coming prepared."

"Uh-huh," I say, "and what exactly is this stuff?"

"All right, well, this is our night-vision camera, *obviously*. Next, we have an infrared thermometer, to keep track of cold spots or sudden temperature changes." He moves along to the next piece of equipment like he's Vanna White. "We have an EMF recorder, which picks up on electromagnetic fields and particularly high levels of unusual energy. This is just a regular digital recorder for picking up sounds. This one is an SB7

Spirit Box. It does a sweep of frequencies and can help us pick up on sounds and voices we might not hear on our own. And this guy—oh man."

He holds up a small square box that looks just like the digital recorder. It's a good thing he'll be the one using this stuff. If it were me, I'd be investing in a fun label maker. Everything looks the same.

I blink a few times. "How much of this did you already have?"

"None of it!"

"And here I thought you were a professional ghost hunter already . . ."

"Well, I had the camcorder and digital recorder, but that's normal. This thing—the Ovilus—contains a database of words and syllables, so if we asked the ghosts a question, this machine would pick up changes in temperature or magnetic fields to give us an auditory response."

I cross my arms. "You have got to be kidding me."

"I'm not. This is how we can communicate with ghosts!" He waves the device like a noisemaker on New Year's Eve.

"Like, if I asked right now what the ghost in this room wants for dinner, it would tell you it wanted steak?"

"It might be a vegetarian," he mutters into his chest.

After we settle, we take a tour of the hotel with one of the staff members. Skroll handled all our permits, and the hotel has allowed us to film on-site. Some of our travels will have to be dictated by where we *can* go.

We take turns behind and in front of the camera. Hayden registers a few particularly cold areas and EMF spikes, but nothing out of the ordinary. I snap photos on my phone, Hayden looming over to look at my screen each time to detect "orbs." We detect none. Following the tour, we break for dinner at one of the Roosevelt's many trendy bars. A bartender brings us our drinks, and Hayden swivels his barstool to face me.

"Have you ever stayed in a haunted hotel before?" I ask.

"I have," he says. "To be fair, I grew up near Boston. Just about everything is haunted there."

"Explains the accent."

"What?" he gapes. "I don't have an accent."

"Oh, yes you do. When you get upset about something, you sound like an angry fan at a Red Sox game."

He drops his *r*'s and widens the *a*'s, and it's another part of the facade chipping away. I never imagined finding a Boston accent sexy, but I never thought I'd find a monster hunter sexy either. The man is too good at poking holes in everything I know.

"Wait until the season starts. We're going to have to schedule our work around games very carefully."

"Uh . . . huh. If you're from Massachusetts, what made you move to LA? You could theoretically podcast from anywhere."

Hayden swirls his drink, picking at the orange peel in his old-fashioned. "It was time for a new start."

"Thank god you didn't say you came here to be an actor."

He laughs, biting the corner of his bottom lip. "*Obviously* not. You saw how bad I was in front of the camera. I *never* would have made it as an actor."

"I'm not so good in front of it, either," I concede.

His shoulders shift, and I recognize the movement as the rattling discomfort that runs through him when he has a point to argue. It unsettles me that he wants to argue *this* point. How could someone who hardly knows me feel so strongly?

What I also can't explain is the coy smile and determined look in Hayden's eyes as he waits for me to find the rest of my words. I feel confused and nervous in a way I haven't in years, full of doubt and certainty at the same time. Something flutters in my stomach and makes my palms itchy, and I'm suddenly so aware of everything: the way Hayden's ice cube pops in his glass, the closeness of his brown leather hiking boot to mine, the scent of his earthy cologne, the rich browns in his hair and beard.

It's the jitters in my stomach, my breath whooshing out of me as I try to speak, and the prickling sensation at the back of my neck. It's the feeling of attraction that I've only felt a few times in my life, and taken chances on even fewer. It's a want I've only followed into the lair once, and I left with bites and scratches. Hayden makes me want to believe in a lot of things, and right now, he's making me believe I won't always need to fear this feeling.

Instead, I smile and swallow the feelings with another sip of my drink. "I think maybe it's time for a new start for me, too."

* * *

By the time the sun goes down, we've relegated ourselves to our room for our investigation. Hayden arranges the camcorder to film both of us on our respective beds, all of our gear lingering between us.

"What's up, ghosties? We're here to hang."

"I don't think the ghosts want to be called 'ghosties,' Hallie."

"Did they tell you that themselves? Through your uvula thing?"

"*Ovilus*. And no, but they might." He picks up his audio recorder and hits Record, setting it carefully on the nightstand. He fetches his handy little Ovilus and places it between us.

"Do we need to chant or something?" I ask.

"*No*. We *do* need to try and engage with the spirits." He passes me the smaller camcorder. "But we need to be respectful. You don't want to piss off a ghost."

"What's it going to do? Make me cold?"

"Ghosts have killed people before." His expression is dead serious.

"Outside of movies?"

"Outside of movies, Hallie." He composes himself. "Okay... spirits of the Hollywood Roosevelt Hotel, we come in peace."

"No," I say. "We don't. We come seeking views on the internet, and if the ghost of Marilyn Monroe is here, can you please tell us what the hell happened with JFK? We're doing an episode on him next week, so any tidbits would be awesome."

"We can't *admit* we're in it for the views. You are making us seem *disingenuous*."

"Hasn't anyone told you to not pay any mind to what people think of you?"

Easier said than done.

"I obviously do not mind what people think of me," Hayden says. "I talk about Bigfoot for a living, for god's sake." Suddenly, he looks nervous, a shiver running through his shoulders. "Okay, not to be that guy, but I just got *really* cold all of a sudden."

"Put on a jacket. Wait, are you *scared*?"

"You don't understand," he seethes. His hands run up and down his arms to sate the goose bumps rising to his skin. "I'm from Boston. I drink iced coffee when it's below freezing. This is cold. *Evil*."

I attempt to smother my laugh. "Do you want the ghost to . . . like . . . fart and warm the room up or something?"

"I don't think they can do that." I'm joking, but leave it to Hayden to fact-check my ghost fart joke. "I'm sorry about her. She's new at this and I'm doing my best to educate her. Please don't come down too harsh on—"

"If you can hear us," I interrupt, "move something—"

"—Do not!"

We both quiet as my phone charger drops off the night-stand. Of course, the cord isn't glued to the surface, but Hayden—all six-foot-something of him—jumps onto the bed. His back presses hard against the headboard, hands covering his mouth.

"It just moved your charger."

"It fell! It was loose in the first place."

"It *moved*, Hallie."

"Doesn't mean it was a ghost."

"It definitely was."

"Fine." I stand up, looking around the room for something I can test our fake ghost friend with. "Can you tell us a name?"

"There are so many famous ghosts here, Hallie—"

I sit beside him, the Ovilus between us. "How thrilling! You'll get to meet a celebrity."

"I like my celebrities alive, thanks," he says.

"What's your name?" I ask again.

We hover over the device. Then, a word pops up on the screen, a digitized voice announcing it for us.

"Little."

Hayden squints, jaw hanging slack, trying to find some hidden meaning.

"*Little*—? Oh my god, there's a little girl that's reported to haunt this hotel."

"Bitch," the device snaps.

His gaze lifts to mine, then back at the Ovilus. And then back at me. "Did that ghost call me a bitch?"

I scratch my head. "It might have been talking about me. It did say 'little.' You're kinda large."

Hayden frowns at the device. "That's derogatory. It's not nice to call a woman a bitch."

"Ass," it corrects.

Hayden and I both shrug.

"That's better," he concedes.

"Gender-neutral, too. I deserved that."

"Of course," Hayden scoffs, pulling his knees up to his chest. "You told a ghost its experiences were invalid. You were just as mean."

"Fine, maybe it'll interact with you." I scoot back, my hands up in surrender. "If you like Hayden better, can you touch him—?"

"*No!*"

"Poke him. I dare you."

The two of us linger in silence. Down the hall, other guests chat. Loud rap music echoes from the street below. A toilet flushes above us. But nothing pokes either me or Hayden. He rubs his arm a few times, but is obviously trying to rationalize his psychosomatic, tender arm strokes.

"This ghost is a Consent King." I whoop. "We love that."

We continue to film periodically throughout the night. Hayden leaves the recorder running to give a thorough listen tomorrow, but I presume the most riveting thing we'll pick up is either snoring or sleep-talk. Meanwhile, I plan to pop two melatonin gummies and try to sleep through whatever mid-sleep recordings Hayden tries to do. I know it's inevitable.

I let Hayden shower first. I try not to think about the prospect of him being naked a room away because we still have to spend the rest of the night together, but it's easier said than done, and my skin feels all kinds of warm. He emerges a couple minutes later in the same clothes as before and we swap.

I run the water and place my pile of clothing on the counter. That's when I realize I've forgotten a change of underwear, naturally. I fling open the door and contemplate the stealthiest way to grab a single pair of underwear from my bag without Hayden noticing, but stealth is clearly not my specialty, because within seconds, I crash into something.

No, not something.

Someone.

I catch a handful of smooth skin and firm muscle, and it feels like an electric shock running through my fingertips. If I could breathe, I know I'd be breathing in the fresh scent of amber and whiskey, mingled with the lemon verbena soap in the hotel shower. But I'm not breathing because I'm touching Hayden, and I can't draw my eyes away from where we touch. I'm at the end of a branch that spreads across the left side of his stomach, attached to a skeletal tree, much like the deer on his arm, inked onto his side, rooted beneath the waistband of his boxers and pajama bottoms.

Now I know that the waves on his arm wash over the shore of his chest and shoulder and the Kraken's tentacles clutch around sails and masts on the top of his bicep, gripping him like I suddenly want to. His torso is toned and lithe, with thin muscles wrapping his stomach and chest. When I run out of ink to gawk at, my eyes track across a thin layer of dark hair on his chest that extends down his stomach, and all I can process is how much more of him I want to explore and the way he catches me with a firm grip on my arm.

"Oh my god," I whisper. I don't mean for it to come out, but it does. "I'm . . . I am sorry. I didn't know you weren't decent."

We yank away from one another. I conclude the best course of action is to cover my eyes, which feels foolish, but I don't want Hayden to see the heat in my cheeks or the way I'm struggling to look at anything else.

"It's . . . okay," he stutters, quickly reaching for the T-shirt behind him on the bed. "Do you need something?"

"*No*," I spit out. I will handle the underwear debacle *later*. "Absolutely not. Bye."

I stumble back into the bathroom and slam the door. Jesus. God. This is horrible. I try to think of something very unsexy—like the Loch Ness Monster or the Yeti—but then I imagine *Hayden* talking about them. Emphatic hand movements, the passionate drawl of his voice. When I step into the shower, I notch the temperature down.

After dragging my brain out of the gutter as I showered, I wipe my makeup off and stand in front of the mirror. A weight sits on my chest. My skin is splotchy, and I should start doing a regular skincare routine. I worry about what Hayden will think about the circles under my eyes and the flatness of my damp hair. Is he going to wish he had a better-looking co-host? Is he going to regret asking me to be on camera with him?

I change for bed, begrudging how I'll have to sleep in a bra tonight, but the last thing I need is for Hayden to know I have boobs. Small ones, granted, but he doesn't need to know. I carefully exit the bathroom, and peer out. Thankfully, Hayden is fully dressed in a pair of spaceship pajama pants and an Emerson College hoodie. He sits on the bed, toying with the Spirit Box.

It begins to thump in bursts of white noise. It's one of the most grating sounds I've ever heard, and I glance back into the room.

"Is there anyone here?" he asks it.

A garbled series of noises echo from the machine. It sounds like radio frequencies, not words.

"How did you die?"

"What?"

"I made contact with someone named George."

"George?"

He nods, so earnest it hurts. There is something so pure about the way Hayden does everything. He waits for each burst of the Spirit Box to give him *something*, even if it's only a blip of an Enrique Iglesias song from a nearby radio.

"What does George say?"

"George—do you have anything to say?"

There's another garble. I'm beginning to get a headache listening to this thing. I'm also partially worried someone will call the front desk about the odd noises coming from our room.

"He says 'lick.'" Hayden frowns at the Spirit Box. "That's not helpful—"

"That's *nasty*!" I cry, through a mouthful of toothpaste.

"Well, if you don't believe in ghosts, you have no reason to be afraid of one licking you, right?"

I spit into the sink and rinse. Returning to my bed, I lean back on the comforter, turning onto my side as Hayden flips open his camcorder again. I'm glad we've moved on from the Close Encounters of the Shirtless Kind without incident.

I wonder if he's made many changes to his nightly routines, like how I'm wearing a bra to bed. Does he wear spaceship-patterned pajama pants every night, or if I weren't here, would he be sleeping in boxers, or nothing at all?

Aaand, then I'm thinking about Hayden sans clothes again.

"Any last words?" He turns his video camera on me.

I cover my face with my hands. "Oh god, no, I don't have makeup on."

"So?"

"So, I look ugly!"

"That couldn't be further from the truth!"

His words shock both of us. He quickly clears his throat as I lower my hands. "What?"

"You look . . ." He mentally bounces between options like he's on *Who Wants to Be a Millionaire?* before eventually selecting the final answer. "Fine. Don't worry, you look fine."

Somehow, this brings a sense of relief. I'm not prepared for what I'd do if he told me I looked pretty. I'm not ready for a compliment from someone like him. Not someone who makes my stomach do flips and looks at me like I matter. He looks at me like he's eager to hear what I have to say. He studies me. I don't think Cade ever even saw me.

"We don't have to film you all ready for bed, if you don't want," he finishes.

That couldn't be further from the truth, I hear him say again. "No, it's . . . uh, actually fine."

Hayden turns the camera on me again with a smile. "Take two: Any last words?"

"Before you kill me?" I laugh.

"No, before one of the *many* ghosts in this hotel kills you."

"They will not."

"They might!" he teases, flipping the camera on himself. "We are about to head to sleep. I had a quick conversation with a ghost named George a few minutes ago, but he proved to be generally uninformative. We'll see if we find anything nefarious overnight, and hopefully we'll survive our stay."

He shuts the camera and sets it on the nightstand beside him. Hayden settles on the bed as my underwire digs into my sides, but it's better than a nip-slip. We aren't on the best in-decent exposure track record today.

I turn on my side to face him as Hayden dims the light between us. His hair is still drying, dark curls forming at the nape of his neck and sleepiness hanging in his eyelids. As he slides under the covers, he tugs the hood of his sweatshirt over his head, bundling up. He removes his glasses and sets them beside his phone on the nightstand. It's the first time I've seen him without them for any extended amount of time.

He'll take them off to rub his eyes or nose, or when he gets *very* into explaining something, but here they are off and it feels like letting down a barrier between us. He's handsome with or without them, but he feels vulnerable now. Without the frames demanding attention, I notice he has light freckles on his nose and great, dark eyelashes. I like this unguarded version of him.

"How much can you see without your glasses?"

Hayden huffs out a laugh. "Absolutely nothing."

"Nothing at all? That's sad. How will you see the ghosts all night?"

"I am going to have to rely on all my other keen senses in

that case. Thankfully, you have that blue hair, so I can generally see you," he says, waving in my direction.

"In case you need someone to snuggle with when you get
scared?"

I'm not sure why I say that, and I'm not particularly proud
of it.

His tiny smile taunts me, but he scoffs to hide it. "Pssh,
me? Scared? Never. Makes you easy to spot in stores, I guess."

I roll my eyes. "Yes, and every mom in the vicinity has to
comment on the fact that my hair is blue."

"It's like how my mom was with all the tattoos. I still have
to wear long sleeves when I visit her because she doesn't like
to look at them," he jokes, but it hardly feels like a joke. My
parents didn't *love* the blue hair at first, but they were never
the grounding and yelling type, so they got used to it and accepted that it was "self-expression."

"I think they're cool. How many?"

"You mean you didn't count before?" His eyebrow quirks
when he laughs.

Of course he noticed me checking him out. I wasn't exactly discreet with it, but it's a conversation I'm not prepared
to have with him. I could ask what he meant when he said I
looked "fine," because it was clearly not the word he wanted
to use.

"The number must be pretty high," I tell him. "The deer on
your arm—"

"It's not a deer."

"It sure looks like a deer."

"It's a Not Deer."

"You already said that."

He breaks into a smile and shakes his head. "No, a *Not Deer*."

"What the fuck is a Not Deer?"

"Urban legend from Appalachia. It's a deer at first glance, but the longer you look at it, it's obvious something is wrong with it—"

"So, it's an ugly deer," I laugh, burying myself against the pillow.

"*Not* Deer."

"Sure, sure, you tell yourself that, Hayden."

Instead of a rebuttal, he offers a small laugh, turning on his side to look at me. I don't know how well he can see me, but he smiles anyway. I smile too.

"You really can't see anything?" I ask again.

"Hardly. Why?"

"No reason," I lie. "Sleep tight, Hayden."

"Good night, Hallie. Don't let the ghosties bite."

"I'm fairly certain they *won't*."

He scoffs and turns over, hitting the lights. As soon as the lights are off, I reach behind me and unhook my bra, wiggling out of it and tossing it into my bag. I'm so happy he is vision impaired in this moment. Within a few minutes, his breathing deepens, but there's no snoring, thankfully. At least if we're going to spend all this time buddied up on our hunts, I'll get a decent night of sleep.

I fall into a committed slumber quickly, only to wake several hours later to voices.

"Siri, what time is it?" Hayden whispers.

Siri, that traitor, shouts, "It's two forty-seven a.m."

A flash from our night-vision camera brightens the room.

Hayden sits at the corner of his bed with the camera turned on himself. Glasses still off, framing himself poorly.

"It's almost three in the morning and I . . . something touched my foot. The room looks empty now." He turns the camera around to scan the room. "It could have been a dream, but it felt really, really real. Man . . . I'm like . . . shaking right now."

Finally, Hayden realizes I'm awake.

"I felt something," he hisses.

I collapse into the covers. "Hayden, please go to sleep."

CHAPTER 8

XoXoGossipCat

Dead. These two are something Else. Why watch all Skroll's cooking videos when there is ThIS?

Notabot283758392

I think this guy puts a little too much weight on the Ovilus. It's not really proven to work. Otherwise, this is pretty good.

Falseflagz

ok but did anyone else know this is what he looked like?

rosWILL @Falseflagz

yeah dude on the website

Falseflagz @rosWILL

oh ok more importantly, do u think they're dating?

' ' '

It turns out people *like* watching Hayden and me antagonize ghosts.

Those ghosts got their views after all.

Later that week, Hayden and I stood in the Nyan Cat conference room as Chloe played our pilot episode for the team— thirty minutes of bullshitting, ghost hunting, and sharp editing. Hayden handled all the storytelling, while Jamie and I did the physical editing.

It was a *show*. A real *show*. One we'd made together, one that I was a part of, just as much as he was.

By the end of the presentation, I was a ball of giddy energy, ready to run and find the closest haunted house. So giddy, in fact, that I hardly heard Chloe give us the go-ahead for a full season. The thrill of making something had never felt *this* thrilling before. It was a good thing I was so ready for it, because we had to pull together another episode in the next week.

I spend the following days at Hayden's apartment, since he has the better workspace, central AC, and an easily accessible library of resources, from morning until evening. I always arrive with coffee, and we expense takeout while we work all day. I know where things are in Hayden's apartment now. He keeps the beers in the lower half of the fridge door; flatware is in the drawer beside the sink. The bathroom is always clean, and there is always toilet paper. I have yet to see his bedroom, but I imagine that's clean, too. Or all the mess is shoved in there.

It's nearly time to break into the takeout menus for dinner when Hayden asks me to fetch him a book from the shelf. This week's mission: Who killed JFK? Was it a cover-up, or was it aliens? Or was it aliens *and* a cover-up? I'm not sure what I buy yet, but the fact that I'd even entertain these ideas is progress.

Some episodes are going to be on location, while others are mostly filmed in studio. Most Skroll shows use a lot of their budget on video and music licensing. Cade used a lot of his getting influencer guest stars on the show. We've set aside most of our funds for travel accommodations. For our in-studio episodes, we'll spend more time on our graphics and editing to make those episodes pop, but driving to Dealey Plaza in Dallas would make us look like tourists and wouldn't actually enhance the episode.

Hayden's been looping a play-by-play of the assassination on the TV for an hour, pausing periodically to break down key moments with his laser pointer that support the alien theories he plans to talk about in the episode. I've seen the video so many times I'm giving the Warren Commission a run for its money. I'm at least grateful for the poor filming quality of 1963 so I'm not seeing high-definition brain matter every ten seconds.

"The book you're looking for should be pretty beat up. I got it secondhand. The author's last name is Haggerty," Hayden directs from the couch. He's face down in his laptop, jotting episode notes in one window, writing a script in the other. Today he's struggling to compile a surplus of information from his four-part podcast series and condense it all into a single half-hour episode.

"But it's all *compelling, Hallie!"*

"You don't understand just how many *theories there are!"*

"I cannot cut the Magic Bullet segment, Hallie. I just can't.*"*

He's spent most of the day frustrated. I'm learning that a frustrated Hayden typically manifests in his face dropped into books, or his keyboard. He paces, and talks through his frustrations (which I often do not understand, but I listen nevertheless), and sometimes hums the *X-Files* theme song under his breath.

I can usually make him laugh or distract him.

I can usually humble him by reminding him I have no idea what the fuck he is talking about.

He has *so* many books in his place and it's going to take me a minute to find what he's looking for. The shelves stretch from floor to ceiling and are alphabetized. What kind of man alphabetizes his books?

One I am turned on by, clearly.

The books on his shelf are either well-loved or not acknowledged at all. Some are crisp, with firm covers—likely self-published or a small press, based off the titles. I don't imagine there's a wide market appeal for something called *Bigfoot and Stonehenge: The True History.*

"Good lord, you have a lot to read." I turn to Hayden.

He smirks, his pencil bitten between his teeth, before it falls and he frowns. "I don't get bored. To be fair, a lot of people *send* me books, hoping I'll promote their work or something."

"Do you?"

"If it's good."

I return to my hunt, hitting the *h*'s. Haddock. Hall. Hamilton. Hargrove.

I backtrack.

Hargrove.

I examine the spines, my fingers running over the titles in front of me. I recognize them from school libraries and entire shelves at the bookstore. There are several editions of the same book for select titles, some older and worn, others in special-edition covers. It looks like a whole collector's shelf.

Tugging one from the bookshelf, I survey the cover. *Serpent Who Smiles*. I'd read it in high school for a horror unit, and while most other students resorted to SparkNotes, I actually enjoyed it. And then slept with the lights on for a few days. They didn't call him the Master of Horror for no reason.

I flip to the author photo and bio. The man staring back at me has dark wavy hair and bright green eyes, a youthful handsomeness that I feel like I've been staring at like a nine-to-five job lately. My eyes drift above the book to where Hayden sits on the couch. Waves of chestnut hair. Bright green eyes.

"Uh . . . were you going to mention that your dad is Everett Hargrove?"

Hayden glances up, hunting for his words. Of course, the clues have been here from the beginning. His name, a father who'd gotten him into this stuff, a nice apartment. I can't believe I didn't notice it before. It's not a detail he advertises. When I'd first looked Hayden up, I hadn't scoured the internet too deep. There's no mention of his father in his bio for *The Out There*.

He swallows. "You never asked."

Our eyes meet. The same solemn clouds linger in the room with us as when he mentioned his mom at the Roosevelt. His mentions of family have been so scant I never thought to fill in the blanks. Come to think of it, he hasn't mentioned much of *anyone*. He sure talks about historic members of the FBI and CIA like he knows them personally, but he hasn't mentioned any friends or romantic partners.

I wonder if, in a way, he's like his own kind of cryptid. Isolated. Elusive. Something that takes some hunting to learn about.

"I guess not."

"Did you not . . . Google me? How did you find my email if you didn't?"

"I . . ." Something in his tone doesn't sound pleased, and if it's something I could have Googled, how could he blame me for uncovering it now? "I just looked up *The Out There*, and it went right to your website. Your website is very informative. I didn't feel a need to go to your Wikipedia page or anything."

Now I'm wondering what *is* on there. Does he have a "Personal Life" section? Controversies? I'll have to find out later.

"Oh. I guess I figured you knew."

"It makes sense. I see how having the Master of Horror for a dad would get you into all of this." I gesture to the wall of odd books behind me. When Hayden doesn't have anything to follow up with, I search for my next line. "Your dad's a great writer."

"*Was.*"

Was. Past tense yet again. When any famous person dies, the internet floods with loving sentiments and acknowledgments of the gravity of their work. When the Master of Horror died several years ago, every writer I knew had something to say.

For all those people who'd been inspired by his work, who felt like they knew him through the pages of his books, it didn't compare to how well Hayden knew him. My throat dries as Hayden stands up and paces across the room to me.

He leans against the bookshelf, arms crossed in front of his chest. His breathing's heavier but controlled. I don't know how to read his emotions now. It looks like right now, the wound is still held together with shoddy stitches, ready to tear open.

"Hayden, I'm so sorry."

His lips tighten, and he shrugs. "Thanks."

I thumb through the titles on the shelf. He must have a copy of every one of his father's books. It's hard to tell; there are too many to remember every title. I stop near the end of the row, slipping a hardly touched book from the shelf. Hayden watches in silence as I run my fingers over the jacket of his dad's final novel, *Phantom Lake*.

"This one, though. This was *my* favorite. I read it while trapped in an airport for a whole day during a polar vortex. It was the only thing that kept me from committing a homicide or ending up on the No Fly List."

His eyebrows rise above his glasses. He adjusts the backward Red Sox hat on his head. "This one?"

"What? You have a least favorite of your dad's books?"

"Well, no, but . . ." Finally, he breaks into a smile. It's tired and half-hearted, but it's a flash of the Hayden I'm growing to like. "It was the last one. He was so sick by the time it came out, we couldn't even really celebrate the release. Still a bestseller. Most people don't want to talk about the content, just that it was his final book. I don't know. I like to think it was good because he wrote it, not just because he died."

"Was *The Out There* his idea?"

"Kind of." Hayden shifts in front of me, rubbing the back of his neck. My eyes trace along the inside of his bicep. I notice something new about his tattoos each time I study him. To-day, it's a small, odd-looking mermaid swimming in the waves around the ship on his arm. When I look up at him, there are words on his lips, but he's weighing each of them carefully.

"I got bullied a lot as a kid. I'm sure that's *impossible* to imagine." His voice breaks off into a teasing laugh. As easy as it is to picture him far thinner with his big glasses, I hope anyone who messed with him realizes the kid they shoved around had a serious glow-up. "I was weird and shy and had a hard time making friends. Whenever I came home sad or upset, my dad would plan something for us to do that week-end. He'd rent a cabin in the woods for just the two of us and we'd go on these monster hunts."

He slides his glasses over his hat, and it feels like a curtain rising before a Broadway show. He's allowing himself to be on display. But this is not the quirky personality behind the mi-crophone at all. Off mic and off camera, Hayden has a quiet presence. For all his height and muscle, he's never once in-timidated me.

"Now, of course, I know he was full of shit on a lot of these hunts. He'd tell me to be on guard for the Pope Lick Monster up in the woods of Massachusetts—"

"Absolutely foolish of him. Everyone knows the Pope Lick Monster—" I jest, leaning against the bookshelf with him.

"Resides in Kentucky," Hayden glares, holding back a laugh.

"Of course."

"But I didn't know that when I was ten. It was the one time I felt like I wasn't so weird after all. He always knew what I needed without me ever having to ask." He twists at the watch around his wrist. "The podcast wouldn't exist if not for him."

"And we wouldn't be here if not for him either."

"Yeah." This is the first I'm hearing about Hayden's life outside of *The Out There*, and I want more. I want to understand everything about him because I'm constantly shocking myself with how much I'm liking every part of him. We couldn't be more different, and yet . . .

The look in his eyes tells me he wants to say more too, but he doesn't know how.

"So, how'd you go from hunting the Licking Guy to running a podcast?"

Hayden frowns. "Licking Guy makes him sound so nonconsensual. Eight years ago, when he first got sick, it was just the two of us. After their divorce, my mom moved to San Francisco with her new husband, so . . . We had this old brownstone in Boston that we lived in to be close to the hospital there. He had the LA apartment for when he came out here to work with his film agent. I was just starting college and I skipped the dorm experience so I could take care of him."

"When you were eighteen?"

"Nineteen," he corrects.

It's still so young to give up the most exploratory years of life to care for someone else. It's a sacrifice not many would make. It isn't a sacrifice many *could* make.

"It's still a lot."

He toys with the bottom of his shirt, picking at a loose string. Today's T-shirt is worn baby blue with two crows and the caption "Attempted Murder." "ALS isn't an easy way to die, but he made it for five years. I needed a job that let me work from home, so I did other audio engineering jobs remotely—student films, indie albums—until I started the podcast. I was only ever away from home for a few hours at a time near the end. I could always pause recording if he needed something."

Hayden says it like it's nothing. He says it with the same obviousness as when he talks about his more confident theories. There's no doubt in his voice when he says it was the clear and easy choice to be at his dad's beck and call.

"I'm sure he really appreciated having someone there to help him."

"Yeah." Finally, he breaks into a shy smile, rolling his eyes. "He'd always tell me to go out and have fun. Go to parties, fool around . . . do normal kid stuff. He'd threaten to hire temporary caretakers so it got me out of the house. It was like he hoped that, one day, I'd come home a drunk mess or get caught smoking pot."

"Did you?"

"Not really. I mean, I'd *occasionally* take a night off to go out for drinks or spend time with my girlfriend. Even then, I was always waiting for my phone to ring in case a nurse would need me to explain something or something would go wrong. I never wanted to do anything that made it hard to switch gears if I had to." Hayden's glasses slide back onto his face. "So, sadly, no passing around a dirty bong in someone's basement."

"You weren't missing much," I assure him, but it doesn't make up for years of time given entirely to someone else. Time he won't get back. "It takes a strong person to do what you did. Your dad was lucky to have such a good kid."

"I was lucky to have such a good dad," is all he says.

"Do you think he'd approve of the direction the show is taking?"

He allows a crinkle of a smile to pass between us. Then he steps closer. "He'd approve of whatever made me happiest, so yeah, I think he'd like this. I think he'd like you, too."

"Even if I don't buy the spooky shit?"

He is so close, and I feel the same smothering sensation I felt in the hotel bar. It's like drowning. His gaze just pulls me deeper underwater, and my heart races as he studies me. The silence is stifling.

He clears his throat. "Even if you don't buy the spooky shit."

I pass Hayden the copy of *Phantom Lake*, and he slips it back into place on the shelf just beside my head. He doesn't back away just yet, leaning against the bookshelf and glancing down at me. My gaze flicks to his mouth as he bites on his bottom lip, then moves lower over his shoulders and biceps. I'm desperate to know if he's thinking the same things as me—what my hair feels like between his fingers, what my lips taste like, what his body would feel like against mine. I'm just as terrified as I am hungry for what comes next. Just as I imagine what his hands would look like exploring my body, he jolts.

"Ow!"

A sad mewl comes from the floor, and Cthulhu's fangs unhook from the bottom of Hayden's jeans. I never anticipated getting cockblocked by a cat named Cthulhu, but "unexpected" is how I'd describe most parts of my life lately.

"That was super rude," Hayden lectures the cat. "I *feed* you."

We break apart as if none of this happened. Electricity fizzles out of the air, and Hayden snatches the book *I* was supposed to be hunting for before we got sidetracked. I dart back to the couch, feeling flushed and thinking that maybe watching the JFK assassination repeatedly will push these thoughts out of my brain. I put my head in my notebook, steadying my breathing before he speaks again. "And thanks."

I look back up. "For?"

Hayden leans against the edge of the couch, flipping through book pages. I catch a subtle shake to his hands. Is that because of me? I look at my own hands. We match. "Listening."

The word feels so heavy between us. Everything in my composure shrinks like a balloon deflating. I linger on how young he looks now. The beard makes him look a touch older than twenty-seven usually, but I don't see that today. I see someone who gave up all their young adult years for someone else, whose late college nights weren't just cramming for exams, but were filled with hospital trips and being ready to wake up and help at all times. Someone who's completely selfless.

"Of course."

"I don't talk about it much, so sometimes it's nice to ... tell someone. There isn't always someone to listen."

It's an admission in its own way, one I know Hayden doesn't take lightly. What he's said is far easier than admitting he's lonely. His gaze hovers on me as I chew on his words.

"I learn a lot about people I *don't* know from you, but it's actually really nice to learn about *you*."

Finally, it's like we can both breathe again. Hayden's eyes drift to the TV, where JFK is seconds away from being taken out by a "magic bullet."

"I haven't even gotten to the good stuff yet," Hayden says.

✦ THE OUT THERE ✦

Episode #2: "The Magic Bullet Is Not a Blender"

On this week's episode of The Out There, *Hayden and Hallie dive into the JFK assassination. They break down the facts and the theories, from plausible to preposterous. Was it a lone extremist who killed the president, or something else?*

HAYDEN

One of the more creative theories is that JFK was killed by the CIA.

HALLIE

That's not that creative. See? I'm learning. There's a "the CIA did it" theory behind almost everything.

HAYDEN

Sure, but the "why" is the creative part, and I'm not sure you're going to buy it.

HALLIE

Try me.

HAYDEN

So in 1947—which is coincidentally the same year as the Roswell crash—President Truman established a secret organization of scientists and government officials and stuff to investigate UFOs. It was called Majestic 12, or MJ-12 for short. There were twelve people.

HALLIE

If there weren't, they are super bad at naming things.

HAYDEN

In October of 1963, MJ-12 issued a letter to the members discussing some questions that "Lancer"—JFK's Secret Service code name—had been asking that weren't going to fly. They referenced a phrase—"it has to be wet."

HALLIE

Gross?

HAYDEN

It means to kill.

HALLIE

Somehow, "kill" sounds better. The CIA is out here like, "we love when things are moist."

HAYDEN

No one loves when things are moist. Well, okay . . . there are some times where it helps, but . . .

HALLIE

Have I told you today that I hate you yet?

HAYDEN

No, actually.

HALLIE

So, we're moistening up the president. Go ahead.

HAYDEN

A month after the moistening, JFK was dead. The theory is that JFK was asking questions about UFOs and aliens and was planning to share what he knew with the Soviet Union. So . . . they killed him.

HALLIE

Why in the hell would JFK want to give info to the Soviet Union? How does that help anybody? He missed the whole Cold War unit of my sophomore year, clearly.

HAYDEN

Yeah, he must have been out sick that day.

HALLIE

What does JFK gain from buddying up with the Soviets?

HAYDEN

I bet the MJ-12 asked the same question. Then they decided to kill him.

HALLIE

Do you personally believe this?

HAYDEN

I find it compelling.

CHAPTER 9

*S*o, you've stayed in a haunted hotel before, but have you ever stayed on a haunted *boat*?"

The *Queen Mary* looks *just* like the *Titanic*: big black hull, tall smokestacks jutting into the cloudless California sky. I'm going to spend the next twenty-four hours pretending I'm some early-twentieth-century socialite, smoking fancy cigarettes and wearing the finest pearls. Mentally, at least. Physically, I'm wearing a pair of jeans, Doc Martens, and Skroll branded knock-off Ray-Bans from last summer's company barbecue bash because I lost my actual sunglasses early this morning.

Meanwhile, Hayden's sunglasses are the same shape, yet not ugly and branded. He wears them all too well, and I hate the way his arms flex as he hauls our bags across the parking lot.

"No," Hayden confirms. "Never a boat. I hope that you provoking the ghosts doesn't make them sink it on us."

"Right? There's totally not enough room for both of us on a door. How do I look?" I ruffle my hair to try and get ready for the camera, and my sunglasses slide off my face yet again.

Hayden pauses like I've caught him in a trick question. He censors himself before he can say anything. He bites one side of his lip. Like the night at the Roosevelt, I desperately want to know what he *wants* to say, but I'm also afraid of what it means.

"Very lovely."

"Is that sarcasm?" I ask.

"Nope, not one bit." He spits it out too fast and pivots even quicker, hitting Record on our camcorder. "Tell us where we are, Hallie."

I spent the car ride memorizing facts about the ship and leaving the spooky stuff to Hayden. I explain a quick history of the ship, from its construction to its time as a troopship in World War II, and then renovation into a hotel as we make our way through the parking lot. We avoid filming other people, but as we step into the elevator, we certainly catch their attention. I can't imagine why.

We're a chaotic mess of two overnight bags, a large bag of camera equipment, and Hayden in a shirt that says, "The Birds Work for the Bourgeoisie," which I do not understand. And I have blue hair. We take a few discreet shots of the lobby, still decorated like it's from another time. Hayden confirms the room we are staying in—the most notoriously haunted one—and when the concierge raises her eyebrows, he follows up with, "Yes, we really do want the evilest room here."

Hayden pats my head and assures me he's making up for disappointing me at the Roosevelt. My hero.

With our keys, we trek down to room B340. The room smells of old carpet and wood, a faint twinge of must and salty sea air. The floors creak under each step as we move inside. Hayden stops dead in his tracks.

"Sorry," I mutter, rubbing the spot on his back I've stumbled into. Hitting him is like hitting a brick wall, and that should not turn me on, but it does. I'm thinking about walking into him while half-dressed, and the touch of his bare chest beneath my fingertips.

Suddenly, his halting makes sense. The room is *small*, a main cabin with a dresser, a TV hanging from the wall, a small couch, and a very dinky bathroom.

And only one bed.

My lips zip together, eyes darting back and forth from the bed to the couch. There's no way in hell either of us will fit on the couch, and the thought of sleeping in a bed with him sends a tingle down my spine and a sudden heat to the pit of my stomach.

"Oh," is all he says.

"Yeah . . ."

Hayden steps farther into the room, setting our bags on the bed and looking to the couch. "I'll take the couch. Or the floor or something. It's no big deal."

"You don't have to do that." I don't want him to sleep on the scary carpeting or volunteer his spinal health for the cause, but I also worry about what it'll do to me if we share a bed. It'll smash the boundary walls I've tried to keep up between us.

"We can . . . figure that out later, I guess."

"Sure, no need to worry about it yet."

I can only imagine what the comments on this new video will look like. Based off our first episode, we have a fair number of fans wondering if we are *together*. Nora read the most entertaining comments at lunch one day, then promptly hunted to see if anyone had written fan fiction yet. I made her promise to *never* tell me if she finds any.

At the Roosevelt, we'd been in the same room, but not the

same bed. Tonight, there's a chance I'll know what it's like to sleep next to Hayden. I'll feel the mattress move as he breathes or turns over. I don't know how to cope with the feelings it might bring up. Because despite *everything*, something keeps drawing me closer to him.

When the Only One Bed shock wears off, we unpack, evaluating our gear and taking the camcorder, EMF reader, and audio recorder with us. We have an appointment to tour the ship at sundown and a bit of time to kill. Hayden and I do our own quick tour, posting photos to our socials that immediately garner more questions about our relationship. Neither of us wants to discuss the shippers.

On our private tour of the boat, we film the history and notable haunts of the *Queen Mary* and marvel at the gutted insides of the ship, cavernous boiler rooms, and hundred-year-old engineering, and I'm actually enraptured by it.

"I can't believe that guy got crushed in a door," Hayden says, recalling one of the tragedies on board we learned about on our tour. He arranges the camera on the tripod in our room. I film him with my phone for some B-roll. "Like, it seems like a bad way to go."

"If you had to pick a way to die on this ship, how would you want to go?" I tease.

"Peacefully in my sleep, obviously."

"That doesn't count. You have to die badly."

"You weren't that specific."

"I am now."

"Oh, come on," he groans, sitting beside me on the floor. Our knees brush as he crosses his legs, slipping his boots off. His socks have tiny ghosts on them. Oh heavens, it's cute. The carpet is rough and tacky beneath my fingers. There is no way I'm letting Hayden sleep on the ground now. Not on *this* carpet. He will get fleas and bring them home to Cthulhu.

"Your accent's out again."

One of his eyebrows rises. "Is it?"

I nod. The harsh *a*'s and dropped *r*'s flare as we bicker, and I enjoy the lilts his voice offers in his frustrated moments. On the podcast and while we film most of our more straightforward content, he's managed to cook it down to nothing. When we let loose, it feels like he's showing me the most authentic parts of himself. Perhaps I like his accent for that reason more than anything else. He also looks criminally good in his Red Sox hats. That may be contributing.

"Is it totally unflattering?"

The fact that he cares sends my stomach flipping.

"No." I shake my head. "It's kind of cute, actually."

We're silent for a terrible moment before I willingly break the silence by reaching into my duffel bag. That changes the subject real fast. Hayden's eyes widen like flying saucers, and fear ripples over him. Nothing kills the mood like a Ouija board.

"What is that?"

"We're going to talk to some ghosties the old-fashioned way," I cheer as he begins to chant "No, no, no, no."

"*Hallie,* you cannot just *whip* out a Ouija board like that. You realize you are *inviting* us to get possessed by a Zozo demon or something."

"What the hell is a Zozo demon?"

He pushes the box away with a single finger. "You don't want to know."

"Whatever, I'll Google it later." I unwrap the box, placing the board and planchette down. "Do you want to ask the first question?"

"No," he spits. "Abso-fucking-lutely not."

"Fine. Are we rolling?"

"Sadly. This is take one, scene one of 'Hayden and Hallie's Found Footage Operation,'" he says to the camera, clapping to mark the take.

Despite his hesitations, Hayden rests his fingers on the edge of the planchette with mine. His fingertips brush against my knuckles, cool and rough, but enough to set my skin on fire. Instead of brainstorming what I'm going to ask the demons haunting the ship, I'm thinking about Hayden's hands running up my shirt or his firm grip on my body. I quickly remind myself of unsexy things—people dying of tuberculosis on this boat, how infrequently people bathed back in the day. God, anything to not think about my co-host manhandling me.

"If there are any spirits here with us, which I doubt there are, on account of ghosts being fake, can you make contact?"

Hayden frowns at the Ouija board. A warm spring wind sweeps through the open porthole. My skin flushes as I think about how stagnant it already feels in here. How much worse will it be when we have to share a meager double bed all night?

The planchette does not move (shocking), but no one is going to tune in to see us sitting over a Ouija board I bought on Amazon. The internet demands spicy ghost content. Softly, so softly that Hayden won't notice, I nudge the planchette toward the "yes" marker on the board.

"It says yes," I conclude. "In that case, do you have a name?"

"Do *not* ask its name."

"Too late," I say. "What's your name?"

A horrific noise shudders through the Spirit Box, running beside us. I have no idea what it says, but Hayden scrambles for his notepad. His handwriting is usually legible, blocky, and *mostly* shorthand (terrifying things only he'd know—CE2K for Close Encounters of the Second Kind, PG Film for the Patterson-Gimlin film).

"How good is your French?" Hayden asks.

"No bueno," I reply.

"It was definitely a French ghost."

"Right. Ghosties, can you *spell* your name for us?"

I rack my brain for any French names. Jacques? Louis? Amélie? I guide the planchette subtly to the *j*, but Hayden interrupts the process.

"Can you tell us if you died on the ship? Did you die in this room?"

There's another crackle of life on the Spirit Box. My pinky toe feels uncomfortably cold and I brush it off as pins and needles, but for a brief moment, I do wonder if there is a ghost with a foot fetish in this room with us.

I shoot the planchette over to the "yes." Hayden gasps.

For someone so smart, he is alarmingly gullible and easy to scare. This is precisely why I cannot let myself believe any of his theories. If I start somewhere, like believing in ghosts, where will it lead me?

One day, it's ghosts. The next, I am wearing a tinfoil hat and trying to steal the Declaration of Independence.

"Were you a passenger here? A soldier, maybe?" he muses. "I mean, I think I would haunt a place if I died and never got to my final destination. It'd be sad to be a transient ghost. You don't even haunt a house. You're just . . . stuck here."

"It's very millennial. Even in death, we can't get a house."

"How did you die?" Hayden asks.

"*Nudes*," the Spirit Box yelps. Hayden sets his pad on the floor.

"Excuse me?"

"Death by nudes," I say. "Obviously."

"It could be noodles," Hayden says.

He flips his pad where he has written "Nudes" and then "Noods?" below it.

"Yes, that is far more acceptable, thank you, Hayden."

Finally, the fear clinging to him breaks into a laugh. He leans his head against the edge of the bed, scrubbing his hands over his face. He saves these moments for us, cutting them from episodes, usually. He frames himself as a generally cool and determined host, but I like these parts best. There's no role, no narrative to hide behind. Just Hayden.

"Just once, I want a helpful ghost!"

"Keep looking, dude. They're not real."

"They're real, Hallie. They're just unhelpful! Are you really not buying any of the stuff we're finding?" he asks. "*None* of it? Of course, there's nothing groundbreaking yet, but you're not even *starting* to warm up to it?"

I purse my lips together. I can't say I'm a believer yet, but my number of groans per episode has decreased, and I'm happy to play along.

"Nope," I assert. I have an image to keep up, after all. It'd blow the whole false flag operation wide open if I confessed. But considering I spent the past few minutes moving a planchette around the Ouija board, I'm not buying what we've found tonight.

We take EMF measurements around the room and down

the hallway before logging off for the night, saving our footage and preparing for bed. I scroll through our social media comments as I lie in bed, liking the positive ones to show *engagement*. The dark and curious parts of my brain lead me to the *Noobie Brothers* Instagram page. They have more followers than we do, but as I scroll through the content, they *don't* have eager commenters. They mostly have grown men insisting they are playing it wrong, which they are—on purpose, of course. I'd much rather have eager teenagers shipping me with Hayden than gamer dudes leaving angry messages. I hope Skroll sees it the same way.

Hayden emerges from the bathroom, ready for bed, and without any prompting, he leans back on the tiny couch. He attempts to settle himself, tossing a few times, scrunching his legs up, but every position looks highly uncomfortable. In fact, all of this is tragic to watch. This bed is big enough for both of us.

I'm so used to the person next to me feeling like an anchor drowning me that I didn't want to sleep beside anyone for a long time. But Hayden is different. He feels like an anchor in the good ways—grounding, keeping something where it ought to be, and reassuring me with the knowledge that I won't go adrift.

"We can share the bed."

Sleepy, hooded eyes flicker up to me. As always, glasses or not, he can find me. "No, it's all good. I'll be fine here."

"You should be able to get a good night's sleep. Let the ghosts keep you up, not the back pain. I don't mind."

I *don't* mind. "Mind" is the wrong word. I am excited, nervous, terrified for what this is going to be like. But I do not *mind*. After a moment's consideration, he paws for his glasses on the coffee table and slides them onto his face. Hayden steps into the bedroom and slowly pushes the covers on his side of the bed back. I try not to watch as he eases himself onto his back with a relieved sigh.

"Okay, much better."

It'll be fine. It won't be weird at all. He's at least wearing pajama bottoms (a grossly cute pair of UFO-print pants) and a T-shirt. Hayden fluffs the pillows behind his head a few times before slipping his glasses off again.

Lying in bed with Hayden now feels strangely intimate. Fresh out of the shower, he smells like his usual musky amber, with a twinge of plain hotel soap, and his hair smells like the generic shampoo in the bathroom ("Lemon verbena!" he'd announced earlier, citing how all hotels had lemon verbena shampoo and it might have been a conspiracy). I can point out every one of the freckles on the bridge of his nose that are almost too light to see, and my fingers long to trace over them.

This will be a game of sleeping as far away from one another as we can, building a pillowed wall between us. The thought of waking up close to him, feeling him breathing, knowing the little sounds he makes in his sleep, will undo me. My entire body shivers at the prospect of warm breath against my back or spending a night falling asleep to the sound of his heartbeat.

"You good?" he asks.

I nod. Our eyes meet in the middle. He can study the blurred canvas of my face, splotches of blue watercolor in his vision, but he can't see me studying every angle and feature of *his* face.

"You know, this show is so much better because of you."

His words catch me by surprise—they've come from nowhere, but after years of feeling insignificant, I don't know how to respond to something like that.

"Oh?"

"I mean it. I never thought about having a co-host. I love the podcast, but doing it alone isn't easy. It's a lot of work, and it's . . . isolating. It's hard to imagine doing this alone now."

Swallowing the tears in my throat is a valiant task. "Thanks. You built some pretty good stilts to stand on."

He flashes a tired smile. "I try."

"Now we just have to hope we don't run out of monsters to hunt."

"Fear not, Hallie," Hayden teases, shutting his eyes. "I am a bottomless pit of weird information, so we'll be good to keep going for at least another ten years."

"Good. Ten years of convincing you none of this stuff is real."

"It's real," he sighs.

"All of it?"

His eyes shoot open. "Well, not *all* of it."

"Tell me one thing you legitimately don't believe in. Aside from, like, the shitty theories you just don't like."

Hayden faces me. I look at the space between us and where his fingers bunch around the comforter. No one has ever felt so close and so far away before. Like we're magnets determined to find each other, it takes everything in me to not reach out and touch him.

"I don't think the moon landing was faked."

"Huh," I ponder.

"Do you know how many people it'd take to cover something like that up?"

"A lot—"

"Four hundred and eleven thousand people, to be exact."

"Excuse me?"

"There was a study done. That's a lot of people. Think about how hard it is to keep a surprise party under wraps. You couldn't fake an entire moon landing with that many people involved."

"On that, we can agree," I say.

"Cool. I'm going to sleep, then, and I'll try my luck on some other theories tomorrow. Good night."

Hayden rolls himself over and flicks off the light. The Port of Long Beach and the moon light the room enough to see the outline of his body beside me. Something rubs against my foot beneath the covers and I jolt away from Hayden.

"Was that you?" I gasp.

"What?"

"Rubbing my foot."

"*No*? That'd be so weird."

"Are you sure?"

"Yes, Hallie, I am not playing footsie with you. Maybe it's a ghost." Hayden reaches for the EMF reader on the nightstand.

"Please do not pull that thing out right now."

Hayden grumbles and puts the device down. I itch the space on the side of my foot that I felt the touch on and solemnly slink back into bed. Hayden laughs into his pillow, and as much as I'd love to kick him for finding this funny, I don't. Instead, I laugh too. Then something sinks in.

"I like how you always say 'good night' before we go to sleep."

The idea of someone wanting to wish me a good night shouldn't make me feel warm and fuzzy. But when Hayden says it, it does.

"Oh," he says, but there's no trace of judgment in his voice. Surprise, yes, but not judgment. He huffs a small laugh. "Then I'll stick with it. Good night, Hallie."

"Don't let the ghosties bite," I say.

He laughs for real this time, and it feels like being at a sleepover with best friends. It feels like the sort of relationship I've always wanted. I've always wanted to fall in love with my best friend—a person I'd stay up past my bedtime with laughing at dumb jokes. Rolling over and saying, "Okay, *now* I'm going to sleep," only to do the opposite. I want to fall asleep to the sound of his laugh, the waves, the creaking of an old ship.

I don't want to fall asleep any other way.

CHAPTER 10

Thank fuck we did this episode in March and not August. I respect the ship's desire to be authentic and give guests an immersive hotel stay, but I could have seriously gone for some air-conditioning. All we have to cool the room is a single wire fan that made a terrifying noise when I tried to turn it on at two a.m. I woke Hayden with my antics and he captured an unflattering shot on the night-vision camera of me trying to reach the fan cord, thinking I was our French ghost.

Birds chirp outside the porthole and a distant cargo ship honks aggressively at the port. They are the first real sounds I've heard all night. No ghosts, no demonic possession. So far, we are zero for two on finding ghosts at haunted hotels. Hayden is an alarmingly light sleeper.

I can't tell if it's from years of caring for his dad or if he just *desperately* wants to find a ghost.

I rub my eyes with the base of my palm, wrapping my arms around the pillow beneath me. My fingers curl around thin fabric that smells like amber and lemon verbena. The horror sinks in immediately.

A pillow should not be this firm and rigid. A pillow should not smell this good.

Nor should it breathe.

I'm not pressed against the starchy sheets beneath me, nor am I swaddling a pillow in my sleep.

I'm hanging on to Hayden.

Everything about him is consuming. His scent, the soft touch of his arm behind my back, the rhythm of him breathing. My head rests against his chest as he lies on his side, an arm draped over my body. Our legs weave together, a brush of knees beneath the covers. Hayden's head rests on top of mine, lips close enough to kiss my hair. His body's firm but inviting, corded muscles along his chest and stomach, cushioning the bony parts of his shoulders and ribs. Heat spreads wherever we connect.

In short, I want to die.

I'm not entirely sure if I want to die in a good way or a bad way. When I imagine a perfect morning, I imagine waking up in someone's arms, someone who cares and wants me there, where nothing is enough to drag me from underneath the covers, no bony cuddles or morning breath bad enough to make me pull away.

Hayden is the one to finally paint the picture for me.

Want simmers in my stomach, the same as it did last night when he first climbed into bed. It's the magnetism in my brain trying to tell me he's different. I fear the mess that could come from falling for another coworker, but what scares me even more is how right everything with Hayden feels, in ways that it really never has before.

I feel him breathing beside me, hyperaware of the soft touch of fingertips on my hip. As much as I want to claw at his T-shirt more and slide closer, I pull myself away. Before I scramble too far, I watch him. He doesn't seem to notice I've left or that I've been cuddling him in the first place. His hair is a messy mop of dark waves. On overnights, he doesn't bother shaving, letting the usual layer of scruff on his cheeks come in heavier. He looks so much more peaceful while sleeping.

Hayden doesn't carry the same concentrated tension in his shoulders that feels like an ever-present wall between him and the world. I think of all the years he must have spent doing nothing but working and taking care of his dad. Shuttling back and forth to appointments, cooking every meal, ready to jump out of bed to help at the first sign of trouble. He gave up *years* for someone else and put himself second.

Because of all this, I let him rest.

                                   , , ,

We spend most of the car ride back to LA in silence.

I stutter out a "thanks" when Hayden brings me coffee after he checks us out. He asks what music I want to listen to in the car, but words are few and far between. I feel his heavy gaze on me the entire time, like he's waiting for me to say something, and he doesn't know how to fill the space.

It's hard to look at him without thinking of how good it felt for someone to keep me close. If the fear of falling for him or dating another coworker didn't fester in the back of my brain constantly, I might have snuggled closer. I might do *something*. I have enough evidence to believe Hayden would reciprocate.

He's kind enough to drive me all the way back home, even though it involves trekking entirely across Los Angeles and over the hill. It's an extra forty-five minutes of trying to pretend I'm not imagining his touch or warmth, not imagining the deep rasp of his voice in the morning.

As Hayden pulls up in front of Nora's place, he beats me out of the car and fetches my duffel for me. I think of the little things Hayden does on a daily basis: compliments my fun patterned leggings, notices when I paint my nails new colors, made it a point to memorize my coffee order early on in our friendship. Having someone who cares the way he does makes me want to *try* and be brave, facing the fears and feelings that bubble beneath the surface.

"Thanks," I say, taking the bag from him.

"Sure." His grip doesn't loosen yet, like he's hanging on to my things and his words at the same time. Finally, he releases. "Hallie, you all right?"

"Yeah," I lie. "Fine. How come?"

"You're just quiet."

Does he know? Hayden wakes up when the wind blows too hard in a room, swearing it's a poltergeist or a death echo or some weird apparition. He must have felt me snuggled against him, the way my fingers tightened around his T-shirt as I clung to him, thinking he was my pillow or a blanket. If he did, what did it do to him?

Maybe I don't want to know.

"Just tired. I don't sleep well in the heat."

Hayden smirks. "*Or* it was something else keeping you awake."

"Your snoring?"

"I don't snore," he shoots back.

I pinch my fingers together. "A little bit. Whatever it was, it was *not* a ghost."

"You keep telling yourself that, Nonbeliever. Rest up."

Nonbeliever. It's a far different nickname than I'm used to, and certainly not one I could imagine finding in a *Cosmo* sex tips article, but it makes something flutter in my stomach.

"I'll text you tomorrow," I say. "We've got some road-trip planning to do."

His smile quirks, and he nods. "We do. Bigfoot hunting is serious business. See you later, Hal."

Nora's at work, leaving Lizzie and me to unpack and lounge for the rest of the day. I'll provide her with a single grape to appease her into not doing anything weird or throwing herself at the walls of her terrarium. I still don't know if it's a hobby of hers or if she's trying to break free. I'm too scared to ask.

I shower, ridding myself of the sweat I've accumulated overnight. By the time I've dried my hair and changed into my cozy clothes, there's a knock on the door. I expect it to be one of Nora's Amazon deliveries or a company asking her to sample their products in exchange for a review and promo on Skroll.

I peer through the peephole and my heart drops into my stomach. A sharp chill shoots up my spine. I'm sure he's heard my footsteps by now and knows—

"Hallie, I know you're home."

It shouldn't shake me the way it does, but Cade is at my apartment—the apartment I'd run to when I ran from *him*. I've always felt safe here, and it feels easy to pretend I'm healing and moving on. Nora's got a dead bolt, and Nora's a security system in her own way. I'm convinced the girl could use anything as a weapon if she tried hard enough. A Taser hangs from the key rack, and I'm tempted to use it.

I would love to see this man pee his pants.

I steady myself before opening the door. I don't even greet him before he steps into the doorframe, keeping me from shutting it in his face again.

"Hi," I say. "What do you want?"

Fear ratchets through my body. We're alone. At work, I can count on him to be unpleasant or sickly sweet in a way that'll discredit me. It's why I've never gone to HR, never tried to escalate the things he's done. It's my word against his, and Kevin likes him. There's no proof, just a whisper network of female employees telling each other not to get involved with him.

"Some greeting."

"What are you doing here?"

We're inches apart, but he deems that insufficient and steps into the apartment. I can't show him the weak spots in my armor that *he* put there. Instead of giving me a forceful tug or shove, Cade lowers my hand from the doorframe, allowing himself inside.

"I need the external trackpad."

I raise my eyebrows. "*My* external trackpad?"

He nods.

"The one *you* bought *me* for my birthday last year?"

Cade toys with one of the picture frames on Nora's bookshelf. "That's the one."

"It's mine."

"I bought it."

"Are you five? This is five-year-old logic, Cade."

His lips turn up in a contentious smile. It took long enough to learn everything about him has a sound. Every one of his movements sounds like: "Are you sure about that?" Every smile sounds like: "Oh, *Hallie*." Everything he does is there to remind me how insignificant I am. Every emotion I have is silly and frivolous.

He eyes me, surveying the worn-in floral-print leggings I'm wearing. I'm not wearing a bra under my hoodie, but it's not like anyone can tell. I'm sure Cade's thinking of all the ways I've let myself go since our breakup.

"It was my money, so I feel like, if I need it, I should be able to use it."

I shut my eyes. "Again, five-year-old logic."

"Hallie . . ."

"Cade," I shoot back.

"It's the least you could do. I could charge you for a lot of things, if I wanted to. I never made you pay for utilities even though you used them. I *could* have. But I did that for you." He turns, approaching me. He rests a finger along my jaw. At one point, I was so flattered by the attention. Now I can't stand the thought of him near me. "I just wanted you to be happy, and you *never* appreciated it."

"You never wanted that."

"For someone who talks about how much I invalidate your feelings, you're sure gung ho to do it to me." Silence burns between us at an impasse. He waits before speaking again. "Hallie, I want the trackpad. *Noobie Brothers* needs it for one of our sessions. I'm not buying a new one. I'd hate to tell Kevin the reason we're late on this episode is because *you* refused to play nice."

My breath catches in my throat. I worry Kevin likes Cade enough to reprimand me or cancel my show because I'm letting my personal feelings interfere with Skroll's business. No show, no job. That's the power Cade has always had. It'll always be his word over mine.

"I think Skroll is fine with some friendly competition, but letting *your* personal grudges get in the way might not be the way to win, Hallie," Cade taunts.

"No," I say, "but getting more views and engagement than you is."

He laughs. "Do you really think people want to watch you hunt for ghosts? You don't believe in this stuff. You're selling out for the sake of spiting me. It's embarrassing."

I think of the past few weeks—sleeping in haunted hotel rooms, snacking on candy and bags of chips late at night while a Spirit Box thumps in the background, spending hours in Hayden's apartment as he runs me through yet another slide-show on the most compelling Bigfoot footage and explains how it cannot be a man in a suit. I may not believe in ghosts or monsters yet, but I *am* having fun in a way I haven't in years. I'm happy, which is more than I could say for a long time.

"The trackpad," he repeats. He holds out his hand. "I'm not asking again."

I disappear into my room and unplug the extra trackpad from my laptop, biting back tears. I hardly use the thing, but the fact that Cade feels like he can walk in and take what he wants from me—that he can *still* take from me—makes it hard to keep my composure. I swallow my tears, storming back into the living room and shoving the device into his hands.

"Take it and go."

He stares me down like I'm a child he can reprimand, and I fear him like a kid fearing time-out. Still. "Hallie, you don't have to behave like this."

"I want you to take your fucking trackpad and get out of my apartment."

"It's Nora's—"

"And mine now."

"You just make it a habit of living places and not being on the lease."

"Shut up—"

"*And* using people to your advantage."

I meet his gaze. He's a few inches taller than me, our eye-lines nearly even. But I've never been even with someone like Cade. He will always look down on me. I can't help thinking about how Hayden physically *has* to look down at me; otherwise he'd miss me every time. Hayden always looks at me like I'm a view he wants.

"Is that what you're doing with this guy, too, Hal? How'd you get him to agree to your show? Is it the same way you convinced me to help you move up?"

The dam of tears in my eyes is about to burst. In moments like this, I hate twenty-two-year-old me, who thought there was any kindness in the things Cade did. I hate the girl who agreed to get drinks with him, who liked the attention and was so desperate to feel special. I hate the girl who agreed to go home with him and thought losing her virginity to some-one like Cade was a good idea. I hate the girl who took so long to walk away.

Deep down, I know it's not my fault, but in moments like this, I want to blame someone for the pain. Cade's good at convincing me not to pin it on him.

"Did this new guy know that he only got lucky because no one else wanted to work with you? If it weren't for me, you would have been let go in one of the rounds of layoffs. But no, you knew getting in bed with me would help you out, so you did. I'm sure your new co-host seems nice and shiny now, and he's probably just grateful you plucked him out of dark-web obscurity, but he'll realize what you are, too. Give it time."

I struggle to keep my tears back and fail, sniffling them away as much as I can. Cade sighs something patronizing as I wipe my eyes.

"If . . . if I am so insignificant, if I matter so little to you and everyone around me, then why the *fuck* can you not just leave me alone and let me live my life?"

I know the answer. It's because I finally had enough of his bullshit. I'm braver than I give myself credit for, but it's the reason everything is broken around me, and the reason Cade wants to keep punishing me.

He looks over my meek composure, smiles, and reaches for the door. He's done what he came to do.

"Looking forward to your next episode."

The door slams behind him, and I can't lock it fast enough. I wait until Cade's out of earshot before the tears come. A stronger person wouldn't have tolerated Cade's torment for three years. Someone who wasn't me would have left sooner. Someone stronger than me wouldn't let Cade *still* treat me this way. I swore I was done with it, too. I wish I was more like the brave and tenacious co-host our fans think I am.

My phone buzzes on the coffee table, drawing me toward something other than my grief. I open Hayden's message. It's a photo of Cthulhu, sitting happily in front of Hayden's sneakers, presenting him with a small, alien-shaped squeaker toy.

HAYDEN (11:42 AM): He will bring me an entire Area 51 after we're gone for almost a week.

I wipe my snotty nose with a laugh, and relief washes over me. I worried my panic would drive a wedge between the two of us, but it evidently has not. I think of Hayden and the small things he does to make me happy, especially when there's nothing in it for him. I think about how he cares, and that despite what I feel about myself, he doesn't see me that way. Our fans don't either. I need to trust them and remember what I'm doing matters. I type out a response.

HALLIE (11:43 AM): He missed you!

Against all my better judgment, I already miss him, too.

he hikers might have undergone something called par-
adox un—dammit—paradoxical undressing. Why is
that word so hard for me to say today?" Hayden fumbles, yet again.

My eyes rise from the script in my hands as Hayden circles
the word several times in red pen on his own script.

My confrontation with Cade over the weekend is still fresh
in my mind. It'd been hard to think ahead for most of the day.
At least when Nora came home, I had something to distract
me. She let Lizzie have some "out" time, where she wandered
around the living room. That night, even Lizzie sensed my
sadness. She gave me a weird lick I didn't like, but I appreciated her concern.

Now, back at work, I'm determined to channel that pain
into one hell of an episode.

The Skroll recording booths are a stiflingly small space to
be confined all afternoon with the man who I woke up snug-
gling days before. I feel way too aware of Hayden's height and
the steady calm his presence always brings as we stand next
to one another in front of the raised mic. The room smells like
him mixed with an elementary school computer lab, full of
warm static and the tang of metal.

"Paradoxical undressing," I say, without flaw.

"Maybe this should be your line. I'm obviously cursed today."

I clear my throat. Behind me, Hayden leans against the padded walls, sliding the pen between his teeth as he studies the script. He's so focused he doesn't notice how long I watch him. The swell of biceps beneath his flannel and the naturally mussed shock of hair keep my eyes hanging on him longer than I care to admit.

"Can I improvise?" I ask.

"Go for it."

As I speak, harsh feedback screeches through our headphones, making both of us jump. Hayden tosses his headphones off with a surprised "fuck!" and the pen flies into the air. He lowers the microphone volumes like they are controls on a nuclear reactor.

"What the hell was that?" I remove my headphones, too.

"I might have moved the computer too close to the mic. No big deal."

Hayden slides his headphones back over his ears. He jumps to the next part of the script and I realize I can't hear him in mine.

"My headphones aren't working," I inform him.

He backs away again and toys with a few settings on the switchboard before returning to me. He steps behind me and heat rises to my cheeks as he adjusts the headphones over my ears. A swipe of a finger runs along the back of my neck, sending shivers all over my body. His laugh comes as a soft puff of breath against my back.

This shouldn't set me off like it does.

I could question it further, but when he finishes adjusting

the headphones, his hands rest on my shoulders, a thumb stroking the surface of my upper back. This is a sick game to play. His touch rushes to the pit of my stomach and lower. I scrunch my neck and sigh softly, leaning closer to him. His proximity is intoxicating and my body wants more. I could do so many things to him in a soundproof booth.

"Can you hear me now?" he says into the mic. His voice comes through the speakers so low, slightly raspy from the amount of talking we've done today. I want him so much closer, to hear his voice right beside my ear, feel him breathing behind me, the rattle and vibration of his words sending chills up and down my body.

"I can."

"Good." It's deep and intentional and it makes my knees wobble.

A single word in Hayden's sultry voice, and I have to unbutton the top of my shirt to cool myself.

As Hayden begins his next line, loud yelping bleeds into the room. He frowns through the window. When I swing open the door, I'm not sure why I'm shocked to find Cade and the boys as the source of the chaos. I pull the door shut behind me.

Instantly, Cade swings back with a smile. "Oh, hey, Hal."

But there's a certain anger behind his steely blue eyes over the fact that I still have not backed down from the show.

"Please be quiet," I say.

"You working?"

"No, I'm sitting in a recording studio trying to meditate." I cross my arms. "Yes, I'm working."

"Right, sorry, I wouldn't want to disturb the little ghosts."

"My little ghost show got sixty thousand views last week."

I know damn well his got only fifty-five K. Cade rakes a hand through his beach-blond hair, pursing his lips.

"You don't need to get so defensive."

"You can call my show by its name."

The recording studio door swings open behind me. Suddenly, an entirely new fear arises. I don't want Hayden to know who Cade is to me. Cade could end everything good here with a single word. I can't bear the idea of Cade exerting his persuasion on Hayden, and I can't stand the unfounded fear that Hayden might believe him. He's convinced everyone at Skroll he can do no wrong for so many years. He's painted a harsh picture of me and I can't control who buys it.

Hayden's hand rests on the small of my back, and now I'm concerned for other (horny) reasons. I can't show Cade any of my cards. I especially can't show him how into my co-host I am. It's information he'd do his worst with.

"Hi," Hayden says. "I don't think we've met yet. I'm Hayden."

Cade holds out a limp handshake, which Hayden accepts. "Cade Browning. You must be the conspiracy theorist guy Hallie picked up off Reddit."

Hayden shrugs, leaning against the doorframe, towering over Cade. "Actually, I was on TV."

"Right." Cade rubs at the fleshy-colored stubble on his chin. "It's funny. Hallie doesn't believe in any of this stuff. I can't believe this is the kind of show she'd do. You know that, right?"

Cade has obviously not watched any of our episodes.

"I'm well aware that young Hallie has a lot of learning to do." Hayden's hand rests on my head, ruffling my blue waves. I swat him away. "We're working on it."

"Best of luck to you. That one's a handful."

I'm sure Hayden's picturing quirky things like my exasperated yelling as he tells me an absolutely batshit theory or asking a Ouija board if a ghost was a virgin or not.

"When she's not provoking demons, she's a delight to work with," Hayden says.

Cade chuckles, and his voice lowers. "I mean, man to man, Hallie was supposed to be *my* producer before I let her go. Chloe only let her make this show so she didn't get fired. No one wanted to work with her otherwise. Not your fault. You didn't know any better."

Hayden's jaw clenches and his eyes narrow. Cade's comment leaves me feeling like I'm going to explode. Cade is like a snake in more ways than one, and when he's threatened, he unleashes more poison. I have to swallow my tears, straighten up, avoid eye contact, and make myself small until this is over.

I visualize what'll come next. Hayden and I will step back into the recording booth, Hayden will ask for an answer, as in: "What the hell was that?" And I'll be left alone again. I'll be without a show, without a future at Skroll, and without one of the first real friends I've found in the past few months. Hayden will have finally learned what I'm scared everyone else already thinks: I'm hard to work with. I don't stand out.

Instead, Hayden straightens up behind me. "It's been going fine so far. In fact, we're busy prepping for our next episode, so we don't have time to chat."

"Of course. Good to meet you, dude."

"You know, it wasn't that nice to meet you." Hayden's arm wraps around me and he shuttles me back into the booth. He lets out a disgruntled sigh and turns around. "Well, that guy's a dick."

"Yeah." I nod slowly and divert my eyes. I used to save tears for the shower or the bathroom in the middle of the night, sometimes my car. I'd save them for a place where no one else could see.

"Hallie?" he asks. His voice is so quiet and confused. "Are you all right?"

I blink away my tears as best I can, but a few slip down my cheeks. "Fine. I'm fine."

I'm not prepared for his touch. It's a soft thumb along the curve of my cheek, sweeping a stray tear out of the way and tilting my chin up. I yank myself away, bending to my knees to find the closest thing to a tissue in my purse. As I dab at my eyes, the stools shift around behind me. Metal clangs against the microphones and Hayden curses under his breath.

When I turn around, he's made his way to the ground with me. The booth is not made for anyone to sit on the floor, especially not someone Hayden's size, but he makes it work.

"Who . . . who is he?"

My lip trembles. "An ex."

"You dated him?" There's no ire in Hayden's voice. Not as he looks me over, hunting for parts of me that need care, or as he runs his hands down my arms, keeping me steady in front of him. No matter how low I feel, I'm not alone. He offers a warm smile and shakes his head. "Oh, Hallie, you are *so* out of his league."

I stifle a laugh.

"You can't listen to that guy, Hallie. He's a total asshole. He had no right to speak to you like that. Besides, he's completely wrong."

There might always be a part of me that thinks Cade is right, no matter how far away from the pain I am. I would so much rather believe in Bigfoot or aliens than believe a word of what Cade says. But that's not how it works. What people like Cade want most is to be able to hurt someone long after they're gone.

"I'm not so sure about that," I concede. "He knows what'll shake me. Three years wasted, just for him to tell me I wasn't funny and how I didn't stand out. I was stupid enough to get involved with him in the first place. Stupid enough to stay that long."

"Hallie, this is not your fault. Cade probably sensed your brilliance. That you are funny and beautiful and great at your job, and used those qualities—*your* qualities—to his advantage."

I linger on one word.

Beautiful.

I'm not sure if it brings me joy, or if I should be chiding myself for falling for someone's pretty words all over again, but I can't find deceit and selfishness in any of Hayden's expressions. All I see is a desperation to make me smile and to fix this.

To take care of me.

"I know that what he did clearly hurt you, but he's so wrong. You're not hard to work with. And you *do* stand out. When you're around, it's impossible to look away. You are the only thing I see. He's an idiot for not knowing you make everything you touch better. Please don't believe anything coming out of the mouth of a guy who still has frosted tips."

I break into a laugh, a few tears dripping down my cheeks. Hayden reaches out, brushing his thumb beneath my eyes. In a matter of minutes, he's made this recording booth change from the scariest place on Earth to the safest.

"Thanks."

"Do you hear me?"

I nod.

Before I can stop myself, I'm in his arms, my head nestled in the crook of his shoulder. I clasp my fingers around his flannel shirt, and I'm so soothed by the sound of his heartbeat.

"It's okay," he repeats. His fingers wind in my hair, the scent of his cologne bringing me back down to earth. It suddenly dawns on me why he brings me a sense of peace: Hayden is the sort of person who takes care of people. He's the kind of person who sees someone hurting and does something about it.

"Do you want to keep going?" he asks.

I nod, pulling myself to my feet. We resume where we left off, and Hayden spews terrible conspiracies, but when it's my turn to speak, I miss my cue. I look down at the script, and I don't know if I can deliver on these words today. I can't joke and tease with him when I feel so much fear in being seen.

"Hallie," Hayden prods. "We can call it for today. We can do double the work tomorrow when you're feeling better. Besides, it's already late."

I don't want to bust my ass tomorrow, but I want to put on a happy face today even less.

"Okay."

He slips his headphones off. "Do you want to go do something?"

* * *

The sun's gone down by the time Hayden says we're close to our destination. He doesn't offer any hints as to where we're headed, but I'm more confused the farther we go. Finally, he pulls into a small parking lot and steps out of the car.

"Where are we?"

He smiles and leads me across a small green space that opens to a ... playground. There are slides and climbing poles, a jumping bridge, and swings. Behind it, though, is a giant rocket ship. I'm even more alarmed when Hayden approaches and slides into the base of it.

"We're going up *there*? We drove all this way to go to a playground?"

"Yep. Come on. It's how the aliens will know to come get us." He holds out a hand for me as I hop onto the platform with him. I bite back a smile as I shimmy up the ladders first and wiggle through holes meant for children until I reach the top. Behind me, I hear Hayden grunting and struggling to navigate the playground. He reaches me at the top, one shoulder after the other, and tugs himself through the hole in the platform. He hardly makes it.

"This is not meant for someone my size," he groans. "Ow."

"You don't say," I tease.

As he takes a seat, he hits my arm, knocking me over. "Don't be mean."

Hayden slides his legs through the bars and looks out onto the city, legs dangling freely over the structure. The brisk March air hits me with a bite. We're closer to the water, catching the wind off the ocean. I shiver and wish I'd taken my jacket from the back of Hayden's car. I hadn't expected to spend time outside.

Without saying anything, Hayden sheds his flannel and passes it over to me. Our fingers brush as I take it and slide it over my shoulders. It smells like him and feels like the hug he gave me earlier. The sleeves come past my hands, and I bundle myself in them, which makes Hayden smile.

"Thanks."

He nods.

We sit in silence, letting the rush of cars on the freeway fill the air—distant honking and loud music blaring. I've always liked the rush of the city. Anything else is too quiet. I've never been one for camping or time out in the wilderness. Our upcoming Bigfoot hunt is going to be a delight. I also hate bugs with a passion, and I've contemplated starting a last will and testament in case I die.

"I'm sorry about today." Hayden rubs his palm with his opposite hand and quiets. His eyes flicker up to mine. The moon glints off the lenses of his glasses, illuminating the bright greens behind them.

"It's fine."

"Not really."

"You defended me more than you needed to. I appreciate it."

"It's still sitting with me, though," Hayden says.

"Why? Because the more you think about it, you wonder if he's right?" I laugh, but it hurts.

"No, because I *know* he's not." His tone feels the same as when he pushes back on his theories, arguing that *of course* aliens are real or that I'm being closed-minded. It's a tone that conveys inflexibility, stubbornness. He's not going to be talked out of this. "Hallie . . . I . . ."

I see so many words on his lips and all of them scare me.

"I've been alone for a really long time," Hayden starts. His voice quiets. The confidence from moments ago is gone. "About three years, to be exact. I think if I'd let more people in near the end of my dad's life, maybe I would have handled it better. But I was so used to keeping my feelings to myself. I never wanted my dad to know how much I was hurting. He'd blame himself or want someone else to step in so that I could breathe. So, I just didn't."

I scoot closer to him, sliding my legs through the bars, too. My boots hit the lower levels, laces clinking against the metal.

"When he died, I didn't want to put that pain on someone else, either. So, I left."

"Left?"

"I rented out the apartment my dad and I lived in in Boston and I moved out here. I could have done the podcast from wherever. I didn't know anyone out here. My mom's in San Francisco, but I didn't want to turn to her, either. I started fresh by myself.

"The problem is that I never *really* started again. When you rebuild your life, you're supposed to grow something new. I came out here with a podcast and a cat, and two and a half years later, all I still have is a podcast and a cat." His voice breaks into a laugh that I match.

"You don't *even* have a podcast. You have a web series now."

"Right." His smile feels bright, and for a moment, I wonder if he's finally putting his pain somewhere. Like he's decided to breathe again. "I haven't made any friends. Haven't really dated anyone. It scares me, so I've been staying the course and keeping every bit of grief at bay as best as I can. Some of those days were so dark and my depression got so debilitating that even when I wanted to try letting people in, I didn't think anyone deserved to see me at my lowest. So, I never did. Then you emailed me."

I lean my head against the bars and glance up at him. He matches my posture with a smile.

"Something told me this was a chance I had to take, even if it scared me." He bites his lip. "It might have been my psychiatrist at first, but I *did* make the choice on my own. The sadness and the hurt are still there. But now it feels like something good is there, too. There hasn't been something good there in a long time."

I reach across the platform, my fingers skimming the holes in the tiles until I find his hand. I tread carefully, running my fingertips along the base of his wrist until our fingers weave together. Holding his hand is so easy. We fit together too well.

Touching him is a conscious choice, and despite my worst fears—falling for someone who could hurt me, dating another coworker, how Cade might respond—when he brushes his thumb against the back of my palm, I know this is what I'm supposed to do.

"I'm sorry he hurt you and that he doesn't see how special you are, Hallie. Everyone should be in awe of you like I am because you deserve it. I'm really lucky that it was me you found and took a chance on."

I squeeze his hand. I don't know what to say to him that can match what he's given me. After a moment, he pulls his feet out of the bars and scoots back, leaning on the platform ground, his eyes cast up at the sky. I join him and trace my thumb over the UFO tattoo on his wrist. If he tells me he has feelings for me, I'll have no choice but to reciprocate. Anything else would be a blatant lie.

I try to imagine the least sexy things I can—alien probing, Loch Ness Monster blubber, the Skunk Ape. But instead, as I look at where our hands rest together, all that comes to mind is what it'd feel like if his hands were on other parts of me.

I spend all my days watching Hayden's hands take notes, edit audio, type scripts, and run through his hair when he's stressed or confused or bewildered. I want to watch him put his hands on me, something light at first, like a stroke of the cheek, hands on my waist, then more forceful. I want fistfuls of his hair between my fingers, the feel of his stubble against my lips, my jaw, my neck.

Like he can read my mind, he turns on his side, claiming a handful of his flannel on me and tugging me closer to him. He holds me against him with a grip on my waist. His body is warm and firm where we connect. Our legs tangle together, his hips flush against mine. Heat pools in my stomach as he leans in closer. My eyes flutter shut as the plastic frames of his glasses leave a cool press against my forehead.

I feel every breath he takes and count them.

One.

Two.

Three.

At four, I reach for what I want. His cheeks are rough beneath my touch, but the curve of his lip is soft and full. I want to taste him and hear the sounds he makes as I kiss him harder. I ponder if they'll sound like the frustrated "hmphs" he makes when something stumps him or more like the heady breaths he lets out as he sleeps.

My heart hammers in my chest. He swallows, parting his lips. Hayden toys with the bottom of my shirt and brushes the sensitive skin along my hip. A soft gasp slips out of me that makes him smile. As his tongue runs along the inside of his lips, I freeze.

I can't do this.

No matter how badly my body wants him—from the ache

that blooms in my chest and between my legs to the tremble in my fingers as I find a lock of his soft hair—falling in love with someone is the scariest thing a person can do, and I know what happens if I fall for the wrong person. I want to believe Hayden is the type of person it's safe to love, but I'm still afraid to trust him with the most fragile parts of me.

"I . . . I can't."

His eyes open as he pulls himself out of his own trance. He studies me carefully, tasting a phantom kiss on his lips. But instead of confusion, there's understanding. He sucks in a deep breath and nods.

"It's okay."

I might not be able to kiss him like I want to—not yet—but I can't fathom pulling away from him. Instead, I weave myself closer to him, resting my head on his chest. He knows just what to do. His arms envelop me, keeping me tight against his body. I fall into him completely, as hard as I'm falling *for* him.

A plane races across the night sky.

"UFO," I say.

"A *plane*." Hayden laughs and it vibrates through my entire body.

"Wow, who's the nonbeliever now?"

⚘ THE OUT THERE ⚘

Episode #4: "Not Even REI Can Save You"

On this week's episode of The Out There, *Hayden and Hallie investigate the Dyatlov Pass Incident, where nine hikers died under mysterious circumstances in the Ural Mountains of Russia.*

Was it an avalanche, government testing, or . . . the abominable snowman?

HAYDEN

Let's go over how each of these hikers died.

HALLIE

Cheery!

HAYDEN

Six apparently died of hypothermia. The other three, however, died of physical trauma, ranging from severe chest trauma and internal bleeding to a fatal skull injury. Some of those who died of hypothermia also had physical injuries and abrasions. Two hikers were missing their eyes and one was missing her tongue. Oh, and another one had missing eyebrows. The final conclusion the prosecutors in the investigation came to was: "The cause of their demise was an overwhelming force which the hikers were not able to overcome."

HALLIE

Wow, give us nothing!

HAYDEN

Doesn't that make you raise your eyebrows a little bit?

HALLIE

Is that insensitive since one of them lost their eyebrows?

HAYDEN

See, you do listen to me sometimes.

HALLIE

I was prepared to tap out when you started talking about the Yeti, to be fair.

HAYDEN

All right, there is some gravity to the Yeti theory, actually. For example, one of the hikers took a photo where there was a blurry, large figure looming in the background and some people have theorized that they could have gotten photo proof of their attacker. What I have also found interesting is the fact that the tent was ripped open from the inside with a knife, and the way the bodies were found does really make it seem like they were running from something, you know?

HALLIE

Like a Yeti?

HAYDEN

Well, yeah. They also were in various states of undress, which gives off a sense of panic.

HALLIE

They were a bunch of college-aged hikers. I don't think the scantily clad part necessarily has to do with the abominable snowman, Hayden.

HAYDEN

It's Siberia, Hallie. You really think they were having tent sex in the middle of the tundra?

HALLIE

Sharing body heat and all that. And like, what else are you going to do?

HAYDEN

Is that what you would do if you were hiking in the tundra?

HALLIE

No, because there is no universe where I would be hiking in the middle of Siberia in the first place. You couldn't pay me to put on a pair of snowshoes and go camping.

HAYDEN

Hmm, sounds like a challenge—

HALLIE

And the end of our friendship.

CHAPTER 12

I'm about halfway through reading a poorly formatted web page ranking the most reputable Bigfoot videos on the internet when a horrible realization dawns on me:

I think I've caught the plague.

"There's one bit of footage," Hayden rambles, pacing in front of the TV and rubbing the bridge of his nose. "I think it's from Siberia. Or Canada? I don't know, it looked cold there—"

"You don't remember?"

"I *know*, it's embarrassing. I'm meant to be the professional here. Anyway, there are *multiple* Bigfoots walking across the screen, and for some reason, I find it *very* compelling." He motions little walking feet with his fingers, then slumps against the couch and begins to scour his computer again. "I should have this bookmarked. What kind of Squatcher *am* I?"

We've been at this for hours, cataloging reference points for our upcoming trip, establishing an itinerary, and making travel arrangements. Our venture would take us to Fresno one night, because Hayden *needed* to look for Fresno Night-crawlers, even if we didn't make it a full episode, then to San Jose to visit the Winchester Mystery House, and two days *way* up north hunting for Bigfoot, before we return home.

I think about a whole five days away with Hayden and my stomach lurches. We almost kissed. I spent an hour resting against his body watching the stars until the glue he'd applied to the places Cade broke me dried. How are we supposed to avoid talking about the almost-kiss for five whole days? We've hardly made it three.

Hayden has not mentioned it so far and nothing's changed, but the way he looks at me is still there and it bubbles furiously between us. There's a sense of affection and longing that hasn't gone away. I don't know how much longer I'll be able to fight it off.

Hayden hums the *X-Files* theme song to himself, typing furiously at his laptop. I don't like the idea of bailing, not when we're on such a good track.

"It's not Siberia! It's Yellowstone," Hayden shouts.

As I shut my laptop and pack up, I cough like a sixty-five-year-old smoker. Cthulhu looks up from his cat tree and hisses. Then Hayden pays attention.

"Hey, don't be rude, man." He turns to me. "You okay?"

I must look *not* okay. His eyes flood with concern and he comes to my side.

"I think I'm going to go home. I should be okay tomorrow."

Hayden presses the back of his hand to my forehead. "Jeez, Hallie, you're burning up."

"Just call me the Jonas Brothers."

"What?"

"Never mind."

I try to sniffle away the congestion in my nose and head, but to no avail. I have no idea how I'm going to drive all the way back to the Valley, but I know I can't stay here.

"Do you want to take a nap?"

"I can do that at home."

"I don't think you're in much shape to drive. Is Nora around?"

I shake my head. "No, Nora went to an indie art festival with Jamie this weekend. I haven't heard from her in twenty-four hours. I think she died of boredom. She won't be much help."

"Uh . . . huh. You can rest here for a bit if you want. I don't want to leave you alone at your apartment all weekend."

"'S okay. I'll be fine."

When I'm sick, I'm used to staying out of the way, sniffling on as few things as I can, and waiting out the illness. Or going to work anyway because I was up against deadlines and filming schedules . . .

"Really, if you want to go rest, you can. I can get you home eventually."

"In *your* bed?"

"Sure. It's clean."

"Does it smell like you?" I ask. My god, delirium is beating me to a pulp at the moment.

His brows furrow. "I imagine so. Is that a selling point?"

I nod.

"You must *really* not be feeling well."

I'm reassured by the soft laugh Hayden lets out as he offers me his hand. I climb off the couch with him. I'm so tired and achy I hardly have time to register that Hayden's bed is probably in his room. In fact, there's a good chance that it is.

The door is always closed, but his room is wedged between the kitchen and bathroom, and I'm not sure what to expect. Hayden keeps so much of himself guarded and behind a shield. This feels like an unarmed version of himself that I might not have a right to yet.

But he doesn't seem to mind, not as I follow after him as a sad flurry of sniffles. For the first time, I think about the fact that I might be getting him sick too. What'll happen if *both* of us can't film? We don't have the time to delay. I'm going to have to drug myself into oblivion on DayQuil to film in a few days. At least if I'm a sick mess, Hayden can go on without me. By now, I'm sure he's figured out how to command attention a little easier.

Then I worry that maybe being *too* high on cold medicine will make me start believing in things like the Jersey Devil. I don't know if that's a risk I'm willing to take.

He pushes the door open, giving a quick peek to evaluate the condition of his room. When it passes his assessment, he invites me in. The back wall is exposed brick with a few art pieces hammered into it. A simple, black-framed bed takes up the middle of the room with an IKEA nightstand on either side of it. The room smells of clean laundry and an earthy musk I attribute to the small essential oil diffuser puffing happily in the corner.

"It's nice," I say. Hayden's already ushering me toward his bed, where I plop onto the comforter. It's black and very, very soft to the touch. "Really, I'm okay."

The last thing I want is to owe someone. It could come up when Hayden and I disagreed on a creative choice, if we needed to cut something he cared about. I'd lose any leverage I had. But when I try to imagine the words, I cannot hear them in Hayden's voice. I can't imagine him saying words that would hurt me.

Not after our talk on the rocket ship. Not from the guy who told me I was the first good thing in his life in years.

I unlace my shoes and drop them beside the bed, crawling

under the comforter cocoon he holds open for me like I'm a sad caterpillar. My head sinks against his pillow, and it *does* smell like him. In minutes, I'm going to infect every thread of his bedding with the plague, but for now—with what ability to smell I have—I breathe in the warm, woodsy scent enveloping me. Hayden drapes the blanket over me with an amused huff.

"You good?" he asks.

I nod.

"Okay. I'm going to keep working, but let me know if you need anything. I'll just be outside."

I'm nearly asleep by the time the bedroom door shuts.

* * *

When I wake up again, it's dark out. The lights of Downtown LA glimmer through Hayden's solitary bedroom window. Now the room smells of cool eucalyptus. I'm not sure if I feel better or worse, but I am warm. And a little sweaty. I make a mental note to offer to wash all of Hayden's bedding for him.

My heavy eyes drag across the room, taking a closer survey now that I'm alone. I register a reusable water bottle with various cryptid stickers, a contact lens case, and a daily pill organizer. Behind the mild clutter is a small corkboard tacked with photos and mementos—badges from a convention, a flying saucer newspaper clipping, and a strip of photo-booth photos. I look for any glimpses into a Hayden different than the Hayden I know now, who lives behind the mic, the glasses, the shaggy hair.

I choke on a cough before I can think any more on it. This summons Hayden. I think about getting out of this bed, and I want to slump to the floor like I'm made of Flubber. I think about getting in my car and driving myself home, and I instantly visualize my car wrapped around a palm tree.

A flash of light from the living room burns the corners of my vision, and I whimper into the pillow.

"Good morning," he whispers, kneeling beside the bed, his weight shifting the mattress.

"It's night."

"It is. How do you feel?"

My eyes flutter open. A person's face has never made me feel better like his does. I see so little of Hayden off duty. I wonder what he looks like cooking dinner for himself or if he lies in bed for hours watching videos of cryptids online, mentally debunking every one of them. I want to know that side of him too.

I sniffle, tucking the covers around my body tighter. Fuck, I really want to take my bra off, but I've already overstayed my welcome. "I'm okay."

"You said that before, too," he chides. "Then you slept for six hours."

"Six hours?" I slur.

The smile teasing at his lips indicates he's not mad or trying to kick me out.

"I feel shitty," I confess.

"I thought so. Come here." He brandishes a thermometer in my direction. "Open up."

I oblige, sliding the thermometer under my tongue. When it beeps, he draws it away. His eyebrows rise.

"A hundred and two."

"That's bad."

"It's pretty bad."

"I think I got the plague," I say.

"I don't think it's the plague. If I had to guess, it's probably the flu." His hand brushes against the side of my face. He feels so cold, I shiver and let out a sad moan. "Fever, chills, some body aches?"

I nod and sniffle.

"Think you can sit up?"

I push myself onto my elbows. My brain feels like it'll melt out my ears, and I'm suddenly freezing again. As I go to slide out of his bed, he stops me. One of his hands catches my leg, a brush of cool fingers against my thigh. "Whoa, whoa, just enough to sit up and eat. You don't have to go anywhere."

But I do.

I don't know how to explain to him that I cannot be a burden. Yet, something in the soft tone of his voice makes me question if I even need to explain it to him. Is this what people are *supposed* to do when they care?

I blink at him a few times as he disappears into the kitchen, holding his hands in a "stay" gesture like I am a poorly trained puppy. It takes a few minutes, but he returns to the room with a bowl of steamy soup and passes it to me. Even though the chicken noodle soup is clearly out of a can, it's one of the nicest things anyone's done for me in a while.

It's up there with Nora offering to sacrifice her liver as we down a bottle of wine and watch reality TV whenever I have a bad day.

I wordlessly slurp at the soup until the bowl is finished. Hayden stays the whole time, taking notes on his phone and doing research.

"I don't want you to get sick, either," I whisper.

"I'll take an extra Flintstones vitamin tomorrow." Hayden

takes the bowl from me and puts it in the kitchen. When he returns, he has a bottle of NyQuil in hand. "Here."

I frown. "You're trying to drug me."

"With love, though."

Love.

Okay then.

Nevertheless, I take the cup of NyQuil from him, and as I am this close to tossing it back like it's tequila in a frat house basement, a brutal cough rips through my chest and ravages my whole body. As I go to cover my mouth with my elbow, sticky liquid douses my hair and runs down one of my cheeks. It smells like Vicks VapoRub and death. *I* smell like Vicks VapoRub and death.

"Oh no," Hayden mutters. He carefully reaches over me, plucking the cup off his comforter and setting it on the nightstand. Thankfully, I haven't gotten medicine all over his bed, the bed he still needs to sleep in tonight.

My bottom lip trembles.

I'm sticky.

I'm sick.

So, naturally, I start crying.

Thankfully, it isn't the first time Hayden's seen me cry, but it's far more embarrassing than last time. I am sweaty, my hair's a mess, and I'm covered in blue cold medicine goo.

"Come here," Hayden instructs, rising from the bed and extending his hand. My sticky fingers slip between his. When we reach his bathroom, he quickly takes out a washcloth and dampens it. I sit on the toilet seat, still frowning, still crying.

Hayden crouches, barely fitting in the scant space between the toilet and the sink. I can hardly smell the musky amber of his cologne through my snotty nose, so I register everything else about him as he dabs at my cheek. On good days, his eyes remind me of spring mornings, bright and vibrant. Sometimes, when we're up late, they darken to a deep forest of endless evergreens. Now, we're somewhere in the middle. It's a soft sage with those notes of brown. It reminds me of cozy coffee shops, rain as it clears, a sharp breeze between tree branches.

"Your bathroom's clean."

Jesus. I've been saying dumb shit to him all day, but the bemused look on his face tells me he doesn't care. That, perhaps, he likes it.

"Is it usually not?"

"No," I say. "You are an anomalous man. Lots of guys don't have toilet paper."

Every one of his touches is so gentle it makes me shake like a leaf. "There are even extra rolls in the linen closet."

"You have a linen closet," I whisper.

"I sure do," he whispers back. "Don't tell anyone."

I run a hand through my hair and catch sticky handfuls of NyQuil. The tears don't come, but I try to shake the stickiness off, and it doesn't work. He reaches for my hand, holding it carefully, wiping each finger, polishing me like a work of art. No one has ever been this careful with me. I'm sure my parents were—especially when I was a baby and it was important to not drop me on my head—but as an adult? Never. I try not to think of myself as fragile, but I like how Hayden cares enough to mind if I break.

"Do you want to wash your hair? You can shower if you want to."

"I want to wash my hair. But I don't want to stand up. And I don't want to be naked. That'd be weird."

Then . . . I'm magically thinking about *him* naked. I know enough about his body that my imagination can do the rest. I visualize soap sluicing around every curve of his muscles, racing down his arms over intricate ink, down his chest and stomach—

I jolt out of fever-dream horny-shower jail when he pushes open the shower curtain. I brace myself for horrifying beard shavings or soap bars melding into the porcelain, but it's a relatively inoffensive bathtub-shower combo. A shower caddy hangs over the head, and I don't have time to survey his products before he guides me to the side of the tub.

"Stay right there."

Hayden returns moments later with a few throw pillows, stacking them on top of one another and patting them for me to sit on them. I wobble but steady as he leans me against the edge of the tub.

"What are you doing?"

"Helping you wash your hair."

Oh no, the lip trembles return. "You don't have to do that."

"Are you sticky?"

I nod.

"Are you sad?"

Another nod.

"Then how about you let me help you? It'll take five minutes." I lean over the tub as he runs the water. When it's warm, he cups a scoop in his hands, pouring it over my hair. And then another, and another, until my hair is fully damp. We could call it a day here, but that isn't sufficient to Hayden, not as he stands and reaches for the shampoo from his caddy.

"I'm going to be using man shampoo," I mutter.

"What does that mean?" He laughs.

"I'll smell like something tough and manly—like cinder blocks."

"...What?"

My eyes open, and Hayden's right beside me, sleeves rolled up, watch discarded onto the sink. God, he is so handsome it concerns me. He's six-foot-very-much of niceness and charming quirks that he might find embarrassing, but I'm left thinking about them long after I've left his apartment. I catch a scruff-hidden dimple revealing that no matter how plague addled I sound, he still wants to hear what I have to say.

"Never mind," I say, anyway.

"Afraid I'm out of cinder block–scented shampoo, so—uh..." He looks down at the bottle. "Crisp Forest will have to do."

"I mean, it's not lemon verbena."

He flicks a small splash of water at me. I shut my eyes as he squeezes shampoo into his hands and begins to lather it through my hair. He keeps one hand at the base of my head, supporting my neck, while the other weaves deep in my blue waves and traces circles into my scalp.

I feel everything about him with a delirious intensity. All I know is that NyQuil has nothing on the careful way Hayden massages shampoo into my hair—a soft press of fingers and even softer drag of his nails against my scalp. His breathing is deafening and lulls me at the same time.

"You know, you could just dunk me. It's only fair, for all the dunking I do on your theories," I say.

"It's also how I get fired."

"That's not true. I can't fire you. And besides, I need you."

"Come on, there're no other weirdos on the internet you'd prefer to work with?"

"*No*," I respond, all too fast.

It makes his eyebrows rise, and he stops shampooing my hair.

"Trust me," I correct.

"We need each other," he says.

I nod slowly. Hayden chews on his lower lip, drawing my eyes there. I imagine the taste of him comes with the prickly bite of his beard and samples of heady sighs from the back of his throat. Everything about him screams safety. Someone who didn't care wouldn't offer me his bed, make me soup, or wash my hair when I've poured cold medicine into it. He's had so many chances to hurt me or hold things against me, but instead he just keeps giving me more.

His focus shifts back to my hair, fingers kneading circles against my scalp again. Back and forth, round and round, like he's learning each inch of me because he *wants* to. My watch sends me a high heart rate notification, a soft buzz at my wrist. If questioned, I'll say it's the fever working its way through me, but I know it's the soft touch of his fingertips against my neck and the way he's looking at me.

Hayden's stare lingers on me for another long, breath-snatching moment before he clears his throat and reaches across the tub to turn on the faucet again. Again, he takes gentle scoops of water to rinse the shampoo out of my hair.

"What *is* your natural hair color?"

"I have eyebrows, don't I?"

Hayden rolls his eyes. "Yeah, but I know people with blond hair who have brown eyebrows."

"Do I seem like a blond to you?" He remains silent. "Are blond girls your type?"

I am an embarrassment.

Absolute buffoonery.

"Bold question, Nonbeliever." He laughs. "Rest assured, you're the only woman in my life right now."

A smile tugs at his lips, like he's trying to reveal something to me in the gentlest way he can. Yet it crashes into me like a train. Obviously, he likes me. He wouldn't have nearly kissed me if he didn't. But to say it . . . It'd back up all the action. I would have no way to disbelieve him. What he does and what he says are so aligned. "Unless you count the Loch Ness Monster."

I break into a laugh, and I am so grateful he's going to ruin the moment so I don't have to. "What the hell is wrong with you?"

"So much. You tell me all the time," he says.

By the time we stop laughing, he's rinsed the shampoo out of my hair and grabs a towel. I wrap it around my hair and sit against the wall of the tub with him. Our shoulders brush, and he looks like he's physically restraining his hands. I wish he weren't. I want them all over me. It's so easy to see Hayden as a normal—okay, *kind of* normal—man who is my friend and who takes care of me and looks out for me. It's easy to see him as the kind of person I could fall in love with.

But if this gets messy, if this falls apart, I lose him and my job at the same time. He holds too much in his hands for me to let them wander all over my body like I want them to.

I'm suddenly not so afraid to lose just my job. I'd be terrified to lose him, too.

I study the brush of his tongue along the inside of his lips, lean closer when his thumb runs along the slant of my jaw.

My god, he wants to kiss me so bad he's willing to risk catching the plague.

So I break the unbearable silence by fake-coughing. Then it turns into real-coughing, which hurts, and I whimper into the bend of my elbow.

Hayden stands and extends a hand to me. In his room, he offers me another dose of NyQuil that I do *not* spill on myself.

"I can stay on the couch," I murmur.

"No, you can't."

"Oh?"

"Cthulhu might eat you."

"Where are you going to sleep?"

"Couch."

"Cthulhu might eat you," I say.

"He won't eat me. I'm his human."

"Right."

"I'm going to change into something more comfortable, then my room is all yours."

As he riffles through his singular IKEA dresser, I pipe up. The NyQuil is beginning to hit me, and in the menthol haze of it, I want Hayden's warmth next to me and to know he's right there. If he leaves, I'm going to spend hours thinking about him on the couch, picturing him curled up with his cat in cute pajama bottoms in a way that will make me feel so fuzzy. "Can you stay?"

He turns. "Stay?"

"Here? I don't want to kick you out of your bed. I don't mind."

His gaze softens. "I . . . yeah, I can stay. Give me a second."

He dips out of the room and returns a few minutes later in another pair of patterned pajama pants, these ones with dinosaurs on them. I hate how cute it looks. When he takes the other side of the bed and stretches out, the bottom of his T-shirt lifts, exposing a thin strip of skin and the waistband of his boxers. One side of his body pale and untouched, the other covered in dark, wiry ink, leading beneath his pants. He smells like minty toothpaste and plain face wash, and years come off his face as he removes his glasses.

As a coughing fit shakes me and tears at my throat, I grasp for comfort. Hayden doesn't object when I choose him. I let out a sad snivel as the choking stops, and he drapes his arm down my back, an affirmation that he wants me close too.

I pick my head up. My vision is blurry and we're on equal footing.

"Thank you," I say.

"For?"

The fact that he has to ask . . .

"Taking care of me."

He wouldn't do this if he didn't care. He tried to kiss me, and I said no, and he still wanted to wash my hair and offer me his bed to ride out my sickness in. He's still here and nothing has changed. Except for maybe the way I feel so much less scared to hand my heart over.

"Of course. I took care of my dad for five years. I think I can handle the flu—"

"Sure, but—"

"Come on, everyone deserves someone to take care of them when they're sick."

I struggle out a laugh and shake my head. "No one's done this for me in a while. Like, not since I was a kid. So . . . thanks."

"No 'good nights,' no one to make you soup or give you cold medicine?" He gapes. "Who's been taking care of you this whole time?"

"Me."

But I wonder the same about him. Who's taking care of him while he's taking care of everyone else? Is there *anyone* Hayden can turn to when he needs help?

"You can consider yourself off duty for a little while," Hayden murmurs.

There's such simplicity to those words, but they make me confident enough to clutch his T-shirt harder, tug myself closer, and shut my eyes. It makes him confident enough to hold me back and turn on his side.

"Wake me up if you need anything," he says. I want to melt, and so I do. Into him. I don't need much more than the sound of him breathing, the soft brush of his fingers against the small of my back, and the way his head rests on top of mine as I drift off to sleep.

It's an almost-snuggle, an almost-kiss to the top of my hair, an almost-admission, and it makes me think I'm *almost* brave enough to do something about it.

CHAPTER 13

By the time Hayden sends his "here" text, I've convinced myself to pack another three pairs of underwear. Five days away means at least twelve pairs of underwear, in case I shit myself twice every single day, and then some for *options*.

I pack a nicer pair just . . . uh . . . in case.

Hayden steps out of his car, popping the trunk and taking my bag for me.

"How do you feel?" he asks.

I shrug. "Better."

What I *won't* admit is how the sight of him in a waffle knit Henley has made me feel exponentially better.

I tried to sleep through the worst of my illness, but doped myself up on DayQuil enough to keep our production schedule moving forward. Even when I made it back home, we spent most of our time on the phone or FaceTime discussing the next episodes and our weekend away. I woke up this morning able to smell, and my voice sounds less like it went through a meat grinder. I'm glad Hayden never caught what I had. Both of us down is DEFCON 1 at this point in the season.

"Good," he smiles. "You've got some color in your cheeks again."

When I slide into the passenger seat, there's already an iced coffee in the cup holder for me. Some painful traffic on the 405 leads us to even more painful traffic on the 5. Hayden tells me to fear not: he has a riveting podcast about the secrets of the Vatican Archives I simply need to hear.

We inch out of traffic as the verbose narrator tells us of a conspiracy about three little Portuguese children who were told creepy-ass prophecies by the Virgin Mary. Hayden's attention is equally split between the road and the podcast, and he occasionally gasps when some real dramatic tea is spilled, though I suspect he knows all of this already.

"Does the Vatican really have the world's largest collection of porn?"

He shrugs. "Allegedly."

"Do you think they'd let us in? We're . . . journalists. In a way."

His eyebrow rises, one arm propped on the window. "I do not think 'journalist' is the best word for what we are."

"Meh."

"Though, there must be some fourteen-year-old boy with a larger porn stash."

"Are you speaking from experience?"

He glares across the front seat over the frames of his sunglasses. "You're typecasting."

"What? Typecasting you as the awkward virgin conspiracy theorist? Never. That'd be totally unoriginal of me. I am sure offering to tell someone about Project MKUltra gets everyone into bed with you. Who could ever turn down that dirty talk?"

His eyes roll, but a smile tugs at his lips. "You know, everyone has a different type of dirty talk, and that's okay."

". . . You wouldn't actually talk about conspiracy theories during sex, would you?"

My cheeks feel hot because I'm not sure if the prospect of hearing about Project Blue Book while getting laid is a turn-on or a turnoff. "If someone asked."

"*Has* anyone asked?"

"No, not yet."

"*Yet?*"

"Not . . . it's not like there's been a girlfriend in recent years for me to ask."

I wonder if there's been *anyone* in recent years, any awkward Tinder dates or one-night stands when he first got to LA. He says he hasn't *dated*, but hookups are different. As we move closer to a tipping point, these are the things that occupy my mind.

"Right. Well, I'll give a heads-up to the next girl you sleep with."

Part of me hopes it's me. His eyes drift from the road to me, then focus back on the curves in front of us rather than the ones on my body. There's a glimmer of hunger in his eyes, and if he keeps looking at me like that, he can talk about whatever the fuck he wants in bed.

We stop for gas north of Bakersfield. We've worked our way through two whole podcast episodes about the Vatican Archives and their alleged porn stash, and Hayden agreed we could take a break, since it was a lot to take in. At least when someone else was talking, we didn't have to confront the tingling attraction that's made his mid-tier sedan feel stifling. I'm at least glad I'm not driving. I've spent most of the ride watching Hayden drive and being unreasonably turned on by it—the sharp angles of his hands, one in his hair, the other on the wheel; the sunglasses that he *thinks* hide all his looks over at me resting on the bridge of his nose.

I've agreed to pay for gas, so I handle filling up while he uses the bathroom and purchases more snacks for the road. Hayden returns with two water bottles, a bag of Twizzlers, and a small bag of chips. As we load into the car, he hesitates over the gearshift.

"Can I talk to you about something?" he finally says.

"Sure."

He fiddles with the keychains on his keys, dangling from the ignition. He spins a small alien head around several times.

"My mom lives in San Francisco."

I know this already, but this isn't a fact. It's a question.

"Okay. Do you want to take a detour?" I ask.

"I think I have to." He rubs the bridge of his nose beneath his glasses. "I've been putting it off, and if she knows I came up here and didn't even . . . I don't know."

"Yeah, we can take some time to go see her," I agree without question. To be fair, any extra time we build into our trip is less time I need to spend in the woods getting eaten alive by mosquitos. I imagine Hayden's mother has a house in the city with actual walls and beds.

I imagine she would *at least* have a mosquito net.

He nods slowly. "Thanks. We could cancel one of the nights at our San Jose hotel and stay with her instead. Do dinner, you know."

We linger in silence. I worry about spending a night in Hayden's mom's house. It's like the first sleepover at a new friend's house. I might not know where the bathrooms are or end up stuck in awkward chats with his parents if I wake up first.

Finally, a signal kicks back into his phone and the soft indie beats Spotify playlist we've been listening to fills the car.

"Do you not want to see her?" I ask over the song.

"I do. I just . . . My mom and I aren't that close. I mean, I see her every few months, and I saw her back at Christmas, but I don't imagine she'll be thrilled to hear that I am here . . . to . . . uh, hunt Bigfoot."

"Most women do want to come before Bigfoot."

He finally looks up, with a laugh. "That's fair. I think she'd be okay if Bigfoot wasn't on the list at all."

"Does she not support the show? I mean, your dad was the Master of Horror. Can she really be that shocked that you're into this stuff?"

"Okay, to be fair, they *did* get divorced." I let him take his time with his words. "I don't know. She's never warmed up to the idea of her only kid hunting monsters on the internet. Or talking about them on a podcast."

I try to imagine Hayden doing something different with his life, and it *is* hard. Even if it was a passion project while he had some pencil-pusher job, I can't imagine a world where he isn't hunting for monsters in some capacity. He's been lucky enough to make it his *whole* job.

"With my degree," he says, "I think she hoped I'd produce music or go into postproduction and that I was maybe turning a corner when I moved to LA. And to be fair, I did audio for some short films and freelanced a bit, but those were *jobs*. Never *my job*."

"Well, won't she feel silly when we make this show huge and have, like, ten seasons of hunting monsters."

He fakes a tired smile, like even thinking about the visit is wearing him down. He doesn't need to take off his glasses to look far younger now. There's something so pleading and childlike in his eyes. "She'll be perfectly nice to you, I think, but there might be some backhanded compliments thrown our way. I'm used to them, but—"

"Hayden," I say, "I can handle a backhanded compliment from a middle-aged white lady just fine."

"I know, but—"

I cut him off, my hand clasping over his on the gearshift. "I won't take offense. I just . . . I care that *you're* okay."

Finally, as our fingers weave together, the shaking in his hands stops and he looks away.

"I'm sorry for burdening you—"

"It's okay. I promise, it's okay."

It's not like Hayden to share things like this with me, and now I know why. He's scared that I'll take it all on my shoulders and that it'll weigh me down. But he's the first person to take on someone else's pain.

His thumb brushes across the back of my palm. He doesn't say anything for a long moment, leaving me to speak up.

"Whatever happens, we'll face it together. I'll be there the whole time."

Somehow, this settles him. "Okay. Thank you."

He hesitates before driving, and I can tell his head is still somewhere else. I unlace my fingers from his. I want to lead him someplace that hurts less.

"Isn't there one more episode in that Vatican series?"

He nods.

"I want to know what they know about the apocalypse."

"No, you don't," he laughs.

"*I do.*"

Finally, he sighs, opens his phone, and hits Play.

* * *

I might be coming around on a lot of things, but I highly doubt I'm going to come around on Fresno Nightcrawlers. While Hayden insists it is possible that little creatures who look like white culottes are viable cryptids, I'm mostly convinced this is a case of kids in weird ghost costumes.

Yet, I still climb out of the car as we reach Fresno and follow him. We're going to be spending most of the weekend in the woods, so I suppose I need to microdose nature where I can. We're in a park, I think. Central California constantly reminds me how little there is up here. In the dark, it's hard to make out much more than brambles, the occasional skeletal tree, and—in the distance—a suspicious-looking bridge. Oh no, I hope we're not going there.

"Remember," Hayden whispers. "*Pants.*"

"They wear white before Memorial Day?"

"*And* after Labor Day!"

"Absolute deviants."

He slides a flashlight into his jacket pocket and clutches our night-vision camera. I think about our conversation in the car earlier, and I'm happy to see the light coming back into Hayden's eyes. I never thought something could dim him so quickly, but evidently, his mother does. I might not know the full extent of it, but I know tomorrow night will not be easy for him.

For weeks, we've been talking about this trip. We've plotted our drives, our hunts, our accommodations. He's always stumbled over his words as our conversations circled around San Francisco. Now I know why.

I feel compelled to try and alleviate whatever pain I can.

So as much as I don't want to wander into this weird park after dark, I follow. At least I'm not alone, and hopefully Hayden likes me enough to fight off some woodsy demon for me.

The spring air is crisp, and I bury my hands in my pockets to keep them from freezing off as we trek across the open land. There are no signs of Nightcrawlers or any other creatures lurking about. Nevertheless, Hayden peeks behind every tree, and tells me to beware of something called a Hide-behind.

"It's how lumberjacks go missing," he explains.

"Oh no, you better be careful. All you're missing is an axe."

He frowns. I hear the ringing in my ears way too loud, punctuated by the rustle of leaves. I am vulnerable to all forms of attack here. Bugs, bears, Nightcrawlers.

"I don't like nature," I lament.

"It's good for the soul."

"Lyme disease is not!" Though, the trees and bushes are not particularly thick here. I'm only in real danger if I fall into one of them, which is a distinct possibility.

Hayden reaches into his backpack and tosses a can my way. I fumble for it, the aluminum clinking against a rock on the ground. He chuckles, shining the flashlight on me as I reach for it. My fingers brush through brambles, leaves, and something horrifically squishy. Then, finally, bug spray.

"Don't say I never do anything for you. You fear Lyme disease and I provide."

"My hero," I grumble behind him. "You know, I did some research on these peculiar pantaloons, and it *is* weird that the first sighting of them—this guy was recording CCTV footage and then *filmed* the monitor with a camera and 'accidentally' deleted the original footage."

Hayden tilts his head like he's a curious puppy and I've thrown him a bone here. "You researched it?"

"Of course. I am a thorough bitch. It seems like a pretty good way to get *shitty* footage that's hard to debunk."

"You believe in Fresno Nightcrawlers, don't you, Hallie?"

I shuffle the leaves beneath my boots. "If I was going to start somewhere, I would not begin with Fresno Nightcrawlers."

"If you were going to start believing in something, what would it be?" he asks. "I just want to know what your jumping-off point is, Nonbeliever."

"I don't have one," I lie. I will never admit it, even if my life depends on it, but I am struggling less and less with Bigfoot existing. It isn't completely unreasonable for a bipedal primate to live in the woods or for a snowy version to live in the Himalayas.

I do not, however, believe Bigfoot is an alien.

"One day," he groans.

"Never."

He turns and glares with a teasing look in his eyes. I think of the way Hayden looks at me a lot. Each coy glance is another opportunity to spar with him and prove I'm just as smart and capable as he is. If I didn't know any better, I'd say he likes it. He comes alive when I push and poke and make him work for it.

This time, he steps closer and rests his hands on my shoulders. My eyes jump to the curve of his bottom lip, the soft pout that forms as he studies me. The woods smell like wet grass and rain, but all I can smell is him: the sharp tinge of amber and whiskey, and I think of how his hair will probably smell like lemon verbena tonight (if his theory holds), and I suddenly want to curl up close to him and take it all in.

It'd be so easy for him to run his hands up my shoulders, fingers brushing my neck. I imagine him tilting my chin up and doing what I secretly wish he'd done on the playground. I worry that my rejection has made him feel scorned, and he may be afraid to make another attempt, but I'm running out of reasons to stop myself.

For the first time in years, parts of me don't feel like they're under lock and key. I'm not as scared of what he'll find. Maybe my mind is elevated like a horny MKUltra experiment, or maybe I've found someone who is looking for answers and not ammo.

His throat bobs and his eyelids hang heavy, like he could shut them and sink into this moment with such ease. So could I. I'm not even thinking about bugs right now, and I am *always* thinking about bugs when I am outside.

The air is full of static around us, like another touch will send electricity rattling all over my body, and I want it to. He'd be the best shock of my life. He *has* been the best shock of my life. I feel him like radioactive particles running through my blood, like I'll never settle. It feels like it's killing me and sparking me back to life all at once. It's the first time I've wanted to believe in something in so long.

I can still sense his body more strongly than I should when he pulls away, and I know it's my own fault.

"Onward, Nonbeliever." Hayden orders us toward a bridge in the middle of the woods.

"I don't want to climb on that."

"A whole-ass train drives over it. I don't think *we* will be the ones to break it. Come on. We have a vantage point here." Hayden flashes his flashlight like a laser pointer and I'm Cthulhu trying to chase it. I don't take the bait, but again, I follow. I step in something squishy and whimper as we approach. I am excited to be on solid ground. Wood is nice. Wood is way better than mud. Then I remember termites exist.

Hayden finally stops dead center on the bridge and sits, shrugging off his backpack. His flashlight floods up to me as I pace warily toward him. Like a true gentleman, he slips off his jacket and sets it on the ground beside him so I don't have to sit on the moist wood. I slip my legs between the bars on the bridge and look out into the darkness. The moon casts a glow over us, enough for me to see him and any Nightcrawlers we happen to find.

"So, we just sit and look for pants?" I ask.

"We could play I Spy."

"I spy with my little eye—something green."

Hayden rolls his eyes. "It's nature. It's all green."

"Sometimes nature is brown."

"Right. That bush?" He points to the closest bush.

"Damn."

"You aren't even trying. I could do better with my glasses off."

"So take them off," I laugh.

He does as I ask and passes them to me. I feel like I'm holding such an integral piece of him, like the bad guy in *Scooby-Doo* holding Velma's glasses out of reach. I hold the frames up to my eyes and stare out at the land in front of us. The lenses are so thick, and the world blurs to a canvas of muddy blacks and blues and sprays of green. I turn to him. The frames hardly fit on my face, sliding down my nose.

"Jesus, you really can't see anything, can you?"

"I told you."

But I can still make out the sharp figure of his body—the

dark blues of his jeans and the chestnut browns in his hair. I can still see his coy smile, and—for once—he's taking advantage of my lack of vision in the same way I always take advantage of his. I can linger on the pinch of dimples in his cheeks or the way his dark eyelashes brush against his skin when he closes his eyes. Right now, the world looks blurry and messy to both of us, but we can both still see what's important.

And, more than that, I can still hear him breathing like it's the loudest thing in the world, and as I wiggle closer to him, our legs brush together. Neither of us pulls away. Every touch is an occupational hazard. Washing my hair, sleeping in his bed, curling up beside him, our hands weaving together in the car. Every single touch convinces me that all I want is more.

"Hayden, I . . ."

"I know. It'll be hard for either of us to spot Nightcrawlers this way."

The shock of his hands coming to the sides of my face rattles my entire body, and I lean into him, one hand resting on the waffle knit of his Henley. I feel every breath, and I can't stop myself from curling my fingers around the fabric and pulling him closer. He swallows loud enough for me to hear, and his thumbs brush along my jaw. One of them is dangerously close to my pulse point, and he must know how hard my heart is beating.

He's so close, and I can hardly look away from his lips. Pressure builds in my chest, like something is sitting on me, smothering me. This is the most dangerous part of a crush—the limbo that hangs between action and inaction, like dry brush in fire conditions. Anything could ignite it and burn right through us.

I'm out of excuses and full of screaming want—for Hayden's lips, the taste of his mouth and bites of beard and every press of his body. As he removes the glasses from my face, there's a split second I can see him failing to talk himself out of this. His tongue runs along the inside of his bottom lip. In my head, I see myself sinking my teeth into it, my fingers knotting in his soft waves, kissing the slants of his neck until he moans my name. Then, when he slides his glasses back onto his face, there's another split second of calm before we shatter the illusions in both of our heads and lean in.

CHAPTER 14

I would like to personally thank every single Fresno Nightcrawler for dragging me into the middle of the woods, onto a termite-ridden bridge, to look for them in all their little white pants glory. Because, if not for them, I might not know what kissing Hayden feels like. Not now, not like this.

I might not know how slow it starts: experimental nips as he explores me, learns me, and studies the soft sounds I make as he tilts my chin down and deepens the kiss. I run a hand up his chest and to the curve of his neck, fingers knotting in his dark waves. I wouldn't breathe if I didn't have to, because tearing away from him for any second feels foolish and unfathomable. As I catch my breath, I nod, telling him we can break this rule and the next.

Hayden's hands work down my body. His grip molds around every curve until he has me memorized, and when he reaches my hips, he tugs me into his lap. I lock my legs around his waist, chest to chest, my forehead to the plastic frames of his glasses as we break away to breathe.

I think of all the days I've spent watching him with desire, from the way his hands move as he speaks to the intense pondering stares and hums he lets out while we work. I've imagined his hands doing all the most intimate things with me, but nothing compares to the way his grip feels on my body: soft, clawing grasps that make me feel like no amount of closeness will ever be good enough for him. Nothing could prepare me for the desperate sighs he lets out with each breath, or the soft "fuck" he mutters as he leans in to kiss me again.

I want him to know that there is no one else I've ever wanted like this. I want *all* of Hayden. I want every inch of height and muscle, every soft lock of hair and harsh prick of his beard. I want to learn every single tattoo on his body and study them and him like it's all one cohesive piece of stunning artwork. I don't know everything about him, and there are still so many secrets I'm working to uncover, but I feel confident I'll want them too.

Hayden pulls away and he struggles to catch his breath. "I've been waiting for this."

I trace the curve of his smile with my thumb. "For how long?"

"Since you woke up holding me on the *Queen Mary*." He places the answer with another kiss.

"You knew?" I say.

He nods, sinking me like an anchor. "I knew, and I haven't stopped thinking about it. Your warmth, your touch—the way you fit like no one else ever has."

My legs are complete jelly. I listen to the sounds he makes as he kisses me, focused, concentrated, like I'm the most interesting conspiracy he's ever heard. He digs deeper and deeper here, too. Tingles of desire sprinkle across my body— my back, goose bumps up my arms, a swelling heat between my legs.

Our hips are flush together as his arms encircle me, luring me closer and closer until there are no gaps between us, just layers of clothing I wish were gone already. As I nibble his bottom lip, he curses and his body tenses, soft fingertips digging into my back, raking up the bottom of my sweater. Heat blooms between us and—as my hips rock against his—I'm left wanting to reach between us, unzip his pants, and make him moan so desperately the local cryptids will know to leave us alone.

He clutches me like I'm the most valuable cargo he's ever held and carefully leans me back against the jacket he's set on the ground. I know his undoubtedly overpriced, waterproof REI jacket will keep me dry and clean, but even if it didn't, I can't argue about a single thing right now. I don't feel the damp wood beneath us or the prick of twigs and wood chips. I can only feel his hands running up my shirt, finding every spot that makes me shiver. He nods in affirmation with each soft whimper and shudder my body makes.

"You feel so good," he breathes, heat smoking each of his words. "*So* good."

I have never wanted to bang someone in the middle of the woods so badly. This is how I get a mosquito bite in a terrible place.

"Tell me what you want." He only comes away from me for ragged breaths and ravaged words. "Anything at all." And then, "I want you to have it all."

I'm contemplating the condom I know is in my backpack and how amazing the rest of him will feel. My heart races thinking about asking him to take those next steps, but there's still something that scares me about it. I don't mean to take this too slow, just one step at a time.

"I don't want to go any further right now."

He pulls away, still tasting me on his lips. "I . . . hmm,

yeah . . . this is a little hotter than I usually get with my first kisses."

I drink in his lopsided, kiss-hazy smile. A smile. There're no signs of disappointment or betrayal.

"Repressed conspiracy theorist with a porn collection."

"Boring Nonbeliever who doesn't know how to spice it up." He kisses me again, teasing, letting me wrap my arms around his shoulders. His kisses aren't a transaction. They're something he wants to do because he wants *me*. He shows me with every trail of his lips down my throat, teasing and using the sounds of my giggles as a guidebook.

"We are also very much in the woods."

"And you hate bugs," he whispers against my lips.

"I absolutely hate bugs."

I drag my hands down the sides of his face, toying with the buttons at the top of his Henley. Now that I've claimed a part of him, I want to take ownership of the simple and sexy details of him. His sharp collarbones, the tease of dark hair where his shirt buttons dip lower on his chest, ink bleeding out at certain angles.

"And yet, your one hand is on my ass."

Indeed it is. It is a very good ass.

"Are you done Nightcrawler hunting for the night?"

Hayden frowns. No, displays abject horror and misunderstanding like a child who had to learn the hard way that there's a seventeen-year-old getting paid minimum wage inside every Chuck E. Cheese mouse. "I'll never be done hunting."

". . . Right. Can we get out of the woods? Go someplace without bugs?"

"*Fine*," he agrees, climbing off me and helping me brush myself clean.

We find the car, and he drives. He reaches a hand over the console, and his fingers weave with mine. I love the look of disbelief in his eyes, like he can't believe I want him back, like he can't believe he gets to have me. Clearly, I've never known being wanted like this. I enjoy the quiet peace of knowing my presence makes someone happy. It's so small and huge at the same time.

We ride in silence to the hotel, with the faint sounds of a playlist called "Mothman Is Real and He's My Boyfriend" in the background, Hayden's thumb occasionally brushing the back of my palm in beat with the soft indie vibes. We check in and claim our room. This time, I don't think either of us will mind if there's only one bed. We take turns showering and get ready for bed since we're set to be up early tomorrow for filming. I feel like, considering he had his hands on my boobs an hour ago, I am safe to start sleeping without a bra now. Hayden settles into bed as he flips through channels on the TV. Finally, he finds something to consume—a rerun of *Cosmic Conspiracies*.

The topic: Was Abraham Lincoln in cahoots with aliens during the Civil War?

As I attack my face with a makeup wipe, I eye the TV warily before looking back at him. Hayden smiles, and I know he isn't planning on changing the channel. Not long ago, he was the thing I found by accident, and now it feels like the opposite of an accident. It feels like fate. A cosmic conspiracy, even.

In bed, I curl my head into the crook of his shoulder. Fresh out of the shower, he again smells like lemon verbena and basic hotel soap, masking the usual musky scent of his cologne. The sound of him breathing lulls me near sleep as he occasionally offers a fact-check or an additional tidbit he thinks

I'd want to know. A month ago, I would have clapped back with rebuttals about how unrealistic his theories are. Now I'll listen to any outlandish theory he has because it's *him* telling it.

"I've met this guy before," he mumbles. "He's a piece of work. We got into an argument about the Stargate Project once. He didn't believe it was real. It's confirmed real. It's a thing."

"I love how you think I have any idea what the Stargate Project is."

He laughs, brushing his fingers through my hair. "Okay, so . . . back in the seventies, the CIA was legitimately trying to study psychic abilities like remote viewing and ESP . . ."

I listen like it's the best bedtime story in the world. We spar and argue over the more ridiculous arcs in the episode, laughing and offering our own conspiracies. I'm too busy being bewildered by other things—his arms tucking me close to him; the way his head rests on top of mine, like he wants every possible part of us to connect. When we're out of bad theories to argue over, he turns the TV off and flips onto his side. His arm drapes over my body, and his forehead presses to mine. There's no sound but the whirr of the hotel room air conditioner and the distant whispers of guests near the elevators. I know what's coming next, but it's going to feel different tonight.

He slips off his glasses and brushes a lock of hair behind my ear, utilizing the shock of bright blue jumping out against the dark. He starts there and trails his fingertips down the side of my face, until he finds my lips and leans in. Much like our first kiss, it's slow and deliberate, like he's still questioning if this is a fluke or not. I reassure him by winding my fingers into his still-drying hair and kissing him, and it feels so good to do. I want every part of him to be all mine.

"Good night," he whispers with one final kiss. "Don't let the ghosties bite."

✱ THE OUT THERE ✱

Episode #5: "HGTV but Make It Haunted"

On this week's episode of The Out There, *Hayden and Hallie travel to San Jose, California, to investigate the Winchester Mystery House. Can they survive their time there without falling through a trapdoor or walking into a wall? More at eleven.*

HAYDEN

I mean, this is a lot of rooms. Like . . . a lot.

HALLIE

And you grew up rich.

HAYDEN

Sure did.

HALLIE

I think that I would run out of room ideas at some point.

HAYDEN

I bet I could come up with a bunch.

HALLIE

One hundred and sixty?

HAYDEN

Yeah. Okay, bedrooms—like, at least twenty, because why not? Then at least twenty-five bathrooms, because every bedroom would have one bathroom attached, then a bunch of extra ones. Not all of them would have showers or baths.

HALLIE

Okay, so you are at forty-five.

HAYDEN

Do closets count? Because—

HALLIE

Definitely not.

HAYDEN

Goddammit.

[BEAT]

HAYDEN

Ten living rooms, eleven parlors—

HALLIE

Why eleven? That's random.

HAYDEN

If I just did ten of everything, that's uncreative.

HALLIE

And more math for me.

HAYDEN

Fourteen dining rooms. Five kitchens. Eight laundry rooms. What am I at?

HALLIE

Ninety-three.

HAYDEN

Fuck. Bowling alley. Movie theater. Two home gyms. Indoor swimming pool. Tennis court. Six libraries.

HALLIE

One hundred and five.

HAYDEN

Five bowling alleys. Four movie theaters—one for G, one for PG, one for PG-13, one for R—

HALLIE

What about NC-17?

HAYDEN

It's like the same thing as R, but you can show more dicks. Oh, and you can't even have a parent get you in. Now what am I at?

HALLIE

One hundred and twelve.

HAYDEN

You know what, fuck this.

CHAPTER 15

By the time we pull up to Hayden's mom's house, Hayden's hands are shaking on the steering wheel. This is not what I imagined when he mentioned he was nervous about seeing his mom. I've watched him speak to ghosts through a Spirit Box and sleep in haunted hotels, but I've never seen him like this.

He's terrified.

We park in front of a European-style home, its large bay windows adorned with overflowing flowers and a well-manicured lawn. Everything about it is picture-perfect, from the dimming sun casting an orange glow behind the house to the shaped topiaries and rush of waves lapping in the distance. Yet it seems like the most uncomfortable place in the world for Hayden.

I don't *love* going home. It's a place I know well but don't fit into anymore. As vibrant as people in suburban New York could be, the bold personas bleeding out from the city, I outgrew it, and I've always known I would. Under my parents' roof, though, my strange self is good enough. I understand Hayden's discomfort, but I've never feared coming home like he does now.

The car turns off, but Hayden lingers on the door handle. I reach across the console and weave my fingers between his.

"You good?"

"I have to be."

"You *don't* have to be."

I wish someone had been there to tell me that years ago. Hayden lingers on it, but the words bounce off him the way some of his wilder theories never sink into my brain. Finally, his thumb brushes against the back of my palm and he slides out of the car. By the time we reach the trunk, I recognize this person so much more, but there's a blankness in his eyes that still feels unfamiliar.

He takes my duffel bag for me and leads me toward the front door and through the house toward a screened-in sunroom. The man and woman who wait there look rich and proper enough to be Kennedys. His mother wears a colorful Lilly Pulitzer dress, and his stepdad has an honest-to-god baby-blue sweater tied around his shoulders above his button-down. It's so New England transplant it hurts. I suddenly feel severely underdressed in my leggings and flannel, but clothes won't help. There's a certain inferiority I feel that assures me, no matter what I do, I could never fit in. I could never step into a living rich-white-people Christmas card like this.

"Oh, sweetheart, it's so good to see you," his mother coos. They share the same dark hair and tall frame, but where Hayden is eccentric, everything about his mom looks like it perfectly belongs at a Tupperware party. Hesitantly, he greets his mom and leans in for a hug. She holds him tightly for a long moment, kissing the side of his head. Despite the strain I can see in his eyes and have seen over the past few hours, he holds on to her tightly.

His mother holds a firm hand out to me. "Ellen. Nice to meet you."

"Hallie," I offer. "It's good to meet you, too."

Her eyes linger on the color of my hair and the comfy road-trip clothes I have on. I brought something nicer for dinner, but both of us are dressed down now. Somehow, it feels like a few hours in the car and working for most of the day isn't a good excuse for how we look.

Hayden moves on to greeting his stepdad with a firm, manly handshake, but the words between them are nothing more than a terse "Hayden" volleyed back with a lifeless "Jeff." I try not to judge a book by its cover, but Hayden's mother is clearly judging me, so I feel no shame in thinking Jeff looks like he causes problems at the local Home Depot.

"Can I get both of you a drink? A little something from the wet bar?" Jeff asks, rubbing his hands together.

"Bourbon on the rocks," Hayden answers quickly.

I cross my arms in front of my chest, stepping closer to Hayden. I feel like a kid at an awkward playdate, relying on my friend to lead the way. "Whatever wine you have open would be great."

Ellen prattles about recent renovations she's done to the house (the kitchen is brand-new, and the wine refrigerator came just last week; the dining table in the sunroom came from an estate sale). By the time Jeff returns, I'm grateful for a drink in my hand. Hayden finishes off half of his bourbon in one sip, while Ellen and Jeff talk amongst themselves over who put the mini crab cakes in the oven.

Neither Jeff nor Ellen asks about the show the entire cock-tail hour.

When Hayden excuses us to get ready for dinner, I follow him outside to the guesthouse. I eye the frames on the walls on the way, looking for any kinds of hints into Hayden's childhood. I pass pictures of a scrawny little kid in glasses, posing proudly in front of science fair projects, track meet photos, old Christmas cards on the beach, and a horribly awkward prom photo.

He deposits me in our room and offers to let me shower and get ready first, and it almost feels like he's offering to be the sacrificial lamb to talk to his family for another hour or so. The guesthouse is above the detached garage, with a bedroom and bathroom and a view of the ocean, slanted ceilings, and a pile of clean towels on the bed.

I quickly shower and blow-dry the blue waves into order. I debate a headband, or anything that'll help block the color, but instead I pull my hair into a half ponytail, letting the curls drape along my jawline. Hayden returns by the time I'm halfway done with my makeup, looking like he's run a marathon. His eyes come back to life when he finds me.

"Hey."

"Hi," he breathes, leaning against the bathroom doorframe. "You okay?"

He nods. I feel like I keep asking, and I don't know why I'm expecting his answer to change. I can't push him to be honest. I can only try to make it better. I drop the mascara wand I'm wielding and step closer to him. I slide my arms around his waist, and he tugs me against him like I'm a life preserver in the middle of the Bermuda Triangle. Hayden dips his head lower, his lips slowly finding mine. This still feels forbidden. I've spent so long telling myself I can't have something I know will be good for me for reasons that are not good for me. But I want him and, when I have him, I feel safe and at ease.

His lips taste like the sharp bite of bourbon and he sinks in deeper for more. He lets out a low moan as my fingers wrap around his hair. His glasses bump the bridge of my nose and it makes both of us laugh. He holds on to me like he feels lucky to have me.

"Does your mom think we're a thing?" I ask between kisses.

"She might suspect it."

"Do they usually respond well to girlfriends?"

"I mean, it's been a while." Suddenly, he pulls away, his hands still cupping the sides of my face. Nerves wash over him. "I . . . Just in case it comes up, I feel like I should be honest with you."

Now my nerves fizzle in the back of *my* brain.

"I was engaged before I moved out to LA."

I have no right to be jealous and I'm not, until I envision a wedding band on his finger that belongs to someone else. Then something flutters in my stomach. Being engaged means at some point, he thought he'd found his person. He'd been so in love or so certain about it at one point that he asked someone to marry him.

To go from that, to completely alone . . .

"We'd been together for four years. I proposed when we graduated college and . . . I don't know . . . my dad was getting worse and I guess I wanted him to at least see me get married if he was going to miss the rest of my life. So, we tried to move on it as fast as we could, but we kept hitting roadblocks. Then he took a sharp downturn and . . . I . . . grief breaks a lot of things. Abby deserved a better husband than I could have been at that time."

As he says this, he keeps his eyes cast down. I trace the UFO tattoo on the outside of his wrist.

"Thank you for telling me." It's all I can say. "And I'm sorry it didn't work out."

He nods. "I think we're both happier now, so it's okay. She just got engaged to someone else, so in case my mom mentions it, I didn't want you to think I was keeping that from you. Not now that we're . . ."

I close my fingers around his. "I know. You said it yourself. Me and Nessie are the only women in your life."

He bites his lip with a smirk and a laugh, and the tension fades.

"We'll get through dinner," I assure him. "And for being a good sport, you can make me watch any weird monster movie you want. I won't even bitch about it."

Oh no, this lights him up. I'm in danger.

"Aw," he hums. Already I see the ideas flipping through his head like a cryptid-movie Rolodex. "You have no idea what you're in for."

I press a kiss against the corner of his mouth. "Maybe I'll just make out with you the whole time if it gets too weird."

He ponders this, an eyebrow quirking. It's not a bad deal for either of us, but I do understand how the decision between making me watch an alien abduction movie and feeling me up might be a challenge for him. Everyone has their kinks, and Hayden sure has his.

"We'll have to see about that," is all he says, and then he swaps me for the shower. I spend the next few minutes setting my face with powder and adding a few bouncier curls to my hair before Hayden steps out of the bathroom, pulling a deep green sweater over his head. It sits on top of a white button-down shirt. We took a quick pit stop at the mall to find me something to wear today. Most of my outfits for this trip were best suited for the woods or long car rides, not dinners with uppity moms.

Hayden hovers in front of the mirror longer than he needs to. His hair is combed and in place, and I can tell he's resisting running his fingers through it like he usually does when he's stressed. What's more noticeable is that his sleeves are rolled all the way down, buttoned at his wrists.

I'm used to rolled-up sleeves with peeks of ink crawling down his forearm. Here, he looks far too crisp and polished to be the same person. His eyes are heavy and darker after his shower, no longer a vibrant emerald; more like a stormy forest green. As he swallows hard and draws away, I can't help but think about how much I'd prefer him in one of his signature dorky T-shirts and a flannel. This person feels like an impostor.

He feels like the kind of person who'd scoff at the idea of aliens crash-landing to Earth, with the least open mind in the world.

If he'd shaved, too, I would have sworn I was looking at a Finance Bro named Josh.

His sleeve slides up, exposing part of the UFO tattoo on his wrist. With a frustrated sigh, Hayden tugs the sleeve down farther.

"How do I look?" I finally ask.

His focus breaks. His Adam's apple bobs, and another emotion flashes through his expression. He eyes my nicer jeans and sweater. I think I look like a high school guidance counselor. A short lock of hair pops out of my ponytail. Hayden smiles, stepping closer and pushing the hair behind my ear.

"Beautiful, as always. You ready?"

I nod, following him across the yard to the main house. As we reach the dining room, Hayden's entire body stiffens, but his mother beams at him.

"You look so handsome all cleaned up."

No, I think. *He doesn't even look like himself.*

A horrible thought dawns on me. Does Hayden's mother not see him for who he is? Does he have to pretend to be someone else to get her love?

We sit as Ellen and Jeff ready the dishes for dinner. I reach over and rest a hand along the inside of Hayden's leg. The muscles of his throat tighten, but instead of pulling away, he rests an unsteady hand on top of mine.

Nothing's gone terribly wrong so far, but Hayden is braced for impact regardless. Of course, Ellen mentions Abby, and Hayden offers a curt response that he already knew about her engagement and he's happy for her. Ellen wants to bait him more, and I can tell, so I interrupt to compliment her orzo salad. Moms *love* orzo salad.

I've learned every detail about Jeff's landscaping routine, but it takes until halfway through dinner for either of them to acknowledge the show.

"Now," Ellen begins, "Hallie, you are producing Hayden's show now?"

"Yes, and co-hosting. At first I was just going to produce, but after the first episode, we decided Hayden should have a co-host."

Somehow, that doesn't comfort Ellen.

"How come?" Jeff gnaws on a carrot. "This was Hayden's show, wasn't it?"

Hayden goes to speak, but before he can belittle himself to them, I intercept.

"He's great at what he does, but sometimes it helps to have a second person. Having someone to talk to makes it more engaging."

"I see. So, you're into all this . . ." Ellen waves her knife like a magic wand, like she's putting a prime-rib-flavored hex on me. "Freaky stuff?"

"Not quite."

"It's weird, isn't it? This was his dad's thing. We always hoped he'd grow out of it."

From what I know, Hayden's dad cared about everything Hayden is and ever was. He cared for the shy kid who came home from school upset after being teased all week; he pushed deadlines and took him on adventures and made him feel important. Despite how ridiculous some of Hayden's theories or these cryptids are, I like how he wholeheartedly believes in things he's never seen. I fall for him most at his strangest because it sneaks up on me, and by the time we're back to "normal" again, I've already lost another part of myself to the quicksand.

"You did?"

I wonder if I'm pressing too hard. Hayden pauses, lowering his fork and looking to me.

"Well, I don't know what kind of career he's going to really make talking about monsters."

"He's doing well so far," I assert. "Really well, actually. He had such a strong fan base already that my bosses didn't even hesitate to say yes to his show."

Ellen and Jeff exchange a look. Jeff shovels another scoop of orzo into his mouth. A piece of it sticks in his mustache. Meanwhile, beside me, Hayden is painfully silent.

"Is it making money?" Jeff asks, now transitioning to a mouthful of beef.

Hayden clears his throat. "I mean, I'm hired as a contractor for the season. If we're the most popular series and win, we'll get a big budget for season two and can profit off the show. I was on hiatus with the podcast anyway, so I was prepared to go without a steady paycheck for a bit."

"I worry about you, sweetie." Ellen reaches across the table, wrapping her perfectly manicured nails around his hand. "I am afraid this isn't helping you move on. I don't want you lingering in the past. You can do whatever you want now."

Hayden's face drops, but he doesn't say anything. Is this the Hayden who came home from boarding school each weekend, quiet and defeated?

"What if this is what I want to do?"

"You want to hunt the Yeti?" Jeff asks.

"This is what I'm good at, and I have never had to come to you and ask for help. I've been doing just fine."

His voice cracks over the word "fine." "Fine" means spending three years alone, trying to heal without burdening anyone or forcing someone else to hold him up when he can't stand on his own. "Fine" feels so desperately lonely when he says it like that.

His mother face-palms. "Hayden, we're not saying that you're not good at it. We're just saying that you can do whatever you want now."

"You weren't there," he finally says.

I suddenly feel like *I* shouldn't be here for this. I debate if it's time to excuse myself and use the bathroom for an hour until they wonder if I fell in the toilet and died. "Every doctor's appointment, every middle-of-the-night trip to the ER— you were *not* there for it."

Rage flushes in Hayden's cheeks, a shimmering coat of

tears glistening over his eyes. This is frustration, not hurt. I know the feeling too well.

"Maybe this isn't the kind of thing you're excited to tell your friends in the needlepoint club about, and I'm sorry if it's embarrassing to have your kid be the guy hunting ghosts on YouTube, but this is the first time I feel okay in *years*. What I have with Hallie—"

I don't know if he means our show or *us*. Either way, if I'm the thing holding him together, I need to hold on tighter tonight. I need to keep him in one piece. I promised I would.

"God forbid I be happy doing something after what I've been through."

"Hayden, sweetie." Ellen rubs the back of his hand. I can hardly watch this. I can't bear to see her belittle his pain and his feelings like this. If he doesn't step in, I'm going to have to. How can she not see the tears building in his eyes or the pain painting every inch of his face? I've remained still for the past few minutes, not even picking at my food, waiting for some cue to step in if this goes south.

"I'm doing my best," he breathes. "I didn't want to do this here. Not in front of Hallie— Fuck it."

He stands, tossing his fancy embroidered napkin on the table.

"Watch your language, son," Jeff chides.

Hayden looks between Ellen and Jeff. "This isn't about you, *Jeff*!"

He's gone before I can step in and try and help him through this. There's a moment of quiet, and Ellen and Jeff look at each other, and then at me. I reach for my phone. They watch me warily, as I pull up one of our videos. I don't play it, but I scroll to the comments.

yessss. this is the best part of my week. I needed this episode so badly.

Thank you thank you thank you for this. This has been the week from hell and this fixed my mood.

I hope you guys know how happy you make people. This show is so full of joy and chaos.

It's just a handful, but every week, our comment section is full. There's a lot of nonsense, some people who want to debunk our theories and findings, but there's also this. I know the first rule of being a creator is to never read the comments. But sometimes, when I know there's things like this buried in there, it's impossible not to. Some days I struggle to believe I'm the spectacular host our fans think I am, too, but there is a lot of love here that tells me stepping into the spotlight was not a bad idea after all.

I pass my phone to Ellen and Jeff. They lean into each other and read what I've pulled up.

"I know that all of this might seem strange, and I didn't imagine myself hunting for Bigfoot or aliens either. I don't believe in any of this, but Hayden's made me wish I did. He has that way with people, and everyone loves him for it. He makes people happy, and it's no wonder he's had the amount of success he has. He's working his ass off and it's paying off. It might look different than what you imagined for him, but you should be proud."

Ellen slides my phone back silently. Somewhere in the house, a door slams.

CHAPTER 16

I excuse myself and follow the sound of the slammed door. It leads me to the huge deck at the back of the house, where Hayden sits on the stairs leading out to the backyard, hands drawn behind his neck, and his head bowed. I can't tell if he wants someone around him, but the thought of leaving him alone kills me. The least I can do is ask. I know he isn't okay. I can't let something like that go ignored.

He doesn't say anything as I sit and drape a hand along the inside of his leg so he knows I'm here. His body tenses, but after a moment, he slips his fingers between mine.

"I'm sorry about that." The words whoosh out of him. "I knew that would happen, and I brought you anyways."

"I don't care. I just care that you're okay."

"It's whatever."

Years of pain weighed on his shoulders, enough to push him to seek help for it. How many times had I belittled my own pain to spare someone else's feelings? I can't let him do the same. I understand the shame he might feel in showing vulnerability. I don't know how long it's been since someone's been in Hayden's corner.

"It's not *whatever*."

Hayden doesn't say anything, but his attempts to conceal how he's feeling permeate the air around us. "What you said . . . you didn't have to."

"Of course I did. They should know how impressive you are and how much what you do means to people. That's way more important than a huge paycheck. And, trust me, one day you'll have that, too."

I sometimes struggle to believe we're good enough to win and get more seasons and worry about how much it'll do to my under-construction confidence if we lose. But for Hayden, I need to be brave. He put his show in the hands of a nonbeliever, and he put his trust in me. I can't show weakness when he needs someone to be strong for him.

"This show . . . It feels like one of those last pieces I still have. My dad listened to me brainstorm every episode, helped me craft a good story. I learned everything I know about writing from him. It gave me something to throw myself into . . . you know, after."

"Yeah." I want to let him continue.

"No one ever had to see me or know when I had bad days," Hayden says. "I could take breaks if I needed them, and people would be happy when I came back. Nobody had to see the worst of it. I guess it made me feel less alone. It didn't feel like there was no one there." He deflates. "It felt like people cared without my having to ask for help. I didn't want to burden my mom with my worst days. Abby, either. I was trying to be as easy as I could be. I just wish doing my best was good enough."

I move down a step and slide myself between his legs. My hands rest on his waist, thumbs brushing his belt loops. His eyes water again, and he looks away from me.

"You know, before I met you, I wasn't really looking to

believe in anything. Then I saw you on TV that night and I knew. I knew right away that you were *it*."

Granted, I was cross-faded and delirious, but finding Hayden was one drunk decision I can never regret.

His thumb brushes along the back of my palm. I feel every bit of tension in his body, and I want to make it go away so desperately.

"I'm sorry your mom doesn't see how special what you do is, but a lot of other people do. Your dad did. All our fans do. *I do. The Out There* makes a lot of people happy, and that's no small feat. What we're doing matters. And you should know you were the easiest choice I've ever made," I tell him.

I hear his words in my head over and over again. He's doing his best, but he needs help. He needed help and there was no one to do it. I can't let him fall back into old patterns. "And if you're hurting, it's easy for me to help too."

A tear slides down his cheek and he wipes it away in a panic, like I shouldn't have seen that. Like asking for any semblance of help would inconvenience me. God, I wish he didn't know this feeling like I do, but it's clear we're cut from the same cloth. He can't take care of other people if he's busy taking care of himself. So he doesn't.

"I'm sorry," he breathes. I cup the sides of his face, my thumb brushing beneath the frames of his glasses to wipe away the tears. My touch clearly comes as a shock, as his hands press against my arms like he's pushing me away because this is something he can't accept.

"Shh . . ." I say. "I promise, I don't mind."

Then he lets me slide my arms around his shoulders. His head rests on top of mine, a few warm tears dripping into my hair. It only makes me hold him tighter. I feel like I somehow have to make up for all those years he needed someone and never had that shoulder to cry on. Hayden's fingers curl around the fabric of my sweater, and he holds on for dear life.

"It's okay to be upset, if that's how you feel."

He holds me so hard it almost hurts, but he can take whatever he needs from me. Anything at all. Finally, he draws away. His damp eyes fog his glasses and I help him finish the job of wiping his tears. He flinches, like he's ashamed I'm seeing this.

"Who's been taking care of you this whole time?"

He chokes out a watery smile, hearing his own words thrown back at him. "Me?"

"That's not a whole lot."

"No," he sighs. "It's really goddamn lonely."

"You don't have to feel alone anymore."

I don't think it's only him I'm speaking to.

"I haven't since I met you."

I try to keep my own eyes from watering, but he's struck me so deep I don't know how to respond. For all the time I spent worrying I was difficult to work with, unlikable, and irritating, someone's life is better because I'm in it, and I have no choice but to believe him, because he does the same for me.

"Good. No more keeping things bottled up, okay? Whatever you need, I'm here."

Hayden cups my cheek, leans in, and kisses me in a way he hasn't before. Slowly, peacefully, like he's falling asleep because for the first time in years, he has a soft place to rest his head. I know that he's closed up his heart and run from love for so long, but when I hold him closer, he doesn't pull away. I don't believe in aliens or ghosts or anything I make my living talking about now, but I believe there is something beautiful between us that makes me feel like for the first time in a while, I know everything will be okay. Hayden sure hasn't smashed my perceptions and beliefs about any conspiracy theories, but he has changed whether I believe I could possibly love someone again.

Finally, we break away.

"I have something for you." I slide away and scurry to my purse, pulling out the tiny plastic bag I'd brought with me. I sit beside Hayden again and pass it to him.

"Is this . . . a joint?"

I nod. "You said you'd never broken the rules. Never got stoned in a shady basement or passed an unhygienic bong around the room. So . . . while we're busy disappointing your mom . . ."

His smile grows as I slip the joint out of the bag and light it. "Are you going to demonstrate?"

"Hayden, it's not that hard."

"I'm a newbie."

"Fine." I suck in a puff. I haven't smoked since the night I discovered him on late-night TV, and I don't make a huge habit of it, but I am a solid five out of ten on the stoner knowledge scale, ten being Nora's parents owning an artisanal weed boutique. I hold the smoke in my mouth for a moment before exhaling. "You want to try and hold it in for a few seconds so it takes effect."

"Right," he says as I pass the joint to him. He takes in a hit, hanging on to it, giving a quick cough, then exhaling like a pro.

"Excellent work."

"Thank you, I try. Good thing I have you with me to make sure I don't do anything crazy."

"It's weed. It makes you want to sit on the couch and eat Cheetos."

"We do not have Cheetos." His voice drops like he's been presented with the world's worst news.

"Or cookie dough. I could really go for cookie dough."

"You know eating raw cookie dough can give you salmonella."

"That's a conspiracy theory." I lie on the deck next to him and look up at the stars.

"Finally," he adds, joining me. "A conspiracy you *do* believe in."

We pass the joint back and forth a few times until it hits the bottom, and I stamp it out.

"How do you feel?" I ask.

My head is floaty. My limbs are light and I don't feel as cold as I did before, but mostly, I'm just hungry and thinking about cookie dough.

"Somehow, I thought colors would look different."

I laugh, rolling my eyes. "That's LSD, not weed."

"Hmm. Next time. It's my own dabble into MKUltra."

I glance over at where Hayden lies next to me on the deck. The moon glints off his glasses and—behind them—his green eyes are bloodshot, a combination of the pot and the tears. But at least now he doesn't seem as self-conscious. I wish there was something I could say to make him understand how I don't mind seeing him vulnerable, that I know how tough it is to break down in front of another person.

By the time our eyes meet, he's already looking at me as well. The first thought that pops into my head is how I'm lucky. Lucky to find him when I did. Lucky to have someone who sees me as an equal. Lucky that at least I can see there was something on the other side of Cade. Something better.

My weed-hazy brain wants to tell him I love everything

about him, but I don't. It's too soon. His Adam's apple bobs in his throat as I inch closer. My fingers rest at the base of his wrist, feeling for the button on his sleeve. Once I find it, I undo the button and roll his sleeve to the middle of his forearm, where he wanted to leave them before. I trace the outline of ink along the inside of his forearm, chills rising to his skin under my touch.

"Deer," I tease.

He shakes his head. "*Not* Deer."

He rolls his other sleeve up, and he finally looks comfortable in his dressy clothes. When I lie back, I move closer and rest my hands on the sides of his face. His cheeks are rough beneath my touch, but the curves of Hayden's lips are soft and full. I want to taste the earthy bite of pot still on his breath and hear the sounds he'd make as I kiss him harder.

But before I can, the porch light flickers on and the door opens. Ellen steps onto the deck with us. Hayden freezes, eyes moving to me slowly like a Not Deer in headlights, and sits up. Surely his mom can smell the tinge of weed in the air, and she'll be able to smell it on *us* in a moment. Of course her son brings home a chick with blue hair and he gets caught smoking pot.

Though, we only did this *because* he never had his burst of adolescent rebellion. I think he deserves at least one pass.

His mom bends down next to him. She runs her fingers through his dark hair and kisses the top of his head. I half expect him to pull away, but he doesn't. It's a step, accepting help when he needs it. Accepting love when he needs it.

His reflexes are a bit slow, but Hayden does lean into his mom when she hugs him tighter. I can tell by that alone how he so badly wants her approval and love.

"I want to see an episode of this show of yours," she whispers.

"They're on YouTube."

Oh, good lord, his words are so slow, and one look at his bloodshot eyes will give it all away. She offers me a soft smile and rests her head on top of Hayden's. "I want *you* to show me an episode."

Hayden looks to me. I think of all our episodes, and I'm proud of them all. But I do wonder what episode I feel the most prepared to show my sort-of-boyfriend's mom. I don't know what'll make a better impression: me explaining that I do not think JFK is the most fuckable president or me finding a creepy room in the Winchester Mystery House and proudly declaring it the "Sarah Winchester Sex Dungeon."

Either way, I am not making a great first impression.

Ellen smiles. "Can I lure you back in with the prospect of munchies?"

I can't tell if I'm registering horror or feral hunger in Hayden's eyes.

"Why would I need munchies?" he mumbles. "Those are for people who are on drugs, which I am not."

Jesus.

Ellen rolls her eyes. "I was a teenager in the seventies. Trust me. Come on."

Finally, Hayden stands, slowly and leaning on me for balance, and follows his mom inside. We'll show them the premiere. Ellen and Jeff guide us into the den, which I am convinced is a room only rich white people have.

When Jeff returns to the den with a small bowl of Cheetos, I decide he is not so bad after all and accept his peace offering. He also offers us artisanal popcorn from their fancy new popcorn maker. Jeff's ready to settle in for the night, though each episode of *The Out There* is only a half hour. I respect how the man is in this for the long haul.

I take a seat on one of the leather couches beside Hayden. I'm not sure how we're playing this yet, so I keep a reasonable distance from him. Instead, Hayden tugs me closer to him, and I lean against his shoulder. I'm something he wants close, and something he wants, period. There's a lopsided, delirious smile on his face when his fingers lace with mine.

Ellen and Jeff look chuffed, and I am, too. I know Hayden's clinging to me for comfort, but I'm happy he's willing to ask for it and to show me what he needs.

"Back in the day," Jeff says, "it was a 'you get what you get and you don't get upset.'"

Hayden raises an eyebrow. "What?"

"The weed flavors. Now you kids have all kinds of fun twists."

"Jeff has smoked a weed," I whisper to Hayden.

"I *know*," he says, a tad too loud.

Ellen and Jeff are subjected to thirty minutes of the two of us provoking ghosts, touring the hotel, and the six clips from the six different times Hayden woke up in the middle of the night because a ghost poked him. Each of them chuckles several times, though they do look confused when Hayden goes off on the finer details of ghost hunting. I assure them I'm usually confused, too.

I expected to need harder drugs than weed to get through watching my most embarrassing claims to fame with my sort-of-boyfriend's parents, but curled up in their cozy den beside Hayden—watching him watch his mom take an interest in what he does for the first time—it's intoxicating enough.

When the first episode wraps, Ellen is the one to press Play on the next episode.

CHAPTER 17

By the time we return to the guesthouse, the high has worn off and we've sated ourselves with enough Cheetos and truffle-flavored popcorn to sober us up plenty. Ellen and Jeff have seen every episode of *The Out There* and seemed to enjoy it. There were a few moments of parental discomfort, which makes me wonder to myself what *my* parents are thinking so far. We haven't talked about it much, and that is okay by me.

Hayden fumbles with the key, and I meet him there, with my hands wrapped around his waist. We began the day curled up in a starchy hotel bed he made feel far more comfortable than it should have. I kissed him good morning, with the thrill of knowing that's allowed now. We muted ourselves in front of his parents, but now, it's just us again.

Before another attempt at the lock, he reaches behind and finds me. I want to go inside and strip off all the parts of him he put behind armor today. I want to get the Hayden I know back. He's bleeding through the seams of a button-down shirt and sweater, but I can help speed up the process.

"Thank you," he whispers.

I nod, pressing my lips between his shoulder blades. His body eases against mine, like he's been waiting to lean on someone all night. "Of course. And I mean it. I am here for whatever you need. You just have to ask."

"I know. There hasn't been anyone to ask in a long time."

"There is now."

He slowly turns. I study him carefully. His eyes are still rimmed red, but his expression is loose and relaxed, unlike the far-too-tight mask he'd been wearing the rest of the day. I hope that progress with his mom has taken a weight off his shoulders.

"Do you feel better?" I ask.

"Much."

"Good," I breathe. I work my hands up his body, wrapping my arms around his neck and finding his lips. I sink into Hayden as he tightens his grip around me. I taste buttery popcorn, sharp nips of whiskey, and I'm consumed by him already.

I bite down on his lower lip and he lets out a smoky groan, his back pressing flush against the door. We push open the door and his hands wander up my sides. The Northern California air is frigid, but his touch sucks me in like a warm blanket I never want to crawl out from underneath.

I'm suddenly desperate to undress him completely. All night, I've been looking at a version of Hayden I don't know. His hair in sharp order, a button-down and sweater that made him look itchy and uncomfortable, hiding all the things that made him unique—from his tattoos to his offbeat career choice to his stupid jokes that I feel like only I laugh at.

The door slams shut behind us and Hayden hardly locks it before I'm kissing him again and my hands shove up the front of his sweater. In a single swift motion, he tugs it over his head. His breathing quickens and I could linger in the sound of his exaggerated breaths and inquisitive hums as his lips slowly find mine again. I taste his smile against my lips as we stumble toward the bed.

I get to work on the shirt underneath; with each button, a new flash of ink bleeds into vision. I submerge in the waves on his shoulder, blow through the space between branches on his side like the wind, brushing my hands over the Not Deer on his arm. I feel the words on his lips between every kiss—questions. He's asking if there's anything about him I don't want, any part he can shove behind armor. I tell him with another kiss that there is no part of him he needs to hide, nothing about him he should compartmentalize for me.

This is the entire point. I want him completely, and I trust him to want me completely.

I trail my fingers down his bare skin and I only want to stop kissing him to look at him. This is the first time I'm stripping him down and can study him. I don't skim over the parts of him I know well already. It's all part of the package. His intricately inked arm, the waves breaking on his chest, every muscle and sharp angle of his body.

I can't believe someone like him is mine. To touch, kiss, *learn*.

I sit on the mattress and Hayden's on his knees in an instant, quickly unlacing my boots and running his hands up my thighs. He reaches for the bottom of my sweater, hesitating before going any further.

"Is this okay?" he asks with a kiss.

"It's only fair if I've got your shirt off." I laugh. As I slip out of the heavy sweater I've been wearing all night, he's on me in a second. Hands spanning across my back, rough scratches of beard, and a swelling ache in the pit of my stomach.

"You must not understand the way I would let you do absolutely anything at all to me, Hallie."

"Anything?" I raise an eyebrow.

"I think you have an idea of what I mean." He flashes a smile. His eyes drag down my body, then he follows with his hands. He's enraptured by every curve. "And I would give you anything you wanted. I wouldn't stop until you had it."

Suddenly, nerves take over the festering heat in the pit of my stomach. Sex has never felt the way I hoped it would. I hoped it'd happen and I'd suddenly understand why everyone never shuts up about it. But then, it was mostly awkward, sweaty, and just another thing to do, like another errand to run or check off the list. With Hayden, this all finally feels right. It's new and confusing, but I don't think I'm scared of it.

"I . . ."

"Or," Hayden whispers, his thumbs stroking my cheeks, "we can stop this here. Whatever you want."

We wait in silence as I find my words and make up my mind. I hesitate to tell him what scares me and what I don't want to admit, but if the Hayden in front of me is the same person who washed my hair for me and held me as I cried, I know he'll listen.

"Sex is . . . I don't know. No one's ever asked me what I liked before. Maybe I don't even know what I like. I've only been with Cade."

"Cade," he huffs. "What an underwhelming man."

"You have no idea." He doesn't know the half of it, and I don't want him to. I want him to keep looking at me the way he is now, and I want to relearn all of this with him. "I've liked everything we've done so far."

"Me too." He brushes a blue wave behind my ear. "To be

fair, it's . . . uh, been a while for me, too. I'm probably a little rusty."

I roll my eyes. "I seriously doubt that."

His nose brushes mine and he presses soft kisses along my cheeks. "How about this? We figure it out together."

"I like that."

"Good." He smiles. "We start small, like this . . ."

Our lips meet again, arms folding around one another like we were made to hold only each other. It's slow, full of quiet breaths and even softer pleas to keep going. I run my fingers over lithe, muscular shoulders, taking what he gives me and offering the same back.

"Even if all we did was this, it'd still pull me apart," he breathes, "piece by piece."

"More of that," I say, "more talking. I want you to talk to me. Tell me everything you're going to do to me."

"See, I knew you were into the conspiracy theory dirty talk." Regardless, he seals our agreement with a kiss before slowly pulling away. Then his eyes darken and narrow. "Ever since last night, all I can think about is how good you taste."

His lips trace a trail of heat to the base of my neck, kisses coming rougher with the slight scratch of his beard. I curve into him as he leans me back on the bed. We discard his button-down, and his lips find my skin yet again.

"And? What do I taste like?"

"Depends." He nips below my earlobe, and his words light up my entire body. "Your lips? Like berries—it's those little lip balms you like. The ones that look like eggs."

I smirk. "Pineapple and passion fruit."

"What?"

"It's pineapple and passion fruit. My lip balm."

"I guess I need a refresher." Hayden draws a hand to my chin and tilts my lips up to his, but I stop him and his brows rise in question. I leave him in torturous wait for a long second before kissing him again. Of course, tonight I've been wearing lipstick—which tastes heavier, and there's little of it remaining, since most of it has left marks on his neck and jaw—but he doesn't care *what* I taste like. All he cares about is that he gets a sample.

"This is different." I hear every heady breath and soft moan from the back of his throat like they're the only sounds in the world. "Still good, *but* you're making a liar out of me."

"Boo-hoo."

He laughs, kicking his boots off, climbing on top of me, and pressing one leg to either side of my body. He slides his hands up my arms, pushing them back against the mattress. There's a split second of hesitation where his eyes ask, "Is this too much?" and it isn't. I don't feel unsafe or pressured or even uncomfortable as his fingers brush the soft skin on the insides of my wrists, like he's ready to let go of me at my command, which won't come.

"Keep going," I plead. With my hands restrained, the urge to touch and learn every inch of him is so strong. I want to trace every line of ink on his body and dress him down until we're even. His hips rock against mine with another kiss, his pants tightening as I kiss him again and again until I can't breathe anymore.

"Do you think about me?" I ask.

"Constantly."

"When I'm not around? When you're alone?"

He registers what I mean now and responds with a shy smile. "Respectfully."

"You have my permission to be a little less respectful," I tease.

He lets go of my wrists and boxes me in against the mattress, his eyes washing over me as he thinks through what he wants next. He cups both sides of my face and begins to kiss from my forehead to the shell of my ear, then lower.

"I'm a little overwhelmed," he confesses against the curve of my neck. There are more rough kisses and wandering hands, and the way his voice pitches down, I suddenly understand why people sign up for phone-sex services. "There isn't a single part of you I don't want to know inside and out."

His hands run up my stomach to my bra. He follows the arc of underwire and slips carefully under the fabric.

"I have, like, no boobs," I laugh.

"I don't mind." He says this between kisses. "If only you knew what you do to me."

I think of all the insecurities other people have put in my head. Stretch marks, freckles when I sunburn, any deviance from a flat stomach. As these imperfections come to mind, Hayden's hands wander over me, as if he's finding all of them too, but instead, he's taking note of his new favorite things. It's so hard to be scared when he treats me the way he does. It's easy to be excited.

"How are you feeling?" he asks.

"Like I want you to keep going."

My body arches against his as he kisses down my throat and chest, learning every curve of me with his mouth. I let out a soft moan that makes him laugh and the vibration sends goose bumps all over my skin. He reaches the button on my jeans and looks back to me. "Still okay?"

I nod, letting him unbutton my pants and ease them down

my hips. Nerves prick at my skin as a brush of scruff rakes above the waistband of my underwear.

"You should know, though," I begin. "I've never been able to finish with a man before."

His gaze shoots to me, and he looks like I've just told him that the only thing on the missing Watergate tapes is the "Macarena" on repeat three and a half times. "Never? Like, Hallie, *really*?"

"Never."

"What is wrong with him?" he whispers. "How was he not obsessed with the idea of making you come?"

His words shoot straight between my legs.

"Great question. Are you?"

His lips tick up. "I am now, if that's what you want."

"Please." It's the shortest way I can say I want his hands and mouth on every inch of me.

I allow Hayden to decide how he best wants to go about this, and he begins by finding my lips again and kissing me softly. Our bodies fold together with an intimacy we haven't shared yet. He's not kissing me like last night was the first time, but like we have years and years behind us and we never tire of each other. Bare skin against bare skin, his hands guide mine as we slip down my underwear together.

"Show me," he rasps against my lips. "I want you to show me what you'd do."

He doesn't need to say anything more. I follow through on his request. He's deathly silent, studying hard as I bring his hand between my legs. I guide him as if it's just me, but I'm already imagining him touching me, hearing the quiet sighs he lets out like I'm the most exquisite thing he's ever seen. I shudder at the chill of his fingertips, following the circles and strokes I trace for him.

"I think I have a good enough idea."

I keep a hand over his as he applies pressure I hadn't given myself. He's slow at first, reading me for signs. I press my thighs together as he strokes harder and faster, and it makes my knees quake. "You feel amazing."

The soft slide of his fingers into me makes my back arch against his body with a sharp cry. I clutch a handful of the comforter beneath me when a chiding laugh comes from the back of his throat.

"If you want to hold on to something, choose me," he says. His free hand weaves with mine, guiding it up his body, burying our fingers deep in his hair as he finds a rhythm that snatches my breath away.

"Better," he says.

I let go of every unpleasant and unwanted touch that lives in my memory and hang on to this. Only this and everything that comes after.

"I want to know exactly where and how you come undone."

His words strike me like a branding iron, so fucking hot and unbearable. How many hours have I spent listening to Hayden speak? Yet none of it sounds as good as him taunting me like this. My hips rock against his hand and he hums in approval.

"Right, because you're out of practice," I laugh.

He rolls his eyes and silences me with a kiss. "Okay, enough out of you."

Fuck, this is the kind of sex I've wanted my whole life. Tender touches and terrible jokes, every action steeped in authenticity.

This is *us*. I love that the commanding side of Hayden can switch back to the absolute nerd he is every day in a split second.

I hook my leg around his body as the build begins deep in the pit of my stomach, toes curling and shaking cries. Hayden nips at my throat, down my chest, and along the cups of my bra.

"You are so gorgeous," he rasps. "Absolutely out of this world."

His touch shifts, and I grab tighter at his hair. He feels so fucking good, and I am so close. My back arches, eyes slip shut, and the tightened coil in the pit of my stomach is ready to unspool.

"It's okay," he whispers just beneath my ear. His other hand grips my hips, holding me in place. He lets out a heady breath against my skin, and I'm too aware of all of him. The press of his glasses as he rakes his lips all over my body, the scratch of his beard on my throat and knowing what my neck's going to look like tomorrow, how hard he is between my legs—I hardly need anything else to come, but his voice lowers as he reaches my lips again. "Don't worry, no one's going to hear except me. And I want to."

I don't have a chance to second-guess myself, because a cord snaps inside me and I'm plummeting. Stars prick at the corners of my vision, and I clutch at him like he's the only thing to hold on to. He whispers things like "beautiful," "I've got you," and "I'm yours" that sound like music.

Hayden extricates himself from me. I still don't know if I can speak, but when he smiles at me, I feel something flood through my veins. Affection and care and safety.

"How do you feel?" he asks.

My body feels weightless, but I'm grounded by the feeling of him hard against my lower stomach. No one's ever pushed me to finish first; no one's *made sure* it happened. For the first time in my life, when I think about sex, I think about something that Hayden and I will do for *each other* rather than do because we have to.

I envision the sex-drunk look in his eyes as he watched me come and how thrilled he was to do this for me. I want the same for him. I want to watch him come undone and lose his composure. Hayden is so good at sliding parts of himself behind armor, but he's unguarded, and I want him as vulnerable as I can get him. I want him to know we're equals and always will be.

"Good," I whisper back. "Can I . . . ?"

He swallows, his thumb stroking along the curve of my cheek. "It's okay. This was for you."

"I want to," I whisper against his lips.

Then he nods, slowly. My hands wander to his waist, where I slip his belt through the loops and unbutton his jeans. His breathing is heavy, and his gaze feels like a pound of bricks on my chest in the best way. I think of how low his tattoos go beneath his boxers and the intrusive-thoughts machine in my brain wonders if he has a tattoo of Bigfoot on his ass or something, but I'm okay to not discover it all tonight.

Instead, I push his jeans aside and slip below the waistband of his boxer briefs. He tilts my chin down and kisses me as I curl my fingers around him. I don't think any *Cosmic Conspiracies* guest star has the right to be this well-endowed. He lets out a heady groan against my lips, fingers clutching the sheets below us.

"Fuck," he hisses. I'm hypnotized by his dark lashes fluttering shut against the tops of his cheeks. His voice breaks off into a sharp cry from the back of his throat.

I follow the signs his body gives me—struggled moans, frantic grips at my hair—and all I can think is that we're even. For every second he drove me mad, broke down every defense until we were both left raw, I'm happy to do the same for him.

"Hallie," he breathes. "*Hallie.*"

I watch his fingers white-knuckle on the sheets beneath us as his release comes with a failed attempt at my name again. Our lips meet, with tastes of fading bourbon and velvety lipstick, both of us swearing each other's names like they're an indisputable theory, answers we've been hunting for for so long.

"I . . ." he starts.

"It's not often you're left speechless," I say.

Hayden strokes a blue wave out of my face with a smile. "No. You're the only person who does that to me."

Hayden leans in for another kiss, this one slow, nothing hungry and desperate like before. He feathers my lips and jaw with kisses, hitting the soft spot beneath my ear that tickles. I laugh and burrow against him, pleading with him to stop.

"I have one request for you," he says.

"Sure . . ." I laugh.

"Get ready for bed."

Considering the past few minutes, asking me to go to sleep feels like a harsh emotional cold shower.

I frown. "Oh."

"That's not *all*. Just step one."

There's a mischievous look in his eyes—and not even in a sexy way—that makes me nervous. Nevertheless, I agree, and we clean ourselves up. When I return from the bathroom, his laptop is pulled out on the bed in front of us.

"You said we could watch anything I wanted," he mumbles into one of the pillows he's snuggled up in. It's so horrifically cute that I'm not even mad at the idea of watching some weird alien movie.

"What are we watching?" I roll my eyes but climb under the covers with him anyway.

His eyebrows rise as he flips through his computer and presses Play.

CHAPTER 18

I swear I have taken a picture of Hayden in front of every single Bigfoot display we've passed.

The Bigfoot Scenic Byway.

A "Bigfoot Crossing" sign.

A ginormous Bigfoot statue at the center of town.

He's like a kid in a candy shop if the candy shop sold exclusively hairy hominids.

It's the cutest thing I've ever seen. I post photo after photo to our social media page, updating the fans on our travels. We stop at the Bigfoot Steakhouse for a late (and underwhelming) lunch before checking into our cabin for the evening. We have an afternoon of Bigfoot hunting ahead of us before sundown. I'm partially glad Hayden doesn't want to camp out here, because while I do not believe in Bigfoot yet, I do believe in bears. And I do believe a bear would eat me.

After finally making it through *The Mothman Prophecies* last night, Hayden and I fell asleep early so we'd be sure to hit the road first thing. Ellen and Jeff sent us off with hugs and Ellen even said she's looking forward to seeing me again. Apparently, I have not made as bad of an impression as I expected.

We spend the six-hour drive listening to more podcasts so

I can be "educated," but it's sometimes hard to learn when Hayden pauses every five minutes to go off on another tangent. My personal favorite comes while learning about an alien named Valiant Thor, who lived at the Pentagon in the fifties and was allegedly a real dreamboat. I have questions about how sexy an alien could be, but Hayden, of course, has an answer. I learn that alien-banging is apparently more popular than I could have expected.

"There's a whole video game series about it. You can date hot aliens," Hayden tells me.

"You can date a lizard man, or a guy who looks like an artichoke, or a blue chick."

"The alien I dated had a compromised immune system, so human fluids would probably kill her."

I immediately ask him to stop.

Our cabin is a short distance from Six Rivers National Forest, particularly the spot where the infamous Patterson-Gimlin film was shot. When we arranged accommodations for this trip, Hayden slowly put a hand on mine and said, "I've got this." So I'm thrilled when I discover that it's just a normal cabin. Hours later, we're in the middle of the forest at a wide clearing that looks strangely familiar.

I cannot believe Hayden has gotten me into hiking boots.

I am going to be covered in mosquito bites.

"So, in 1967, Roger Patterson and Bob Gimlin weren't *actually* hunting for Bigfoot out here. They were *into* Bigfoot, but they weren't trying to *find* him—"

"Unlike you," I comment, following him with the camera. I flinch as a mosquito sucks my blood like El Chupacabra (I'm learning, clearly). "Ow."

"Damn straight. I am going to find Bigfoot if it fucking

kills me!" Hayden shouts into the forest, before promptly tripping over a rogue root and completely eating it on camera. A gaggle of birds flee the scene.

"Yeah, that's staying in the episode."

He frowns as he brushes the dirt off his jeans and strides forward toward a specific part of the clearing.

"Am I projecting okay?" he yells.

"Yes, loud and clear, Hayden."

He flashes two big thumbs-up. "The film is some of the most famous Bigfoot footage ever recorded and has been picked apart to death, with re-creations attempting to debunk it. Patterson and Gimlin were on horseback—coming right to this clearing. The horses noticed it first—so intuitive—"

"—so we needed to bring horses? I don't like horses."

"Why don't you like horses, Hallie?" He squints, pawing at his backpack for his sunglasses. The afternoon sun glints off his thick black frames in a way that'll look terrible on camera, but I suppose part of the appeal is how we're amateurs. Neither of us is an expert filmmaker. Since we're hiking through the woods today, we'll mostly be taking turns behind the camera and can set up the tripod in Hayden's backpack if we need it. When we have Jamie with us, at least the quality is higher, but without Nora and him staying behind, Cthulhu would starve on all our trips. Without them, I wouldn't have made out with Hayden in the woods and he wouldn't have given me my first man-induced orgasm.

As much as I adore my little pressure wave vibrator, it's not the same.

It doesn't tell me I'm beautiful and it doesn't look anything like the extremely handsome man in front of me . . . investigating . . . tree stumps.

Huh.

"Horses are big."

"So am I, but you like me." He slides his sunglasses down the bridge of his nose and flashes me what I *think* is a wink.

"Is that meant to be a euphemism?"

"Wouldn't you like to know, Nonbeliever!"

"Hayden . . . I *do* know."

He smiles across the clearing, disgustingly cute and earnest. Euphemism or not, after the past two nights, I am thinking about undressing him again. Maybe this time, we'll take it further.

"That is *not* going into the episode."

I nod in agreement.

"*Anyway,* when the creature emerges, Patterson scrambles for his camera, and Gimlin draws his rifle. The two of them cannot *believe* what they capture. While the footage is grainy, the large, apelike creature strides across the clearing, arms swinging, back hunched over."

"Are we positive this isn't the world's hairiest man?" I shout.

"Hallie, this is *really* hairy. I mean *really*, really hairy. *Astonishingly* hairy. It's also a female Bigfoot, for the record."

"We love that. Representation matters."

"As the creature makes its way across the screen, Patterson's hand now steadied, our Bigfoot takes a single glance over its right shoulder before escaping into the woods. There's been decades of debate over the authenticity of the film, but I personally think it's real. And I'm about to prove it. On camera. Right now. Once and for all."

I lower the camcorder. "Why does this make me nervous?"

"Don't be nervous. Just film me."

I purse my lips and raise the viewfinder again. Hayden

takes his place at one end of the clearing, bouncing and waving, as if he isn't the only thing in sight.

"There are some rough estimates about the creature's height, ranging from six feet to seven and a half feet. For reference, I'm six-four, so this creature would be *slightly* taller than me. If we're going for the six-six estimate that a lot of people go with, I am a decent stand-in for Bigfoot."

"That's a horrible sentence."

Another mosquito bites my arm, and at this point, it feels like bullying. I do not like the woods. I do not like Bigfoot hunting, but I am beginning to hope we find something, because the money we could make off genuine Bigfoot footage would pay for a lot of calamine lotion.

"All right. I'm going to walk across the clearing here and mimic the video as best I can. I'm going to show you that humans don't look like this when they walk. There is no way this was a man in a suit. No way at all. Watch."

And so I do, against all sane judgment. Hayden takes long, precise strides across the clearing and the most horrifying part is that it looks like he has this *rehearsed*. He knows every movement and all the timing of the most famous piece of Bigfoot footage. Most people have probably *seen* the Patterson-Gimlin film, whether they know it or not, but nobody . . . has it memorized. Jesus, he has it *memorized*.

Though he's a man who is a "decent stand-in for Bigfoot," I am still thinking about him taking all my clothes off when we get back to the cabin.

His arms swing haphazardly, his back slumps, and then . . . he turns and gives the money shot. Except instead of Bigfoot's noncommittal glance, he smiles and flashes the Scout's Honor sign before moving toward the forest. I wonder how far into the woods he's going to go before turning back. I don't know how method of an actor Hayden is, but this is Bigfoot we're talking about. I simply do not know how dedicated he is to authenticity when it comes to his favorite cryptid. I don't know what Bigfoots eat. Do I actually have to worry about Hayden getting eaten by a Bigfoot?

Should I be far more concerned?

I waver between my obligation to make sure my co-host doesn't die and staying here and *hoping* he returns. I turn the camera on myself.

"I'm getting bitten to shit by mosquitos, and I have no idea how long Hayden plans to be out here. We might die, and this *might* be the last episode. Whoever finds my body . . . Tell my parents I love them and that, in my life insurance policy from Skroll, they split it fifty-fifty."

Eventually, Hayden stumbles down the nearby ravine with an emphatic grunt.

"WAS THAT CONVINCING?"

Oh good, he's back.

"Yes, very much so, Hayden," I holler.

When he emerges and returns to me, Hayden's sweating, wiping his forehead with his flannel. Patches of dirt coat his jeans and there are traces of plant life stuck to his shirt. His dark waves slip away from his face and he bends at the waist.

"Did you overexert yourself mimicking Bigfoot?" I ask. I squat in front of him, framing the camera up to capture his expression. I can't say it's flattering, but this is good fucking content. As we record more episodes, it feels like the dynamic between us tightens, and our fans have latched on to us week by week. The number of teen girls wanting us to kiss and admit we're dating grows. If only those teen girls knew what Hayden and I have been up to lately . . .

Hayden straightens and takes a deep breath. "All right, if we're going to attract a Bigfoot, I think we need to have a Bigfoot mating call—"

"Oh, *fuck* no."

"Come on."

"What happens if Bigfoot comes running out of the woods with a full hard-on? What do you do then?"

"Well, in order for Bigfoot to have a boner, he has to be real, so check and *mate*. But if that happens, I suppose," Hayden ponders, "that's how God wanted me to go. Either that, or in the process of freeing an alien from Area 51."

"Never met someone who'd be crushed to not peacefully die in their sleep . . ."

Then a crack of thunder echoes above us.

"We live in California. This doesn't happen," Hayden seethes.

It only takes a few seconds for the rain to descend on us. He's right. This doesn't happen in California. Perhaps in Northern California, but I don't know the landscape as well. In LA, rain means everyone drives horrifically and Mulholland Drive is full of rocks and mud.

I hope that at least this slaughters every mosquito that had my blood for happy hour.

"*No*," he hisses. "We're Bigfoot hunting!"

"Hayden," I shout over the pouring rain. My jeans and boots take on water. "I think Bigfoot hunting needs to take a rain check."

We both take a moment to giggle at my joke before I close the camcorder and slide it into my bag. The content is too good to damage. Besides, Hayden might kill me if I lose the footage of him re-creating the Patterson film. His fingers slide between mine as we trek to the car. Our journey takes us through sloshing ravines and has us gripping damp tree bark. I spend most of it laughing, catching him as he slips into the mud, and we stumble up the hill to his car. By the time we reach it, my clothes are soaked, my legs weighed down by wet denim, and—due to the Amazon reviews telling me these hiking boots are waterproof—I conclude that everyone is a goddamn liar. My socks are wet, and death is upon me.

Hayden opens my door for me before racing to the driver's seat. The rain pelts the steel frame of his car as he slides his glasses off and tries to dry them, with little success. He puts the car into drive and we speed down the hills toward our cabin. I crank the heat, tugging my T-shirt away from my chest to dry it against the vents. It takes us a few minutes to reach our lodging; not long enough for us to dry off. Hayden throws the car in park and snatches his backpack from the back seat as we rush toward the porch. I step into a tragically large puddle. I am not safe here.

The cabin is all one room, a bed, living room, and open-concept kitchen with large windows spanning the front. It has the perfect porch to drink coffee on, overlooking an endless army of green trees scraping the sky. I may not like being *in* nature, but it's lovely to look at, and the fresh air is a nice reprieve from LA's smoggy haze.

I hustle up the steps as Hayden tosses me his keys. His hair is soaked, glasses fogged, Bigfoot T-shirt clinging to him. It takes the shape of his body and I drink him in as he shoves his hair out of his face.

"Bigfoot obviously doesn't want to be found," I laugh, missing the keyhole on the first try.

"So he sends us a wet T-shirt contest instead."

Hayden's hands rest on my waist, his laugh rippling down my spine. His lips hover beside my neck, each breath coming in deep, heavy pants that ground me here. Here, in a moment that smells like crisp amber and timber and fresh rain, with Hayden's hand spanning across my stomach, softly clutching the fabric of my T-shirt.

"Hallie," he says.

He inches lower to the waistband of my jeans, fingers knotting in my belt loops now. My only answer is a simple nod, and he grips me by the waist and spins me to face him. My back spreads flat against the wooden exterior of our cabin, and his hands are on me before I have to plead for his touch.

Hayden cups my jaw, tilting my head up and finding my mouth. He hesitates with a sharp intake of breath, studying me through his fogged glasses before drowning me in a slow, delirious kiss. His hard, corded muscles press against my chest. I'm ready to strip off the damp fabric of his dorky T-shirt to find the ridges and angles of his stomach, the fine lines of his tattoos running across his chest and side. I daydream about how far below his boxers they go.

He moans against my mouth, teeth sinking into my bottom lip and his stubble marking me as his as he kisses along my jaw and down my neck. I savor each hungry sip he takes of me. Hayden's hands find a home in the back pockets of my jeans, grip tightening around my ass. I feel his desire pressed to mine, and I know this is it. This has to be. I've wanted him plenty of times, but right now, I don't question it. Not one bit.

We curse between kisses, fingers knotting in stretched-out wet fabric. I snatch a handful of his T-shirt, claiming all of him as mine. Against the unrelenting storm, I hear his words from last night in my head. *I'm yours.* Now I decide I'm his, too.

He fumbles with the keys and door, shoving us inside. Hayden hardly bothers to lock it before we drop both our backpacks to the ground. He only lets go of me to tug his flannel off his shoulders. The backs of my knees hit the mattress as he presses me against the comforter. Then he clutches me tightly, yanking me away from the bed.

"We are so damp," he laughs.

I match his giggles, wrapping my arms around his shoulders. "So you have to undress me *before* we hit the bed?"

Hayden cups my face, thumbs stroking my cheeks. It feels like waiting for permission or a question in itself. In this moment, we're deciding if this is going to go further or not. As our lips meet again, slow and savoring, he waits for my reply and is patient as ever. Every touch lets me know I'm cared for no matter what I answer with. I know I can back out at any point with no consequences, but I love how, with Hayden, there is no point of no return.

"Hallie, we don't have to do this."

I nod. "I know. But I want to if you do."

"Do you have to ask?" he teases, nipping my bottom lip. His eyes darken as his glasses unfog inside, deep stormy green like the forest we left outside. He hums in affection, kissing my cheek, jaw, forehead—he's not going to leave any part of me untouched. "I've wanted to make love to you since the night I met you."

That long? I think. He'd wanted me to be his since the tiny alien in his drink, our doomed ghost tour with Gary. My breath catches in my throat for a moment before he snatches it from me with another kiss.

"Really?" I tease. I want more of his voice. I want to hear every dirty thing he has to say, and I want him to do them all to me. More of last night. More of his moans and taunts and more of his body.

"Yes," he laughs. "I knew I had a nice cold shower in my future after that ghost tour."

I shove my hands up the front of his T-shirt. His body shudders under my cold touch with goose bumps rising to his skin. "I hear Gary the tour guide has that effect on people. It's in the Yelp reviews."

Without having to ask, Hayden pulls his T-shirt over his head in one swift motion. My eyes dance over waves and branches, and the intricate line art I have yet to identify all over his body. Trees and waves and Not Deers. I follow it below his pants, tempting me to work harder. It feels like a game of "X marks the spot."

As I unbuckle Hayden's belt, he halts my progress with a deep, rumbling laugh. "You next. Take something off."

I mean, I'm glad it's my turn. My clothing is so wet and uncomfortable I can hardly stand to keep it on another minute. I find the bottom of my T-shirt and pull it over my head, only for it to snag on my face. The wet fabric latches on to my head like a Facehugger, and I am trapped in the least sexy moment of my whole life.

"*Help me*," I hiss between laughs.

I can't see a thing, but I feel Hayden's strong grip work its way up my body until he's untangling me from the brutal clutches of my T-shirt. It hits the ground beside us with a damp thump. When he finally looks at me again, it's like he's seeing me for the first time. Relief, passion, excitement.

"You're safe now," he teases, kissing me again. I feel his words in more than one way.

Beneath us, he's kicking off his boots and socks. I follow and do the same.

"Everyone on Amazon said these were *waterproof*," I lament. "My feet are wet!"

"No damp socks, no bugs. What *do* you like?"

I rest my hands on top of his belt buckle and tug him closer to me. He leans me back against the mattress, a hand behind my head, the other teasing my lower stomach like it's taking everything in him to not get to work on my pants. "Those are completely normal things to dislike. Who *likes* wet socks?"

"I'm sure someone out there does."

"Sounds like a conspiracy theory."

I grab one of Hayden's hands, arching for him and guiding his fingers to the center of my back. He unhooks my bra with ease, slipping each strap down my arm. He sucks in a bewildered breath as I strip closer to nothing.

Chilly fingers brush over my quickly hardening nipples and all of me aches for him. He kisses down my chest and stomach, finding the coldest, most sensitive parts of my body with his mouth and dousing them in his warmth.

"Is this okay?" he asks, just above my waistband.

I offer a nod. We did more the night before, but he doesn't take that as perpetual permission. The thought alone makes my eyes water, and when our glances meet, he cups my cheek.

"I mean it. The second it's not—you tell me."

I have a feeling it will never stop being okay, but I love that he's asking. I love that I can learn to love this with someone like Hayden. For so long, all I pictured was a lifetime of uncomfortable encounters. Now I don't know what to imagine. All I know is I'm excited to discover it with Hayden.

"I will."

"Good," he breathes. Hayden draws away, watching me unbutton my pants. I hadn't planned to get naked with him when I dressed in my REI catalog–chic. I had not planned to wear my hottest underwear Bigfoot hunting. But considering the sheer amount of underwear I packed, I really could have planned this better.

When our lips meet again, our bodies fold together. He takes the chill out of my bones with every soft touch and warm press of lips to my skin. Each kiss of his is dizzying and my body feels like loose stitches coming apart one by one. Hayden plucks at another as he curses under his breath, tasting the slant of my jaw.

He leads my hand to his belt buckle. This time, I slip the leather through it and infiltrate to his button and zipper to reveal a pair of boxer briefs with vectored Bigfoots on them. I have no idea where a person gets these articles of clothing.

Shame washes over his expression. "I . . . uh . . . I forgot what I was wearing."

"It's okay," I laugh. "I think it's cute."

There's a sample of his smile in his next kiss, his arms tightening around me. "Good. You still okay?"

I nod. "Yes. I want you to keep going."

Hayden wets his bottom lip, tasting my lips on his. I want to suggest he take a taste of something else, but he's one step ahead of me. His fingers lace under the waistband of my underwear, carefully inching it down my legs. I don't absorb the fact that this is the first time he's gotten me completely naked until he sucks in a deep breath like he's been physically struck.

"Fuck," he stutters. "I cannot believe no one has ever taken the time to worship you like you deserve."

I tilt his face up to me. "Then why don't you show me what I'm missing?"

Hayden slides my legs over his shoulders as a touch of fingers dances up and down my outer thighs, tracing circles, hearts, whatever he can manage. He takes his time over every imperfection—the stretch marks and spidery veins along my hips, the uneven skin between my legs.

His tongue slides between me and, at once, I feel like I'm on fire. Every drop of water has dried up as my skin burns. I lean my head back against the mattress and shut my eyes. He is slow, methodical, and he breaks me down like he does with every theory, explanation, and story he tells. I worry about breaking his glasses as my legs contract around his head and the build burns in the pit of my stomach.

"Holy shit," I cry. The moan I let out is enough to let Bigfoot know not to come by, because we're more than busy. The ink on his chest and shoulder contracts and tightens with each movement and shift of muscle. He plucks at another stitch of composure with a deeper stroke, making my toes curl, voice crack, and heart race. Each taste, touch, kiss is an inch closer to bleeding me dry.

I shudder as I come, tugging at his hair. My entire body feels light and heavy at the same time, the sensations rushing through me so good it's almost painful. I can hardly feel my legs, but do I feel the prick of his beard moving up my body until he presses his forehead to mine.

He wraps me in his arms like something he's desperate to call his.

"How do you feel?" His voice is a fire hazard, low and smoky. My response is a weak nod and a pleading sigh for more. He laughs, kissing the side of my head softly, caressing my jaw with his thumb. "Good."

We meet in the middle for lazy but demanding kisses once again. I am so captivated by the feeling of his damp, silky waves between my fingers and his hard erection between my legs that I barely register him reaching into the duffel bag beside the bed and fishing out a small box of condoms.

"Did you just *have* those?" I ask. Presumptuous, but prepared. I won't Boy Scout–shame him in this moment.

"At the last gas station. After last night," he jokes, "I figured I should be prepared for anything."

As I help him tear open the top of the box, he finds my lips again and again.

"Yes, because you were clearly gunning to sleep with a hot Bigfoot you found in the woods."

His smile feels bright enough to break through the stormy rain clouds outside. "I was actually hoping that this girl I just can't stop thinking about would be interested. I have this conspiracy theory that she might like me back."

"Do you now?"

He gives a sure-as-shit grin and nods. I think of all the ways I can tell him I want him too, but the best I can imagine is sliding his boxers down his hips. The ink on his side bleeds down his hip beneath the waistband of his underwear. I follow the roots down his body like a map, and words dry up in my throat. "I'm optimistic about my findings," he assures me.

He tears open the condom with his teeth, tossing the wrapper aside and sliding it over himself with my help. I can't drag my eyes away from him—every sharp curve and angle of his entire body—and "distracted" is such a small word for how I feel. No man who makes his living talking about aliens has any right to be this gorgeous.

"Don't worry. I am fully ready to get illumi-naughty with you," I say, unable to keep my laugh in.

He smiles as his eyes darken, taking me in. I've been sitting on that one for a hot minute, knowing it'd be that final push toward a barrel full of gunpowder. He runs his fingers down the side of my face, down my chest, and holds on to my waist as he nudges my legs apart with his knee. He holds me against him, positioning himself between my legs. My eyes slip shut as he pushes into me, exploratory and teasing at first.

"Hayden." It slips out at the same time he gasps my name and tightens his grip on the bedsheets beneath us. Fuck, he feels so good and so made for me.

"You're okay?" he whispers, pushing strands of hair out of my face. His voice is so low, like even though it's just the two of us, he wants this moment to be as intimate as possible. I nod. Our fingertips meet at the frames of his glasses. Together, we slip them off and I place them on the nightstand beside us.

"Don't worry. I can see you perfectly fine." His lips dip to mine, and his hips rock into me. He is precise and methodical, but open to improvising as we learn each other.

Learning is exactly what it feels like. We listen to one

another—this feels good, this could be better . . . don't be afraid to go harder. I like the way his hands wander all over my body, the soft curses he lets out between kisses, and how each one is laced with a smile, like he feels lucky to have me. Our lips drift away like a boat tethered to the shore, but we always find our way back.

With his glasses off, Hayden might not be able to see every detail of this, but I'm so glad I can see all of him. I want to see the look on his face as I clutch his hair tighter, bite his lips, and tell him how good he feels. I never want to look away from the dark curls that fall around his face, still damp from the rain, brushing the hardly-there freckles on his nose and cheeks. I take a picture in my head at the way he weaves our fingers together, holding my hand against his chest. He cares about every second of this just as much as I do.

My legs hook around his back, and my nails rake against his shoulders. He laughs, he smiles, and he tells me I'm beautiful every chance he gets. I'm wanted as I am, as more than an object, and he wants to do this with me because it's *me* he cares about. I didn't believe sex could be like this—full of teasing, communication, and love.

He has my heart, and I can't imagine asking for it back.

"How do you feel?" he breathes.

His beard pricks beneath my fingertips, and when our eyes meet, I trace his lower lip with my thumb. I don't know what he can see, but even if I'm a blurry canvas of blue watercolor in Hayden's eyes, he looks at me like I'm his favorite work of art.

"Shocked you're not talking about Finland not existing right now."

"That . . ." he begins, trailing his lips along my jaw, down my throat, "is a very niche conspiracy theory, my little Non-believer. If I didn't know any better . . ."

I silence him with a kiss as heat festers in the pit of my stomach. Hayden grips my waist, the rolls of his hips coming quicker and more desperate. His lilts and moans more unhinged with each push. Hayden's voice cracks, stumbling over my name like it's a foreign language.

My legs tighten around his waist, one hand clutching the headboard behind me, but it's all he needs. We stumble over the finish line together. I nip at his lip a bit too hard as I come, but he doesn't mind. All he does is kiss me harder. I taste a twinge of blood in all our kisses as I lose feeling in my legs. I shudder around him, riding out the high spreading all over my body. Hayden whispers my name like he's learning it for the first time, kissing me softly yet desperately as my senses return to me.

All I can do next is wrap my arms around him where he collapses on top of me. I study each vertebra of his back, I listen to his breathing, and nothing feels like home like he does. I press lazy kisses against the top of his head, toying with the sweaty, rain-soaked waves that curl against the sides of his face.

"Hallie, you good?"

"Yeah, pretty good."

He laughs. "Good. Good, I'm glad."

"Can you excuse a rain check on Bigfoot hunting for this?"

"Yes, yes I definitely can."

CHAPTER 19

The cabin smells like bacon when I wake up.

Granted, the bacon smells a little burnt, but *any* bacon sounds good right about now. I push myself to my elbows. The space beside me in bed is cold already, but it's no reason for concern. Hayden has a few red-flag personality traits—mainly knowing where so many US military bases are and far too much about horrifying murders and monster sightings—but he also goes for runs early in the morning. I haven't willingly run anywhere in fifteen years.

The sheets still smell like him—no, like *us*—a woodsy musk mixed with rose and vanilla. As I pull myself out of bed, I hunt for my underwear and the first piece of clothing I can find, which so happens to be a heather-gray T-shirt that Hayden's left on the floor.

I pad into the kitchen, following the smell of breakfast. I find Hayden hovering over several browning pancakes and see bacon popping in a frying pan next to them. I eye a pot of fresh coffee, too. He's still wearing a sweaty Red Sox T-shirt and gym shorts, looking unfairly handsome. When I finish working out, I look like a damp gremlin. Except I don't duplicate. I lie on the couch until the pain stops.

Hayden finally looks up as I lean against the island counter, immediately breaking into a coy smile.

"Morning."

Before I can answer, his eyes drift lower to my shirt. He leans against the stove, arms crossing in front of his chest. He's beaming. Of course, we had an excellent time banging the hell out of one another several times the night before, but this is something else.

"What are you smiling about?"

"Your shirt—well, *my* shirt."

I finally look down and roll my eyes. The shirt's been run through the wash countless times and smells like him, like he's woven deep into the fabric itself. I drown in it, and if I belted it right, it'd be a trendy dress for brunch with Bigfoot. On the front of the shirt is the "I Want to Believe" image, and suddenly it all makes sense.

"You look good."

"You kill me," I spit back.

"You must *really* love me if you're willingly wearing an 'I Want to Believe' shirt. Like, *seriously* . . ."

Love. I stumble over the word and the way he *doesn't*. There are more and more moments lately where I look at him and the same word pops into my head, but to say it would be a confession. Someone wanting to love me sounds like a conspiracy theory I am not ready to relent to yet. I swallow my skepticism and slide toward him.

"I'm wearing it because it was the first article of clothing I could find. I'd never wear something like this publicly. *Ever.*"

Hayden's eyebrow rises as I wrap my arms around him.

One arm tends to the crackling bacon beside us and the other pulls me into a kiss. He tastes like coffee, mint toothpaste, and a skipped day of shaving. His kisses come rough and scratchy, but I can't argue or think to pull away.

"So, I'll know this is the real deal when I catch you wearing my *X-Files* T-shirt in public."

I nod. "Sure, we can agree to that."

"Good. You can keep it. I have three others."

I blink rapidly. "You . . . have three . . . you know what, no, I'm not going to ask you to elaborate."

"It's better that way," Hayden says with a wink.

Many things are better when I don't ask, like whether he wrote *X-Files* fan fiction in high school or if he'd actually be willing to get shot by a laser beam storming Area 51. I'm afraid to know.

"What are we having for breakfast?"

"Well," he begins, raising the spatula emphatically, "after my run, I realized we didn't have much food, so I went to the store. So, pancakes, some bacon, another box of condoms—"

"Are those in the toaster?"

"*No*. I mean . . . we have them now, is what I mean. The tiny pack I got at the gas station might run out before we get back home, at this rate."

I laugh and slide against his chest. He takes hold of me and kisses the top of my head. The forest is quiet, and we're the only cabin for some distance. The gutters drip rain outside, but the sun's breaking through the trees and into the heavily windowed living room. Hell, a bird even chirps in the distance somewhere. And the person I'm with wants to make me happy. It's more than I can ask for.

"Don't like me too much," he teases. "We still have to make up lost ground hunting for Bigfoot."

I grumble. "I was hoping you'd give up."

Hayden tilts my chin up, brushing his nose with mine. "Never."

♪ ♪ ♪

I return home to Nora watching HGTV with a grape-eating Lizzie nestled on her lap. As great as a weekend away was, I missed my bed, and I cannot wait to shower the woods from my hair and skin.

"Good job," she whispers to the lizard before looking up to me. "Hi. Did you find Bigfoot?"

"We did *not* find Bigfoot," I confirm, shedding my bags on the armchair. "We didn't find any Fresno Nightcrawlers or ghosts in the Winchester Mystery House, either. Though, if you ask Hayden, something untied his shoe in the house, so the verdict is still out. Good content. No cryptids."

"*That* should be your tagline. Of course, Hayden will never support that, but it's *true*."

I unzip my backpack, hunting for my phone, and Hayden's gray "I Want to Believe" shirt falls out of the bag and onto the floor. Nora's brows rise as she studies it.

"Wow. You've drunk the Kool-Aid, I guess."

"No, I . . ." I debate if I want to lie and say I do, in fact, have a UFO shirt, or if I would rather fess up and admit that it's not mine, but it's Nora. Nora, who saw me at my absolute worst. Nora, who was so strange and offbeat herself that she embraced everyone else's quirks too. Nora wouldn't judge me.

And I have an image to uphold, goddammit.

I can't have anyone think I believe in aliens.

"It's . . . uh . . . it's not mine. It's Hayden's."

Her eyebrows don't lower. "Uh-huh. I see you've hit the sharing-clothes stage of being co-hosts."

And *discarding* clothes, clearly.

"Never know when I'm going to need a costume for the show." I'm about as convincing as a poorly photoshopped picture of a cryptid, of which there are many, I've learned. Has it been clear to Nora that Hayden and I were falling into each other's orbits this whole time?

"Right."

Nora whistles the *Jeopardy!* theme song, tossing the T-shirt back to me. I shove it into my bag and let out a long sigh. "Fine, I slept with him."

"See?" She cheers. "That's a *far* more reasonable explanation."

"I . . ."

"Oh, come on, Hallie. It's like you haven't even watched any of your own episodes. Why do you think you have fan fiction written about you two—?"

"YOU PROMISED TO NEVER TELL ME!"

Her hands shoot up in surrender. "Okay, sorry. I did. It exists. It's . . ."

"Don't you dare."

". . . Out There."

I throw a pillow across the room at her. "I hate you."

"Your shippers are going to be so happy," Nora says.

"I don't know if we're going to talk about it yet." We haven't discussed it, but—for the sake of the show—I'm not sure we're going to go from zero to one hundred that fast. "I don't want it to cause . . . I don't know."

She's quiet as I sink into the couch, too. I cross my arms in front of my chest. All weekend, I was in a trance. Even in the most intense moments, I didn't stop to think about the implications of us being together.

"What'll happen is the internet will explode. At least your corner of it."

"Yeah . . ."

"It's something else?"

"It's Cade. Skroll."

"What about them?" she asks.

How could I tell her that I feared someone I'd cut out of my life? I still did things and worried what Cade would think. His claws dug into me for years, and now that he's pulled them out, it's like one of them has broken off and left itself embedded in my side.

"I knew this would happen when I eventually started dating again," I say. "I worried what Cade would say—"

"Who the fuck cares what that jerk-off thinks?"

"I *don't*. I worry about the repercussions. I worry what he'll say or do to me or my partner. I don't want them to get stuck in the cross fire of his bullshit."

"What could he do? Realistically, what could Cade do?"

"I don't know, Nora—tell people how terrible I am, or—"

She nudges my knee with hers. "So? He's arrogant and he only cares about himself. If he stops doing nasty shit, it's like he'll die or something. If he starts spewing bullshit about you or Hayden, I think it says more about his character than yours. Your fans aren't going to listen to a word of it.

"And if you let him dictate your happiness, you'll never be happy. You can't let him do that, Hal. If you pull away from the good and happy things in your life for the sake of easiness, where does that get you? You can't quit on yourself just because Cade sucks. He's always sucked. He's always *going* to suck." Her arms wave eagerly over her head. "The man is made of suck! But you left him so you could be happy. So that you didn't have to deal with his shit anymore. And I know it's hard to break that mindset, but you can't let him control you. He doesn't get to do that."

I pull into myself. I don't want Cade to have that power over me anymore. But I worry no one could love someone who paid as much mind to my ex as I did. How much of hearing about my hurt could Hayden handle before he decided I wasn't worth the trouble?

"How do you feel about Hayden?" Nora finally asks.

I don't know what I can tell her. What I do feel isn't easily put into words. It's the feeling of a warm bed, a crackling fire, a tight hug. It feels like being safe and brave at the same time.

"It's like I believe in something for the first time in so long."

"Like aliens?"

"Absolutely not."

Hayden's made his entire life about taking care of other people, often at his own expense. He's never expected something back. He doesn't expect me to hold him up, because he's so good at doing it himself, but I don't want to let him do it alone anymore. He finds the things that mean a lot to me and keeps doing them. He knows my coffee order, he consults with me before making choices. He wishes me "good night" every night because I mentioned I liked it *once*.

This has to be what falling in love feels like, and I know because it's unlike anything I've ever felt before.

It hurts in the best way.

"If Hayden makes you feel the way I think he does," Nora

says, "and trust me, it *is* obvious, then that's between the two of you. Cade doesn't get to decide what you can and can't do. Cade doesn't get to decide what makes you happy. And don't worry," she continues, "I think, if it came down to it, Hayden could take Cade in a hot second. Amazing—for someone who puts protein powder in everything he eats, Cade is surprisingly flimsy."

"In all ways."

"Except being an asshole! He's a real pro at that," she muses. "Shit, I *really* hope I get to see Hayden punch Cade at some point. That would make my life."

⸰ THE OUT THERE ⸰

Episode #7: "Fill Out the Survey So We Can Improve Future Abductions"

This week on The Out There, *Hayden and Hallie dive into cases of alien abductions. They cover probing, crop circles, and the extraterrestrial's apparent passion for latex bodysuits. Strap into your flying saucer, kids.*

HALLIE
  I have a question about crop circles.

HAYDEN
  Yeah?

HALLIE
  Are there crop circles accompanying every alien abduction?

HAYDEN

No, that'd mean the whole world is covered in corn. Which it's not. Crop circles are weird, and a lot of people think they're fake. Some people have come forward and claimed they made crop circles themselves, which is very possible.

HALLIE

It still seems like a lot of work.

HAYDEN

It is! That's why I don't even know what I believe. Obviously, it could be done by humans looking for clout, but some of them are so large and utilize sacred geometry so well that it would be way easier if you were hovering above in a flying saucer with a little laser.

HALLIE

True. But I guess what I want to know is, why would aliens make them in the first place? Is it to send a message? Is this the alien equivalent of writing "blank was here" on bathroom stalls?

HAYDEN

It's way cooler than that. They at least display skill.

HALLIE

I do like the idea that aliens come to Earth to do arts and crafts. That's nice.

HAYDEN

Did you just say that "aliens come to Earth"? I want to hear it again.

HALLIE

Hypothetically. I meant hypothetically. And I'm going to follow it up by saying that they aren't just *doing arts and crafts*—the little green men are ass-men.

HAYDEN

Excuse me?

HALLIE

The probing! Why do they have a thing for butts? Of all the parts of the human body to pick . . . it's always your ass.

HAYDEN

It's not meant to be sexy. It's for science, but to refute your point, there have been cases where they've gone in through the belly button, so when you do get abducted by aliens, make sure to let them know you'd like the belly-button option instead of the ass option.

HALLIE

They'd ask?

HAYDEN

Oh yeah, they ask you at the door.

COMMENTS

SlimGiggly

Call me a conspiracy theorist, but they're looking at each other differently in this episode . . .

Blucifer

@SlimGiggly agree

FlatwoodsBabe201

@SlimGiggly @Blucifer if it's of interest to you, another fan put together a breakdown of how many times they touch each other per episode. The number has gone up at least two touches over the past several episodes. It's exponential growth.

DeanVengeance

@FlatwoodsBabe201 that is not how exponential growth works

FlatEarthRoundAss

For the Haylie Shippers, check out the latest installment of my multi-chapter fic "five times Hallie didn't believe Hayden (and one time she did)"

<link>

CHAPTER 20

For years, all Cade wanted was to be a regular guest around the convention circuit. He begged Kevin to get him into the big ones—SDCC, WonderCon, NYCC—and there'd been no luck. I feel an alarming sense of pride in the fact that I have been asked to attend a convention before he has.

Of course, Cade would not be caught dead at CON-Spiracy—and several months ago, neither would I, but I'm on a *panel.*

Take that, asshole.

"I'm typically not one of the more normal-looking people in a room."

Blue hair makes me stand out everywhere I go and makes little children think I'm cool and adults think I am a witch. While Hayden has opted for his usual casual uniform of jeans, an offbeat T-shirt (today it's a Majestic 12 T-shirt), and a flannel shrugged over his shoulders, I've tried to look as serious as I can. Jeans and a gray turtleneck with a black blazer on top. I look like a contemporary Dana Scully, which explains why Hayden hasn't been able to stop eyeing me.

But compared to the attendees of CON-Spiracy, I look like I should be taking calls for a very important lawyer or something. It's a convention in LA, exclusively dedicated to the strange and unexplained. It's not a place I ever expected to be, but I fit in alarmingly well.

"You know," Nora chirps, fixing a stray hair coming from my bun, "me either!"

"Everyone misses you because you're too tiny," Jamie says, propping his elbow on her head. Her face and entire body scrunch in annoyance. She wiggles out from underneath his grip and clutches her notebook.

"*You* don't," she replies.

"I must have taste."

"You go to Fathom Events at the movie theaters."

Hayden steps into our meeting room at the LA Convention Center, four badges in hand.

The small plastic badge is shaped like an alien head, but in place of big beady eyes, there's a sticker at the center:

HALLIE BARRETT
TALENT
THE OUT THERE

Giddy energy courses through me. I guess I never expected to be *known* for the things I did, not publicly. My name was on Skroll videos for years, and I appeared in some of Cade's videos here and there, but it did little more than garner me a small bundle of Twitter and Instagram followers. I was "The Girlfriend." I just *happened* to be there.

Since *The Out There*'s premiered, my following has expanded tenfold. I feel more pressured to post because people *care* what I have to say. They want pictures of the two of us goofing off and our B-roll. For some reason, they want to know what hair dye I use.

People ask my opinion, and when I give it, it's valued.

This is all new and unfamiliar, and if it brings me to a conspiracy theory–themed convention, so be it.

I do wonder if I'm going to be a pariah here with my sheeple aura. Will they know right away I am the resident skeptic? Granted, I'm less concerned while reading the program than I would have been months ago.

Worms from Space: A Dive Underground

Portals & Points of No Return

Bohemian Grove: Woodland Hanky-Panky
or Something Worse?

I do wonder if I'm best off playing my role. If we've been invited as Hayden and Hallie of *The Out There*, the people will be expecting me to poke holes in everything he says and play the straight man onstage.

Hayden drapes my badge over my head before passing the other two to Jamie and Nora.

"All right, we're official. That'll get you two into any panel you want and into several of the autograph signings."

Jamie raises an eyebrow. "Excellent, I was really hoping to get my copy of Bigfoot erotica signed. Regardless, this is great press for the show. This isn't an audience that would be tuning in to Skroll's content."

I wonder if it'll be enough to knock *Noobie Brothers* from the top spot. Our Bigfoot episode raked in larger-than-usual numbers, but *Noobie Brothers* saw a spike as well. The rest of the shows are trailing far behind both of us.

"No," Hayden agrees, "they don't know Skroll. But they

know me, and soon they'll know Skroll too. I knew buying Bernard that drink two years ago would come in handy one day. Shame about Mark, though."

"What . . . happened to him?" I ask. We hadn't originally planned on attending CON-Spiracy. It came to us as a happy accident when Mark Larkin, an allegedly hip and renowned ufologist, suddenly couldn't make it. Bernard, another researcher Hayden met at a *different* conspiracy convention, needed a last-minute replacement on a panel.

"He took a trip to Mount Shasta."

"And he extended?"

Mount Shasta wasn't too far from where we hunted Bigfoot. Northern California is lovely, so I understand why a guy would want to take a nice long vacation up in the mountains.

"No. He took a trip to *Mount Shasta*. Remember what we talked about? Mount Shasta is a portal to another dimension. He isn't coming back."

"You are awfully concerned."

Nora and Jamie usually see us at Medium Professional. When we get to the Skroll offices, we have scripts, clips, and talking points. They see us flub words and break character to laugh. They do not see all . . . this.

They're not subject to the shouting matches where Hayden and I volley back and forth on some of his more ridiculous theories. We aren't really *arguing* with one another. It's not personal. If Hayden chooses to take my dismissal of the theory that George Washington met with aliens at the battle of Valley Forge personally, that is something he needs to work out himself and discuss with his psychiatrist.

Hayden holds his hands up in surrender. "He knew the risks, and he went anyway."

"Harsh."

We migrate through crowds of attendees, lined up for book signings and photo ops with notable figures in the Fortean community. A few giddy young girls stop us and ask Hayden for a picture; another random man asks him for an autograph. A third random man intercepts us entirely. I'm lost but listen intently anyway. There's something about monoliths in Antarctica and ley lines. Hayden answers politically, saying he can't offer comments on the matter right now.

We make our way to our exhibit hall, a small room with a hundred or so chairs rowed up against an elevated stage with a long panel table. Attendees filter into the room, and other panelists claim their seats behind the placards. Hayden casually chats with the individuals he knows, introducing me as his "partner." I like this better than "co-host." We are partners. What we do is *ours*.

We find our seats and I snap photos of our nameplates because this is fucking cool, and a sudden rush of anxiety sweeps over me. I'm about to face an entire gaggle of conspiracy theorists with my skepticism and I don't know how that'll be received. I wonder if they'll throw tomatoes. I'm afraid of the kinds of questions we'll be asked.

When we're blocked mostly by the table, Hayden gives the small of my back a rub, sensing my nervousness. Meanwhile, he's in his element.

The topic is "The Unexplained in the Digital Media Age," which I feel confident I can talk about from a technical standpoint. My producer background might come in handy here. I know how to market a lot of things. I even know how to market cryptids and monsters.

The moderator runs down the panel, listing renowned

ufologists and demonologists who've gone viral or hit it big with their shows on streaming sites. Hayden covertly informs me how the moderator, Nina, got famous reacting to scary videos on YouTube. As she reaches Hayden and me, she notes quickly that Mark Larkin couldn't make it and sends his apologies.

"No, he doesn't," Hayden whispers away from the mic.

There's a smattering of applause before Nina begins leading the panel. Her first question centers on how the panelists choose to use more contemporary mediums to display their work. Hayden offers a curt response about how it allowed him to do what he loved but be close to family. We volley through questions about work histories, most intriguing finds. Finally, Nina refers to Hayden's earlier statement and directs the next question to him.

"Now, Hayden, I am glad you brought up what you did earlier. Obviously, we're at a point in time where everyone has a smartphone, everyone's heard of YouTube, all in the palm of their hand. How would you say the digital age has made hunting for the otherworldly more accessible?"

He leans forward, clearing his throat. "Well, the most important part is that *anyone* can do it now. I think about people's viral videos and their experiences that they've documented, and these are *normal* people. You don't need fancy ghost-hunting equipment or anything to share what you've lived through. I think it highlights how *odd* the world is and how often people encounter these types of things."

Nina laughs. "Now, considering what you've said, I want to hear from Hallie—he says the world is odd. Meanwhile, you are a known skeptic. I've been having such a fun time with *The Out There* these past few weeks, so congrats on the quick success. But you *are* dismissive of a lot of the things Hayden wants to talk about."

I lean forward on the mic. "Well, isn't that evidence enough that *anyone* can get involved in this?"

A small series of giggles. "I suppose so. How did you get involved in the first place?"

"Well, I've been with Skroll for several years now, and a lot of what I did was produce other series and other things behind the camera. When I was looking for a prospective show, I stumbled upon Hayden on *Cosmic Conspiracies.*"

"Great episode," one of the other panelists says.

"Hayden here was talking about how Bigfoot might have been an alien and, granted, it was super late at night, and I might have been inebriated, but it was the most captivating thing in the world—"

"But you don't believe in it," Nina argues.

"Sure, but orcs and elves and stuff aren't real either and we watch twelve hours of *Lord of the Rings* without question. And whether you believe in it or not, it *is* interesting. Plus, Hayden is a spectacular writer. He made someone like me want to work with him right away."

"So maybe it's genetic?" Nina proposes.

Hayden shifts in his seat and bites on his lip as she says this. He's had people ask him to sign his dad's books here, which he kindly refuses, understandably so. Instead of opening up about his dad, he leans into the mic. "It's either genetic, or all the *X-Files* fan fiction I wrote in high school."

"I knew it!" I shout, garnering laughs. Then I pivot back to the actual conversation. "I wasn't initially supposed to be on the show with him, but—"

"Everything's better with her involved," Hayden interrupts.

"*The Out There* would only be half of what it is without her co-hosting. She brings a charm and perspective to the show that it never had before."

I bite my lip and his hand rests along the inside of my thigh. I know the look I give him is telling, but I can't help it. I spent months questioning if anything I did was worth it, if anyone wanted to hear what I had to say. I did stand out, and I did matter. I made things *better*.

"No one can antagonize me like Hallie can," Hayden continues. "And that's not necessarily a bad thing. It's good to have someone challenge me, otherwise it's just me talking in circles. It tests the rigor of my theories, too. As much as I tried to be well-rounded, nothing humbles you like someone telling you you've lost your mind in front of God knows how many viewers."

"And how does that translate off-screen?" Nina asks.

We're silent for a moment. How does that translate off-screen? Taking each other's clothes off, banging while we're supposed to be Bigfoot hunting, me only getting bits and pieces of *The X-Files* between kisses.

"I don't take the arguments we have personally," Hayden asserts.

"And I don't hold the weird parts against him," I finish. Clean save. "Where we butt heads is where the magic happens. Regardless of what weird shit Hayden says, I respect his right to say that weird shit. He's also great in that he doesn't let the harmful conspiracy theories have much attention. If he does, he's going to point out why they hurt people. I can respect that. And he does make you think . . . sometimes I don't know what he makes me think about, *but* I am thinking."

"As someone who listened to the podcast beforehand,"

Amara, one of the other panelists, adds, "I think it's made the show more personable. And the way Hallie pushes your buttons is hilarious. Honestly, she has some good points."

"Uh, but I do too," Hayden scoffs as I cheer, "Thank you!"

We wind down the panel. Most of the Q&A questions are oddly specific and directed at the other panelists, but that is perfectly fine by me. Another asks about my hair dye. I'm going to have to ask the company to pay me, at this rate. I guess I have to keep the blue hair as part of the brand™.

As we disembark from the stage, we reconvene with Nora and Jamie, who have been taking photos and posting to the socials as we spoke. I feel hopped up on energy and importance. I feel *seen* and like I've stood out and—the whole time—Hayden was happy for it. He never tried to drag me down, instead bouncing questions to me when he *knew* I'd have something funny to say, and he never scowled at me as I interrupted to banter with him. This is how we are. We love each other's weirds.

In fact, I think I fall for Hayden most when he's at his strangest.

Hayden advised—as a third-time attendee of CON-Spiracy—that the exhibit halls aren't terribly large, so we did not need to spend an entire day there. We wander around the central hall a few times, posing in mock alien test tanks, and he makes the rounds on writers and researchers he's featured on his show. This is so his element it hurts, but I love this side of him.

The second Hayden steps into a world where he knows he's accepted, he thrives. He's kind and considerate, taking time for even the most curious fans, and I have yet to see him miss a beat.

The four of us agree on drinks at a nearby bar after we've checked our CON-Spiracy boxes. Over a whopping plate of nachos and beers, I know there's a place for me within this weird little world. I never anticipated the comfort it'd bring me, and I have to believe there are more good, exciting things ahead.

At one point, both Jamie and Nora disappear to the bathroom, leaving the two of us alone together.

"You were spectacular today."

I smile. "Really?"

"Really."

"So were you. I like seeing you like this—"

"Peak weird?"

"*No.* Smart. Comfortable. Authentic. It's what I saw that night on *Cosmic Conspiracies.* I knew there was something special about you. It's uncomfortably sexy."

Hayden's lip twitches up, and with a quick glance toward the bathrooms, he leans in. Our lips meet with the taste of blond ale, and I wince at the mild twinges of jalapeño from the nachos.

He finishes with a kiss on the nose before anyone sees us together.

* * *

It's well past sundown when my phone buzzes on Hayden's counter. I ignore it for the moment.

"You cannot *teleport* an entire battleship," I insist.

"Um, have you tried? Look, they're talking about how some of the crew's arms and legs were embedded into the hull of the ship. While they were still *alive*," Hayden says, gesturing wildly with a carton full of lo mein at the docuseries on TV about the Philadelphia Experiment.

My phone continues to buzz. This time, I pick it up. My screen is ablaze with notifications. I partially expected it to be my mother or someone telling me that a family member died, but no. It's all social media comments. We'd been more active than normal today. But nothing we've ever posted has gotten us *this* much activity.

"What is it?" he asks.

I scroll and my heart rate picks up.

I KNEW IT.

Omg y'all

screaming, crying, throwing up

Do u think they will break up by the time I turn eighteen? I'm fifteen now. I was so hoping he wouldn't find someone until he had the chance to meet me.

There are so many heart eyes and crying emojis I don't know what to make of it. I see how many new photos I've been added in, and it's a lot for one day at a passably well-attended convention. CON-Spiracy is not San Diego Comic-Con by any means. Then, I see exactly why.

It's a photo from happy hour when Jamie and Nora went to the bathroom. Hayden's hand spans the side of my face and I'm clutching the fabric of his flannel. There is no question what we're doing. I can feel the taste of his lips against mine, the soft kisses that follow the first, teasing and adorable. But now it feels like a secret spread too wide and nausea builds in my gut.

"Hayden . . ."

I slide the phone across the kitchen island to him, and he

softens, blushing. I wish I could share his enthusiasm and affection.

"Aw," he says, head tilting like a puppy, then he registers my expression. "We look cute, but I guess this isn't exactly how we planned to go public. Are you okay with the world knowing you're banging the conspiracy theorist?"

"No," I huff. "It isn't like that at all."

After a moment's consideration, Hayden drops his food and leans across the table, clutching my hands. "What is it, then?"

"I'm not ashamed of you. I don't think you're weird or feel embarrassed about what you do. I just . . ."

"Everyone knows now?"

I nod.

His fingers weave between mine.

"We weren't going to be able to keep it under wraps forever," he says. "I was going to suggest we go public in the season finale."

The way he talks about it, it sounds like there's such a future here. I think of a day when I don't co-host *The Out There*, and I suddenly don't know what I'll do. I'm so proud of what we've built together, and I'm proud of what this show has done for me personally. I feel invigorated to create again; I am full of ideas and excitement, and I thought that part of me had died out.

What's happening now isn't a short fling between us that'll fizzle out if we get canceled. For the first time in so long, I believe there's a chance I could love again. I don't know when I'll be ready to say it, but the itching, tugging feeling in my chest tells me it's not as far away as I think.

"The more attention on us, the more they have to use against us."

Hayden rounds the counter and takes the barstool beside me, tugging it closer to my chair. "What do you mean? Are we not allowed to date? Is that a Skroll rule? I thought we just couldn't get arrested."

"No, there's no rules about that. Everyone knew I was dating Cade, but now that I'm with you, that's two in a row. That might look . . ."

"I get it." His fingers trace up and down my arm. "I'm not ashamed of anything we've done together, or anything we've built. The two of us are a team. Whatever someone throws at either of us, Hal, they're going to throw at both of us."

I know he's formulating scenarios in his head. Since I'm a woman in the media, the guillotine will always come down much harder on me. There'll always be someone commenting on how I dress, what I weigh, if my voice is annoying or not, and I've learned to live with that. Fuck, I learned to live with someone doing it in my own home. But I don't have to anymore.

"If anyone tries to say anything that hurts you, I hope you know I'd be the first person to fight back," Hayden promises.

"I know."

Hayden brushes my hair out of my face. "There isn't anything we can do now that the cat's out of the bag—"

Somewhere, deep in the apartment, Cthulhu mewls, and we both laugh.

"He's mad we're eating and he isn't."

"Feed your child, Hayden."

"He has kibble."

"He needs wet food," I say, leaning in. Hayden toys with the bottom of my sleeve, parting his lips as he meets me in the middle.

"He has *kibble*. Let a man eat his noodles first."

He finishes with a kiss before cracking open a can of cat food that has Cthulhu bolting faster than a shambling cat should. He leaps onto the counter, ignoring me, but mewling eagerly as Hayden feeds him. He flops happily on the counter. Hayden gives him a soft belly rub and a kiss on the head.

For the moment, I forget about our furiously happy fans and the people who might use our relationship against us. All I can think about is the rest of tonight: eating takeout, drinking beer, and curling up with Hayden as we work our way through *The X-Files* together.

CHAPTER 21

There are plenty of things to dislike about corporate company bullshit, like inspirational All Hands meetings, appreciation pizza parties instead of raises, and the word "synergy" as a whole.

But it's hard to dislike the open bars at the swanky quarterly parties Skroll throws for the employees. Tonight's "Skroll into Spring" mixer is going to be held at an uppity rooftop bar and boasts everything from said open bars to a photo booth and the chance to win "exciting prizes" that are not raises either.

It was a Skroll party that started my entire relationship with Cade. Clearly, Skroll parties do not lead to good life choices.

I can tell tonight is going to be different. I spent years needing to be seen, trying to grab whatever pockets of spotlight I could, but tonight, I know I have the chance to bask in it.

In the wake of our appearance at CON-Spiracy, we saw a small bump that we expected to plateau, but our numbers kept growing. Our backlist saw plenty of action, too. Our comment sections fill up minutes after posting a video, our social media posts garner everything from "omg" to "stop" to "I ship this so hard." The fandom is still torn on what our ship name is, but "Haylie" tends to win out and seems to fit better in a weird white lady's pregnancy announcement or what someone incorrectly shouts when my Starbucks order is ready.

If Skroll were to pick a winner right now, we'd be full speed ahead on planning season two.

"So, I know you didn't ask, but *that* is why I have Zak Bagans blocked on all forms of social media." Hayden concludes the tangent I indeed did not ask for as he runs his fingers through his hair. We're crammed in his tiny bathroom together and the air smells like hairspray, heat-damaged hair, and a more expensive, sharp, citrusy musk of his cologne he only whips out for "special occasions."

"... Right." I've lowered my mascara wand for the time being to lessen the chances of an eye-makeup catastrophe in the middle of his tirade. "Well, you showed him, I guess."

Hayden meets my eyes in the mirror and his track down my body, taking in my outfit for the evening. There's so much joy in the fact that Hayden likes me in whatever I wear, but I also like the look of hunger in his eyes as he studies the off-the-shoulders blue dress I have on.

The only thing that'd feel better than his gaze would be his hands all over me.

"What?" I tease. "I look good or something?"

"I don't hate it, that's for sure." I feel his voice against my bare shoulders with the brush of scruff along my skin. Then he finishes with his lips. I lean into him, the satin of my dress meeting the sharp crinkle of his black button-down. The sleeves are rolled to the center of his forearms. The Not Deer on his arm crosses in front of me, claiming me as his.

"You're going to mess up my hair and makeup," I whisper as his lips climb to the side of my neck.

"I think as Skroll's hottest show at the moment, we can afford to be a few minutes late." His voice comes out near a growl, so low it hooks something in my stomach and has me pushing him toward the door and into his room.

I fall onto his comforter, enveloped in the taste, smell, and feel of him as his lips catch mine. Our kisses taste like fresh-brushed teeth and fruity lip gloss and each one is the best kind of drowning—little room to come up for air before I'm tasting him again and dying for the soft, heady moans that come from the back of his throat.

Hayden's hand grips my thigh, teasing under the hem of my dress. He works his way down my legs, sliding his fingers behind my knee and hooking my leg around his body. Every intimate moment with Hayden is a "eureka" in itself. When he kisses me, I realize this is how it should be. With each laugh and giggle when someone elbows the other, I know that I don't need to impress him, because it's me he wants. It's him I always want, too. *This* is what everyone talks about and yearns for.

"And if we do get in trouble," he breathes against the curve of my neck, "I'm blaming you."

"Uh, rude," I laugh, smacking his shoulder.

"*You're* the rude one for looking as beautiful as you do."

"And you're not half-bad either," I tell him. He does look good and I think he knows it. It's amazing what a little hair-spray can do for a man. His dark waves are fluffed higher, usually how his hair looks after some mild to moderate sexual activity, and he's kept his beard trimmed into a strategic five-o'clock shadow. I kiss him one final time before sliding from beneath him. I put the finishing touches on my look while he feeds Cthulhu and hails an Uber to the bar.

The rooftop bar is decorated with lined plants and globe lights stroking against the night sky. Skroll has infiltrated the bar with pop-up photo spots and gimmicky props. There's an open bar at every corner, and we hit the nearest one. Funky indie beats blast over the city above the hum of cars stuck in traffic. Typical LA.

Across the rooftop, Nora and Jamie have stationed themselves in the photo booth, her propping a fedora on his head as he lovingly drapes a neon pink boa over her shoulders. It's hard to read Jamie sometimes, with his quiet stares and deliberately chosen words, but around Nora, he's an open book. Happy, vibrant, like she's unlocked the box full of all of the things he tries to keep under wraps.

Drinks in hand, Hayden and I decide how we want to tackle this. He doesn't know many people, and Skroll has never been a firm nine-to-five-type office, so I see most people in passing. But the truest shock is the way we don't even get to pick who we talk to first, because there's a line of people who want to talk to *us*. Other producers I've worked with over the years express admiration for how well I've transitioned from behind to in front of the camera, and everyone wants to meet Hayden.

It's how I discover that many of my coworkers are closet *Cosmic Conspiracies* fans, who have relatives who did camping trips to hunt for Bigfoot, too, who visited Roswell and claim to have seen a UFO before.

It doesn't take long for Chloe to push through the crowd to reach us. She meets me with a hug and pats Hayden lovingly on the cheek, as if she's known him for years. Clearly, she's had a three-martini happy hour already.

"Well, look at you guys," she says. I'm suddenly so aware of

Hayden's fingers woven between mine. It's where Chloe's eyes go too. "I can't say I saw this when you pitched me a show about hunting for ghosts."

I wonder if she means our success or the blossoming relationship between us.

"Neither did we," Hayden agrees. "We may not have found Bigfoot yet, but . . . I think we've found something good."

Chloe softens. "There's a reason your show is doing so well. It's because the two of you . . . have something. I don't know what it is, but there's something magnetic about your chemistry. I think there's a lot of people wanting to see you two succeed. Oh—Champ!"

"Oh, this guy coming? You need to call him Champ," I whisper to Hayden.

Hayden's eyes widen, then narrow. "You mean like the lake monster?"

"No, absolutely *not* like the lake monster."

I stiffen as she ushers Champ Kevin over to our group. He hardly comes up to Hayden's shoulders and he's dressed like he's trying to be cool—trendy skinny jeans, a white T-shirt, and a leather jacket, holding a can of hard kombucha. But it doesn't matter. I'll tell him he looks good anyway.

"Champ, you of course know Hallie," Chloe says. Kevin offers me a half hug and a kiss on the cheek, telling me I look wonderful. "And her new partner, Hayden."

"Ah, the real Man in Black himself." They exchange an unbalanced, manly handshake. "Huge fan of your father's work, too. It was a huge loss when he passed."

Hayden bristles beside me.

"And I'm obviously sorry for your loss as well."

"Thank you," Hayden says. "I like to think he'd be proud of

what we've been doing these past few months. The ghosts and monsters were always his thing."

"You know, I liked the idea when Hallie first pitched it, but I wasn't entirely certain how people would respond to it. It turns out people really do like this sort of content. I never would have guessed."

"I never would have expected I'd be so happy hunting for Bigfoot, either," I add.

"So . . . it's really not an act?" Kevin asks me. "Like, you really don't believe any of this?"

"It is absolutely not an act," Hayden says, sipping his drink.

"Champ, I promise you, I am not *nearly* that good of an actress." He lets out what I think can only be described as a snicker. It's weird and makes Hayden let out a nervous laugh because he's not sure how to respond either. But a snicker from Kevin is a good sign. Hell yes for snickers.

"And to think we were hiding you behind the camera that whole time." He crosses his arms and his eyes are wide in bewilderment. "I know you were so busy helping Cade out all those years, but—"

Kevin should consider a career in demon summoning, because just as he says the name, Cade exits the elevator with Skroll's new social media manager on his arm. She can't be more than twenty-three to his thirty, with full lips, a tiny waist, and a killer pair of hips. She looks like she came right out of a sponsored Instagram picture. Someone as gorgeous as her could have anyone she wanted. My stomach clenches. I feel like I should have warned her about what a monster he is.

Immediately, this asshole spots Kevin and infiltrates our conversation. I reach for Hayden's hand as Cade approaches us. Hayden's fingers curl around mine in a way that tells me nothing can hurt me. I love the safety he offers, but I know I'm strong enough to hold the net up myself. Cade is only a monster to me if I let him in my closet, under my bed.

"*Chaaaaamp*," Cade coos at Kevin. They embrace in a garishly corny hug with large backslaps, for some goddamn reason. "Good to see you, my man."

As if they don't see each other several times a week in the office.

"And you too, Chloe."

"Cade," Chloe acknowledges, but she acknowledges her gin and tonic even more after the fact.

Cade turns back to his date. "Babe, grab me a vodka soda, please."

His date looks ready to say something or enter the conversation, but when Cade's eyes narrow with a sickly-sweet glare I know so well, she backs away and waits in line at the bar.

"We know you know Hallie," Kevin says.

"A little too well," Cade says, nudging Kevin's arm. "I'm just kidding. I've met her new partner, too."

"We were actually just talking about you."

"Oh, really? What about?"

"Well, really, about Hallie, actually." Kevin course corrects and Cade deflates, the life fading from his sparkling eyes. "We were talking about how she was working with you for so long, but was never really the star of the show, you know? She'd pop up here and there, but she was never center stage and I can't believe it. We had a star on our hands this whole time, and never knew!"

Kevin talks about me like he's discovered gold in them there Hollywood Hills and Cade's nothing more than another dull rock. I know the look of rage in his eyes—a calm facade, the eye of the storm before whipping winds wreak havoc. He won't cause a scene here, at least.

"It's true. I mean, Chloe," Hayden starts, "you remember how that first episode went. I was wooden as hell until Hallie stepped in. *The Out There* would have been canceled after like ten seconds—"

"Oh, come on!" I say. "I knew you had something magic in you, too. I didn't pick you out from *Cosmic Conspiracies* for no reason. You being astonishingly pretty was only seventy-five percent of the rationale."

"Yeah, I sure misled you on the acting part. That first episode was abysmal."

"Oh, that isn't true," Chloe says, then reconsiders. "Okay, that first episode was rough."

"*So* rough," Hayden replies. He glances over at Cade. "It totally explains how you got the platform you did, Cade. She's brilliant on-camera or off-camera, so I can't imagine how lucky you'd be to have her guiding you to stardom all those years."

My god, he's gone right for the jugular. I try not to smile, but the pride I feel is ready to burst out. Hayden might be right. The reason Cade has what he does is because of me. He was just the pretty topping to it all, but none of the ingredients.

Cade bites down on his lip, eventually settling on a resigned, tight smile. "Of course. All thanks to Hallie, no doubt."

I lean in closer to Hayden, his hand slipping back to my hip, visible so Cade can see his hands on me. His lips meet the side of my head and my fear about being spotted with him and flashing our relationship out in the open dissipates as Chloe coos and Kevin looks as happy as a weird little clam.

"I have to tell you," Kevin begins, "it is so inspiring that you and Cade have maintained such a strong professional relationship and that stunning careers like yours have all bloomed at Skroll. That's what Skroll is all about."

No, Skroll is about clickbait and sponsorships.

"And I'm so happy to see our two exceptional shows here tonight. Obviously, every show in the program is spectacular, but the numbers we're seeing from both *Noobie Brothers* and *The Out There* are fantastic. It's going to be hard to choose just one."

"I don't envy you," Cade adds. "You've got a tough decision to make, but it's a testament to how skilled you are at finding superb talent, Champ. I mean it."

My stomach churns hearing him kiss Kevin's ass like this. He won't hurt Kevin like he'd hurt me, like he's probably bullying poor Madi now to get extra posts on Skroll's socials, but it sucks to see another person falling into his web. There is no person Cade doesn't view as potential prey to feed his ego.

"We're looking forward to the rest of the seasons, though," Kevin finishes, raising a glass. "And we'll see where these shows go."

We clink glasses in the middle and Cade's eyes wander over to me. I want to tell him I know what his game is and no matter what he does, Hayden and I are going to beat him. I stand up tall and even as he tries to strip down my defenses with his glares, I don't let him claim a victory over me.

He isn't going to beat our show, either.

"Champ, if you don't mind," Cade interrupts, "I have something timely I'd love to have a word about."

Kevin, like the obedient puppy he is, agrees. Chloe's quickly whisked away and, once we're alone again, I let out a deep breath. Hayden rubs the small of my back and takes a *long* sip of his drink.

"We're going to crush that asshole," is all he says, his inner Angry Boston Man coming out to the party. I clutch a handful of his shirt and step closer, standing on my toes to reach his lips.

"Oh, you know it," I say with a kiss.

We schmooze our way through the party and our popularity doesn't wane. As more coworkers arrive and more drinks get flowing, it seems like maybe we should set up an autograph table or something. People who flocked to Cade at every other party give him a passing wave on their way to us.

We take a few photos in one of the photo booths with Nora and Jamie, and I imagine the strip going up on the corkboard beside Hayden's bed.

When Hayden and I part so he can use the bathroom, I form an alliance with the food table and the last coconut shrimp and am actually a little grateful to take a break. We've been so busy being the talk of the party that I missed all the mini spring rolls being paraded around, dammit.

"I'd watch out, if I were you." A chill runs up my back. "Your dress is already looking tight."

Cade's touch runs along the curve of my hip before he circles around me and leans against the table. I'm suddenly glad I haven't had much chance to eat, because I might be sick, but instead of allowing Cade a win, I suck in a breath and turn to him.

"Do you really want your new girlfriend to see you touching some other girl?"

He chuckles and mischief brims in his eyes. "Somehow, I think she'll be okay with it, like you were years ago. I hope she stays a nice girl. You sure didn't."

"She's pretty. Out of your league."

"So I should be with someone more like you? Average?" When I don't have a response, he drops the joking act and steps closer to me. "I know what you're up to, Hallie. This game you two are playing—"

"What game, Cade? The one where I beat you in this program fair and square? Is that what you're so scared of? Is that why you lash out every time I get a win over you?" I step closer to him. Since I'm in my heels, our eyes are nearly even. There is no big and small now. Cade doesn't know what to do when he can't punch down. "Are you terrified that everyone will find out it was *me* making you look good all those years? That you have little to stand on without me, and your talent's running out?"

"Do you have anything to stand on aside from spreading your legs for every—?"

Cade quiets as Hayden's arms slip around my back again.

"Cade," he says. His voice is icy and sharp as a knife. He's shed the easygoing, charismatic host persona he's been carrying so well all night. Now, this is someone who knows the worst things Cade's done to me and brushes the lies Cade tells about me off as easily as I brush off his wackiest theories.

"Hallie and I were catching up." Cade takes a step closer to me. Before his hand can rise to toy with one of my curls, Hayden's hand shoots out, clutching Cade's wrist.

"Did Hallie say you could touch her?"

Cade holds his hands up in surrender and laughs. "Damn, you're awfully protective of a girl who is only using you to beat me. You do know that, right? She doesn't actually care about your show and she probably doesn't care about you either. She won't if you two don't win the program." I still and watch Hayden's eyes darken as Cade continues.

"I warned you, dude," Cade continues. "Hallie's a tough one to work with. A tough one to love. Being with her . . . it's a bad choice, man."

I can't break my composure now, no matter how badly I want to. Tough to love sounds so much worse than tough to work with. Tough to work with means the unbearable parts of me can go off duty. But . . . tough to love . . .

"I think I can make my own bad choices, thank you very much," Hayden says. "So far, the only bad choice I've made is starting a conversation with you."

"I'm just trying to temper your expectations. One day, she'll leave you just like she did to me. She'll find another ladder to climb at Skroll and start fresh." Hayden's entire body radiates heat and anger. His fingers tighten around the fabric at my hip. "When you can't deliver her a win, trust me, she'll be over fucking the conspiracy theorist she found on Reddit *real* fast."

Hayden finishes his drink and sets the glass on the table with a harsh thump. "You can say whatever you'd like about me. I've heard it all already, and I don't lose sleep over the opinions of a thirty-year-old frat boy. But you leave her out of it . . ."

I've never heard his voice slip this deep before. There's no lovable sleepy rasp from late nights recording or researching, or the lazy mornings where we stay in bed too long. It's deliberate and chilling in a way that makes Cade blink faster and take notice of how much larger Hayden is. If one of them *were* to throw punches, I know who I'd have my money on.

"I could grab another drink, sit around, and tell you how much I care for Hallie—how special she is—and what an *idiot* you are for mistreating her. But you wouldn't listen, so I'm not going to waste my breath. I can't believe I already have."

Hayden slips me behind him, creating a barrier between Cade and me. "If I hear of you trying to hurt her and, so help me God, if you ever lay a hand on her—"

"What?" Cade chuckles. "What'll you do? Skroll's still pissed about Eric's legal trouble. Wouldn't want either of us getting canceled over something silly. Are you really going to get your show canceled over her? Trust me. She isn't worth it."

"Hayden," I interrupt. "He's right."

We are too close to fuck this up, way too close, no matter how much I want to see Hayden punch Cade. The only thing worse than losing to Cade is losing to Cade over something stupid.

Finally, the tension breaks, and Hayden steps away from Cade. I usher him out of the confrontation, but he quickly jerks back toward Cade.

"Oh, and just so you know . . . Madi? Your date? I let her know if she's looking for someone who knows how to satisfy a woman, she might want to look elsewhere." He slips his arm around my back. "You know, I'm just trying to temper her expectations. Come on, Hallie. I have some ideas about season two I want to run by you."

Cade seethes, drops his glass on the appetizer table, and skims the party for Madi, who evidently isn't here anymore, and for a moment I think Hayden might have actually told Madi he's terrible in bed. I can't imagine what kind of open bar conversation that was.

"If that's how you're going to be," Cade says. Then he backs away and heads for the elevator. I cling to Hayden until he's gone and we both let out a sigh of relief before he turns to me.

"Are you okay?" He cups the sides of my face. He's surveying every micro-expression to figure out where his help is needed. It's like he'll never understand that his presence alone helps more than he'll ever know.

"I'm fine."

"Are you sure?"

I nod. I feel the way I always do after standing up to Cade, the equal parts adrenaline and fear of what he'll do to get back at me. But there's nothing he can do. Hayden and I have Skroll's biggest show and everyone at this party swarmed to us like Mothmen to a flame. As new as it felt to bask in my well-deserved admiration, it felt all the easier to do it with Hayden at my side. And even if I'm scared to say it, scared to feel it, I am falling in love with Hayden, too.

I'm falling deeper and deeper into his confidence and bravery, his unwavering support and care. I'm falling for all of it and I reason that it's far better than falling for the conspiracy theory that birds aren't real (which he tried to explain three days ago by showing me a Vine, of all things).

"I'm good. I promise." It's not a lie, not at all, but Hayden watches me for a long, quiet moment, stroking the curve of my cheek. There's still anger in his eyes and a soft shake to his fingers, and it makes me wonder how I could ever question his loyalty or affection for me. He's so quickly brought to his knees at the mere idea of someone hurting me. I shift topics so he knows I'm okay. "Did you really tell Cade's date that he's bad in bed?"

Hayden's steady face breaks into a proud smirk. "Sure did."

"*Really?*"

"The opportunity was right there." He wraps his arms around my waist, pressing a kiss to my forehead. "I had to take it."

⚹ **THE OUT THERE** ⚹

Episode #8: "The Kokomo from Hell"

Don't be fooled by the beautiful sandy beaches and vibrant sunsets, folks. Hayden and Hallie dig into the mysterious history of the Bermuda Triangle, from ship and aircraft disappearances to the rumors that the Lost City of Atlantis lies deep beneath the waves. This was not what The Beach Boys were singing about.

HALLIE

I guess going to Bermuda is out of the question. I was going to suggest it for an end-of-season trip, but . . .

HAYDEN

Absolutely not. When I was a kid, my parents tried to do something nice and take me to Disney World and, at first, I didn't want to go because I knew part of the Bermuda Triangle touched Florida.

HALLIE

So you've never been to Disney World?

HAYDEN

No, I have. They showed me a map and that it was a different part of Florida, so we went. I had a great time, but then my mom yelled at my dad for telling me about the Bermuda Triangle and freaking me out and traumatizing me. I'd read about it in a book, and didn't learn about it from him, but alas. Maybe I should have known divorce was in the cards.

HALLIE

Were you really that traumatized by the Bermuda Triangle?

HAYDEN

To be fair, I thought I would have to deal with it a lot more in my adult life than I have. It doesn't occupy my thoughts that often.

HALLIE

Oh good. I was worried.

HAYDEN

No, you were not. Wait, what are you doing?

HALLIE

Looking up all-inclusive resorts in Bermuda.

HAYDEN

No!

HALLIE

Look at it. It looks so pretty. Why can't we go?

HAYDEN

That's how they get you. They show you a pretty resort where you can get drinks with umbrellas in them, and then you die.

HALLIE

Damn, I had no idea the Bermuda Triangle has a master's in marketing.

CHAPTER 22

"This guy *never* skips leg day."

Hayden and I gaze up at the statue of Mothman, who could cut steel with his abs. I don't know who designed this statue, but I imagine this is what it's like in the darkest parts of Hayden's brain—for example, the part I think secretly lusts to get in bed with a cryptid. The statue towers over us like a knight in shining armor, with razor-sharp wings and bright red eyes glaring out over Point Pleasant, West Virginia.

This thing has intense abs and pecs, and as I round the statue with the camcorder, I observe the back of the sculpture.

"He's got an ass that won't quit, too," I add. I cannot believe Skroll is letting us expense a trip to film Mothman's hard, steel ass.

Hayden joins me behind the statue, one hand planted firmly on a cheek. "I think you've seen better."

"You're fishing for compliments."

"Maybe."

A few weeks ago, we'd have cut that segment in a heartbeat, but now, the secret is out. Our fans know we're together, and while we haven't outwardly said it ourselves, we're not trying to hide anything. We appear in each other's social media stories and posts, never minding how close we look, and like the occasional comment about what a cute couple we are, just to keep things interesting.

So for now, I let the camera linger on Hayden for a moment longer, capturing his sly smile, raised eyebrows, and soft laugh as he carefully peels his hand off Mothman's ass. I lean in, grabbing him by his jacket collar, and kiss him.

"See? You're not mad at me," he taunts with a smirk.

I've suppressed most of my memories from our camping escapades last night. I shove my bugbites and the feeling of blades of grass stuck to me back into the bowels of my brain with the part in *Pinocchio* where they turn into donkeys. The horror of peeing in the woods will live with me until I die, but at least I didn't need to use a leaf.

We did not find Mothman, but I didn't *hate* being in the woods as much this time. Hayden's an alarmingly good camper—he can cook on a little fire he builds himself, he knows how to make sleeping bags comfortable, and I feel fairly certain he'd fight a bear for me. A few doses of tent sex hadn't hurt either.

"No," I agree. "I'm not *mad*, but I am making you promise, on film, that you will not make me go camping until at least halfway through next season. Please. I am begging you."

"So, there go my hopes of a Skunk Ape episode in the first half of the season?"

"Yes, I banish those hopes to the Bermuda Triangle, thanks."

"Back to the drawing board. Now," he continues, slipping back into his Narrator Voice. I steady the camera on him. "Mothman is an omen of doom. His appearance has preceded many catastrophes, from the Silver Bridge collapse in 1967 to Chernobyl to 9/11."

"Chernobyl? You're trying to say that Mothman caused Chernobyl. What'd he do? Hit the nuclear reactor button with his thick ass?"

"No, he *warned* them, and they didn't listen."

"Are we in danger being this close to him?"

Hayden shakes his head with steadfast confidence. "No, he's a tourist attraction. Not the real thing. You know, I think we need to come back in September and come to the Mothman Festival. It's a whole festival. A whole *festival*, Hallie."

I could die at the way he practically bounces on his toes in excitement over the prospect of a whole Mothman festival. It's like Coachella for conspiracy theorists.

"I don't know if there's enough for us to do in West Virginia to warrant coming twice in one year. That's only like three months away."

"We can hunt for the Flatwoods Monster, too."

"What about the Not Deer?" I stop recording and hang the camera strap over my shoulder. Hayden's smile grows, his fingers clasping around mine as we slowly fold together, shielded by Mothman's washboard abs and juicy ass. After spending the night in the woods, we checked into our hotel and quickly showered, but Hayden still smells like fresh air and crisp pine, and hints of lemon verbena shampoo.

"Are you ready to eat a pizza with Mothman on it?" He says this like it's supposed to turn me on or something.

I nod. "Sure, but not as ready as you are."

He pulls away, offering me a hand as we move through the center of town toward the pizza place. As we wait at the crosswalk, my phone buzzes and I extract it from my pocket. One notification jumps out amidst the many social media comments and likes.

NORA (2:15 PM): Have you seen this?

NORA (2:15 PM): I want this man to eat shit and die.

NORA (2:16 PM): he starts talking shit 6 mins in

I hover over the link she's sent to our chain and click it. I know right away it's not going to be good news.

⸙ WHAT THE FOX ⸙

Ep. #321 with Special Guest Cade Browning

Fox Evans is Cade's knockoff Joe Rogan former roommate from college, who has hit it surprisingly big with the fuckboy podcast crowd. Against all better judgment, I press Play, right in the middle of the square.

FOX EVANS

And this is a competition, so like . . . I need you to win. Everyone listening—he needs to win. None of the other shows are competing at his level. Not a one.

CADE BROWNING

Yeah, there're some odd shows in the lineup.

By now, Hayden's swung back to me, listening in, too. He quietly asks "Cade?" and I nod before we continue.

FOX EVANS

I couldn't help but notice a particular ex-girlfriend of yours is also working on a show in this competition.

CADE BROWNING

Yeah.

FOX EVANS

What's up with that?

CADE BROWNING

It's a free country. She wasn't right for Noobie Brothers—

FOX EVANS

Yeah, she's got some features none of the other Brothers have.

When I look back up at Hayden, he has his hands drawn behind his head, his green eyes stormy and furious beneath the lenses of his glasses.

CADE BROWNING

[CHUCKLES] And I mean, like . . . I don't want to say it and sound like a dick—

FOX EVANS

You don't come on What the Fox to sound like a nice guy. There are so few spaces for men to just be themselves anymore.

CADE BROWNING

Fine. I mean, like, she is not the cute, bubbly girl she seems like on camera. Trust me. I know her quite well off camera. People love her, but they don't know her. But I have no control over how she behaves anymore.

FOX EVANS

Now, I don't want to poke the bear or anything here, but I was looking at some numbers. For some reason, her show is averaging higher viewership than yours—

CADE BROWNING

Yep.

FOX EVANS

How come? I mean, look—it's a show about ghost hunting—

CADE BROWNING

Mm, can't forget looking for the Loch Ness Monster.

[BOTH LAUGHING]

CADE BROWNING

She randomly found this guy—

FOX EVANS

From, like, the bowels of Reddit or something—

CADE BROWNING

Or his mom's basement.

Hayden sits down beside me on one of the benches and rests a hand on my leg. I think of a childhood full of bullying and how hard it must be to hear someone dragging his name through the mud. I pause.

"We don't have to keep listening," I choke out. My eyes burn, and as much as what Cade is saying is child's play compared to what he'd say in private, so many other people are going to hear this. So many other people will eat up whatever he says like I did for years.

Hayden shakes his head and his voice comes out icy cold. "It's up to you. I don't care what he says about me."

I press Play again.

FOX EVANS

I feel like I can't even articulate how bizarre and embarrassing this show is—let me just play a clip for you . . .

[CLIP OF *THE OUT THERE* EPISODE #6]

HALLIE

What if that Bigfoot burger you're eating is made from Bigfoot meat?

HAYDEN

It obviously isn't. That'd imply that someone found and caught a Bigfoot and carved it for serving.

HALLIE

It'd be a shame to shove Bigfoot through a meat grinder. But I have a question.

HAYDEN

Shoot.

HALLIE

How come no one has ever found a Bigfoot skeleton?

HAYDEN
 There's been a few people who have claimed they found one or killed one, but none have been proven to be real. They're always these sketchy guys who say things like "well, I can't tell you where it is, but I have it."

HALLIE
 Not sketchy at all.

HAYDEN
 I know, says another sketchy guy.

[BOTH LAUGHING]

HALLIE
 So, Bigfoot's immortal?

HAYDEN
 Anything's possible.

HALLIE
 Right. It's Out There. How's the burger?

HAYDEN
 Honestly? It's kind of dry.

[BEAT]

FOX EVANS
 You see what I mean?

CADE BROWNING

You don't gotta tell me, dude. Whatever she can do for the attention, I guess. This is just what she does. She's so insecure that she needs someone to be tooting her horn all the time. She's needy, and clingy, and if she didn't sleep with all her coworkers, she'd be out of a job.

FOX EVANS

Shit. That true?

CADE BROWNING

She's two for two that I know of.

FOX EVANS

This guy?

CADE BROWNING

Yeah, came out a few weeks ago that they're together. She's clearly using him and it's really upsetting that she'd do it to another person just trying to make their mark.

FOX EVANS

Match made in weirdo heaven, I guess. You know, that's why you can't trust women like her. You want to believe they're being genuinely kind and nice, but then they pull shit like this and it makes us look bad. You know, there's a name for girls like her. We can't say it on my show, but there is.

CADE BROWNING

[LAUGHS] Yep. If I get you taken off the air, you'll never have me back.

, , ,

I close the episode with shaking fingers and I feel like I'm going to be sick. I don't want to look at Hayden and face that maybe this time when he hears Cade say it, he'll buy it. But one peek at him tells me he won't. His hands ball in fists against his jeans and his jaw is a tight, straight line.

That should bring me comfort enough, but it doesn't. Not now. More notifications buzz at my phone, responses to my latest post from earlier this morning—a photo of me frowning at our collapsed tent after I tried to disassemble it—and I start to read. The earlier comments were punny jokes and quips, the occasional serious conspiracy theorist telling me that the reason we didn't find Mothman is because we weren't "deep woods-ing it" enough, which I shall never do.

Now the conversation's shifted.

Do u really think she's just dating him for the attention? To get on the show?

I rly hope not:/ Hayden deserves better than getting played by some bitch

Don't care. 2 for 2 on sleeping with her coworkers is low and why no one roots for women to succeed. Done watching this show now.

I think I'm out, too.

Before I can read more, Hayden rests a hand on top of mine and nudges me to put the phone down.

I always knew the risks of stepping into the spotlight. The hammer will always come down harder on a woman than a man, so any step out of line I took would be met with vitriol and angry virtual pitchforks. I know there are people who don't like me, or who find me annoying, but they seem to be a small minority I can ignore easily when so many of our fans flood our comments with love.

I've spent months disproving all the conspiracy theories Cade's spread about me and let fester inside my brain, only for him to throw the evidence back in my face. Only for him to find some way to sabotage my hard work at the finish line. With each negative comment that pops up on my screen, I know one other person is believing him and turning our fans against us.

All because I fell in love with the wrong person. Then because I fell in love with the right person.

And I knew better.

I knew better than to be fearless and blaze my own path. I knew better than to claim any space being seen.

I look up at Mothman, and his titanium, jacked body stares me down. Who the fuck made this statue? Mothman has abs and a tight ass. Mothman goes to CrossFit. Mothman flips tires for fun.

An omen of doom is fucking right.

I stand, and before I can break down in front of nice little families trying to take pictures with Mothman, I flee. Hayden follows close behind me, guiding me back to our rental car. We arrive at the gray sedan that smells like smoke and stale French fries, and Hayden quickly opens the back door and I realize what he's doing.

I slide into the back seat with him and as soon as the door slams behind him, I give in to the tears. Hayden sweeps me into his arms, his lap, and holds on to me like it's his personal responsibility to keep me from falling apart. I cry into his jacket, hot tears sliding off the waterproof windbreaker fabric, in broken, heaving sobs that won't stop until it feels like I can't breathe anymore.

"It's okay," Hayden whispers. "I promise it'll be okay."

I struggle to believe him, but I don't struggle to believe that other people will take Cade's words at face value. If our fans turn against me, it'll run *The Out There* into the ground. It's only been a few hours and the Skroll fans have already gotten wind of this. We got cocky, showed our hands, and Cade retaliated. He knows he's going to lose, so he did whatever he could to hurt us. To hurt me. No, to punish me for being brave enough to tell him "no" time and time again.

It scares me the most that even now—when I have someone who cares for me so unconditionally, a job that makes me excited to go to work, fans who hang on to everything we say and post, who tell us every week how happy our show makes them—I might never be free of the scars Cade left behind.

Hayden's grip tightens on my jacket, like he's restraining himself from acting out, and I suddenly wish he'd punched Cade back at the Skroll party. It'd make Cade's retaliation worse, but at least he'd have a fucked-up nose or something to make me feel better. I follow Hayden's breathing, though it's heavy and angry, to calm myself enough to wipe my eyes, talk, put the pain into words.

He brushes away the tears with his thumb and hangs on to me tighter.

"What do you want me to do?" he finally says.

"What?"

"What do you want me to do? I don't know," he starts, his voice slipping into a frantic ramble. "I could . . . I don't know,

I could sue him if you want. He used a clip of our show without our permission. Or . . . I don't like resorting to violence, but I'd totally punch him for you if you asked."

"Hayden, you don't have to do anything." It's not the answer he wants, because he restrains himself from fighting me on it. "You don't. It won't make a difference. He did this because we made him look bad. Because we were going to win."

Going to.

Now, if our views tank because our viewers hate me, think I'm using Hayden for attention, or believe that I don't love him with everything I have . . . Skroll could change their mind. I'd be a liability for them to keep around.

"I don't want this asshole to get away with this, Hallie. He can't just go around saying things like that about us, about *you*. It's not true and he can't just *do* that."

"Cade does whatever he wants and he *never* pays for it. He's never seen consequences for a single fucking thing in his life, Hayden. Whatever we say, he'll spin it to make it about us. This is how . . ."

This is how I stayed for so long.

Because I am terrified of stepping out of line and of being seen—a fear that didn't exist before Cade. I just wish it didn't exist after Cade either.

"Okay," he breathes, leaning his head back against the seat. His eyes flutter shut and he rubs the bridge of his nose under his glasses before returning to me. He wipes away my remaining tears and presses a kiss against the side of my head. "Then what can I do *for you*?"

"I just want to go back to the hotel."

Hayden slides out from under me and we climb into the front seat, driving back to our hotel room. It's hardly a refuge,

full of concerning-colored comforters and even scarier carpet, but at least it's not a tent in the middle of the woods. The
mosquitos are far less bountiful here. Since we missed our
chance at Mothman pizza, Hayden disappears to find food
for us once he knows I'm okay.

With him gone, I slide out my phone again and continue to
read the comments that flood in. Cade shares the podcast episode and quotes on his page about eliminating toxic people
from your lives, and the comments are full of supportive fans
telling him to keep his chin up, ignore me and *my* negativity.
Good for him for *overcoming*. We don't talk about how *women*
can hurt *men* enough.

I move to Hayden's profile and find a picture of the two of
us together. There are so many new comments, like people are
desperate to swarm and tell him he's better off without me. I
wonder if his phone is buzzing constantly, too. I wonder if he's
reading any of this, and what's going on inside his head.

I know it won't do me any favors to look at my own comments. For every loving fan, I'm afraid there's ten more mean
troll-termites that'll crawl out of the woodwork on me.

When I first discovered Hayden and *The Out There*, the entire point was to make it about him. He was going to be my
show and I was going to guide him on a path to success. I was
never supposed to share the spotlight. Now I do, and it could
be the downfall of years and years of work.

I set the phone aside as the hotel room door opens again
and he steps in holding a box of pizza in one hand and a bottle of wine in the other. He slips off his hiking boots and
jacket and places the pizza between us on the bed. I can't help
but smile because I already know what's inside.

"This asshole is not going to keep us from our Mothman

pizza," he says, pouring a glass of wine for each of us into the flimsy plastic hotel cups. I sip at it, but wine out of a plastic cup tastes far worse. It's just science, no conspiracy. Regardless, though, I am going to drink all of it.

Hayden leans over the side of the bed, grabbing my phone off the nightstand and placing it on silent beside his on the other side of the room. There's a digital storm brewing for both of us, but he's trying to make this as safe a shelter as he can. He'll board up the windows and doors to keep anything that might knock me down or sweep me away at bay if he has to. He kisses my forehead and asks if I need anything else. I can only give him a weak shake of my head.

He flips open the pizza box, and I know I'm not the expert in the room, but this really doesn't look like Mothman. Mothman stares back at me with weird little tomatoey eyes and a pepperoni body, an ungodly amount of mushrooms for wings, and scrawny bell pepper legs. I don't know if I prefer this Mothman or the bootylicious one in the town square.

"I'll let you take the first piece."

"My hero," I tease. I claim one of Mothman's legs, which seems to have a somewhat proportionate amount of pepperoni and bell pepper. It's not a New York slice by any means, but it's the thought that counts, I think. Hayden claims a more shroom-smothered piece and we dig in and eat in silence for a few minutes. Half the bottle of wine and an inconsistent half of Mothman's body are gone too quickly.

Both of our phone screens keep lighting up across the room and it's painful not knowing what everyone is saying about it. But watching our follower counts drop, notifications rise, DMs filling up because one person wields so much power would hurt worse than holding back.

"Hallie, don't pay them any mind. Please."

"Are people spamming you, too?"

He nods. "Yeah."

"With what?"

"Does it matter? No matter what we do, there are going to be people who have nothing good to say. I've been doing this long enough—"

"Sure, but what happens when this bullshit ruins our chances of winning? What happens when I am too much trouble for you to work with?"

His eyes soften and he sits up. Our knees brush against each other and he takes my hands in his. I stroke the outline of the UFO tattoo on his wrist, pushing the band of his watch out of the way. I think this might be the closest I come to believing in aliens, but at least I thought maybe I was starting to believe in myself again.

"I have spent the past five years talking about Bigfoot and aliens and that time that the US government researched astral projections, found monsters, and was like 'well, fuck *that*.' People are constantly picking fights with me online and I have plenty of enemies in the conspiracy theories community."

"It's a super weird community."

"Yeah, sure is. But I don't listen to them and they don't get to tell me what to do. People are constantly telling me I'm an idiot—you included." He tilts my chin up with a smile. "Remember what I said that first day we hung out at my apartment?"

My eyes widen. "Hayden, you gave me an entire Power-Point presentation. You need to be more specific."

"That some people just believe what they're told. Others don't."

"We've already established that I'm not really a conspiracy theorist. I thought you knew that about me."

Hayden wipes my eyes as another flood of tears drips down my cheeks. "I know that very well, Nonbeliever. But what I'm trying to say is that for this moment, it might help you to be a little out there like me."

"Why?"

"Because there's no reason you should listen to what this jerk-off says. Just because he says it, doesn't mean it's true. You can choose to not believe in him just like you don't believe in Bigfoot, or aliens—"

"Or Mothman."

"Ouch," he hisses. "In his own hometown, even."

"No mercy for Mothman."

"See?" he laughs.

"It's not that easy. I wish I could brush what Cade says off so easily. It'll just be harder now that he's got more people who believe him." My phone continues to flash with a cascade of new notifications. I'm afraid of what every one of them will say.

Hayden draws me back to him. "I know it's not, but I don't want you to think about Cade. I don't want him to get a second of your brainpower, because he doesn't deserve it. He used your brilliance enough. We've created something amazing together. And there are always going to be naysayers who are quick to jump with their holier-than-thou attitudes, but there are also always going to be people who love what you bring to this show. *I* love what you bring to this show."

The more I think about stepping in front of the camera, the more it makes my stomach churn. I want to keep hunting monsters I don't believe in with someone I *do* believe in for as long as I can. I want to follow Hayden into the woods and complain the whole time, jab at all his theories until he sounds like he belongs in *The Departed*, and watch our success grow and know *we* did that. Together.

But with each win, I'm terrified Cade and the fears he's planted will be right behind us, dragging me—no, *us*—down... and Hayden deserves more than that.

I think I do, too, but it seems like the only ghosts I do believe in are my own doubts looming over my shoulder and keeping my worth shoved down so far I don't know how to show it off. I can't imagine following Hayden out to Area 51 and hunting for aliens, pretending everything is fine and like I'm the brave girl who stands up to him all the time, who takes no shit. I thought I was her.

I've just been reminded that I'm not all the way there yet and that healing isn't always linear. It's full of Bermuda Triangles and wormholes and portals that I can't explain, too. This is one of them. All I can hope is that I am one of those cases where there are answers on the other side.

For now, my brain just feels like a series of unhinged conspiracy theories about myself, and I'm not sure which of them is the truth.

CHAPTER 23

I turn my phone off. Hayden ignores his.

    While the buzzing stops and I don't see the speculation and fights in the comments, I know it's all happening and I know Hayden's fully aware of it, too. Before we take off to return to LA, he confirms people are still talking about it. He confirms that Cade is still fueling the fire, leaving cryptic comment responses on posts, liking posts tagged with #TheOutThereIsOverParty, asserting to his haters that people would change their minds if they knew what I was really like.

As always, Cade chooses the right weapons to fight with.

The flight back to LA is actually kind of nice because neither of us can focus on the comments and spiral going on online. For a few hours, it's like it's not even happening. The plane lands and Hayden reaches for my hand. Our fingers weave together and he keeps me close as we wait for our bags, as wandering eyes catch us with a sense of vague familiarity around the airport. We're not A-listers by any means, but we *do* get recognized in a "is that that person from the internet?" kind of way. None of it makes Hayden pull away.

Nothing I've said or done can make him back away from what we've built together. So why do I want to run so badly?

He does what he can to cheer me up, buys me a coffee from the Dunkin' in the airport because that might be the way to *his* heart, puts on a particularly ridiculous podcast episode about the fact or fiction on certain internet Creepypastas in the car and feigns rolling his eyes to engage with me.

When we arrive back at Hayden's apartment, Cthulhu comes bounding toward him at the door, flopping over and demanding belly rubs and treats.

"Hello, Mr. Chunks," he coos at Cthulhu. "I know, you want snacks."

Cthulhu trots behind Hayden as he opens the treat jar and nibbles at them for a few seconds before turning and giving me a wary slow blink.

"Slow blinks mean trust," Hayden whispers.

"He looks like he's going to eat me." I set my bag down on the couch as Cthulhu waddles over to me and rubs his head against my leggings. Cthulhu and I have a tenuous relationship. He doesn't attack me, per se, but he will nudge me out of the way to snuggle with Hayden to prove that he is *his* human, not mine.

"See?" Hayden says.

I bend down and rub the back of the cat's head, and for the first time since I've known him, he purrs. Much like the rest of Hayden's apartment, this has become a home. I spend most nights here, have a half a drawer in his dresser for pajamas, a toothbrush, and a spare change of clothes for when I do stay over. I live on Hayden's couch with my laptop, amongst a sea of his weird conspiracy and cryptid books. When I stepped in just now, it felt like falling into the world's softest bed.

"Do you want to hang out for a bit? We can order takeout and take it easy before hitting the ground running on the finale tomorrow." He's already riffling through menus in one of his kitchen drawers, but I feel like I'm walking on thin ice again and I'm about to shatter. "What's up?"

"I just . . . Maybe it's not such a good idea for me to be in the finale."

I've been dreading saying the words, but I keep thinking it's what's best for both of us. There'll be no victory of beating Cade like I want, there'll be no hunting for aliens in the middle of the desert with my favorite person. But if I know Cade, as long as he has a platform, and as long as he has Skroll backing him, he's not going to stop making my life a living hell.

For years, I gave in because it was easier, and I hate that I'm going to do it again, but I don't know what other choices I have. I don't feel brave enough to choose anything else.

"Why wouldn't you . . . Hallie, that's like saying 'what if we made *The X-Files* but there's no Scully.'" He crosses his arms in front of his chest. "And to be fair, they did have episodes like that, and they are *not* favorites of mine."

"I know it's not what you want to hear, but I think with all this stuff going on, with all the hate and attention, maybe it's better if you do the finale alone. The more I poke the bear, the worse it's going to get, and it could jeopardize your chances of getting a season two. I'm supposed to be the one pulling the strings to make the magic happen, not be the reason you fail."

Hayden thinks over what I'm saying and his Adam's apple bobs, jaw tightening. "You do realize that this show wouldn't exist if you hadn't stepped in to co-host. We wouldn't have even gotten a full season if it was just me and you know it. Trust me, *I* know it."

"That was then and this is now. Circumstances change. Hayden, there are a shitload of *our* viewers who think I'm using you for attention, that I don't really care about you or the show."

"Well, if they take the word of some asshole on a podcast so easily, I don't want them. We're better off without them."

The bad part is that in the Skroll competition we've chosen as our battleground, numbers *do* matter. We stand in silence, arms folded across from each other in the kitchen and no sounds but the hum of the refrigerator and Cthulhu chasing a piece of kibble around in the living room.

"This is exactly what he wants," Hayden finally says. "You realize that? He wants you to back away because he's threatened by how great you are and he knows he doesn't stand a chance on his own. And if you walk away from the last episode, we're handing him a victory, because on my own, I am nowhere near what I am with you to bounce off. And I don't *want* to do this without you, so please don't make me."

I struggle to swallow my tears, and I am so goddamn tired of crying. "I'm scared. That's why I want to back away. Cade's going to do whatever he can to make sure everyone in the world sees me the way he does. Our fans . . . you . . ."

His eyes flicker up to mine and he shakes his head. "I could never."

"I might seem brave. I'm not jumping at every breeze in a haunted hotel room like you . . ." Hayden frowns to himself. "Or worrying about getting eaten by Bigfoot, but I'm not really brave. I let someone push me around and belittle me for years because I was too scared to leave and risk the consequences."

"But you did . . ."

"And I'm still paying for it. I know what it takes to stand up for myself like this, and Hayden, I just don't know if I have that right now. I'm trying my damn best to heal, and you have no idea how much you've helped with that, but I don't know the best way to do that right now. So, I'm sorry to disappoint, but this has all been *a lot* and I need time."

Hayden watches me for a second before scrubbing his hands over his face and sighing. I sniffle my tears away with the bottom of my sleeve and reach for my duffel bag again. As my hand curls around the doorknob, he speaks up.

"Hallie, before you go, can I say something?"

I turn and nod. "Sure."

He thinks over his words carefully and I recognize the nervous, uncertain person he is now from our first day working together. I think of all the ways we've made progress together. I've let myself love someone when I swore I never would again. I stand in confidence next to him, knowing I can say what I want when I want to, and he's going to either listen, or playfully argue and volley my nonsense right back at me. He lets people see his worst days. He doesn't hide the daily pill organizer of antidepressants anymore or come up with a lie when I can tell he's stuck inside his own head. I don't want either of us to lose that progress, but I already have one foot out the door.

"I only know half of what Cade put you through and I can't imagine the pain he's caused. And god, I wish I could take it away, but I can't. I can only do the best within my power. But I know how hard it is to let people see you. Trust me, I do. I spent three years completely alone because I didn't want to show anyone all the ways I was broken.

"All I can tell you is that being alone *sucks*. And I know it's not the answer, even if it seems like the easiest thing to do. But I really don't want to see you take what he says to heart. Not when we're so close, not when we have thousands of fans who love us and who want seasons and seasons of us being stupid on the internet. And especially not when he is wrong about *everything* he says about you."

"Not all of it," I choke out. "I did very much so date the last two people I've worked closely with."

Hayden cracks a smile that makes the tears in his eyes fade away. "Fair, but the rest of it? He's completely wrong. You're not hard to work with or hard to love. Loving you has been the easiest thing I've ever done."

Our eyes meet and I can hardly see him through the sheen of tears blurring my vision. I can only gather the tight and nervous composure and tension in his body, the dorky Bigfoot T-shirt he's wearing, and the red flannel over his shoulders. But I know him well enough to fill in all the gaps. I know the heavy fear that weighs down the lightest greens in his eyes, and the shake he has in his hands because being this open terrifies him more than our brushes with ghosts do.

But I also know the slight nod of his head to tell me he means everything he says. And the truth is that he loves me. *Loves* me. Easily, happily, and completely. Just like I feel for him, too.

"What?" I ask, even though it's a stupid question. I heard him loud and clear.

"I love you so much, Nonbeliever. And you should know that of all the ridiculous conspiracy theories and monsters I believe in? I believe in you the most." His chest heaves in heavy breaths like he's just a second away from breaking down and begging me to stay. "I don't want to do a single second of *The Out There* without you. It's you and me now, Hal. Whether you believe it or not, you're the magic that was always missing and anyone with two brain cells knows it. Even Cade does, because otherwise, he wouldn't be having the hissy fit he's having right now. It takes a lot of bravery to even live through what Cade's done to you. It takes even more to walk away from it and forge your own path without him. You've done both. Don't underestimate yourself for a minute. And know that no matter what, you have me in your corner.

"But more importantly than what I want, I want you to feel safe. Supported. So, if you're scared of what Cade will do, what our viewers will say, and you don't feel comfortable finishing this season . . . If it's going to do nothing but hurt you? If you need to step away for a bit, I want you to do that."

"Hayden . . ."

"I mean it," he says. I know he does. "Really. And it won't change how I feel."

But how could it not? In a few weeks, after I sit out this episode and Skroll makes their choice, it's likely there won't be any more *The Out There*. Not the one Hayden and I knew. He might go back to podcasting, or start something new, but I chose him and got him to put his trust in me. It feels unforgivable to let him down like this.

All because I'm not brave enough to believe in myself and drown out the skeptics.

I don't hear Hayden cross the room and approach me, but he draws his hands to the sides of my face and wipes away my tears. It only makes them come harder, and I crumple into his chest. His shirt still has the faint tinge of airplane on it, but his hair smells like lemon verbena and I'm convinced he is carrying extra hotel freebies around everywhere to prove a point.

He holds on to me tightly, one hand woven in my hair, the other tucking me snugly against his chest. So warm, so safe, so loving, but I wish it was enough to give me that last kick of bravery I need to pick happiness over anything else.

"It's okay. I want you to do whatever it is you need to do to take care of yourself." Hayden tilts my head out of his chest and brushes his thumb along the curve of my lip. "Even if it's backing away and taking the time you need. I'll always be here for whatever you need."

I lean into him, sliding my arms around his shoulders and meeting him at his lips. He makes it so easy to love him and he makes me so unafraid to be loved, but right now, kissing him feels like he's pleading for me not to leave, which I can't promise. He clutches my shirt and pulls me tight against his body. I run my hands up his chest, tracing the tattoos I know are underneath his shirt, and bite down on his lip in the way that makes him sigh and hold me tighter.

"I love you," he repeats. "Just tell me what you need from me."

I know I could tell him I love him, too, but I've always wanted it to be at the *right* moment. I want it to come when it feels like a celebration instead of goodbye, so I keep that to myself for now. I pull away, brushing the curves of his cheeks. "Right now? I need some time to think this over. To process these past couple of days."

Hayden lets go of me and nods. "Of course."

I break away before I convince myself to do something I'm not ready for and grab my bag. I give Cthulhu a pat on the head before heading to the door.

"Hallie," Hayden adds. He wipes his eyes beneath his glasses and sniffs away the rest of his tears. "Don't be a cryptid. People *should* see you, and God knows we have enough cryptid-hunting work ahead of us. Don't make our job any harder than it already is."

He finishes with a soft smile that makes me feel like it'll be okay. It's a sliver of light I can hang on to as I walk away and try to figure out what I'm supposed to do next.

CHAPTER 24

- *Sugar-free gummy bears*
- *Laxatives in the kombucha machine*
- *Replace protein powder with baking flour*

I look up from the list on the sloth-shaped notepad between Nora and me. Her handwriting leaves much to be desired and I think the bottle and a half of wine we've split between us has something to do with it. But I am enamored by the pure evil she's jotting down in pink, glittery gel pen.

"Nora, who are these for?"

Her eyes narrow over her wineglass. "*You know who.*"

Unfortunately, I *do* know who. For the past several days, as much as I've tried to ignore the world outside my apartment, Cade keeps seeping into my brain and the curious gremlins in the back of my mind want to know what kind of shitstorm is brewing online. I wonder if people have moved on and forgotten about it, or if the actual fans of *The Out There* have prevailed and pushed the haters back into the dark.

But I am far too scared to look and definitely too scared to ask.

I haven't even turned my phone back on since I left Hayden's. I'm sure I'm going to turn it back on to a million notifications and "good night" texts from him each night. It's hard to fall asleep without hearing him say it, but I can't face up to all I ran away from yet. I know Nora's been keeping him updated, and at the very least, letting him know I'm okay.

I thought taking time to process what happened and lie low was the right call. Now I just feel like a coward.

"What's the deal with the gummy bears?"

Nora's eyes widen. "Just go on Amazon. Look up reviews for sugar-free gummy bears."

"I don't have my phone."

She groans. "Fine, they make you shit yourself. Like, violently."

"So do the laxatives."

"Yes."

"So, you want to get back at Cade by making him shit his pants?" I ask. I mean, it'd be satisfying as hell, but it wouldn't actually *fix* anything.

"No, not all of it. The flour won't do that. It's just gross."

"R . . . right. I'm going to . . . go back to watching the movie now."

Nora thinks the other best way to get through a crisis is by getting high and watching *Big Fat Liar*, because apparently, Frankie Muniz strikes again. I don't know if that works or would even show up as a *Cosmo* sex tip, but by the end of the movie, I am most definitely not thinking about Cade or Hayden or *The Out There*. I am thinking of Paul Giamatti's blue skin and orange eyebrows, wondering how the hell he ended up in this movie. I did, however, force Nora to wait several days before subjecting me to this. I needed time on my own to process my grief and do private sad activities like watching Sarah McLachlan ASPCA commercials on repeat.

To be fair, it hasn't *all* been terrible. Nora's great at distracting me with everything from building an obstacle course for Lizzie to deep, honest conversations about our feelings that are tough, but oddly cathartic. One of them leads me down a rabbit hole of Googling the phrase "gray asexual" that I find comforting and feels like finding the last hidden word on a word search puzzle about myself.

When the movie ends, and I have nothing to distract me, I start to cry again. I blame the wine and weed and potentially PMS.

"Oh no!" Nora wails. "We were doing so good! Should we watch the live-action *Scooby-Doo* movies next?"

"No!" I cry. "They solve mysteries. That's what *we* were doing."

". . . Right. You know, I've never seen anyone triggered by the Mystery Gang before."

"Hayden looks like Velma. But a *man*."

"He . . . yeah, he does. That's a fair reason."

"I'm upset. And confused."

I collapse into my hands. I don't even have Cheetos. I must mumble this at some point, because Nora pats my back and waves her phone in front of my face.

"Don't worry. Jamie is bringing Cheetos."

"Jamie's on his way here?"

Oh god, Jamie is going to see me crying into a bag of Cheetos. I thought the segment of me brainstorming Bigfoot mating calls was bad.

"Yeah, I told him we were really going through it."

"You? I think it's mostly *me* going through it."

"*No*," she drawls. "I'm sad because *you're* sad and because I want to rub Cade's balls through a cheese grater, but I *can't* because I *think* that's a *felony*."

"It's totally a felony," I sniff. "But I'd bail you out of jail."

"I'd still have a criminal record."

There's a knock at the door.

"How'd he do that so fast?" I gasp.

"You said you wanted Cheetos twenty minutes ago."

"I *just* said it."

"That was *not* the first time."

"Oh . . ."

Nora pops off the couch and opens the door for Jamie. She lets out an elated squeal and throws her arms around him. Jamie, ever the good sport, takes her in his arms and gives her a squeeze.

He only interrupts their sad hug to shove a Crunchwrap into her hands. Then, there's another squeal.

Jamie joins us on the couch, shrugging off his backpack and passing me my large bag of Cheetos. I resolve that the next time I'm in the Skroll offices, I'm begging Chloe to give him a raise. He deserves it.

I dive into the Cheetos like an Olympic swimmer.

"Thank you," I say. "You really didn't have to do this."

He shrugs. "I'm expensing it."

As Nora happily chomps on a Crunchwrap and sips her glass of wine, I look at the way Jamie looks at her and how he loves the tiny, weird parts of her without even thinking about it. It makes me think of the way my heart feels when Hayden does something particularly goofy or ridiculous. I fell in love with him in moments where he hummed the *X-Files* theme song while perplexed, or how he'd mouth the words to Bill Pullman's *Independence Day* speech. Some people are authentically themselves, and Hayden is one of them. I loved that about him. I still do.

"Did you come from the office?" Nora asks him.

He nods, reaching his arms behind his head. There's a look of weariness in his expression like he's spent the entire day nose down in his computer with few chances to look up. "Mothman episode is almost done being edited. It's looking good, by the way. You two are getting better with a camera."

Were getting better with a camera, I want to correct. Before I can, he groans.

"The Area 51 episode, though . . ."

"What about it?"

Jamie rubs his hands over his face. "It's rough. We spent all of today shooting and reshooting the talking head parts and it's . . . Hayden's, uh . . ."

"Awful?" Nora chimes in. I frown.

"No," Jamie hedges.

"He's floundering, isn't he?" I ask. Jamie doesn't need to say it, because it's all over his face. I knew this would happen, and no matter how brave Hayden tried to seem, he knew this would be how it ended too.

"Floundering's a good word for it."

I try to swallow my guilt with another chomp of Cheetos, but it doesn't work. "How so?"

"It's a lot like it was at the start—relying on his script way too much, wooden, and he keeps looking next to him like you're going to have something to argue, but . . ."

"I'm not there," I finish.

Another nod. "I think he's only doing it to finish out the season strong, but it's clear he doesn't want to be there if you aren't."

"*The Out There* is Hayden's. He doesn't need me," I push back, but even I know that's not true. *The Out There* is something wonderful that Hayden and I have made *ours*. I think of future seasons where I follow him around the world, bringing out his bright colors and emotions as I tell him ghosts are fake, as I punch holes in his conspiracy theories.

"Need you or not, I think he *wants* you there. If I didn't know any better, I'd say you were even coming around on some of this stuff," Jamie teases.

I choke on a Cheeto. "Absolutely not."

"You sure?" Nora asks.

"Positive. I have an image to uphold, dammit."

We sulk on the couch for a few more hours until the high starts to wear off and Jamie heads home. When I change for bed, I hesitate over my drawer of T-shirts. One sticks out to me. Hayden's "I Want to Believe" T-shirt. I curl my fingers around the worn fabric and hold it against my chest. I haven't washed it yet, and it still smells just like him.

If this were any other night, I would be curled up against him, going to bed early before we head to Area 51 tomorrow. I keep making attempts at packing my bag, like I'm going to suddenly find the bravery to face whatever lies ahead for us.

I slip the T-shirt on and step into the bathroom I share with Nora. She's brushing her teeth but stops when I enter. Then she looks at my T-shirt. In the mirror, her eyes flick up to me. Then my shirt. Then me again. "Girl."

"What? It was in my drawer."

Nora spits into the sink. "Remember when you showed up here asking for a place to stay? I asked you what made you change your mind. You told me that you were done letting Cade do this to you."

It'd been one of the hardest nights of my life, but I survived it. And I survived him. I decided to make a clean break when he told me he didn't want me on *Noobie Brothers*, but that if we wanted to keep sleeping together, we could. When I said no, the verbal claws came out, when they'd merely been poking into my skin for years.

I knew it wouldn't be easy to unlearn it all, but I stopped him from winning once before.

I think I can do it again.

I *want* to do it again.

"You fought for yourself before," Nora says. She begins to apply a face mask. "Just saying. Oh, and since you're being a hermit, maybe you should see this."

She slides her phone across the counter to a post Hayden's shared on his page. It's a photo of the two of us up north while Bigfoot hunting. Hayden was tired of not getting me in any of the pictures, so he asked two old fishermen to take the photo for us. It took both of them to figure it out.

We look too happy. Everything felt simple then, both of us lost in the excitement of what our relationship could be. I wasn't thinking about Cade or about how anything I did would be perceived. I was thinking about Bigfoot hunting, how I was going to dodge all the mosquitos I was about to encounter, and how hard I was falling in love with Hayden.

I read his caption, full of snarky quips and his usual exceptional skill with words, and most importantly, an entire section about me. His words are hardly different from the

ones he's said to me in person, but I appreciate them nonetheless.

> Over the past few days, there's been a lot of talk online
> about our show and Hallie and I and not all of it is great.
> I know it's the nature of being a public figure, but when
> it gets personal, it's hard to stay quiet.
>
> I think how people treat others says a lot about
> them and little about the people they mistreat. It says
> a lot when someone uses their platform to spread hate
> and rumors when they could be, I don't know . . .
> promoting their own show, but that's none of my
> business, I guess.
>
> What is my business, though, is our show and my
> co-host. @theoutthere began five years ago in my
> closet because I hadn't figured out how to build a
> recording booth yet and I brought listeners stories
> about every conspiracy and cryptid I thought people
> should know about all from one desk. Now the show has
> me traveling around the country looking for ghosts and
> monsters and has a wider audience than I could ever
> imagine. I seriously can't believe you guys are all here to
> listen to us argue about alien corpses, like . . . damn.
>
> But all of that is because of @halliebarrett, who
> plucked me out of obscurity and made a decent show
> great. For someone who doesn't believe in any of this
> stuff, she believed in this show from the beginning and I
> am so grateful for that. But I'm even more grateful that
> she's the one I get to do it with.
>
> Not only does Hallie seem to always know what to
> do to make our show kick ass, she's one of the kindest,

funniest, most incredible people I've ever known, and spending every day with her makes me the luckiest guy in the world. Anyone who disagrees obviously a) doesn't know her that well or b) sucks. Case closed.

I know the fans of our show love her as much as I do, but if there's any question about it, I am always proudly Team Hallie. Partner in crime. Best friend. Favorite Nonbeliever. 👽

P.S. If you respond with nasty comments, I know how to use a block button. Just ask Zak Bagans.

I click open to the comments. The first one—from a user named ZaddyBigfoot—simply reads "why tf does this guy have zak bagans blocked on ig??" and it feels like an unexpectedly promising omen. I've been avoiding everything online for days now, worried that people would latch on to Cade's words like my brain does, but a quick read of these comments tells me I might have been so scared of a small but loud minority. And that the vitriol hasn't survived.

Omg obsessed with these two.

If there is no season two I am going to eat my arm i s2g.

Hallie's the best thing to happen to this show.

We love both of you so much.

Ok fandom agreement to refer to CB as "bitchfoot" from here on out?

No, that's insulting to Bigfoot.

"I'd guess a few of them at least would be really upset if you didn't show up at Area 51 tomorrow," Nora remarks, eyebrows raised. "You can believe them, or Cade and his fuckboy army."

I pass her back her phone and disappear into my room. For the first time in days, I turn on my phone. It short-circuits and has to hard restart because of all the notifications, but once it calms down, I start working through the comments. There's so much love and support and cute compilation videos I'm tagged in of all our funniest moments on the season thus far. It's overwhelming to a degree I hadn't expected. I don't know how much of it has to do with Hayden's post, or if people *really* care about me the way it seems like they do.

When the social media apps stop blowing up, some of my texts come through. A couple spam, a few from Nora of weird cat videos she found online, and most importantly, a good night text from Hayden every night we've been apart.

I sit in bed for a while, overwhelmed and working my way toward shoving my fears to the furthest corners of my mind. I Google the drive to Area 51. I sign up for an online therapy service and am quickly matched with a kindly middle-aged woman named Maggie, and she sends me a message asking what I want the most help with. I tell her to buckle up, but she seems ready for anything. I stare down the plastic alien from Hayden's drink, who now sits on my nightstand. I even watch an episode of *Cosmic Conspiracies*.

And then, I open my laptop and I listen to Cade's podcast episode again. I listen to him belittle and berate me. He told me I didn't matter, that I didn't stand out, and that I was hard to love for so long. I believed him because I didn't know how to believe in anything else.

But I don't have to do that anymore.

I believe in myself and in *The Out There* and anything that comes after.

I believe in the love I have for Hayden and that it's worth fighting for.

I open a new email to Chloe, cc Kevin and HR, paste the link to Cade's podcast into the body, and begin to type.

Hi Chloe and Champ,
I want to bring something to your attention.

CHAPTER 25

I finish packing my bag for Area 51.

I make sure to pack enough for the several days we planned to be away and plenty of underwear, as always. I zip the duffel and tuck my "I Want to Believe" shirt into my jeans. That, arguably, is the most important part.

After sending my late-night email, I checked the shared Google Doc we've used to plan our travel to see if Hayden's made any changes. He hasn't.

8:00 a.m. Hayden drops off Cthulhu at cat hotel.

8:30 a.m. All meet at Skroll offices to load up car.

9:00 a.m.–4:00 p.m. Drive to Rachel, NV.

Nora and I load into my car bright and early as we head into Hollywood to meet at the Skroll offices as planned. She tries to reach Jamie, but her calls and texts go unanswered. I try to call Hayden several times, but he often turns his phone off on trips to not mess with EMF readings, so I don't expect to reach him.

It's still early and most of the company hasn't made it into the office yet, but among the sea of clear and white desks and computers, we do not find Hayden or Jamie. Fuck.

"I'm going to check the kitchen," Nora huffs, still out of breath.

I still don't know what I'm doing. I don't know if laying out Cade's years of torment and my disgust at his comments online was a good idea, but it felt like the only thing I could do. I have no idea if it'll get me fired or torpedo *The Out There* more than I already have.

But I had to try.

As Nora vanishes and I try to catch my breath, Kevin swaggers his way through the office with a young girl at his side. She's tall, with muted dark hair, clutching a notebook, pencil behind her ear. I like her style—offbeat, like she's trying to make bolder choices but is afraid to.

"Hallie!"

Well, that doesn't sound like the voice of someone who read my email this morning . . .

I fake my best smile and decide to play coy. "Morning, Champ."

"Hallie, I want you to meet my niece, Effy. She's going to be interning here this summer and she mentioned how much she enjoyed your show. I figured she'd want to meet you, if you were around. I wasn't sure if you'd already be heading to shoot the last episode."

I'm not sure if I want to curse the garbage truck that held us up for five minutes or sigh in relief that Kevin still *wants* a last episode. It's still another chance to prove our show is worth it and proof that sticking up for myself did not bite me in the ass.

"Yeah, Nora and I are meeting them there," I say. "It's nice to meet you, Effy."

There's a hardness to Effy that I wish I'd had at her age—a firm handshake and a determined gaze.

Kevin's phone buzzes and he looks down. "Sorry, you two. I have to step into a quick meeting, so feel free to talk amongst yourselves." Kevin slips into a conference room. Do I need to show her around? Am I supposed to teach her how to work the vending machine? As nice as this girl seems, I'm kind of in a rush. Once Nora comes back, we're out of here.

"Thank you for watching," I say. "We really appreciate it."

"Of course. I can't wait for the last two episodes, and hopefully season two."

I struggle to find the right words. So much is still in limbo, but I hate the idea of disappointing a kid. She can't be more than twenty. Thankfully, Effy continues for me.

"I've been begging my uncle Kevin to—"

"He lets you call him Kevin?"

"As opposed to?" she asks.

"You know what, never mind."

"Can I ask you something?" Effy says.

"Of course."

She picks at the corner of her notepad. "How do you stand out against all these guys?"

My brows rise. "How do I . . . stand out?"

"Yeah. I've been watching Skroll's videos for years, and they were always fun, but it was just . . . all guys. There were so few people who weren't just average white guys. Then your show got made."

Skroll has always been a bit of a boys' club. Nora and some of our other writers and contributors show up in passing, but there have been so few other women featured prominently in their shows. I was so busy trying to please Cade I didn't realize how much work there was to do here.

"I don't know," she continues, her words picking up speed. "I feel like you found a way to be yourself and be successful. I guess from where I'm standing, it's tough to imagine being yourself and having that be enough. You always said what you wanted and didn't care if Hayden disagreed with you. And he respected you for it. I like that you don't care what people think."

Words ball up in my throat, and I'm not sure what to say. Sure, the girl I came across as on *The Out There* was vibrant, always ready to fight and stick up for herself. With Hayden, I always knew I could. I was fun and on for the cameras, but I haven't always been that way.

For years, I did what I believed I had to to succeed, to please Cade. I was so angry at the girl who did that for so long. How could anyone believe Cade had my interests in mind?

But, if I've learned anything, it's that beliefs can change.

"This is my first *real* job. I guess I'm nervous about being good enough." There's a look in her eyes that says *I want to kick ass*, and I respect that. I wish I had her tenacity back then. "I want to be taken seriously."

I think of what I needed to hear years ago. What would have given me the worth to stick up for myself? What would have made me braver? I can't lecture past-Hallie. I can only move forward. And I can only do what good I can.

"I think . . . I think you find the people who believe in you as you are, and fuck the rest of them."

She laughs. "You make it sound easy."

"It isn't," I say. "Not always, but I guarantee it's worth it."

"Right." She clears her throat. "Thank you. Really. This is

kind of embarrassing, but I bought a box of the hair dye you talked about on Instagram. But I got the pink color. Influencer culture at its finest, I guess. I'm not sure how it'll look."

"Damn," I say. "They really have to start sponsoring me."

My phone buzzes in my pocket and yelling echoes from the Shocked Pikachu conference room. Both Effy and I glance up at the door. Right away, I place Kevin's voice . . . and then Cade's.

The door swings open and Cade storms out and charges directly for me. At one point, his blond locks and big blue eyes felt like the key to my success. He'd listen to me talk for hours, tell me I was brilliant and smart and there was no one like me. He told me we'd do great things together. He told me he loved me because it kept me going. He took so much from me that I didn't even know who I was by the time I left. But now, I have a far better idea.

His hair is a mess, cheeks blown red with rage. I've seen this side of Cade so many times. If I didn't put his dishes away, if I took too long in the shower or getting ready, if I didn't want to go along with his plans. He'd yell, belittle me, never relenting until he'd won. I believed it was what I deserved. I believed I had to endure to matter eventually.

Now I know I don't have to.

I'm brave (I have spent so many nights in haunted houses and went camping once), I'm smart, I have a great eye for talent, and I'm somebody who deserves to be taken care of. I'm someone who deserves to be loved, and loved by someone far better than Cade.

"What do you want?"

"What have you done?" Cade seethes.

Ah, so Kevin *did* read my email. I don't know what to

make of this yet. I'm not sure if Skroll is giving Cade a slap on the wrist I'll pay the price for, or if they will *actually* do something about his bullshit.

"I need you to tell them that none of it is true—"

"Cade." My glare narrows. "You said it all yourself. You *promoted* it. Everyone knows what you said, and you were so damn proud of it. What changed?"

"I am going to lose *everything*. Because you are a lying bitch. Tell them it's not true—"

He grips my wrist. His voice is angry but *desperate*. Cade doesn't *ask* for anything. Cade takes what he wants and he always wins. Always. For the first time in my life, I'm hearing him plead for something.

I don't flinch at his words. He can call me what he wants. I yank my hand away, shaking him off me like water from a public restroom, where he belongs with wet toilet paper.

"Why should I care? After all you've done to me, why should I care?"

"Because they fucking *fired* me, Hallie."

"I'm sorry, *what*?"

"I am getting *fired*!" he repeats, like I need to hear it in another sentence to understand it. And hell, maybe I do. My brain stops in its tracks. *Fired*. Cade is *fired*.

It might be the first time he's ever not blatantly gotten away with his shitty behavior. Naturally, this brings me joy. He won't have a job.

He won't have *Noobie Brothers*.

With *Noobie Brothers* out of the running . . .

So, instead of giving an answer or anything useful, I laugh.

"You're laughing? I'm getting fired and you're *laughing*? It's not fucking funny, Hallie."

I shake my head. "Sure, but why do I care?"

"Because you can't let them do this. Skroll is *everything*. If I lose my show, if I lose my job—what am I supposed to do? I'm nothing without it."

"Shame."

The world doesn't need any more assholes playing games.

"Hallie—" Cade begs, his hands coming to my face. His gaze softens and he pleads with me. I know this tone of voice from some of his vilest moments.

Don't take it personally.

I only want the best for you.

No one will love you like I do. You know that.

With Effy hovering behind me, probably wondering what kind of a workplace Skroll is, I need to prove my point. Fuck the rest of them.

I swat his hand away from me and he backs up like he's been smacked. He's very close *to* being smacked. "Don't touch me. Ever."

"Don't be like this—"

"I'm going to be like this."

"Please, Hal. I'm *begging* you."

"Begging me?" I smile. Begging has never sounded so good.

His expression drops. Again. "Yes. Please. *Please*. Call this all off."

I spent three years caving to Cade's desires and putting them above mine. Three whole years of choosing someone else over myself. Why should I allow him any other victories?

"No," I say.

"*No*?" he snaps. Now I know the rage in his eyes. It'll be followed by words like "What did you say?," "Do you want to repeat that?," or "I think I misheard you." But not today.

"No. I think I'm going to let them fire your ass."

His eyes widen, and he's too frozen to fight back.

"And I will not take back what I said. I think you've given them more than enough reason to believe me."

I turn to Effy. Maybe it's not in good taste to tell off my shitbag ex in front of an intern, but judging by the way she covers her mouth with her notebook to hide her smile, I don't think she's going to say anything. I rest a hand on her shoulder.

"I think your hair would look great in pink. Uh, if you don't mind . . . I have somewhere I need to be."

Just as I say this, Nora skids back into the office on her heels. "They're not here anymore!"

"I know, we need to go." Nora looks to Cade and scowls. I wave her in my direction to hurry up. "Come on. We need to give him time to clean out his desk."

"Are you fired?" she asks Cade. She bounces on her toes when his glare only becomes more intense. "That is *hilarious*."

"Nora!"

I'm already booking it toward the door as she turns to me and hops to attention. "Okay, what now?"

"We need to get to Area 51."

CHAPTER 26

*A*rea 51 really is in the middle of bum-fuck nowhere, I realize as we cruise down the Extraterrestrial Highway toward Rachel, Nevada. The actual closest place we can get to Area 51 is technically a mountain we'd have to trek twenty-five miles on a dirt path to get to, and then hike up.

I'd nixed the hiking idea weeks ago, and Hayden eventually relented, telling me that we'd spend our time in Rachel and get as close as we could *without* hiking a mountain.

"Hayden, it's me," I say into my phone. "Again. I know your phone is off to avoid messing with EMF readings, but Area 51 is supposed to have aliens, not ghosts, so if you could turn your phone back on, that'd be great. I'm, like, five minutes away and I'd like to know where you are. So, uh . . . call me back. Thanks?"

I've left five other similar messages, all gone to voicemail. If it were anyone else, I'd consider this a red flag, and perhaps it still is, but I know it has nothing to do with *me*, and everything to do with Hayden's unwavering trust in ghost-hunting equipment he got from Amazon.

As we arrive, I realize it cannot possibly be that hard to

find him. Rachel—population under one hundred—is a single strip that's hardly a mile long, with few businesses.

"All right, this might not be too hard," Nora says, slowing the car. She looks to me. "You okay?"

"Fine."

"You sure?" I don't have anything to say to her that we haven't already talked about in the car for the past six and a half hours. She is a champ for being willing to drive me all the way out here since my car was in desperate need of maintenance. I have promised her many alcohols when we hit Vegas on the way back. She also wants a trip to the Hoover Dam because she wants to see where they keep Megatron on ice.

"I'm proud of you, you know."

I glance up. "Why?"

She shrugs. "You came to me a few months ago at your lowest because you didn't know what else to do or where else to go. You were afraid to go into the office or to see Cade at all. You didn't think you were going to last much longer at Skroll, and now you're the co-host of one of their biggest shows. And you told Cade to go fuck himself and now he has nothing."

I let her words soak in.

"But you got that spark back. You had ideas and you weren't afraid to share them and work and create, and that made *me* happy. You shouldn't ever waste your time on someone who is going to stop you from being your most brilliant self."

The last thing I expected was to find so much joy in talking about monsters and aliens. I didn't expect someone to get me racing across the desert to Area 51. I especially didn't expect someone to get me racing across the desert to Area 51 in an *X-Files* T-shirt.

I smooth my hands over the heather-gray fabric and swallow. It makes me think of that sleepy morning in our cabin with the smell of bacon and fresh air and rain, burning pancakes because we were too distracted with one another. Months ago, I wanted to stand out and matter. But now I know that I do—to the people who matter. And what I want is a lifetime of those mornings, someone to say good night to me every night, someone to take care of me when I'm sick, and someone who lets me do all the same right back.

The fans, the attention, the success, and the knowledge we beat Cade at his own game—it's all icing on top of the cake.

We pull up to the Little A'Le'Inn, where we'll be staying tonight, and where Hayden and Jamie are setting up a tripod and camera in front of a small UFO hanging from a tiny crane beside the entrance sign. Nora swings into the parking lot with a screech, yelling "TOKYO DRIFT!" and I'm sure we're going to be banned from a town that has only one hundred people in it.

Nerves churn in my stomach and I clutch the tiny plastic alien I've taken on my trip. My shoes feel full of cement and all of my clothing feels too tight. I can't tell if it's anxiety or the scorching desert heat that makes me feel like I might as well be on another planet.

I swallow my fear and step out of the car. Nora's *Fast & Furious* moves have captured their attention, with both guys squinting and covering their eyes to see who has interrupted their shot. It's hot as balls out here, but Hayden's still in jeans, too, adamant he's too tall and looks stupid in shorts that aren't for the gym. He's already sweating through his "Property of Area 51" T-shirt and Nora's about a second away from attacking us both with her translucent powder so we don't look dewy.

"Hey!" I shout. "You better not have found any aliens without me."

Hayden smiles, and it's a look that says *I knew you'd be here.* "Nope. Just this one."

He points to the spray-painted alien behind him on the sign. As I approach, his eyes drift over me, until they land on my T-shirt. I wonder if he's remembering what he said that morning at breakfast, because I am: "You must *really* love me if you're willingly wearing an 'I Want to Believe' shirt."

I've suddenly forgotten everything I want to say, but I don't need to say anything, because Hayden reaches out, feeling the fabric of my T-shirt.

"There's a camera nearby," he says.

His voice has never sounded this nice. Not even the night I discovered him on TV and realized he was my golden ticket to keeping my job. I didn't realize watching the world's gaudiest conspiracy show was the key to all my happiness.

"Yeah, I know."

"Someone might see you wearing that."

"Yeah," I agree. "They might. But remember what you said? I must really love you if I'm willingly wearing an 'I Want to Believe' shirt. I must love you even more if I'm willing to be filmed in it."

The heat is oppressive, and the words stick between us like humidity. It's the first time I've said it, and I've left him hanging on for a return for days now. This feels like the perfect moment I was waiting for.

"And that's pretty crazy, because you know how I feel about all this stuff. I think they're doing normal suspicious government things over that hill at Area 51, and I do not think there are aliens there—" He shuffles, a rebuttal bubbling on his lips. "*I know.* I know, you don't agree."

But I can't hide my affection for the fact that, without fail, the way to break through the walls and find the real Hayden is to . . . insult aliens. Or Bigfoot. Or Mothman.

"I didn't think I would ever love doing something like this, and part of me had given up on finding those things that felt important. But then I met you . . . We couldn't be more different, and we disagree about more than we actually agree on, but we've always been equals. We've always respected each other and taken care of each other because it'd make the show stronger, but it made *us* stronger, too. I'm a better, happier person because of what we've accomplished together and a better, happier person because of the love I have for you.

"I told Skroll everything. I sent them the Fox Evans podcast. I told them about how Cade treated me. I didn't know if it'd make a difference, or if it'd hurt our chances at another season, but you were right. I can't let Cade control me. And I won't. Not anymore.

"I want to keep following you all over the country, hunting for things I don't believe in because I believe in us and what we're making. And our fans, who want to see us do this together. It's us. Partners. The Mulder to your Scully."

He frowns and steps closer. Despite the stifling desert heat, his touch is exactly the warmth I want. It's perfect. His fingers brush against my cheek as we come together.

"It's the other way around," he says. I don't get to respond before he pulls me into a kiss. It's slow and long-awaited, bites of five-o'clock shadow and tastes of tongue. I breathe him in as our bodies mold together. His arms wrap around me, enveloping me completely. I clutch the fabric of his sweaty T-shirt, and I swear I won't let him get away from me again. I love him too much to even think about it.

"Right," I say, pulling away. "The Scully to your Mulder."

"Better." A wry smile spreads across his face. "You look good."

"This shirt changes *nothing* about my beliefs."

"Right," he smirks. I hit his shoulder and shove him away, but he grabs me, pulling me into a hug so tight it nearly hurts, but I'm too busy squeezing him back to care. Our breathing is staggered, frantic, and desperate. I've longed for Hayden's touch and comfort for days, and maybe without knowing it, I've longed for it my whole life. I could kiss him until my lips fell off, but a hug . . . a hug is perfect right now.

He pulls my chin out of the crook of his shoulder and tilts my head up. "I love you too, Nonbeliever."

He kisses me again, making up for days without. My nose knocks into his glasses and I giggle. He doesn't bother to fix it. His hands run over the fabric of my T-shirt, yanking me closer.

"This is such a good look for you," he says against my lips.

"Don't get used to it. You get it for this episode and this episode only. And my cover story is that I spilled something on my other shirt in the car—"

He nods. "Right. We have a farce to keep up—"

"It's not a farce. I do not believe in aliens."

"Then why did you race to Area 51?"

"Because I love you. And I can't bear the idea of you doing this without me."

He ponders this, tasting me on his lips. "You came to find aliens."

"I came for *you*."

"To watch me find aliens," he whispers. "It's okay. You can admit it to me. I won't tell. I knew you'd be here."

"How?" I ask.

"Just a theory." He smiles and bites down on his lip.

"Sounds like a conspiracy." I pause, toying with the curls at the back of his neck.

"So . . . what do you say, Hallie?"

"I say, 'Let's see them aliens.'"

He smiles again, leaning in for another kiss. "That is the sexiest thing you could have possibly said."

• EPILOGUE •

Six Months Later

*A*s established last season, you do *not* want to sleep with the Loch Ness Monster."

Hayden rubs his gloved hands together. The chilly Scotland air bites at his cheeks, painting them pink behind the frames of his glasses. He blinks a few times, trying to figure out where I'm going with this. He should know by now that there's no destination.

"Uh, yeah, it seems like a bad time."

"Can you elaborate?"

"Honestly, I'd rather not. Besides, I'm taken, aren't I?"

"Yeah, but if the Loch Ness Monster were to come barreling out of the water, I don't know if I'd fight her off for you. I'd lose."

Hayden frowns. "Ouch."

"You wouldn't protect me from the Loch Ness Monster?"

"I'd lose, too." He steps closer as I put the camera down. The fans were more than elated when we formally announced our relationship in the season finale, so there's no secret to keep now. But there are still some things we can keep for ourselves. "We'd both die a big, sad, blubbery death."

"Exactly how I want to go out."

He smiles with a warm press of his lips to my forehead. In front of us, Jamie and Nora set up equipment, rigging an umbrella over our cameras. They evaluate the lighting and test our mics to make sure we're not picking up excess noise. A higher budget means letting them come *everywhere* with us because it's all coming out of Skroll's pocket now.

"No bagpipes in the background?" Nora asks.

Jamie sighs, already tired. "No, Nor. There are *no* bagpipes in the background."

"You should have worn a kilt. You'd look dashing in one."

"No," he asserts. "I would *not*."

"Oh, come on, Jamie," I jest, rejoining them. For season two, we've also resolved to include more of Nora and Jamie *in* the season. So much of our success rests on their skills and assistance. They should share some of the limelight, too. "This is your homeland. You should be more excited about this."

"I'm not Scottish."

Hayden waves his hand in circles, and it occurs to me that he might not know the shape of the UK. "Scotland is part of the UK, mate."

"Don't say that. Your British accent is really bad—"

"Wait until you hear my Scottish."

I rest a hand on his shoulder. "Please don't. I'd love to still be attracted to you."

Scotland is one of the most beautiful places I've ever been. Rolling green hills and foggy moors. Everything is quaint, and there are so many sheep. It's very damp and the wind off the lake makes it feel far colder than it is. The inn we've booked rooms at is small and local, with a pub downstairs.

Hayden and Jamie have worked their way through the entire tap list in two nights and I'm worried neither of them will want to go back to California.

Skroll hit us with a formal renewal the day the Area 51 episode dropped. Not only did it premiere to our largest numbers yet, but Skroll removed *Noobie Brothers* from their site almost immediately.

When we sat down to brainstorm our new episodes, with a new, bigger budget, Hayden's immediate thought was to go big. Really big.

"I think we should look for Atlantis."

"How do we do that?"

"How comfortable are you with scuba gear?"

We decided on Scotland. What better way to go big or go home than to hunt the most blubbery of all monsters? Our production schedule is more flexible because we don't have to do it all ourselves. It's going to allow us to actually take a *vacation*. We can travel the world hunting monsters and ghosts, and I get to do it with my favorite people at my side.

Once we've conquered the Loch Ness Monster, we plan to milk a few extra days of castle tours and exploring Scotland together. We are still not allowed to go to Bermuda, much to my chagrin.

As Nora and Jamie prattle on about lighting and positioning to get the most of us *and* the lake in case of any action, Hayden slips his hand in mine and we face the water. His eyes narrow, hunting for any signs of the elusive dinosaur lurking beneath the surface. His gloved thumb brushes against the back of my palm, and we settle on a rock near the shore.

Hayden's lips press against the side of my head, a welcome warmth against the brisk air.

"Are there any cryptids that live in warm climates?" I ask.

His eyes widen, and he begins to hum the *X-Files* theme song. "Well, El Chupacabra—"

"I'd go to Puerto Rico."

He beams, realizing I know where El Chupacabra originates from. "There's also the Skunk Ape—"

"I am *not* hunting through a Florida swamp for a hairy, smelly man."

He shrugs with a laugh. "True. You don't have to go to Florida or a swamp to find hairy, smelly men. I think it's worth the investigation, though. Not that we did great with hunting Bigfoot. But one of these days, we're going to have some success. We're going to find something so irrefutable that even *you*, my favorite Nonbeliever, will believe."

"Doubtful."

These are the types of conversations we have all the time. Over dinner, in the car, at Ralphs while we grocery shop. Several months after wrapping season one, when Nora's lease ended, she let me know she was looking to move. Specifically, that she and Jamie wanted to move in together, so it made sense that I move in with Hayden. Three months in and I have not tried to push him into the Bermuda Triangle. The jury is still out on whether we can make it through the whole trip without me shoving him into Loch Ness.

His hands rest along the sides of my face with a smile. I taste the pint he drank at lunch on his lips. His hair smells like lemon verbena (pushing his conspiracy forward, even across the pond), and I sink into the warm, musky amber scent that lives between the fabric of all his clothes.

"You love me anyway, right?" I ask between kisses.

He purses his lips and pulls away. "Ehhh . . ."

As my eyes drift, something breaks the surface of the water in the distance with a soft splash. Hayden offers an apologetic kiss, but my eyes focus on the lake. A ripple disturbs the water, and right in time, I punch Hayden in the arm.

"Look!"

He turns back to Nora and Jamie and shouts for Jamie to begin filming. He slips off the slick rock and into the muddy grass beneath us. With a defeated "ow," Hayden climbs to his feet. I keep my focus on the water. A blubbery fin—or something like it—pokes into the air. I don't know what to make of it, running through a checklist of dolphins (definitely not), big fish (possible), eel (not sure), but something tells me I've seen something *else*.

Which excites me. It feels the same way I felt that one night watching *Cosmic Conspiracies*.

"Did you see that?" I ask.

"Jamie, did you get it?" Hayden's hovering over the camera, replaying the footage, because the creature is long gone now. Our cacophony probably didn't help either. "I didn't get a good look at it."

His voice is so quick and frantic, hands shaking, too. I scrabble up the side of the hill to reach him. I clutch his hand as he pulls me through the muck and I cling on to him. Being muddy has never felt so invigorating. Seeing a potentially blubbery monster never felt so invigorating, either. "What do you mean, you didn't see it? *You didn't see it?*"

"No!"

"Oh my god." I smack my hand against my forehead. What kind of monster hunter is he?

Jamie rolls the tape back and we circle around. It's far away, but after a few seconds of still water and Hayden and me kissing in the foreground, the water breaks and a blubbery mass emerges. I watch Hayden's reaction the most. He strokes his chin inquisitively and surveys every frame. He runs possibilities through his head in seconds and bites his lip.

"Replay it."

Jamie does.

"It could be anything," he finally concedes. "It's a good spot, but we can't *know* it's Nessie."

"Ye of little faith," I tease, elbowing him in the side. "Who would have thought *I* would be the one spotting a cryptid?"

It shocks me, too, and I'm hopeful that we *will* find something one of these days, in equal parts because it'd make Hayden happy, and it would make *us* a shitload of money. With that money, we'd be able to equally supplement our travels to woodsy places with all-inclusive vacations to places without cryptids in our time off.

"Do *you* think it's Nessie, Hallie?"

A year ago, I would not have hoped to see the Loch Ness Monster. I would have written it off as an odd duck flopping in the water and called it a day.

I am on the fence about the Loch Ness Monster. Clearly, this thing is a dinosaur, but whether it was the *one* dinosaur that the asteroid missed . . .

A year ago, I would not have wanted to believe.

"I think it's fun to believe it *is* Nessie. Good for views, good for press, good for your soul." I shrug. "We'd make a lot of money if we did find proof. Can we milk it?"

Hayden beams, all too dorky and sweet, and rests his head on my shoulder. "I won't tell anyone."

"Tell them what?"

"That you believe in the Loch Ness Monster."

I glare at him. "I don't think I do."

"You totally do."

"I believe I'm willing to suspend my disbelief for the sake of our views, Hayden."

"Ehhhh," he groans beside me. "I think you are saying that now, but you were *very* convinced you saw something. Like I said. It's okay. I will *never* tell. We have a false flag operation to keep running here. The Scully to my Mulder. I understand, but one day, you will admit it to me and it'll be the best day of my life."

The verdict is in: Hayden's going to get shoved into a lake.

CASE CLOSED

• ACKNOWLEDGMENTS •

Love and Other Conspiracies is a truly special book that came from the warmest and weirdest parts of my heart, but it would not exist if not for so many other people who helped me on this journey.

None of this would have been possible without my spectacular agent, Jill Marr. I couldn't ask for a better cheerleader and partner in this journey, and I am so eternally grateful for your support in letting me tell my strange little stories.

Mary Baker, editor extraordinaire. I don't know how you do it, but you have such a magic way with taking my ideas and words to the next level and always knowing how to make something better. Your guidance, kindness, and enthusiasm throughout this process cannot be understated.

Thank you to the wonderful Berkley team, including Hannah Engler, Kristin Cipolla, Christine Legon, Jennifer Lynes, Jennifer Sale, Lindsey Tulloch, and Sasha Grossman. Thank you to Vikki Chu for the stunning cover and book design that captured the vibe of *Love and Other Conspiracies* to absolute perfection.

To my family: you all had every chance to tell me to go to business school and work a desk job my whole life and you never took it. I am nothing without your lifelong support and encouragement to follow my dreams and do what makes me happiest. Mom, Dad, Nick, and Stephen (and Lilly, Bear, and Cali), I love you all dearly. I'll love you even more if we just never discuss Chapters 17 and 18.

Maria—you are truly the Scully to my Mulder. You have listened to every good and bad idea, every panic spiral, and all my nonsensical tangents for over ten years now. For that, you deserve all the awards, but even more for being the best friend that anyone could ever ask for. It's extremely lucky and rare to find someone who you never get sick of hanging out with and who knows and accepts you for who you are. I'm really glad you decided I wasn't as mean as my high school Facebook pictures made you think I was. (And a special thank-you to Grubby for reminding me to take involuntary breaks by trying to bite my hands while I'm typing.)

Laura and Nicole—I haven't had the Sunday Scaries in nearly three years because of you guys. Our weekly critique meetings are the highlight of every week. I'm forever in awe and grateful that a random CP group matchup introduced you both to Maria and me. I know I can be vulnerable, share my hot messes and "maybes" freely, and somehow, our hive mind always finds the solution. I love you guys.

Dallas, Julie, and Nikki—You three are some of my closest writer friends who have become *real* friends. You are not only some of my most trusted readers and CPs, but you're always there for a good brainstorm, rant, or gossip session. I'm so grateful to have found you all.

Love and Other Conspiracies would be a very different (and messier) book if not for the help of my Kiss Pitch mentor, Kat Turner. Kat's wisdom made all the loose threads in early versions of this book knit together to be something that was ready to go forth into the world. Many thanks also go to all the Kiss Pitch mentees, organizers, and other mentors who had such enthusiasm for this book, too.

Writing is a terribly isolating passion to have, but great communities like the Romance Friends and SF 2.0 have made it feel so much less lonely and much more fun. I'm so grateful for all the Berkletes and the way they welcomed me with such open arms. Y'all are way cooler than me, but never fail to be so deeply kind and supportive. I'm lucky to be among such rock stars.

Thank you to the amazing authors who took the time to not only read *Love and Other Conspiracies* but give such wonderful blurbs and kind words; to the early readers who helped shape this book into what it'd become, including Ashley Hawthorne, Alona Stark, Sarah Slusher, and Vienna Veltman; to Mary Jo, for coming up with the title "The Out There," which is the one thing about this book that *has* remained consistent and top-notch through all these drafts.

Dearest Zak Bagans, I am so sorry for all the slander in this book, but I promise *I* do not hate you like Hayden does.

Last but most definitely not least—to my readers. Anyone who has picked this book up, told their friends about it, requested it at the library—you are making my dreams come true and I hope I can impart even a tiny bit of joy with my words. You guys are the best.

Keep reading for a sneak peek at
Mallory Marlowe's next romance,

LOVE AT
FIRST
SIGHTING

*O*nce you put something on the internet, you can never take it back.

Which is why I think extremely hard about how I'm going to push this sponsorship.

I prop my tripod on a flat patch of ground and take a few establishing shots to guarantee the best lit angles, especially the ones that'll hide the aggressive boob sweat currently dripping down the center of my chest. For an athleisure company that boasts extreme moisture wicking, the product is extremely moist.

The sun's setting behind the Santa Monica Mountains, casting an orange and pink glow onto the ocean behind me. It matches my agreed-upon color palette—blue (my sports bra and yoga pants), orange and pink (the sky), and tan (of the spray-on variety). But I'm in a race against time to get these shots. A lunch meeting ran into a happy-hour collab, and then I had to hike—but slowly, so I didn't sweat everywhere. It's late August in LA, so mission failed a little bit. I step in front of the camera and shoot a few test shots. The lighting looks good, my skin is glowing, and all that's left is the hard part—making it look like I'm not trying too hard.

Of course, I have to try a *little*. No one climbs up to the top of a mountain at dusk, alone, with nothing but a tripod, a camera, and a water bottle. This is a prime way for a nice girl like me to lose a kidney or get abducted by aliens. This would be easier, and safer, if I had someone helping me, but despite the cash from my sponsorships, I don't know if it's financially worth it to pay for my own private photographer. And God knows I'm not inviting my roommates to help.

I hustle through a few poses.

A hand in my hair, laughing at an unhilarious patch of bramble—passable.

Taking a sip out of the trending, overpriced water bottle of the moment—blocking my face, and showing off mixed branding messages.

Facing the ocean, a hand on my hip, glancing back at the camera—this is just weird and feels like a bad attempt at a Bond Girl pose.

I take one final shot, glancing down at my waistline, like I've just slid into the best pair of buttery yoga pants (which these pants are *not*), water bottle in the other hand, competing brand name turned around, and flash a smile to no one in particular. Bingo. This is the one. The right cocktail of casual and capitalism.

To anyone looking at the picture on Instagram, they probably see a stunning model with sculpted curves, flawless makeup, and a sports bra that costs as much as a small mortgage. They'd see someone who has a perfect life. Yet, as I look at the smiling woman in the picture on the screen, all I can see is the lifelessness in her eyes that a filter can't fix. She's got no reason to want for anything. This is the picture-perfect life she's always wanted, but I'm feeling woefully underdeveloped.

However, for the sake of Spinx yoga pants, lifeless and plastic is more than good enough. In fact, it might be exactly what their brand is looking for. I transfer the photos from the DSLR to my phone, run a few tried-and-true Lightroom presets over them, and they're ready for public consumption.

I draft up a caption, throw in a Thoreau quote and something inspirational about how these yoga pants make me feel closer to nature, apply the proper Spon-Con labels and tags, and hit Post.

Even a few years ago, there was a thrill to every post, especially as I migrated from my teen beauty pageant era to my lifestyle influencer era. Brand transitions are never easy, and the transition from done-up Toddler-in-Tiara to "I'm a Real Woman, I Swear to God" felt near impossible sometimes. They're even harder when you have to face them alone.

Now, I see through the filters far faster.

Notifications roll in almost immediately—hearts and harassment that I ignore. My feed refreshes and a post from Alaka-Sam floats to the top.

In theory, nothing about a grown, borderline-skeletal man in leather pants and a sapphire-sequined pirate shirt should make my stomach knot, but it does. He poses in his dressing room at Houdini House, a swanky and private Los Angeles nightclub, fashioned like a knockoff Haunted Mansion—because Los Angeles, Vegas, and children's parties are possibly the only places where magicians are cool.

He's dappling moisturizer onto his alarmingly sharp cheekbones and the caption reads "Magic Is Skin Deep" because now he's got his *own* sponsorship with Epidermée cosmetics and doesn't need me. Of course, I can't be too upset. While he might have been mostly interested in me for my sponsorship connections, I was mostly interested in him for his open invite to Houdini House. There was a period of time when *everyone* and their mother wanted an in there, and I had to be the It Girl. But the second their brand ambassador DM'd him on Instagram, there was no need to keep dating me.

Needless to say, I was not devastated to be dumped by a man named Alaka-Sam, but it felt like a particularly harsh blow to my ego nonetheless.

I do not Like his post.

Instead, I close up shop and begin the trek down to my car now that the sun has dipped behind the horizon. I no longer match the backdrop, so it's time to go.

I will be the first to admit that I've climbed *way* out of my way to take these pictures. I'd broached quite close to a rusty gate that *might* have had a "No Trespassing" sign on it, but the letters looked more like "No Ass" at this point. I can see someone rolling their eyes as they listen to a true crime podcast about my murder, wondering why I didn't just go to the populated overlook near the highway. Answer: I'd look like a tourist and that's not part of the Brand.

I traverse the dirty brambles and rocky hillside to the symphony of rush hour traffic and lapping waves in the distance. I kept my sneakers out of the shots because they and my lower legs are full of plumes of dust and dirt, but now that I don't have pictures to worry about, I'm fine with getting a little messy. I like to think a willingness to get your hands dirty really sets apart a microinfluencer from a macroinfluencer.

Above me, the sky is a deep cerulean with twinkling stars that look like the face glitter I wore to Coachella a few months ago. My phone buzzes in my back pocket and I slide it out. I'm well used to my notifications popping off, full of comments from my fans, fair-weather friends, and fraudulent bots. Usually, they're full of affectionate emojis, ads for suspicious clothing giveaways, and pleas to "please come to" whatever country happens to want me that day.

Today, at the very least, there's a text from my mom.

MOM (7:22 PM): contractor said the kitchen would look better with a backsplash. Can you send $

Our green and white ping-pongs of a conversation are scarcely full of love and care. The last few messages aren't much different than this one. I wonder if the repetition is really that lost on her. There's no inquiry into how I'm doing nor a desire for a catch-up. Just a favor. A *financial* favor. I shouldn't be shocked, and yet, the pinpricks of pain stab in my chest. This is how it's been for a long time.

She'd been delighted when a modeling scout hawked me down at age five at the Fashion Fair mall in Fresno. Once the scout and ultimately photographers saw dollar signs in my cherubic cheeks and big doe eyes, so did she. I wouldn't have any of *this* if I hadn't spent my childhood years bouncing from pageant to pageant. I was able to take Miss Teen Central California out of my bios within a few years of the hustle because El Martin had made a name for herself on her own.

I have more than most people could ever dream of and there's no need to keep it all for myself. Most people give me something in return.

Usually it's a promo, a collab, some freebies.

The one thing no one ever returns is love or care.

EL (7:23 PM): Of course, just send me the invoice.

I seal it with a heart emoji. In return, I get a thumbs-up reaction. Instead of letting it get to me, I keep trucking forward, when suddenly the sound of traffic and waves is punctuated by a soft whirring. It's not the thunderous staccato of a helicopter or deafening drone of a landing plane. This is something that doesn't want to be heard.

I peer over my shoulder and see a faint shimmer against the deep blues and stormy grays of the mountainside. I blink and wonder if it's a trick of the light, but it can't be. There's something *there*. The backdrop ripples around it like a funhouse mirror as it inches closer to me.

I pick up my pace and begin to move quicker through the ravine to reach my car. I'm a sitting duck out here; the inevitable murder podcast begins to play in my head.

Because it took so long to find Ms. Martin, her body was fully decomposed and a small family of rabbits had made a home in the tented sanctuary of her blue yoga pants.

I don't get very far before a blinding white light floods behind me. I panic for a split second before I begin to run. It's the first time that I realize whatever this *thing* is, it might be after *me*. Instead of my life flashing before my eyes, I'm imagining the post Spinx will make when they hear I died shooting sponsored content for them.

Ariel "El" Martin died the way she lived. Wearing Spinx leggings. We know she was comfortable in her final moments.

It whirs faster as I dash away, stumbling over rocks and downed branches as I try to remember my path back to the car. I pass the same "No Ass" sign and trip over a shrub. A scrape bleeds through my poor Spinx yoga pants.

"Fuck," I mutter, rubbing at the wound. I haven't skinned my knee since I was honest-to-god eight years old. At least now I know how to photoshop it out—if I live through this. Using my tripod to get me back on my feet, I feel my stalker practically breathing down my neck with its floodlights. I still have no idea what it is. Or how big it is. I can't see anything about it except this light.

What I do know is that if these are my last moments, I'm not going to go quietly.

I pull out my phone, flip the camera on myself, and go Live.

"Hi, guys," I start, squinting and still trying to focus on fleeing. "So I was out shooting that really great Spinx content that I just posted and I'm on my way back to the car, but there is something *following* me. I can't see what it is, but it looks like a ship or something. I don't know, but look, it's just behind me."

That makes it mad. The lights flash from white to red to blue and it picks up speed. So do I. Then a horrible thought crosses my mind: Am I getting abducted by aliens?

Aliens are so not my brand. I think they're real because the universe is too big for us to be the smartest things out there, but I did not expect them to come to Earth. I did not expect them to follow me home from my photoshoot. I know I'm hot, but I didn't think they'd pick *me* to follow. My brain plays an Instagram carousel of photos of what's to come—little green men standing over my bed, a hovering ship, probing. I sincerely hope that whatever this *thing* is, it will pay no attention to me and intends to abduct someone far more interesting.

I have a meal delivery service and a snail face mask to promote by the end of the week.

I do not have *time* to get abducted by aliens this week.

"Holy shit . . ." I gasp as I stumble backward to the ground. Dirt and rock shards dig into my palms and my phone tumbles from my pocket. I scramble for it and the tripod and my water bottle, which I've dropped. As I grasp the bottle and the craft hovers closer, I get an idea. I hurl the aluminum water bottle into the air at full speed and hope my one season of softball in fifth grade prepared me for this. It clangs hard against metal, and I anticipate that maybe a laser beam will sear me in half, but instead, the craft wobbles.

Then it spins.

Then it crashes.

Then I realize that this Well bottle could definitely be considered a murder weapon.

The lights along the front flicker as they die, and sparks pop from the pile of sheer dark metal. It looks like *translucent* scrap metal, but far thinner, far more silky. It actually looks a bit like the dress I wore to Corbin Bleu's fragrance release party a few years ago. The craft is not nearly as large as it seemed. The flashing lights and shimmering iridescence made it seem massive and unknowable. I reckon *maybe* it's the size of a pint-sized Smart car, but lying crumpled and destroyed, it seems like much less of a threat.

I grab my phone and turn the camera back on myself as I move closer to the crash.

In California, fire season has become an all-year event, so I role-play my best Smokey the Bear and scuttle down the side of the hill to the wreckage.

Thankfully, the smoke dissipates by the time I reach it. My trusty water bottle is only half-full and I don't think it'd put out a whole brush fire, but what do I know? I'm no firefighter.

"I don't know what I just saw, you guys." I'm out of breath and my Apple Watch tells me my heart is racing, as if I didn't already know. "I have no idea what just happened, but I hit it with my Well bottle and it crashed. It's like . . . busted, oh my god. Not only was it a lifesaver, but I'm glad I have my Well bottle here to . . ."

I sprinkle water over the sparking embers to make it clear I am preventing a forest fire like a true friend of the environment. There's been debate after I nearly got canceled for taking a private jet from LA to Coachella. But that's when I realize even with the flash on, it's near impossible to *really* see the iridescent, reflective sheet metal on camera.

I kick aside another piece of metal and it flips over. It displays something that looks like a serial number and product info. It's stamped on, mostly smudged, but it could be enough to find the culprit. I flip on the flash and zoom in.

"What does that say?"

The logo is a circle with three letters printed along the inside and three stars beneath each letter.

P.I. . . .

The final letter is scratched and charred, and I can't make out the rest of it. But I take a photo of it anyway. If only I knew who to tag . . .

For the first time, I feel like I can breathe. The craft is destroyed, I stopped a forest fire, but I still feel a sense of looming dread and adrenaline that'll take hours to get rid of. Whatever this was, it could have killed me. I could have *died* in Spinx yoga pants.

And the brutal reality is that I'm not sure anyone would have cared.

I'm scared, and I'm alone, and there's no one to call. My

survival instinct is to film. To put things on the internet because I have *no one* else. It's never felt as lonely as it does
standing in the middle of a desolate hillside, alone, with a
smoking, crashed drone.

"Guys," I say into the camera. "I doubt anybody is going to
believe me, but I need to share this. And in case someone murders me on the walk back to my car, you'll know what happened and where to find my body. Uh, peace and love. Bye?"

I end the video.

I'm breaking my own content rules, breaking the laws of
Influencer-dom. It feels different from any of my other vulnerable posts. I try to keep them to a minimum. For a girl
with a seemingly picture-perfect life, I can't let people know
it's not. I can offer mild candid shots on a few select topics. I
can reveal I get periods (only if I'm selling expensive au na-
turel menstrual products). I have to confess my hair gets
greasy in order to sell shampoo. I can take one makeupless
photo a month to prove I do have a face under all the sponsored foundations and blushes.

One time, I posted about feeling sad after a bad string of
sponsorship deals fizzled and I felt weird about it the entire
time. Usually, I would say "probably going to delete this" like
I do on those other posts, but I *want* everyone to see this. I
want them to see it more than my yoga pants photos or anything I've ever posted before.

None of this is smart. But I don't think I care.

I also email the video of the Live to myself, at two different
email addresses, which seems smart. I once lost an entire
vlog because I deleted the wrong video off my phone. Can't let
it happen with this.

I haul my ass (which does look great in these yoga pants)

back to my car and am so grateful for any kind of security. All I hear is the thundering of my own heart, a newfound case of tinnitus, and Shakira as she pops back on the speakers as I turn the car on.

My hands hold steady on the wheel, trying to fight the shake to my fingers and the nauseous feeling in my gut. My heart slows and my fingers stop shaking, enough for me to put the car in drive and get the hell out of here.

I spend the drive focused only on the road, but I jump at every set of headlights that appears behind me. Every vibration from a plane above or rattle that my car makes sends me into a spiral. It's a miracle I make it back to the Hollywood Hills in one piece.

I am still full of dread as I pull up to the Nest and park. The Bird's Nest has been my home for the past two months. I haven't fully unpacked and gotten comfortable yet. The most lived-in part of my room is the corner with the best lighting, which I dubbed "Content Corner." Half my stuff is still in a storage facility in Sylmar. It might be an ostentatious, modern, multimillion-dollar home located up in the Bird Streets of the Hills, but it's still the closest thing I have to home at the moment. As I pull into the driveway, I see Bex, the house leader, through the wide front windows filming a makeup video. I'm hoping I can avoid her en route to my room.

As I step out of the car, another one whooshes past, sending a harsh blow of wind my way. I jump and scurry toward the door. Meanwhile, in my back pocket, my phone is buzzing off the hook.

Wtf is this shit

No one pays you to talk about your feelings

> I would love to see this bitch deal with a flat tire on the side of the road
>
> I guess it's true—the pretty ones always die first in horror movies

Of course, there are more positive messages, too, but I know that I've committed influencer crime numbers two *and* three.

1) make it look effortless
2) stick with a cohesive color palette
3) always consider The Brand

I trudge inside. The Bird's Nest is horrifically white and sometimes looks more like an *American Horror Story* billboard than a home. Everything is open concept, with wide-open windows that look down on Los Angeles. It's a killer view that tacked on an extra fifty grand in "air rights." When Bex's father, a wealthy real estate developer and the owner of the house, struggled to sell it because the last owner died from a botched liposuction inside, she concocted a simple plan—let some influencers live here and we'll gain a sponsorship and turn it into a cash cow like the Hype House.

I got an in through a mutual sponsorship with How Glow Can You Go?, a do-it-yourself spray tan kit. When I first moved in a few months ago, I was living with two girls—Maddie and Becca. Maddie has over six million TikTok followers and she makes bank becoming an expert on the crisis of the week. She has a Bachelor's degree in photography, but her bio reads "International Relations Commentator" this week. Last week, she was an "Anti-Crypto Environmentalist."

"'Bout time you made it back here!"

Two months ago, Becca was trying to break into the young Christian mom influencer circles for some reason. But on account of having no kids and claiming no particular religion, it didn't go so well. So, she did what any wealthy influencer does when they're in a crisis and she went to Europe. She spent three weeks in London and came back with a new Brand and the most horrifically fake British accent I have ever heard, and insisted she was no longer Becca, but "Bex."

Apparently, a few weeks experiencing another culture shifted her entire perspective and her time in the UK made her feel seen. Adopting the accent was inevitable when she heard it *so* much. For three weeks. She's clad in a checkered skirt, a pair of Oxford shoes, and a Union Jack crop top, and she smells like her new signature scent. It smells like Earl Grey tea, so I can't complain, but she insists we call it "cuppa," which I'd rather get canceled on the internet than do. Time has yet to tell if the British gimmick is actually working for her.

If I had to pick two roommates to bring to Houdini House with me, I would take Maddie twice, just so I didn't have to take Bex.

"We gotta 'ave a chat."

"Right now?" I try to hide the fact that my hands are still shaking.

"What the bloody hell is *this*?" Bex raises her phone, showing the glaring black void of my shared Live. I don't even want to look at it. I don't want to remember anything about it. I can't explain what about it rattled me so much, but there was a clear moment when I wondered if I was going to die.

"Did you watch it?"

"Of-*fookin*-course I did. So did probably a 'alf a million

people. A 'alf a million people watched you throw a wobbly on the telly—"

"It was Instagram."

"You know what I mean." Bex's overplucked eyebrows rise. I know her goal is to be as British as possible, but it seems to be that day by day, she's morphing into a sixth Spice Girl, named Desperate Spice. "If we're going to have sponsorships comin' out our arse, we can't have you acting off your trolley."

I bite my lip. "Pretty sure that's still ableist even if you say it as British slang."

"You're right, sorry. I can't do two Notes app apologies in a month. But your profile looks like shite now. Are you even *thinkin'* about your Brand?"

"No," I push back. "I was trying to make sure if I *died* for real, someone knew about it. What if I died?"

"Okay, well, you're safe now, love. Delete it."

Anger furls in my stomach. I don't *want* to delete it.

I want to be believed. I want my own stories to be bought as much as my sponsored content.

I want someone to care, even if there's nothing in it for them.

"No. If you don't mind, get out of my way. I want to go upstairs and shower."

I push past her and up the stairs. I lock my bedroom door and strip out of my athleisure. When I turn on the shower, the faucet vibrates and lets out a bellowing moan. I slam it off before it can make any more noise. I live it all over again. The noise. The lights.

I sit down on the cold tile for a minute and watch the video again. And again. Fear shakes my voice and each time, I think I pull some new detail out of the darkness. And the comments just keep piling up. I can already see the headlines that'll emerge out of this by morning. By the time I finally muster the courage to shower, I've hit another fifty thousand views. I wash off the fear left behind with several freebie shower gels I've been given, customized shampoo I promoted six months ago, and a loofah infused with authentic volcanic ash and charcoal.

My entire life is a facade of my own crafting. No one really knows me. No one really knows the truth.

Now, I need them to.

I've wrapped a towel around myself and stepped back into my room when there's a knock on my door. With a grunt, I stand on the other side of it but do not open it.

"What?"

"Thank you!" Bex shouts.

"For *what*?"

"For deleting the video!"

Deleting . . . I didn't . . .

All it takes is a quick scroll through my page to realize my Live video is gone. There's no notification of it being taken down for violating guidelines or anything. It's like it was never there.

I don't know what I saw, but I now know I was not supposed to.

˒ SKROLL NEWS ˒

Published 3 hours ago

NEW BRAND ALERT?
INFLUENCER EL MARTIN'S CHAOTIC VIDEO BREAKDOWN

By now, if you're not living under a rock, you know who El Martin is. The twenty-eight-year-old social media influencer has been on the scene for nearly ten years now, but has gained recent popularity after joining The Bird's Nest, a Hype House wannabe in the Hollywood Hills. Raking in almost a million followers, the model is most known for her scorching photos and beauty tips.

[Photo from @elohelmartin, featuring a white woman with dark hair posing in a black bikini on the beach.]

But is she about to be known for something else? Like UFO hunting?

[Gif of an alien dabbing.]

Last night, Martin posted a peculiar video to her Instagram, featuring the influencer out and about in the mountains, followed by a series of bright lights coming from an invisible source. "I have no idea what just happened and I doubt anybody is going to believe me, but I need to share this," a clearly flustered Martin tells her followers.

[Screenshot of a blurry video from @elohelmartin, featuring the subject with bright lights casting behind her.]

Eventually, Martin was able to defeat and evade her follower and posted the below video to her social media page to get the word out. "In case someone murders me on the walk back to my car, you'll know what happened and where to find my body. Uh, peace and love. Bye?" the influencer concluded before uploading the video. However, the video quality makes it difficult to see exactly what she's filming.

[Embedded video from @elohelmartin reading "This video has been deleted."]

It's a sharp contrast to her usual content—sponsored ads for shampoo, makeup, and athletic gear—and certainly doesn't match the perfectly aesthetic image she's cultivated over the years. Could this new freak-out be a hard launch of a new brand?

In recent years, other influencers have taken to film and TV projects, including Mikey Mayhem, who has been making waves in the new streaming show Clean Break, about a surfer recovering from an addiction to nasal decongestants. You can read Skroll's review of Clean Break here.

Perhaps El's video is a hidden trailer of some sort. Internet sleuths have begun picking apart the influencer's latest post for clues, but the reactions are SENDING us!

cobrakyle23

it's giving cloverfield

xMeggyx

I've given up on believing anything I hear from these "influencers." They'll do anything to sell a product. Can't wait to see the brand of flashlights or LED headlights she's trying to promote in a week. Also, a terrible actress.

jason52612456

If aliens come to earth and she's the first person they make contact with, they'd just go back to their planet

alltherave @jason52612456

lmao or they'd try to sleep with her and then go home. She's hot.

Whether El's launching a new creative venture or is suffering a public meltdown, we're intrigued to see what she does next! Perhaps her next collab should be with the hit Skroll series The Out There??

> [Embedded video "The Out There Episode #15: Swamp Girl Walks with the Skunk Ape."]

El Martin has declined to comment for this story. Skroll News will update this article as it develops.

MALLORY MARLOWE is an author and video game writer living in Los Angeles, California. She's been seriously right-brained since childhood, and her love of telling stories began with highly elaborate plots for her Barbie dolls and taking elementary school writing projects too seriously. She studied Writing for Film and Television at Emerson College. When she isn't writing, she's likely reading, stuck in LA traffic, or has fallen down a weird internet rabbit hole. *Love and Other Conspiracies* is her debut novel.

VISIT THE AUTHOR ONLINE

MalloryMarlowe.com

MalloryMarloweWrites

Mallory_Marlowe

LOVE
AND OTHER
CONSPIRACIES